M000202191

Soul

Forge

Soul Forge by Richard H. Stephens

https://www.richardhstephens.com/

© 2018 Richard H. Stephens

All rights reserved. No portion of this book may be reproduced in any form without permission from the publisher, except as permitted by U.S. copyright law. For permissions contact: richardhstephens1@gmail.com

Cover Art by Marco Pennacchietti

Paperback ISBN: 978-1-775-1036-7-7

2nd edition, August, 2019

Acknowledgements and brief history

Soul Forge has been in the works for over 36 years. The story came to me one fall evening in 1982 while sitting at home and listening to music. *Run to the Hills*, by Iron Maiden, came on and a switch tripped inside my head. I quickly jerry-rigged my old Underwood 88 typewriter, with long elastics attached to the leg of my bed to advance the broken carriage, and began my journey with Silurian Mintaka.

Soul Forge was originally titled, *The River Styx*. I loved that title until it dawned on me that the story has nothing to do with Greek mythology. The title went from, *The Evil Within*, to *Saint Carmichael's Blade*, to *Where Have All Our Heroes Gone*, but I was never happy with any of those. At the beginning of 2017, I had an epiphany. *Soul Forge* is about Silurian's journey through life. Faced with many hardships at an early age, he was one of those people who somehow managed to see the good in everyone, despite what they said or did to him. He was pure of heart and possessed a courageous, giving soul. The day eventually came when everything life threw at him, broke his spirit and plunged his soul into a darkness so deep that even his closest friend walked away.

Soul Forge is the story of Silurian's quest to forge his lost soul anew, despite the evil forces attempting to keep him on a path to destruction.

As with any great work of the imagination, there are certain elements beyond the control of the author, but are vital to the satisfactory completion of their vision. *Soul Forge* would never have left the ground without the incredible support of my beta readers, Joshua Stephens, Paul Stephens, science fiction author Louise Spilsbury, and Christopher Smith. Also, my amazing artist, Marco Pennacchietti, and my godsend editor, Michelle Dunbar, who maliciously beat me into submission in an effort to improve the way Soul Forge is written. Finally, I want to acknowledge my loving wife, Caroline Davidson, who has logged more hours on this project than you or I will ever know. Putting up with myself and my story, she truly has the patience of a saint.

Soul Forge is dedicated to Paul, Joshua, and Rebecca. Thank you for keeping me young while the years pass me by.

Soul

Forge

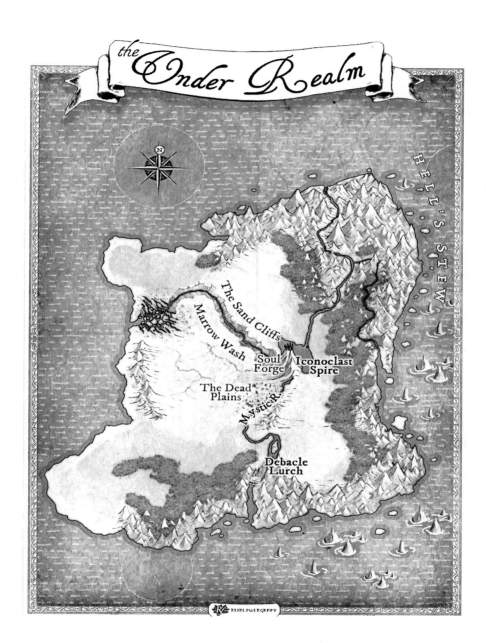

When the shadow stabs,
the life-giving sun,
forth shall he ride,
leaving nothing but ruin.

Freedom will be denied,
to those who fall,
within his shadow,
death dealt to all.

Upon naive waves,
he unfurls his sail.
Fear ye who live,
for only he shall prevail.

We live now only to await,
our life blood courses nigh.
The Stygian Lord comes again,
blighting the land, razing the sky.

Only one hope remains,
for those foolish enough to pursue.
Onto the Under Realm,
into hell, but never through.

Venture forth to unknown power,
a cradle of evil disgorge.
A quest of unspeakable terror,
at journey's end, Soul Forge.

For those who search,
death shall follow.
For those who persist,
shall be riven hollow.

As does the Innerworld,
also does hell.
A drinker of souls,
'ware the Sentinel.

Contents

To view the full colour maps in the Soul Forge realm, please visit: www.richardhstephens.com

Foreward

"**I** must see the Stygian Lord," a naked red demon panted, scrabbling along a steep, rock strewn trail—its clawed feet seeking purchase upon the unsure terrain. Pebbles cascaded over the brink of the ledge, plummeting thousands of feet to the violent froth of a river below. The unkempt path spiraled upward around the edge of a mountain peak, terminating at a cave's mouth near the summit.

The demon rounded the last bend in the trail and commanded the two large sentries warding the cave's threshold, "Quickly, let me pass."

The guards resembled the smaller demon, but much larger, with sinewy arms thicker than the lesser demon's chest—the horns sprouting from their temples more defined. Clawed hands clasped tridents twice as big as the one the little creature dragged along. Neither guard took an interest in the insignificant beast.

"Step aside, I say." The eager demon attempted to run past the sentries—its reckless flight brought to an unceremonious halt as the guards crossed their tridents, barring its passage. It may as well have run into a granite wall.

Before it knew what had happened, the small demon hurtled through the air, landing in a crumpled heap close to the trail's edge.

Gasping for air, it gained its feet and searched for its errant trident.

The guards stood at ease once again, their pole-arms resting at their sides.

"You must let me pass. I carry important news for our Lord. The queen still lives. I saw…" Its words caught in its throat as the mountain shook.

When the tremor subsided, the demon stuttered, "I-I mean, we were supposed to prevent the queen from locating the lost sword, m-my Lord, but before we slew her, w-we were beset by swamp creatures…"

The mountain heaved.

All three demons scrambled to avoid being pummeled by falling debris shaken loose from above.

Swallowing a lump in its throat, the little demon whined, "They were too much for us. My minions fought b-bravely. We b-battled until the last of us was slain. Except myself, of course. Someone had to deliver the news. The queen and her men have slipped into the Mid Savannah. I came straight here to report our failure to obtain the b-blade the b-bishop sought."

The demon dropped to its knees, prostrating itself, begging for mercy—hopeful that its effort to deliver the news had convinced the Stygian Lord to invite it into the cave as a reward.

Another tremor shook the mountain.

Terror filled the lesser demon's eyes. A scream of agony escaped its lips. Ever so slowly, it melted, dissolving into a viscous red puddle that trickled down the gravel path and slowly absorbed into the soil underneath.

Soul

Forge

Soul Forge

Wizard

The Hog's Head Inn, quieter than most nights due to the storm, still had its share of excitement. The two men huddled together at the bar weren't the only ones talking about the mysterious hooded figure occupying a table in the corner shadows of the tavern.

The barkeep approached the two men. He leaned in and motioned with his chin. "That guy asked me if I know anything about someone living in these parts. Someone who years ago fought for the king. Someone special, he said. Who do you suppose that could be?"

The larger patron grumbled, "We all fought for the king."

The smaller patron stole a quick glimpse into the shadows. "Surely it can't be anyone from this cesspool. Nordic Town is about as far away from special as a person can get. Nothing exciting ever happens here. Where did he say he's from?"

The bartender tried his best to appear inconspicuous. He leaned in closer. "He didn't. Just asked if I knew any middle-aged warriors living around here."

The large man snorted. "We're all warriors when it suits the king."

"You're lucky he didn't turn you into a toad," his companion declared to the barkeep.

The barkeep gave the short man an odd look. "Aye, but the way he said it made it seem as if the man he's looking for is different…I don't know. I *do* know I'll be happier when he's gone." He stepped away to tend to another customer.

The larger patron hazarded a glance at the stranger and elbowed his buddy. "Aye laddie, he does have the look of a wizard."

Lightning flashed. The building shook with the ensuing thunderclap. Both men gulped.

The barkeep rejoined them. "Hey. Do you think he's looking for that guy living off the old Gulch Trail?"

Soul Forge

The two men considered the question. The smaller man nodded. "Aye, perhaps. What's a wizard want with him, though? That guy hasn't left his cabin in years. He's probably dead by now."

The larger patron rubbed his chin. "This reminds me of when our beloved Quarrnaine died, may the gods bless her soul. Remember? The king's men came in search of Silurian Mintaka, up by the Gulch."

The two patrons spat on the ground at the mention of the name.

"Hey," the bartender said, spitting himself, "isn't that the same place you and the boys went to lynch that crazy, son of a—"

A chair scraped the floor, grabbing the attention of the few patrons inside the Hog's Head Inn.

The mysterious man in question stood beside his table. He reached into the folds of a black-hooded cloak and plunked a few coins down. Without a word, he grabbed a wooden staff leaning against the wall.

All eyes followed the white-bearded man as he shuffled toward the exit. A rapid succession of forked lightning silhouetted his frame when he opened the door, blinding those within the dimly lit room. By the time their eyes recovered, he was gone.

Before anyone had a chance to catch their breath, another hooded figure rose from the opposite corner of the tavern. Where he had come from, nobody knew. The hunched figure slipped across the floor like a wraith and followed the wizard into the night.

Soul Forge

To Find a Legend

A quarter day's walk north of Nordic Town, smoke wisped from the lone chimney of a ramshackle cabin. A small window above the front door gave evidence of a second floor.

The lone occupant slouched within the embrace of his favourite chair, staring blindly into the fathomless depths of a sputtering fire. He swallowed the last contents of a glass decanter sitting upon his knee. Today, like every other day, he drank himself into a stupor to numb his mental anguish—only to dread the fear that unconsciousness would bring. He shuddered. The memory of discovering his family murdered, refused to leave him even now. His eyes became heavy…

The sound of shattering glass made him jump. Springing to his feet, he grasped for the sword that no longer hung about his waist. He steadied himself upon the cold fire mantle. He must have dozed off.

He fixed an icy stare upon the front door. Taking a step toward it, a stabbing pain shot through his foot. He staggered against the mantle and cupped his injured foot in both hands—blood dripping to the dirty floorboards. He cringed at the large shard of glass embedded in the meaty part of his heel. The sound of breaking glass had been his decanter hitting the floor.

He had had the dream again. The nightmare of his homecoming, twenty-three years ago. Ghoulish images flitted about his mind. From the great feast hall at Castle Svelte with wine overflowing, the vision always transformed into a pool of blood at his feet as he clutched his wife's headless body in his quivering arms.

Shaking the image from his head, he sat down and gingerly dabbed at the gash with the hem of his grubby tunic. He scrunched up his face and extracted the shard.

3

Soul Forge

The tears dripping from his unshaven chin had nothing to do with the stupidity of impaling his foot. The hut was so quiet and empty. So ever lonely. The ache in his heart, unbearable.

Holding blood-covered hands over his face, he attempted to squeeze the mental anguish from his head. The more he pressed, the ghastlier his visions became. His wife's severed head lying beside the fireplace, her face disfigured by a broken vase. His three-year-old daughter dangling from a meat hook driven through her thigh, embedded into her bedroom ceiling.

The panic from that day still crept along his skin twenty-three years later. From the horror of slipping and falling in the blood splattered hut to his frantic search for his sons.

He had found his eldest son behind the hut, staked to a tree by two crossbow bolts—one fired through each eye. He never did discover the whereabouts of his four-year-old, which in hindsight was worse, as his tortured mind envisioned unspeakable images of what the butchers might have done with him.

What gnawed at him most, beyond the horror and the pain, was the senselessness of it all. While he was off saving the kingdom, someone had taken away his reason to live.

His hands released their excruciating hold upon his face and bashed the arms of the chair. He punched at the air with violent speed. When his arms tired, he slouched into his chair and wept.

These fits of rage had stayed with him for over two decades. His inability to control them was the primary reason he shunned visitors—fearing an episode might seize him at any time. He constantly battled against the lingering insanity gnawing at the edge of his mind.

His lust for revenge, and his loathing of those who had done nothing to prevent his family's murder, weighed heavily upon him. He had sacrificed everything to deliver the realm of Zephyr from the clutches of a diabolical sorcerer, only to be left with nothing.

As the sun ceded its light beyond the woods, he wrapped his foot in a dirty rag and made his way to bed. Toward the ever-present darkness that came with sleep.

Restless nights drew into dreary days since the day he had sliced his foot. Days into forlorn weeks. Despite his poor ministrations and filthy hygiene, his foot healed, but his mind continued to fester.

4

Soul Forge

During one of his less disturbed days, a knock startled him from a rare, restful nap. Springing upright within his chair, he stared at the door, not knowing what to do.

The rap repeated.

It had been a long time since the last brat child from Nordic Town had come to harass him.

The knock sounded again. Harder.

Fear froze him. He didn't want contact with the outside world, and yet, deep down, he yearned for another's company.

He recalled a similar occurrence a few years back when the king's men had come searching for him. They would've found him too, had he not fled out the rear door to lie amongst the thickets beyond his backyard. They had broken into his house and ransacked it before moving on. The same men he had fought beside while someone else had taken his family.

Time passed without another knock. He unclenched his fists and sank into his chair, daring to hope the caller had lost interest and moved on.

A shadow passed before his front window and stopped. Years of neglected dirt encrusted upon the glass prevented him from seeing the intruder. Thankfully, it also prevented them from seeing him.

The silhouette leaned against the window with cupped hands.

He slipped from his chair and pinned himself flat against the wall between the window and door, his heart hammering.

The shadow straightened itself, offering a sleeve to the pane. The old window rattled under the pressure and shattered. A curse sounded from outside as shards of glass crashed inward.

His resolve to remain unseen snapped. Stepping over the debris, he launched himself at the door, unlatched the restraining bolt, and threw it open, prepared to attack. The white bearded visage staring back at him gave him pause.

A man much older than himself, stood waist deep in the wild grass surrounding his dilapidated hut. A black cloak hung upon the old man's slouched shoulders, covering flamboyant white robes beneath.

Eyes devoid of colour scrutinized him from either side of a slightly upturned nose. A breeze toyed with the visitor's long, white hair as he leaned upon a staff almost as tall as himself.

5

Soul Forge

The man in the hut quelled his urge to lunge at the old man's throat, to choke the life from him. Instead, he greeted him with an icy stare.

The old man cleared his throat, a strong voice betraying his fragile appearance. "I humbly beg your pardon, kind sir. I appear to have broken your window." He hefted the staff to point at the damaged window. "I am Alhena Sirrus. I have urgent business with the Chamber of the Wise and cannot afford delay."

Getting no response, Alhena persisted, "When no one answered, I hazarded a look inside. I search for a man who used to live in these parts. Within this very hut, unless I am mistaken."

Receiving nothing but an eerie glare, he continued, "You are not, by chance, Sir Silurian Mintaka?"

The man in the hut wavered but shook his head. He stared hard at the white-bearded visage. There was something oddly familiar about the old man.

"No? I didn't think so," Alhena said. "How long have you lived here, if I may be so bold as to inquire?"

The man on the step glared. "What are you? A wizard?"

"Me?" Alhena laughed. "Oh no, but you are not the first to ask that."

"You look like a wizard. What's with your eyes?"

"Ah, my eyes. I was born this way. I see fine though, let me assure you. At least for my advanced years."

The man on the step grunted.

Alhena shuffled his feet. "Do you recall the family's name that lived here before you?"

The man on the step said nothing.

"Have you heard of the name Mintaka?"

The man on the step didn't respond at first. After a moment, he shook his head.

Alhena opened his mouth to speak but closed it again. He appeared to be undecided about something, but in the end, he stepped toward the broken gate. "Well, I shall leave you to your peace, then. It has been nice chatting with you. Again, I apologize about the window." He paused, thinking. "I shall be glad to send a craftsman up from Nordic Town."

The man on the step said nothing.

Soul Forge

Alhena neared the gate. "The Chamber of the Wise shall pay for it, of course."

When the man on the step didn't reply, Alhena added as he passed through the gate, "I will be on my way then." He tried to close the broken gate, but its rusted hinges protested. He gave it up and turned down the path. "I guess it is high time I find Rook Bowman."

The man of the hut almost stumbled off the step. Against his better judgment he called out, "Hold!"

Alhena stopped, concealing a smile.

The hut's occupant gave him a slight wave, his voice lacking enthusiasm as he disappeared into the hut. "Come."

Alhena reentered the yard and mounted the single, broken step. He stopped upon the threshold—the total disorder and filth inside gave him pause. He raised his eyebrows, took a last deep breath of fresh air, and stepped into the dimly lit interior.

The hut's occupant had seated himself before a crumbling fire mantle, paying no attention to him. The man retrieved a filthy decanter beside his chair and raised it to his lips, not bothering to offer Alhena any.

Alhena walked over to stand before him. He placed his back against the soot covered mantle and clutched his staff tight. "As I said, I am Alhena Sirrus, senior messenger to the Chamber of the Wise. I am on an urgent mission to find this Silurian fellow, but I fear he cannot be found."

The man in the chair grunted, hefting the decanter to his lips.

"Does the name Rook Bowman mean anything to you?"

The man in the chair glanced up, the flask almost slipping from his grasp. His reply, however, was anything but enthusiastic. "I know the name. He fled Zephyr years ago."

Alhena nodded. "Aye. After the Battle of Lugubrius, Rook Bowman and Silurian Mintaka left together." Alhena waggled his staff. "If you trust wizards, the king's magician conjured up a vision of Sir Rook residing alone, shrouded by a peculiar golden haze. The wizard has never determined where this place is."

The man of the hut leaned into his chair. "'Tis probably the light of the netherworld the fool sees." His hands trembled. Lifting his jug, he swallowed deeply, before asking, "Why do you seek Rook Bowman anyway?"

"Unfortunately, my good sir, that answer is for either of the men in question."

The man in the chair sneered. "Then spill your guts. You're looking at one."

Soul Forge

The Foreboding

The soot covered mantle prevented Alhena from stumbling backward. The audacity of the haggard man to claim to be one of the two men in question was preposterous. The alcohol surely befuddled his wits. He choked down the urge to laugh. "You jest?"

A log rolled in the hearth, dispersing a shower of sparks, and cast the room in an orangey-golden hue.

If not for the white knuckled hold on his staff, Alhena would have stumbled. "Rook Bowman? The king's wizard was right. You are alive. The golden light that has baffled the Chamber all these years, is but the light of your fireplace."

The man in the chair drained the decanter. Setting the empty vessel on the floor with a thud, he gave Alhena a cynical sneer, and shook his head.

Alhena's smile dropped, his eyes widening. "Silurian?"

The man in the chair nodded, eyeing him over steepled fingers.

Alhena's eyes fell on an empty scabbard sprawled over the chair's arm, embossed with intricate carvings. He appreciated the worth of the dazzling gemstones embedded in its surface—as encrusted in dirt as they were, they would still fetch a king's ransom.

He recalled seeing a similar one resting behind the king's supper table during the great victory feast following the Battle of Lugubrius. It had belonged to the man on King Malcolm's immediate right. The king's champion. The realm's favoured sword.

He squinted, trying to envision the man claiming to be Silurian in a different light. This man appeared so frail. A husk of a man. As if his next breath might prove to be his last.

According to the Chamber of the Wise and King Malcolm, the kingdom's salvation lay at the tip of this man's sword. Alhena wanted

9

to laugh. Strap a rucksack over the man's shoulders, weigh him down with a sword, and before he reached the front gate, he'd need saving himself. As far as the people of Zephyr were concerned, Silurian was believed dead. Perhaps it would be kinder if they were allowed to maintain that belief.

"Tell me, old man. What news is so important that the Chamber risked someone as close to death as you to carry?" the man asked.

"That is privy for Silurian or Rook. Convince me you are who you claim to be. Tell me about your family."

The man tensed.

"Silurian Mintaka was married, with a son and a daughter. I see nothing here indicating their presence—"

Murder exploded from the man's eyes—pain evident behind his ice-blue stare. He thundered to his feet and faced Alhena, nose to nose, facial muscles twitching.

Alhena tried to back away, but the mantle prevented him.

Releasing a heavy sigh, the man disengaged and stepped to the broken window, careful to avoid the scattered shards, and gazed out.

The room's contents sharpened in Alhena's heightened awareness. Years of cobwebs decorated the log walls. Candle stubs flickered, their drippings forming tiny stalagmites upon filthy tabletops.

So enrapt in his assessment of the shabby hut, he practically leapt from his skin when the man whispered in a harsh voice, "I had a daughter and two sons. Now, get out."

Alhena's eyebrows lifted in surprise. Silurian Mintaka did indeed have two sons. The question had been a ploy to allow the man to betray himself.

Yellowed oil paintings atop the mantle's ledge caught Alhena's eye. Ignoring the man's demand to leave, he retrieved the middle picture. Years of accumulated grime all but obliterated its surface.

He blew off the most recent buildup and gaped. In the picture, five people stood before a new log cabin—a small window above the door. A young man and woman each held a baby, while a boy, not much older than a year, hung onto the man's breeches.

He lifted his head and compared the man's grizzled features with the person in the painting. Though much younger in the painting, Alhena couldn't deny the picture matched the image of the man watching him now. Zephyr was doomed.

Alhena closed his eyes. What was he going to tell Chambermaster Uzziah? That the man the kingdom placed so much hope upon stood drunk across the room, demanding to be left alone? Perhaps he should just return to the Chamber and inform them that they would have to find someone else to champion their cause.

Silurian glared at him, his ice-blue eyes flicking to the door.

"I apologize if my query about your family has upset you. I needed to ensure you are who you say. I admit, finding you here like this after all these years, gives me some concern. I believed you dead. Perhaps after what I have to tell you, you may wish that were so."

Silurian grunted, his hands clenching and unclenching.

Reaching into the folds of his robes, Alhena withdrew a tightly coiled scroll sealed in red wax, embossed with the chambermaster's sigil. "This writ is for your eyes only."

Silurian accepted the scroll and turned it over several times before he broke the seal. Unrolling its short length, he regarded it blankly and let it snap back upon itself. He tossed it to Alhena. "Read it."

Alhena flailed his hands out in surprise, almost dropping his staff as he caught the scroll in his arms. "The contents are for your eyes alone. A Chamber messenger is not privy to such a decree."

Silurian's sneer turned ugly. "I care nothing of Chamber protocol. Read it."

"If you insist." Unrolling the parchment, Alhena began to read.

"Out loud."

"Oh." Alhena cleared his throat. "Dated this twelfth day of Septomb, six hundred and forty, at the Chamber of the Wise, Gritian. Only the intended recipient may bear witness."

He stopped reading, but Silurian's murderous glare gave him all the permission he needed.

"By urgent request of his Excellency, King Malcolm Peter Svelte, we, the undersigned, respectfully command your immediate attendance at Castle Svelte or the Chamber in Gritian, whichever destination you deem most expedient. By the time this missive reaches you, Zephyr may already be lost. An invading host has entrenched itself deep within the Altirius Mountains, systematically assimilating the hill tribes under its shadow. Helleden Misenthorpe has returned."

Silurian sneered at the mention of the sorcerer's name.

"We trust you appreciate our peril. Our lives rest within your most competent hands." Alhena glanced up. "It is signed, Archbishop Abraham Uzziah, Chambermaster of the Gritian Council, Primate of Zephyr, and endorsed by the remainder of the Chamber."

Silurian's indignant tone accosted him. "The scroll is wrong. Helleden Misenthorpe died upon the plains of Lugubrius. I slew him with my own sword."

"I feared this might cause you some distress. Return to Gritian with me and I shall answer your questions along the way."

He had to lean in to hear Silurian's next words.

"Surely that cannot be true."

Alhena swallowed. "You have not heard about the queen?"

Silurian frowned. "Quarrnaine? What about her?"

Alhena took a deep breath and extended an arm toward Silurian's chair. "Come, seat yourself. What I have to say will come as a great shock."

Silurian's gaze never left him as he unfolded his arms and returned to his chair. Taking a seat, he stared hard at Alhena's staff.

Soul Forge

Bishop's Gambit

Alhena took a moment to compose himself, drank from his waterskin, and related Queen Quarrnaine's tale of four years ago…

…Unshaven faces and bloodshot eyes sat around a well-littered table, deep beneath Castle Svelte's main keep. The fiftieth morning since King Malcolm led his forces west, taking the battle to Helleden Misenthorpe's minion army.

Quarrnaine Svelte occupied the king's ornate chair at the head of the table while pages toyed with the fireplace behind her, awaiting further duties. Four men-at-arms faced each other at the hall's far end, warding a massive, double-doored entrance.

Quarrnaine rapped her scepter upon the oaken table, bringing the ragtag assembly of nobles to order.

She locked troubled eyes with the gruff man on her right, High Warlord Clavius Archimedes, an intense man of big stature. He offered her a grim smile.

Quarrnaine averted her gaze to High Bishop Abraham Uzziah, sitting across from Clavius, and nodded for him to proceed.

The bishop's bloodshot eyes remained on her as he gained his feet and performed a perfunctory benediction over his breast.

"Your Majesty." He bowed his head. "May your reign be fruitful, your health fair, and your blessings plentiful." He paused to reverently kiss the silver crucifix dangling from his neck. Letting it fall to his white vestment, he addressed the council, "My lords. My ladies. I hereby declare the Royal Council emergency session open, this ninth day of Octomb, six hundred and thirty-six."

Clavius gave him a scornful glare.

Soul Forge

Abraham removed his conical headdress and placed it upon the table between himself and Clavius. Picking up the golden goblet on the table before him, he studied the glum faces—everyone aware of the fact that the king's forces were being well beaten in the west. Swallowing loudly, he put down the goblet and pulled a yellowed scroll from inside his vestment, brandishing it like a weapon. "A few months ago, my deacon uncovered a scroll from deep within the castle's catacombs that I believe may interest this council. The scroll is written in an ancient text unknown to most, though remarkably, its contents speak of recent affairs."

He held out the scroll to the queen. "No offense intended Your Majesty, but I do not believe the script will prove intelligible to you."

She studied the scribbling briefly, turning the scroll over in her hands, before returning it to his care. "No offense taken, Your Grace." The trace of a smile tugged at the corner of her lips. "I trust it is to you."

"Aye, 'tis, my queen, though I admit, even I had to consult the chief archivist to fully appreciate its content. The scroll is dated the year of the tree, six hundred and nineteen. Two years after the Battle of Lugubrius. You probably wonder why a text written seventeen years ago is transcribed in ancient script?"

Despondent faces looked back at him.

"We don't know. Nor can we fathom how the scroll found its way into the oldest section of the vault."

He allowed his audience time to mull that over.

"The text begins with the Battle of Lugubrius. I shall spare you its retelling, but the latter passages delve into a powerful myth that has split the church factions for hundreds of years.

"I trust you are familiar with the Sacred Sword Voil legend?" He studied the mixed reactions while taking a sip from his goblet. A few blank faces greeted him. "For the benefit of those who are not, I shall endeavour to briefly retell it."

Ignoring a grunt from across the table, he recited, "Legend has it, the Sacred Sword Voil was forged upon the fiery summit of the world's highest peak by the hands of Saint Carmichael. He had planned to use the sword against factions intent upon bringing down the church. Alas, while placing the finishing touches on the blade, he was ambushed,

14

and brutally slain. Before he died, however, the legend infers that he imbued within the sword a part of himself. One of his disciples snuck into the raiding party's camp that same night and escaped with the sword. This individual sailed to our shores, and with the aid of a cult commissioned in Saint Carmichael's name, erected a shrine. The sword became the focus of the main altarpiece."

Across the table, Clavius fidgeted with the goblet before him. He heard the warlord utter under his breath, "Oh, come off it."

Abraham glanced briefly at the queen but was met with a stoic glance. He took a quick sip of his wine and continued, "The Sacred Sword Voil is reputed to have retained a measure of its magical property. The sword in question is the same sword wielded by Silurian Mintaka nineteen years ago..."

Clavius rose to his feet, his dark-green surcoat unfolding around his legs. Heavy brows accentuated his contempt. "Forgive me, my queen. I am certain everyone assembled here grows tired of listening to our good bishop's folklore. He speaks of a sword whose magic is lost. I implore we stop wasting precious time discussing hokey, religious myth. Must I point out, it is no myth battering at the king's heels? Nor is it conjecture, while we sit here fantasizing, that the realm is being laid to waste. Within the next fortnight, this great bastion known as Castle Svelte, the essence of everything we hold dear, shall fall beneath the sorcerer's shadow. I say we stop with this fairytale and get on with the business at hand." The high warlord pounded the table with the side of a clenched fist, before easing his brawn into a protesting chair.

Abraham received the harsh criticism with practiced composure.

The queen merely raised her eyebrows.

"Thank you, my queen." Abraham turned to the council. "I'm well aware of good Clavius' concern. Time is a commodity we can ill afford to waste. Thus, I implore the council to hear me out.

"The scroll reveals much, much more. It recounts the story of Silurian Mintaka's personal crusade to find the resting place of the healing saint, Raphael. Silurian believed that by locating Raphael's tomb, he might invoke the saint's spirit. The scroll states Silurian found Saint Raphael's resting place along the banks of Saros' Swamp, somewhere deep within the Forbidden Swamp. In return for restoring

Soul Forge

the blade's magic, Saros bade Silurian leave the sword under his protection.

"It's further written that the magic imbued in the sword cannot be utilized until a royal member from the House of Svelte transports it back to its resting place upon the altar of the lost shrine of Saint Carmichael. The scroll states that by placing the sword within the statue's sheath upon the altar, it will evoke an ancient magic that will restore balance to the sword—and thus, the kingdom."

Clavius spared no time getting to his feet. "Your Highness! We gain nothing listening to the prattle of religious hokum. How much time must we squander entertaining the fanatical whims of our spiritual friend? Even if there were credibility to the legend, we can ill afford the time pondering such an incredulous quest, let alone find the manpower needed to traverse the Forbidden Swamp in search of this fabled Saros' Swamp. The enemy will be at our doorstep before a fortnight is past." He hammered the table three times with a clenched fist, rattling goblets. "That. Is. Fact."

Clavius glared at Abraham, his breathing laboured. "I say, go find the hallowed sword of yon, *good* bishop. Better yet, search out Mintaka and have him lead you to it. But do it alone. This conjecture is nonsense. Utter and complete drivel."

Abraham put down his goblet. "Your Majesty, if you will be so kind as to let me finish, I assure you, I am not wasting this council's precious time."

Quarrnaine gave the high warlord a stern look. "Very well, Your Grace. Your counsel has been invaluable in the past. You deserve our undivided attention now."

She rose regally to her feet. "Further outbursts from the floor will not be tolerated." She smote the table with her scepter. "You may proceed, Your Grace."

"Thank you, my queen," Abraham said softly, his next words strong and sure. "Only a member of royal lineage, be it by birthright or religious rite, may deliver the Sacred Sword Voil to its proper resting place. Silurian Mintaka falls into the latter category. In answer to my friend, I dispatched troops weeks ago to search for him.

"My senior messenger arrived last night from Gritian. If Silurian is still alive, he cannot be found." Sipping from his goblet, he eyed

16

Soul Forge

Clavius over the cup's brim and said, "The sword *must* be sheathed upon the altar of Saint Carmichael, within its original scabbard. The script warns us that a certain condition governs this action."

"Oh, here we go," Clavius muttered.

The queen cast the warlord an ominous glance.

"Once the sword has been sheathed, its power shall be spent. The Sacred Sword Voil is one of the last remaining relics of the long-ago, Age of Saints. Should we elect to use it now, we shall be forever more left to our own devices."

Clavius rose to his feet. "Well I guess that settles it then!"

The queen jumped to her feet. "Clavius!"

The entire chamber erupted into pandemonium.

Queen Quarrnaine glanced over her shoulder only once. The morning's war council had been a tumultuous one, but in the end, she agreed with the high bishop. Something had to be done. Her small entourage of knights, accompanied by their squires, led her away from the highest house in Zephyr—her home for the past twenty-seven years.

Ranging south of their position, unseen by the company, six fleet scouts warded their flank. Trailing the queen's procession, four horse drawn wagons creaked along, laden with supplies and several spare mounts.

An acute pang of loss turned her stomach with a foreboding that she might never lay eyes on the castle again. Its massive girth. Its graceful spires. The aura of strength emanating lifelike from its lofty heights and crenellated ramparts. To Quarrnaine, the reality of her home seemed to be fading into myth—as surreal as the fable High Bishop Abraham Uzziah had her chasing. Her heart lingered with the throng of well-wishers surrounding them. Her people. They parted just enough to allow her procession passage, many extending hands, attempting to touch her as she went by. She fought unsuccessfully to prevent the tears from rolling down her cheeks.

17

Soul Forge

As she rode amongst her well-wishers, she second-guessed her decision to leave them behind. Her husband fought for his life along the Madrigail River, as did her sons in the northwest reaches of the Spine. Castle Svelte prepared for the siege surely coming, and yet, she fled eastward in search of some fantastical talisman.

She stiffened in the saddle, wiping away the tears. She had no time for self-doubt. She had to be strong. The kingdom crumbled around them. It was time she took matters into her own hands.

Turning her attention forward, the forest rose before them. The company tromped down the road leading around Castle Svelte's southern ramparts, following the shoreline of Ring Lake.

Against the vehement protests of High Warlord Clavius Archimedes, she had decided to exercise the high bishop's gambit.

Eight grueling days of hard riding netted her small band of knights the coveted Sacred Sword Voil, exactly where High Bishop Abraham claimed it rested. On the banks of Saros' Swamp, inside a small shrine, swaddled within a bundle of well-oiled cloth.

There was no doubt in Abraham's mind that the sword was the mythical weapon they sought. He recalled the intricately etched blade that had hung from Silurian Mintaka's waist during the great victory feast after the Battle of Lugubrius. Ten exquisitely etched runes; five on either side of the gleaming blade.

Four days after recovering the sword, Abraham led the envoy in double file across the gently rolling hills of the Mid Savannah. Outcroppings of exposed rock and small stands of low trees dotted the nondescript terrain.

To Abraham's right rode his personal military commander, the Warlord of Gritian. They brought the company to a halt many times, realigning their course via landmarks, and setting off again. Though the terrain proved easier to traverse than the sodden swampland, progress was slow.

Immediately behind Abraham and his commander rode the queen and her personal aide, the king's champion, Jarr-nash Sylvan Jordic.

Soul Forge

Jarr-nash had been hurt recently defending the king and had been sent back to Castle Svelte. He had been about to rejoin the king's forces, but after the tumultuous chamber meeting, the only way High Warlord Clavius would even consider allowing Queen Quarrnaine to accompany Abraham was if Jarr-nash went along as her personal protector.

Pushing their steeds to near collapse, the company charged across the Mid-Savanna, dust billowing in their wake. They had rested twice, but briefly, since breaking camp in the wee hours of dawn. Riding four abreast, with scouts on the flanks, they followed Abraham's lead.

Near sunset, a white bearded man, Alhena Sirrus, urged his mount to the front of the column. Slowing to keep alongside Abraham, he said, "Pardon my breaking rank, Your Grace, but I must confer with you."

Thunder sounded in the distance.

Abraham stared into Alhena's queer, white eyes. "Granted. What weighs you?"

"Perhaps it is nothing, Your Grace," Alhena said, raising a hand to rub at his bearded lower lip. "But I sense something foul afoot. The sky's usual brilliance has left it. More so than the sun's setting justifies. Nor is there evidence of wildlife about."

The lead riders knit their brows in unison, scanning the countryside.

The warlord spoke, "I see nothing amiss. With all the commotion of our passing, I'd be surprised if we encountered any wildlife at all. Consider your concerns noted. Return to your file."

The lead riders smiled at the warlord's next words. "The sweltering heat has affected your eyes, my aged friend."

"Aye, my Lord. Indeed, my eyes are not what they used to be, but I speak not only of the absence of animals, but also of the carrion birds that have dogged us since we left the Forbidden Swamp."

Abraham spoke up, "Alhena. Need I have someone escort you?"

When Alhena's pace didn't drop off, the warlord snorted. "You're a worthy messenger, there is no doubt, but I am thinking age has taken—"

His words caught in his throat.

A shadow fell across the landscape—black wisps of unnatural cloud coalesced upon the horizon.

The quest ground to a halt.

Soul Forge

Abraham groped for the crucifix about his neck. "What in God's name?"

The countryside darkened again—swirling black mist thickened overhead.

The warlord ordered the company into a gallop. The pikemen and wagon train quickly dropped behind.

The sky continued to darken. Large blots of black mist swirled together, transforming overhead into an ebony ceiling. The sun had all but disappeared, offering no more than an eerie glow. A strong wind blew up, throwing dirt and small debris into their faces, forcing them to hunker down in their saddles.

As the last vestiges of sunlight faded, the blackened sky burst into a blood red glow. Alhena looked up to see a massive, crimson fireball hurtling earthward.

Terrified horses threw riders to the ground and bolted away. The few who were able to control their frantic mounts, spurred them away from the fireball's path—the crackling power of the plummeting ball of flames drowned out the roar of the wind. All sense of rank and order were abandoned.

"Keep moving!" the warlord shouted.

Another blinding flash illuminated the countryside as a second fireball coalesced overhead.

The first fiery globe detonated before it hit the ground, shaking the land and exploding into thousands of fist-sized globules of burning rain that pelted the hapless riders.

Men and women fell writhing to the ground, consumed by the deadly fire. The baggage train took the brunt of the blast, turning the wagons into instant funeral pyres.

Jarr-nash plucked Quarrnaine from her faltering stallion, and set her before him, hefting a great shield over their heads.

Another flash illuminated the pitch at the same time the second fireball burst into a shower of flames. Screams of agony and terror echoed above the fiery roar.

Soul Forge

The countryside lit up. Another fireball formed. In the bright glare, a large outcropping of rock appeared on Jarr-nash's left. He uttered a silent prayer and summoned a thunderous shout from the depth of his being, "This way!"

The skies opened up. Sheets of rain slashed across the countryside, soaking them instantly. When the next blinding flash flooded the landscape, Jarr-nash saw what appeared to be a large statue standing guard over a stone building. The statue stood with arms folded and its legs straddling a set of wooden doors nestled between its feet. One of the doors flapped wildly in the wind.

Trees flared up like great torches, providing an eerie light to ride by. Another flash illuminated the countryside.

Abraham rode his horse dangerously close to Jarr-nash, his mount fighting to retain its footing in the slick mire of grass and mud. "The shrine! The shrine!"

Jarr-nash nodded. The remote building could be none other than the lost shrine of Saint Carmichael.

The ground heaved. A scream sounded to Jarr-nash's right as a knight toppled from his saddle engulfed in flames. The knight's horse bolted away into the darkness.

Jarr-nash ducked. A fireball hurtled by and impacted the midsection of the statue they headed toward. The ensuing concussion obliterated the statue and threw the remaining horses to the ground, pelting them with shards of blasted rock.

Jarr-nash's horse went down hard. He clutched his queen tightly, but the impact proved too much for him to hang on. She slid into a large chunk of blasted statue and bounced into the path of their sliding horse. One of its flailing hooves clipped her head.

Jarr-nash arrested his slide and ran to her, ignoring the patches of fire spreading from the base of the destroyed entranceway. He fell to his knees, shocked by the blood washing over Quarrnaine's beautiful face.

The sky brightened. A new fireball formed.

Ensuring the Sacred Sword Voil remained strapped across his back, he scooped the queen into his arms, and attempted to stand. Quarrnaine's unwieldy weight, combined with the slippery mire underfoot, made the simple feat impossible.

21

Soul Forge

He fell forward, spinning his body to avoid landing on her, and hit the ground hard. Quarrnaine's weight crushed the breath from him. Gasping for air, he tried to get up. He needed to release his queen but couldn't bring himself to do so.

He panicked. The burning wall of grasses advanced upon him—hungry flames driven by the wind, only an arm span away. The intense heat and black smoke, suffocated him.

A pair of hands grasped him by the armpits and helped him to his feet as another flash illuminated the chaos. Sparing a quick glance over his shoulder, he almost fell again at the sight of Alhena's unusual eyes.

He forced his way through the encroaching wall of flames, not daring to see whether the old man followed them. The queen's life was paramount.

Again, he slipped and fell. The raging fires nipped at his heels, but he refused to release his burden. He'd no sooner hit the ground when Alhena's hands lifted him back to his feet.

He slipped and stumbled the rest of the way to the shrine, somehow managing not to fall again, and stopped at the top of a stone stairwell. The chipped steps descending into the earth were blocked by statue debris.

Left with no choice, he laid the queen amongst the rubble. With Alhena's help he began digging.

From out of nowhere, Abraham, two knights, and the Gritian warlord joined them.

One of the knights uncovered the splintered remains of a door, but they still couldn't find any sign of the entrance proper.

A thunderous detonation rocked the land. The pile of debris they stood amongst lurched and collapsed upon itself, taking everyone down with it. To Jarr-nash's relief they had tumbled into the relative calm of the shrine's interior—the spot from which they had fallen, engulfed in fire.

They lay in disarray within a small chapel. The flames crackling from above cast an ethereal light upon a larger than life statue matching the one that had stood guard over the entrance. Jarr-nash's eyes focused on the empty scabbard hanging from the statue's waist.

Soul Forge

He pushed aside the crumbled rock that had fallen on him and went to his queen. She lay half buried in debris but her even chest falls reassured him she was alive.

He freed her from the rubble and with Alhena's help, stood up with Quarrnaine clutched in his arms—silt and small debris sifted from her limp body to the floor.

He traversed the nave and mounted the altar steps. Kneeling before the sacred presence, he gently laid Quarrnaine upon the dusty altar.

Behind him, the bishop prostrated upon the top step, mumbling incoherently to the altar piece. The warlord remained amongst the pews, halfway between the cleric and the two knights who had remained at the entrance.

Alhena stood at the base of the chancel steps, glancing anxiously from warlord, to bishop, to the statue.

Jarr-nash shook the queen's shoulders. "We are here, my lady. We found the shrine. We need you to wake."

She didn't stir.

A crimson flash illuminated the shrine, causing all but the queen to turn and gasp. Framed by the flaming doorway, one of the knights shouted, "It's coming right at us!"

Jarr-nash's eyes grew wide, his attempts to awaken the queen more animated.

The knights shrunk away from the doorway, yelling for him to hurry.

Jarr-nash reached over his shoulder. With a euphoric 'swish' the blade slid from its sheath. He jumped to his feet, facing the serene altarpiece staring back at him.

The light in the chapel increased, a harbinger of the fireball's approach.

Jarr-nash raised the Sacred Sword Voil, positioning its gleaming tip at the small slit atop the marble scabbard.

Bishop Uzziah's cry diverted his attention. "No, you fool! You'll destroy the blade!" He appeared to be having an apoplectic fit.

Jarr-nash stared dumbly at the bishop, unsure what to do.

A frantic movement near the chapel's entrance caught his eye. The knights were bent over, covering their heads with their arms. The unnerving whine of their approaching doom rose to a deafening roar.

Soul Forge

Jarr-nash hesitated for only a moment longer before doing the only thing he knew to save his queen. With a loud clang, he drove the blade home. The sword's hilt shuddered to a halt atop the dusty scabbard at the same moment the fiery globe impacted the shrine's entrance.

Jarr-nash's last images were of the knights disappearing in a wave of flame as it swept through the chamber on the heels of a powerful concussion.

The sound of grating rock sounded above the din as the granite roof collapsed into the bowels of the blasted shrine.

Dust motes danced amid the moonbeams filtering into the desecrated shrine of Saint Carmichael. The only sound wafting across the destruction, other than the occasional popping from the dying fires outside, were of pulverized mortar sifting its way down the remnants of the shrine's walls.

At the base of the altar's dais, beneath a layer of black soot and splintered rock, High Bishop Abraham Uzziah stirred. A feeble cough escaped his throat. He lay upon his back. A heavy weight pinned his left arm but he was thankful to be alive.

In the shrine's relative darkness, he whispered a solemn prayer to his good fortune as the dreadful events of earlier in the day washed over him.

Ignoring the throbbing pain in his shoulder, he pulled his injured arm from beneath the small roof slab lying upon it. He sat up and looked around, his bloodied arm hanging uselessly at his side.

He flinched as a piece of broken rock fell somewhere in the darkness behind him. When the chapel became tomblike again, he heard the faint breathing of someone buried next to him.

With his good arm, he searched through the rubble until he discovered a leg. The moon's position in the early morning sky blanketed the shrine floor in shadow, preventing him from seeing who it belonged to. Reaching into his vestment, he fished out his tinder box. From another pocket he withdrew a scroll. Hoping the parchment wasn't too important, he set it aflame.

Soul Forge

As his eyes adjusted to the new light, he discovered the leg belonged to his personal messenger, Alhena Sirrus. The archivist with the strange white eyes. The deacon who had discovered Saint Carmichael's scroll.

Abraham shook him a couple of times to no avail. He would have to be content with the soft exhalations escaping the old man's lips.

The queen!

Doing his best to ignore the pain in his shoulder, he struggled to his feet and made his way over the rubble, mounting the steps to where the statue of Saint Carmichael had stood. The scant light from his makeshift torch revealed the toppled statue's feet. Large pieces of its broken legs led back toward the steps.

Directing the rapidly diminishing flames to follow the broken statue, he abruptly stopped his progress. Near the base of the steps, two motionless figures lay crushed beneath the statue's torso. He picked his way through the rock fragments, dreading what he already knew to be true.

At his feet lay the lifeless bodies of his queen and the king's champion. Pulling smaller pieces of statue and broken roof from them, he discovered Jarr-nash wrapped tightly around Quarrnaine—protecting her even in death.

Tears welled in his eyes, streaking his dirty face. He reached out to touch their necks. His body shook with grief as his touch confirmed his fear.

He dropped the remains of his makeshift torch amongst the rubble. The scroll unfolded, sputtered and went out. Darkness enveloped the ruins.

As throes of despair wracked his body, he noted the serene stillness outside. The winds had subsided, the rain abated, and the thundering detonations of exploding fireballs were but a distant echo within his fragile mind. Pungent smoke of burning grass wafted upon a gentle breeze. A blanket of stars sparkled in silent spectacle around a three-quarter moon.

He shivered. Goosebumps prickled his exposed skin. A cool breeze swept through the broken walls, swirling granite dust around the silent chapel.

Soul Forge

Unseen, crushed beneath the halves of the statue's broken head, two hands firmly clutched the hilt of a finely wrought blade. One hand slender and delicate.

The Sacred Sword Voil pulsed softly within its unbroken sheath.

Soul Forge

To Live Again

Alhena swallowed hard. The fire had fallen to a hungry glow during his lengthy recital of the events that had led to the queen's death, entombing the hut in shadow—the heat insufficient to ward off the evening chill.

Silurian uttered a barely audible groan. Bending over his knees, he covered his face with his hands, grieving the loss his seclusion had cost Zephyr and her people. The random pop of cooling embers was all that disturbed the silence.

Silurian lifted his dirt smeared face from his hands. Darkness had fallen. At some point Alhena had stoked the fire.

The few candle stubs around the room flickered and danced in the half-light, exuding a warm, cozy atmosphere, a direct contrast to the mood of the hut's occupants.

Alhena stood where he had for most of the afternoon, his colourless eyes radiating empathy.

Silurian wanted to hug him. Cry into his shoulder. Experience the embrace of another human being, but his damaged pride wouldn't allow it. Self-loathing overwhelmed him.

The price the kingdom had paid four years ago, because he had hidden from the king's men, made his anger boil. The iron grip of grief threatened to choke him but his mind kept returning to the fact that the people of Zephyr were not there for his family during *their* time of need. It was irrational—he knew it. Even so, the bitterness refused to leave.

27

Soul Forge

Not knowing how to deal with the strong emotions, his dark thoughts turned on Alhena. Who the hell did Alhena think he was? Silurian didn't need pity. He craved only to understand the fairness of life.

Deep down, he appreciated Alhena's valour and the courage he had shown in relating the tragic events of Quarrnaine's demise, and yet, Silurian wanted nothing more than to choke out of him for having the audacity to care.

He dropped his head into his hands, fighting the urge. He forced himself to mumble, "Thank you. The story must be difficult for you to tell."

Alhena's eyes brightened. "Aye. It is not a tale I care to remember. With your leave, I shall find your pantry and fix us a long overdue meal."

Silurian's throat tightened. All he could do was nod.

After a scant meal, Alhena set his empty plate on the floor beside him.

Silurian's anger simmered, but he still felt it darkening the periphery of his mind. "What do you know of Rook Bowman?"

"If you mean, where is he, I do not know. The last I heard is that he left Castle Svelte shortly after the Battle of Lugubrius in search of his wife, Melody, but I believe you already know that. Rumour has placed him in the Forbidden Swamp."

Silurian nodded. He had accompanied Rook as far east as Saros' Swamp, following the trail of her abductors, before returning home. He had also travelled extensively afterward with Rook, looking for answers, but he kept those memories buried deep.

"You have remained locked away within this hut for twenty years? I find that difficult to comprehend."

Silurian scowled. "I tried fitting back into the real world. More than once." He searched for a way to explain his true feelings, but the proper words were beyond his grasp. Wiping his eyes with a dirty wrist, he stared at the floor. "It never worked out. Each attempt ended worse than the last. I did unspeakable things. Things better left unsaid. Trust me when I tell you I am better off here where I can't hurt anyone."

With that admission, he withdrew into a trancelike state, no longer acknowledging Alhena's presence. Although he dreaded the dreams

28

sleep would bring, he preferred their company over trying to control his conflicting emotions about Alhena's presence. In the uneasy silence, he drifted off.

Alhena awoke to the ominous creak of wooden planks above his head. Silurian's chair was empty.

Gathering his cloak around him to ward off the morning chill, he stood, listening. The sound of footfalls creaked their way to the rear of the hut.

In the full light of the new day, the cabin's interior appeared much worse than it had yesterday evening. He spotted a rickety stairway along the back wall of the hut.

Cresting the last step, he entered a dark hallway and stopped to listen. The roof continued to creak above him. At the hallway's far end, the worn remnants of wooden rungs led up to a dark recess in the ceiling.

He climbed the uncertain ladder into a poorly constructed shed. Dusty shelves, laden with small urns in various states of repair, cluttered the walls. Sunlight filtered through a door left ajar.

Easing the door open he was shocked by the sight of a poorly tended garden vying for space amongst a thick growth of weeds upon the rooftop. Strange, he hadn't noticed the garden from the ground.

Movement from the roof's far corner caught his attention. Silurian knelt, twisting tomatoes from their stalk, not paying any attention to him as he walked through the garden.

"Wonderful day for travelling, eh?"

Silurian grunted.

Casting his gaze about the rooftop, Alhena admired the self-contained garden, as shabby as it was. He shook his head. The kingdom didn't have time for home garden admiration. He needed Silurian's answer, but he didn't know how to coerce it from him. It should be simple. 'Are you coming or not?' But the issue was more complex than that. If Silurian refused, what then? Throw him over a shoulder?

Soul Forge

Seeing the man up close, he debated whether Silurian agreeing to accompany him was a good idea at all. By the looks of him, he required months of hard training with sword and horse if he were to become even a shade of his former self. The kingdom didn't have that much time.

There was also the man's mental state to consider. Silurian was, without a doubt, unstable. Zephyr might be better served if Alhena were to inform the council that his search had come up empty. He shook his head. He couldn't do that. Or could he?

He took a deep breath. "I see how you have kept yourself alive all these years."

Silurian didn't respond.

Alhena cursed himself. *Think, you old fool. Ask him and be done with it.*

Silurian rose to his feet, wiping his hands on his pants. "Tell me, old man. What use has the Chamber for me? Even your strange eyes can see I'm not the man I used to be."

"I am not privy to Chamber deliberations."

"Bah. Do you believe I can just pick up where I left off?" Silurian's voice rose, "Look at me. I'm not worthy to wield a sword in the king's name. Hell, I probably couldn't pick up a sword in my own name."

Alhena didn't shy from his glare.

"People died because of my inaction. Great people. How can the Chamber honestly think the king's men will rally behind me after what happened to Quarrnaine?" Silurian's eyes were red.

Alhena surveyed the garden, trying to find something meaningful to say. Perhaps he should have waited before relating the story of the bishop's gambit.

"It is not for me to say, though I think you have the way of it. The people will not take kindly to you. At first. Once they realize what happened to your family, they may think differently. All I know for sure is that Zephyr will not survive without some kind of divine intervention. It is the elders' respected opinion that such intervention can only come from one of two people. You, or Sir Rook. I would be amiss not to tell you, and you did not hear this from me, but the council believes that if you *and* Sir Rook are found, even together, you may not be strong enough to defeat Helleden this time."

Soul Forge

Sweat beaded upon Alhena's brow despite the cool temperature. "So, I ask you, Sir Silurian Mintaka, former king's champion, and Group of Five member, will you accompany me to Gritian?"

Silurian's lips curled with sarcasm. "You forgot Liberator of Zephyr."

"So I did, but the question still remains."

Silurian's breathing quickened. He reached behind his ears with both hands, entangling his fingers within his long hair. "And how are we supposed to get to Gritian? Didn't the Chamber bother to give you a horse?"

Alhena flinched.

"Well?"

"I lost him."

"So, we have to walk? All the way to Gritian?"

Alhena shrugged. "I just need your answer. Are you, or are you not, willing to accompany me back to the Chamber?"

Silurian glared at him for a moment before the life faded from his eyes. His vacant gaze fell to the rooftop. "I cannot."

Although Alhena expected that answer, had actually hoped for it, hearing it felt like a slap to the face. Unable to keep the disgust from his voice, he said, "Then my usefulness here has expired. With your leave, I shall return to Gritian with your decision."

Silurian's subtle shooing motion of his hands dismissed him.

Alhena lingered for only a moment. He strode briskly across the earthen rooftop to the shed door. Pausing on the threshold, he glanced back. Silurian stood with slumped shoulders, his head lowered. Swallowing the words he wanted to throw at the sorry man, Alhena stepped into the shed and slammed the door.

The clear blue sky above the ramshackle hut crackled with energy.

Alhena stumbled. A faint trail of lightning careened erratically across the cloudless sky. He passed through the broken gate and stopped to look around. A strange sensation tingled in his mind, warning him that something wasn't right. He debated going back to the hut but a stern voice brought him up short.

"Messenger! Hold!" Above the cabin's eave, Silurian waved his arms.

Alhena frowned. Hold for what? He slowly turned in a circle trying to identify the source of his misgiving.

Shortly, the front door burst open. Silurian emerged, toting a weathered leather rucksack and the pommel of an old sword protruding from the top of his fancy scabbard. He didn't stop to close the door.

Crouching low beside the southwest corner of Silurian's hut, the black cloaked figure from the Hog's Head Inn watched as the hut's occupant scrambled through the broken picket gate to join the older man. The pair ambled up the faint trail toward Zephyr's main road.

Making sure no one was around, the hunched stranger scampered in their wake, darting from tree to tree, never losing sight of them.

When the two men turned north along Redfire Path, the figure stopped, content. Searching around one last time, the figure stole across the main road and slipped down the lesser used, Nordic Wood Byway—heading west, toward the Gulch.

Soul Forge

Return to Fear

Rook Bowman had come to the Forbidden Swamp long ago in search of his estranged wife, Melody. He had been allowed in because of who he was. He had been allowed to stay because of who he had become.

Musty air and the smell of rot and death permeated the swampland, mixed in with the fragrant scents of blossoms festooning the region's multitude of bogs, fens, swamps, quagmires, and little lakes—a perfect biosphere for the varied species calling the marshland home.

Middle aged and battle weary, Rook had once been the leader of an infamous band of vigilantes the kingdom had affectionately called, the Group of Five. Before the Battle of Lugubrius had changed everything.

Rook had chosen to live as a recluse out here in the wilds and his past deeds drifted into obscurity—forgotten by all but old men. In the Forbidden Swamp he had little need to maintain his fighting prowess with his fabled bow. The swamp creatures defended the borders, requiring little support from him. No one entered the swampland undetected. Known locally as the Innerworld, the Forbidden Swamp thrived in its symbiosis. No hunters. No prey.

Over the years, Rook built two small structures on the shores of a small pond. One to live in, the other, a shrine to St. Raphael and a place to house his best friend's priceless artifact, now gone. Taken by Queen Quarrnaine on her ill-fated quest a few years ago.

A peculiar golden aura emanated from the water of the pond he referred to as Saros' Swamp, illuminating the area and basking its shores in a warm, yellow glow.

Deep beneath the placid surface dwelled a creature reportedly possessed of an ancient magic—Saros, the warder of the Innerworld.

Soul Forge

Rook stood in front of his hut staring at the placid water of Saros' Swamp, anticipating a message from the creature. Indiscernibly at first, inches from his feet, the auburn glare dissipated, revealing a man-sized rectangle of black water.

Thirteen red images coalesced upon the surface before him— thirteen simple ovals with dots of deeper crimson in their centres— thirteen eyes. Red meant death, but he couldn't comprehend what the eyes represented. They swirled around the perimeter of the viewing area. The largest eye detached itself from the circle and drifted into the centre. The remaining twelve eyes circled around it several times before the entire image dispersed back into the flotsam from which it had been constructed.

Saros had displayed this message before, but Rook struggled to determine its relevance. Communicating with Saros was never easy.

He entered his mud and grass shack to lie down for a nap, but sleep refused to come. Something wasn't right and the thirteen red eyes were at the heart of his unrest.

He stared at the brown thatched roof. A peculiar sensation sent a wave of cold flooding through him. *Did the symbols hail the return of Helleden Misenthorpe?*

He calmed his breathing. In an effort to get that thought from his mind, a memory of Silurian Mintaka jumped into his head. As usual, thoughts of Silurian started out happy, but always turned dark.

Rook's throat tightened. They had shared so much together, but in the end, they had lost so much more. Fighting back tears, he smiled. Did the crazy bugger still make that awful swill he called Dragonbane? An appropriate name for sure. Grimacing, he could almost taste that dreadful swill to this day and the way it hit like a warhammer.

He let out a heavy sigh. What had driven Silurian to do the things he had done? Silurian had been the epitome of goodness. Through all the bad times they experienced before the Battle of Lugubrius, Silurian had always been the one to find the best in a dire situation. People often commented that the sunlight shone from his arse.

The murder of Silurian's family had played an instrumental part in his mind shift. How could it not? During the dark years that followed, something deeper had taken root in the beleaguered man. During their quest to locate Melody, he had lost sight of the virtues that had made him so great. Fueled by his need to make sense of his family's murder and his sister's disappearance, his mind had slid down a dark path and eventually lost its grip on reality altogether.

Rook loved Silurian like a brother—perhaps even more so. Their falling out had torn him apart. The worst part of those years had come when Rook realized he was powerless to prevent Silurian's demise.

Oh, Silurian, what transformed you from the saint the world cherished, to the malevolent creature you became? We were fortunate to survive at all.

Thunder sounded in the distance.

Rook swung his legs over the edge of his cot. He must've dropped off, but it didn't feel like he had slept for long. Hobbling to the food cupboard, he stopped, sensing a foreign presence. He made his way to the doorway and gazed out at the perpetual mist.

Nothing appeared untoward.

A breeze toyed with his shoulder-length, black tresses. The presence grew stronger.

He squinted through the golden haze suspended over the water, past St. Raphael's small shrine, into the mist clinging to the scrub. Nothing moved.

The air became deathly still. No sound reached his ears other than his heavy breathing. The hairs on the back of his neck stood on end. Something wasn't right.

The pond's golden hue faded and winked out. Gooseflesh prickled his skin.

He wanted to retrieve the bow hanging inside his hut, but his feet refused to move. The unknown presence felt so malign it threatened to suffocate him. He could taste the vileness in the air.

Helleden?

He wasn't prone to jumping to conclusions—fear wasn't a frequent companion, but at this moment, in this place, with the strange sensation enveloping him, fear overwhelmed him.

The sun disappeared behind ebony clouds.

Soul Forge

Redfire Path

The first day of travel along Zephyr's main artery was done in uneasy silence. Redfire Path originated in the southern seaport of Ember Breath and ran the length of the kingdom, culminating at the gates of Cliff Face. The well-trodden roadway jutted around lofty oaks and majestic maples, traversing an occasional bluff as it undulated through the peaceful Nordic Wood.

The path was wide enough for four men to walk abreast, but Silurian chose to remain a few steps behind Alhena, preferring to keep his own company.

Alhena had tried to introduce conversation when they first set out, but received little response, so he tromped on, setting a slow enough pace for Silurian to keep up.

When the forest darkened with evening shadow, Alhena located a small clearing off the path, edged by a babbling brook.

Silurian limped in after him and dropped his shoulder pack.

"We should gather wood," Alhena suggested, but his suffering companion simply unrolled his bedding, and slid beneath it. The half-day's journey had exacted its toll.

Reflecting on the state he had found Silurian in, Alhena was amazed Silurian had made it *this* far. He might yet prove himself someone to be reckoned with if he hadn't just curled up to die.

Settling against a large rock, Alhena mulled over the events of the last few days as a slight drizzle fell, forcing him into his bedroll for the night.

Silurian stirred violently twice during the night, waking suddenly with a yelp and harsh breathing, scaring Alhena half to death.

In the morning, Alhena built a fire to dry out his damp cloak and provide them with a hot breakfast. Stirring the contents of a shallow

36

pot, he watched Silurian yawn awake. He bowed his head in deference to the warrior. "Good morning to you, Sir Silurian."

Silurian grunted. "Don't bob your head at me. I'm no king."

"Forgive me, Sire. Should my formalities offend you, I shall cease them forthwith."

They ate a hot meal of cooked elderberries, crushed in a paste and chased it down with a mug of an exotic root juice, all of which Alhena provided.

Silurian took one sip of the root juice, gave the cup a look of disgust, and tossed the contents into the fire, choosing instead, a bottle of homemade liquor he pulled from his pack.

Alhena glared at him. His rations were proportioned to get him back to Gritian. On horseback.

Silurian never lifted his glare from the wooden bowl, grumbling from time to time at the meagre fare.

Before Alhena had cleaned the dishes and packed his bedroll, Silurian left the clearing without him. Alhena threw his pack over a shoulder and hurried after the impetuous man.

The day promised easy travelling. By mid-morning the forest gave way to an expanse of golden grass that stretched north toward a chain of mountains rising purplish-black across the horizon. The Undying Wall.

Alhena paused to stare vacantly at the grassland to the west. His throat constricted and a tear threatened to escape his left eye.

Silurian gave him a curious look.

Swallowing hard, he snapped out of his momentary melancholy. Without a word, he strode into the grassland trench that marked Redfire's passing.

The joyous cacophony of birdsong in the forest gave way to the annoying drone of biting insects. Clouds of gnats were drawn to their faces while grasshoppers and crickets scattered into the heather at their approach.

As the day drew on, Alhena struggled to keep walking through the insufferable, mid-afternoon heat. Being exposed upon the grassland provided them little reprieve from the scorching sun. He pushed on, however, because the Chamber had demanded his speedy return.

Soul Forge

He was reluctant to look back lest he discover that Silurian had collapsed, but the cadenced scuff of the man's leather boots, and the occasional slosh of liquid as Silurian consumed his liquor, provided proof of his continued existence.

"There aren't any bloody rivers near this forsaken path," Silurian commented during the afternoon. "No wonder there's no bloody trees." He took a long look at an empty liquor bottle clutched in his hands and pitched it into the tall grasses. The bottle thudded to the ground and rustled briefly before the sound of it breaking announced its final resting place. He pulled the stopper from his waterskin and swallowed deeply. "You picked a fine time to lose your mount."

Alhena shot him a pained look and called a halt to their slow march.

Neither man spoke while they ate. Alhena drank sparingly from his waterskin, while Silurian quaffed the contents of another liquor bottle.

Alhena shook his head. *That's all the realm needs. An out of shape, middle-aged sot who hasn't seen battle in years.* Using his staff to assist him, he stood. "We should put a few more leagues behind us before nightfall."

He left Silurian staring at the bottle between his knees.

Trudging along behind Alhena, Silurian thought about all the predatory animals that might be lurking about, hidden within the tall grass. Boars, wildcats, snakes, and worse. He scanned the undulating wall, searching for telltale signs of movement. Besides palm-sized dragonflies flitting about, and the ever-present cloud of gnats, nothing moved.

He clenched and unclenched the leather hilt of his old practice blade. Other than the tall stick Alhena carried, the messenger appeared to possess no other weapon. Fat lot of good he was going to be in a fight. Unless he *was* a wizard.

In the waning sunlight, Alhena led them off the path. Picking a spot, he trampled a clearing to use for the night.

Supper consisted of dried bread and salted meat, that again, Alhena provided.

Soul Forge

Silurian drank himself into a stupor and passed-out beneath his bedroll.

The next morning dawned warmer than the last. Alhena ate a cold breakfast of nuts and fruits while Silurian drank half a bottle of spirits. Alhena offered to share his meagre fare, but Silurian merely snarled at him.

Disgusted with the way he continually treated Alhena, but too proud to apologize, Silurian kept his eyes on the ground at his feet while Alhena stowed his gear and waded through the tall grass to rejoin the path.

It was some time before he joined Alhena patiently waiting for him down the trail.

They plodded along in silence until the sun rose above the wall of grass, heralding another day of intense heat.

Sweat fell steadily from Silurian's face, due in no small part to his alcohol consumption. His mind felt bleary and his leg muscles screamed. The fact that the Undying Wall didn't seem any closer today did little to alleviate his weary soul.

At one point, he said, "Hey, messenger."

Alhena stopped.

"What makes you so brave?"

Alhena frowned, jabbed his staff into the baked earth and started forward again. "I do not know. I am not, really. Why do you ask?"

Silurian matched his pace. "Evil things flourish during times of trouble. Wars draw out the scum. Cutthroats, thieves, and their ilk. They crawl out from beneath the rocks. Roadways are unsafe."

Alhena offered no response.

"Why did the Gritian council send a defenseless old man like you? Why not an armed escort? If the need is dire, why just send you?" He stared at the staff. "Unless you *are* a wizard."

Alhena stopped. His milky eyes stared back. Silurian couldn't tell what emotion was behind them.

Alhena shrugged out of his rucksack and placed it between them. Unlashing the sack's leather thongs, he reached into the bulky bag and withdrew two bundles wrapped in rags. Within the rags rested two sets of four, five-inch steel spikes, each set anchored to a leather strap.

Silurian's eyebrows knitted. "What in hell's name are those?"

Soul Forge

Alhena lashed the spikes to his hands. Eight deadly shanks extended from his knuckles. "I call them knucklettes."

"Knucklettes?"

"Aye. A weapon I discovered north of the Kraidic Empire.

"North of the Kraidic Empire? There's nothing but snow up there."

"True, but the people that live in the harsh climate have found ways to adapt."

Silurian wasn't impressed.

"You see, I am not as helpless as you think." Alhena flexed his hands before slipping out of the knucklettes and repacking them. Slinging the pack over his shoulder, he continued walking.

"Humph," Silurian managed. *A fat lot of good they were going to be in a sword fight,* he thought, but he wished Alhena had kept them on. If they were attacked, he would spend more time defending the old fool while he donned his weapons, than he did nullifying the threat.

The afternoon drew on. Mountainous clouds sailed lazily across the sky, casting them in appreciated shadow for brief periods of time.

Silurian's sword hand twitched. His ever-searching eyes darted all around.

"Do you think we are in danger, Sire? Out here?" Alhena asked, his gaze directed at Silurian's hand.

Silurian grunted. "I'm always prepared. It keeps me alive."

Alhena faced him squarely with those damned, haunting eyes. "Hmm. Surely, I have outlived my welcome in this world, but still, here I am. Yet, I am not on end—"

"I'm not on end, damn it. If you wish to remain of this world, you'd be better served wearing your weapons. Or do you just plan on swinging that stick around?"

Alhena didn't dignify the question with an answer. Instead, he said, "My stomach tells me it is time to eat."

After a brief stop they set off into the sunset; the Undying Wall, awash in evening sunshine, still a full walking day away.

As the sun lost its grip upon the land, Alhena trampled down another camp away from Redfire Path. They ate sparingly, both men cognizant of the fact that their diminishing supplies wouldn't see them all the way to Gritian.

Soul Forge

The next day dawned hotter than the last. The looming wall of mountains, iron grey in the morning sunlight, appeared closer this morning than they had last night. Fluffy, white clouds cast drifting shadows across the lofty heights.

Alhena stopped to strap on his knucklettes as they closed on the small foothills at the base of the Undying Wall.

Silurian unsheathed his sword. "What is it?"

"Simmer yourself, Sire," Alhena laughed.

Silurian spun about, searching for things unseen.

"We are a few hours from the pass. There has been much unrest within the mountains of late. I exercise caution, is all."

Silurian harrumphed. He lowered his blade and stormed ahead. "It's about time you took our safety seriously."

Alhena started after him. "You needn't worry about me."

Silurian grunted, "See to it that you live long enough to get me back to Gritian."

Alhena caught up to him. "I have outlasted many worthy adversaries by surrounding myself with company such as yourself. I believe I shall reach Gritian once more before I expire."

Silurian didn't know what to say to that. He stopped and sheathed his sword. Shrugging out of his rucksack, he dropped it to the ground and rummaged through the worn leather bag. Locating what he sought, he withdrew a bundle of oily rags and caringly pulled aside the blackened cloth. Buried within the beggarly rags rested an exquisitely crafted dagger. Tiny gems were inset along gilded ribbons adorning the blade.

Alhena gaped as Silurian nonchalantly flipped the gleaming dagger through the air, catching the ivory handle unerringly in his left hand.

With no regard for the priceless relic, Silurian threw the dagger to the ground near his feet. The knife easily sliced into the hard earth, coming to a quivering rest halfway up its blade.

Alhena winced. "Isn't that...?"

"Soulbiter." Silurian rummaged deeper into the folded rags and withdrew a magnificently tooled sheath matching the dagger's blade. He extracted Soulbiter from the ground, grit audibly grating along its length, and wiped it upon his thigh; his filthy pants barely registered the stain. Thrusting the dagger into its sheath, he jammed it into his

41

belt, and walked off with a grunt. "It isn't of much use, other than shaving."

Redfire Path ascended into the foothills, rising out from the grassy trench toward the forbidding granite grandeur looming before them. The Undying wall rose straight up from the sparse foothills, its lofty crags drifting in and out of view behind skulking clouds.

As the approach into the mountain pass came into view, the jagged peaks were obstructed by the mountain's bulk. The foothills terminated at the entrance to the pass; a trenchlike passage that split opposing cliff faces.

Alhena stopped before entering the trench's murky shadows. "We sleep here tonight. We should spend as little time in there as possible."

Silurian walked a couple of steps into the gloom, examining the trail. Remembering his youth and the many run-ins with a particular troll, he didn't relish the prospect of entering the lower trench at night. He rejoined Alhena in the fading sunlight.

Skirting a house-sized boulder on the eastern side of the path, they made camp.

Silurian dropped his bedroll to the ground and plopped himself on top of it. He retrieved an unfinished bottle from his pack, pulled the cork with his teeth, and spat it on the ground. Swallowing several mouthfuls, he uncharacteristically held the bottle out for Alhena.

Alhena had scrounged enough fuel to keep a fire burning. "No thank you, Sir. I don't hold liquor well. Perhaps when we reach the Undying Pools."

Alhena prepared the fire and waited until it burned of its own accord before unrolling his bedroll close to the meagre flames. It wasn't long before he dropped off to sleep.

Silurian studied his travelling companion in the flickering light as he set to work sharpening Soulbiter with a well-used whetstone. He wondered how old Alhena actually was? Much older than himself, certainly, and he was pushing forty-five. Or was it forty-six? He shook his head. Who really cared?

A sudden shiver tingled his skin. What would the Chamber think of him? From what Alhena had said, it might be better if he didn't return to active duty. What if the king discovered he had blatantly avoided his attempts to locate him four years ago? He didn't think he could face King Malcolm.

He winced. Perhaps he should slip into the night and return to the false security offered by his fireplace.

Clouds rolled in, obscuring the stars. He dropped his millstone into his pack and wrapped himself in his bedroll to ward off the chill.

The clouds thickened as the night slipped by. An empty bottle lay beside him. Fumbling through his sparse provisions he pulled out his second last bottle. He considered conserving his dwindling supply, but in the end, he unstopped the bottle with his teeth and took a healthy swig, smiling as it bit his pallet and warmed his throat.

Looking about, the dark mass of the mountains gave him pause. The hidden heights seemed to be reaching down to smother him.

A breeze kicked up. The sputtering fire threw ghastly shadows upon the rock face beside him.

He unsheathed Soulbiter and slipped from his bedroll. Walking around the small perimeter of light given off by the struggling campfire, he perceived an evil presence stalking him from just beyond the fire's glow. The firelight dimmed, sputtering for life—the suddenness of it made him jump.

He crouched and looked around but saw nothing. Calming his breathing, he located the bundle of sticks Alhena had scavenged and tossed the whole pile onto the embers. The fire flared to life, giving audience to the mischievous shadows dancing upon the wall.

Alhena sat bolt upright.

Silurian's heart caught in his throat. "By the gods!" he swore. "I nearly threw my dagger at you."

Alhena squinted, peering beyond the fire's light. "What's the matter? Did you hear something?"

"No," Silurian snapped. Embarrassed with his outburst, he raised the bottle to his lips.

Alhena knuckled sleep from his eyes. "Do you fear something?"

"No! I don't fear anything, you milky-eyed fool." He sucked back a mouthful of homemade brew and spouted it into the fire. The flames jumped wildly. "Go back to sleep."

Alhena scowled. "Were I not duty bound to the Chamber, I would take exception to your harsh words."

Soul Forge

Silurian's pulse quickened. Spitting on the ground, he resisted the impulse to round the fire and throttle the old man. "You threatening me?" He located Alhena's staff, unattended by his side, and watched for a tell-tale movement from his fingertips.

Alhena held his deadly stare for a tense moment. Without another word, he crawled beneath his bedroll and turned away.

A long time passed before Silurian's breathing settled. Alhena's snores meant he was alone again amongst the flickering shadows. He had to hand it to Alhena, the old man had spunk.

He placed the unfinished liquor bottle back in his leather sack, pulling the drawstring tight with trembling hands. An unpleasant wave of desire to release his pent-up anger gripped him. He wrapped his arms tightly around his body and rocked back and forth.

He had feared this would happen. He struggled to quell the urge to kill the only friend he had in the world—if he could call the strange, old man a friend. He forced himself to think of something else, but his thoughts didn't drift far from his primal yearning. He grimaced at the prospect of facing an insolent member of the public. How was he going to handle the impending reception of the Gritian council?

The fire sputtered and hissed. A light drizzle fell. He adjusted the bottom blanket of his bedroll and pulled the top blanket over his face, but sleep wouldn't come.

Alhena had prepared every fire. Cooked every meal. More times than not he had used his own supplies, without ever a grumble, because he, Silurian Mintaka, former king's champion, legendary Group of Five member, was too self-important to help out.

He peeked his head out from beneath his thin leather blanket. He had to squint in the increasing drizzle to locate Alhena across the glow of the dying fire.

The old man tossed and turned but didn't waken.

With a heavy sigh, Silurian climbed out from under his waterproof blanket, and carried it around the fire pit. With more care than he thought himself capable of, he removed Alhena's damp blanket and replaced it with his own.

Returning to his wet bedroll, he climbed under his ground cover blanket and struggled to find a comfortable position upon the cold rock. After a while, he gave up. Lying on his back, staring into the

44

Soul Forge

underside of his wet blanket, he promised himself to never let pride overshadow his judgment again. A promise he had no ability keep.

Soul Forge

Redfire's Fury

Raindrops clung to the scrub grass—a million sparkling diamonds surrounding their soggy campsite. Grey clouds meandered slowly northeastward, disappearing beyond the heights as the early morning sun broke free of the snowcapped peaks in the east.

Silurian shivered, his bedroll soaked through. Throwing off the wet blanket, the aroma from Alhena's cooking pan made his mouth water. Wiping away the wet hair clinging to his cheeks, he noticed Alhena watching him.

Alhena turned his eyes to the fire.

He thought of apologizing for his actions last night, but the words wouldn't come. He dug through his satchel and withdrew two slightly bruised apples. Waiting until Alhena finished dispensing the steaming fare into wooden bowls, he shoved the larger apple at him.

Alhena accepted the humble offering. "Thank you."

They ate their scant fare in silence.

Alhena had cleared up the campsite and put the fire out by the time Silurian finished eating.

Standing, Silurian noted that his feet seemed to be toughening up. His blisters didn't hurt quite as bad this morning. Packing his bedroll, he realized Alhena had returned his blanket, brushed, dried, and folded just so.

Alhena sat upon his own packed bedroll, waiting. "Thank you for the blanket."

Still embarrassed by his actions, Silurian simply nodded back.

Soul Forge

Entering the canyon proper, the walls on either side of Redfire Path rose perpendicular into the shadowy gloom—the air noticeably cooler within the confines of the trench as it climbed its way toward an unseen pass many leagues distant.

The eerie corridor followed a due north course for most of the morning before veering northeast. After the bend, the walls dropped away to an almost scalable slant but by midafternoon the path reverted back into a trench as the walls narrowed—rising roughly two times Silurian's height, before sloping away, out of sight.

Silurian wanted to ask about the events that had shaped the world over the last two decades. Who notable had died? Who were the prominent nobles at court? How had Zephyr's neighbouring kingdoms faired? He'd love to know more about his old friend, Abraham Uzziah, apparently now the high bishop *and* chambermaster. If he were to fight again, he wanted to meet up with the present high warlord and discover what the military leader was like to deal with. Had Jarr-nash succeeded him as king's champion all those years ago, or were there others in between?

Shame denied him these questions. The queen had died defending the realm in his absence, and the people of Zephyr blamed him. It was going to be tough facing these people again.

They travelled carefree for most of the day, but when Silurian stopped and unsheathed his sword, Alhena jumped.

"What is—" Alhena started to ask but Silurian raised his hand.

Alhena dropped his rucksack to the canyon floor, tore it open and donned his knucklettes with practiced alacrity.

A shower of loose earth cascaded over the trench's western lip behind them.

Silurian assumed a bladed battle stance, the action instinctive, as a huge wolf ran along the lip of the trench. Closing on them, it launched itself into the air. It had no sooner become airborne when another wolf appeared and took flight, followed by a third.

Silurian met the first wolf head on, driving his sword deep between its ribs. The beast's momentum toppled them to the canyon floor in a bloodied heap.

Soul Forge

Alhena had no time to consider Silurian's struggle as the second wolf leapt his way. He swung his staff and ducked low, the wolf's breath hot on the back of his neck as it passed overhead, snapping at him. Its trailing claws raked his back, driving him to the ground. Unable to stop its forward progress, the wolf slammed into the trench wall.

Alhena regained his feet and prepared to face the wolf as it righted itself and came at him. With a feral growl, the shaggy beast leapt for his throat.

Alhena swung his staff and threw himself to the ground.

The wolf twisted, avoiding the swing, and rotated in the air. Its snapping jaws grazed his scalp, taking with it a patch of wispy grey hair. It landed heavily upon its side and sprang back to its feet.

Alhena rolled to his back, unable to free his staff from beneath the folds of his robes.

The wolf approached, nose low, lips pulled back, fangs bared, circling. Without warning, it pounced.

A sword whistled inches from Alhena's face, clunking off the wolf's skull, taking a furry ear with its passing, and changing the course of its attack.

With a yelp, it retreated out of reach of Silurian's advance.

Alhena rolled over and shakily got to his feet. The third wolf already lay dead several feet away from the first.

Another round of pebbles cascaded into the trench. Alhena's warning shout spun Silurian around as three more wolves ran along the western wall.

The pack animals spilled over the edge, one after another. With a quick sidestep and an even faster stab, Silurian dispatched the lead runner.

Soul Forge

The other wolves landed gracefully before him, teeth bared, emitting angry snarls. Crazed eyes followed his bloody sword as he brandished it between the two. They closed in on him.

Silurian backed away, closely watching their yellow eyes. His temples pounded with adrenaline as he fought to control his ragged breathing.

Alhena shouted out a warning a moment too late as Silurian tripped over the corpse of the original wolf he had dispatched—the action spurring the remaining wolves to attack.

From his back, Silurian slashed at the beast on his right, stopping it dead in its tracks, his sword lodging itself between the animal's ribs. The weight of the wolf falling away twisted the blade from his sweaty grip.

The second wolf landed heavily upon his chest, its claws rending his flesh as it snapped at his throat.

Silurian reacted without thinking, grabbing the shaggy fur around its throat, trying desperately to keep its slavering jaws at bay—the animal's fetid breath hot on his face. Its jaws snapped a hand's span from his chin.

A new weight drove down upon him, forcing what little breath he had left from his lungs. His fingers lost their grip on the thick fur. Turning his head, he expected the wolf to tear his throat out, but death never came.

The wolf toppled from his chest with a high pitched, truncated yelp as Alhena drove his knucklettes into its neck and rode the wolf to the ground. The messenger rolled sideways and violently twisted his weapons.

Struggling to catch his breath, Silurian got up and pulled his sword free of the wolf it had lodged itself in. Ignoring the painful claw marks to his chest and the blood running down his face, he directed his concern to Alhena's blood covered head.

Alhena wiped at the straggling hair clinging to the side of his face. He forced a smile through his obvious discomfort and leaned upon his staff for support.

Silurian couldn't help himself. "You're one sorry looking wizard."

49

Soul Forge

They spent the rest of daylight hours tending to each other's hurts, cleansing them with the remains of Silurian's second last bottle.

The ensuing darkness masked the grizzly signs of battle staining the canyon floor. Silurian and Alhena sat uncomfortably upon the hard ground before a small fire. Making the best of their situation, they dined on wolf meat.

The moon won free of the towering eastern summit, providing more light than their small fire. Alhena leaned back and sighed. "I fear my days as a messenger draw to a close. I am too old for this nonsense."

Silurian stopped caring for his sword to study him before returning his concentration to the blade. After a while he muttered without looking up, "Aye. Dark times are no place for the weak or aged."

Alhena shot him a dirty look.

"Had I made this trip alone, the wolves would be dining on *me* tonight," Silurian said, raising his head to stare Alhena in the eye. "You still have an adventure or two left in that worn body of yours."

They spent the next morning redressing their wounds and preparing wolf meat to take with them.

Alhena stood up, wincing at the pain in his scalp. "If we want to reach the Mountain Pools by sunset, we had best get a move on."

Silurian yawned, shouldered his pack, and followed quietly in his wake.

Alhena trod along quietly, bearing his hurts with dignity. If a man who hadn't left his hut in twenty years continued the trek to Gritian without complaint, he wasn't about to wallow in his own misery.

A couple of hours into their walk, he stopped to take a swig from his waterskin. "We will not reach Gritian before the full moon, as Chambermaster Uzziah requested. Too bad I lost the horses."

"Horses? You had more than one? How the hell do you lose *horses?*"

Alhena snorted. "Of course I had more than one. You think I set out from Gritian with only one horse, expecting you to walk behind me? As a matter of fact, I had three. My own, one for you, and a pack horse."

He fell silent, the painful memory tightening his throat.

"And?"

He kicked at a small stone, sending it skittering ahead. "I was set upon by villains."

"Where? In this pass?"

Alhena kept his eyes focused on the ground. He silently admonished himself as his eyes watered. "Aye. I left Gritian a fortnight ago. I stopped during my second night on the road at the top of this pass." He paused to steel himself. "During the night, I was awakened by Starbourne's nickering. Starbourne was my horse. Named after the white, star-shaped blaze on his face."

Silurian nodded, his expression sympathetic.

"Starbourne alerted me to the presence of the three nasty men who had snuck into my camp. They untethered the horses, and were about to set upon me unawares, but for Starbourne's whicker. There was naught I could do to fend them off. Luckily, I was able to sidestep their advance and Starbourne spirited me away.

"Sure enough, two of them gave chase through the night, but there was no way they were going to catch us as long as Starbourne drew breath. Our flight south, down the dark pass, was treacherous to say the least, but Starbourne never faltered.

"They pursued us into the grasslands. I thought the best way to lose them would be in the grassy plain below the Wall, but they were relentless. By the time I finally lost them, poor Starbourne was blown." Tears dripped off his cheeks.

Silurian said nothing.

"Blacker than the night, Starbourne. Magnificent animal. King worthy." His voice cracked. "I put him down, out there upon the plains." Choking back a sob, he turned and walked away.

Silurian hurried after him.

Alhena muttered, not caring whether Silurian heard him or not, "Going to miss the old bugger. He was the only family I had."

Soul Forge

The day passed in silence, their injuries forced them to stop frequently. Prior to nightfall, the path ascended out of the trench's shadowy clutches toward a plateau in the distance.

A dull roar reached their ears above the gusting wind. The higher they tramped, the louder the roar became. Cresting the rim of a broad plateau, they were greeted by a fine mist.

Alhena craned his neck, marvelling at the magnificent view. Water cascaded from heights unseen, plummeting into a series of interconnected pools that stretched away from the trail in either direction.

The plateau was oval in shape, elongated north to south, and almost entirely submerged in water. Redfire Path offered the only way into and out of the pass. At the clearing's centre, three dark pools rippled beneath a slender waterfall—shimmering mist whirled across moss-covered shelf rock at its base.

Without hesitation they made a beeline to the base of the waterfall, the mist intensifying the closer they got, soaking them to the skin. When they couldn't walk any further without stepping into the lethal deluge, they ducked into a hidden cleft behind the falls. Short of building a raft or swimming, the slick fissure was the only way across the plateau.

Exiting the cleft on the far side, they followed a faint path angling up toward a ring of stones, built along a causeway bordering the northern edge of the main pool and a separate pond beyond.

Soul Forge

By the time they had the wolf meat cooking over an open fire, and their waterskins refilled, stars sparkled overhead. They had scrubbed the grime and gore from their skin and clothes and warmed themselves by the crackling fire. But for the flickering light the fire provided, and the few torches Alhena planted along the water's edge, the basin was lost in darkness.

Silurian uncorked his last bottle. He was about to take a swig but stopped himself and offered it to Alhena first.

Alhena took a tentative swallow and coughed. "Whoa. That is strong enough to kill someone." He shook his head, staring at the grimy bottle. "How do you drink that swill?" He took another pull, before handing it back.

Silurian took a large swallow before examining it in the firelight. "Dragonbane? With much practice."

"Dragonbane, indeed. I am surprised it does not render you unconscious."

Silurian offered him a wry smile and took another long swallow. "Oh, trust me, it does." *Sometimes it's the only way to cope.*

They finished their meal, took stock of their wounds, rekindled the fire to ward off the chill creeping down from the heights, and settled into a Dragonbane induced sleep.

Soul Forge

Silurian's eyes opened suddenly. The moon shone bright between two towering crags as he slipped from his bedroll into the chilly night. The only noises in the pass came from the incessant cascade and an occasional pop from the dying fire.

The torches lining the pond's edge had gone out, but the moonlight was sufficient to navigate the rocky terrain. He felt the need to stretch his cramping muscles and clear his troubled mind.

Passing beneath the waterfall, he walked around the water's southern edge until he passed beyond the soaking mist, gooseflesh riddling his skin. He went as far as the terrain allowed and stopped to stare at the moon's rippling reflection. What in the gods' names was he doing here?

A few mangy wolves had nearly killed him. Most people may have thought themselves fortunate to have fended them off but he wasn't most people. Good luck wasn't going to save the kingdom.

Years ago, he had commanded a rare arcane ability, albeit through the enchantment of his sword, yet he clung to the belief that he possessed an ability of his own. When the lightning appeared over his hut several days ago, he fancied it was his doing, but during the skirmish with the wolves he had felt nothing.

The campfire jumped back to life across the water. Alhena must've woken.

He picked up a stone and pitched it into the water. The battle with the wolves certainly indicated that he was indeed merely a conduit of his old sword's magic, not the source. If this were true, he was in trouble. Zephyr was in trouble. His prowess with a sword, however fine it had once been, was no match for Helleden Misenthorpe's sorcery.

Caught up in his contemplation, he barely heard Alhena cry out.

Soul Forge

The clang of Silurian's scabbard as he rose and walked away, stirred Alhena awake. Groggily, he watched Silurian walk beyond the embers' glow, past the dead torches along the shore—his footfalls fading into the distance toward the waterfall.

Alhena wrapped his arms about himself, shivering, trying to ignore the pain of his pulsating scalp. Gritting his teeth, he climbed from the warmth of his bedroll to address the dwindling fire.

The fire burning well once again, he walked to the edge of the pool, beside their camp. A recurrent thought dogged him, leaving him wondering whether dragging Silurian out of seclusion was the best idea. Sure, Silurian had accounted for himself against the wolf attack but he had still needed saving in the end.

The water's glass-like surface reflected the sparkling sky, commingling near the centre around a gently rippling, full moon. He fingered his tender scalp, grimacing at the rawness of the scabbing skin. Was that Silurian he could see way over on the far side of the falls?

Memories of the Battle of Lugubrius assaulted him. He remembered standing beside his lifeless king—the ramparts of Castle Svelte unreachable in the distance—watching the horror of Zephyr's fractured army being slaughtered around him. He had stood over dead King Peter with a knot of knights fighting ferociously to protect their slain sovereign's corpse. When all had seemed lost, the Group of Five had come out of nowhere and changed the tide of battle. One fateful swing of Silurian's blade had sent the minion horde scrambling for their lives.

Empathy filled him. What in God's good world had reduced Silurian to such a wretched state? He grunted. Zephyr was going to have to come to grips with the fact that Silurian wasn't the same man he had been twenty-three years ago.

He turned away from the water's edge but stopped short and looked over his shoulder. Of the three main pools, only the centre one, fed directly by the waterfall, churned and rippled with any significance, but the water's edge nearest him bubbled and churned.

He backed away, unable to wrest his eyes from the pond. The water parted to reveal a set of glowing, crimson eyes. The sight of the creature that pulled itself from the murky depths stopped him in his tracks. He tried to call out to Silurian but wasn't certain he had.

Before him, a massive reptile rose up from the pool, emerging in a wash of water to stand upon four muscular rear legs. It reached out to him with a short foreleg—its slimy body glistening in the moonlight, beneath a massive crocodile's head that topped its ten-foot frame.

Alhena stumbled backward through the campsite, trying to distance himself from the creature.

The creature's gravelly voice surprised him. "Where is the other one who travels with you?"

"I-I don't know…"

The creature's eyes shone brighter. With a sudden leap, it covered the distance separating them, landing heavily beside the fire.

Alhena fell over his bedroll.

"You lie," it growled, and bent low over him.

This creature wasn't natural. Alhena's instincts screamed at him to get away but his body refused to move.

A shout sounded from the direction of the waterfall.

The reptile rose to its full height, craning its neck.

Silurian emerged from beneath the waterfall, charging toward them, sword drawn, struggling to maintain his footing upon the slippery stone.

"Alhena…Don't…Move."

Alhena frowned. There was no worry of that happening.

The creature turned to intercept Silurian.

Alhena cringed as the two collided. His jaw dropped. They embraced each other.

Stepping back, the creature said, "Silurian Mintaka. After all these years, I thought you truly dead."

"You should know better than that, Seafarer, you walking handbag."

For the first time since Alhena had found Silurian, he saw genuine happiness upon his face.

"What brought you back to life, my friend?" The reptilian creature settled down upon his stomach before the fire, reminding Alhena of a massive crocodile.

"'Tis a long story," Silurian said. "Truth be told, I probably shouldn't be here."

Soul Forge

Alhena stoked the fire as he listened to Silurian relate their adventure thus far. When Silurian mentioned the wolves, the creature nodded.

Silurian had barely finished his tale when Seafarer suddenly froze, his eyes glowing brighter.

Alhena followed the creature's concerned gaze to the Mountain Pools.

Seafarer rose to his four back feet. "Remain here. I must deal with something, but I need to speak further with you before you face the Chamber. It is vital you await my return."

Without another word, Seafarer ambled down to the water's edge and slipped beneath the surface.

Soul Forge

The Portent

Helleden! Rook shuddered. Black storm clouds brooded overhead, coalescing into an unnatural domed ceiling and blotting out the sun.

He forced his feet into motion, walking to the swamp's edge for any sign of the magical creature.

The air thinned. His breathing quickened. A cool breeze stirred his unkempt hair, and quickly became a gale. He leaned forward to prevent himself from being blown backward.

The skies opened, drenching him.

Fear gripped him. He wheeled about and staggered to his hut. Grabbing the door latch, he threw the bolt. The door whipped open, just missing him.

Hanging onto the jamb for dear life he retrieved his bow as the wind ripped the door from its hinges and cartwheeled it into the ethereal darkness.

He pulled himself into the turmoil within his hut—parchment and debris swirled about as if caught up in a mini twister. He grabbed his quiver and ducked to avoid being hit by sections of the hut's disintegrating roof.

He stepped clear of the teetering structure just before it collapsed upon itself and shattered into unrecognizable pieces, following the door into the maelstrom beyond. Grasping the remnants of the last remaining corner pillar, he dropped to the ground and wrapped his arms about its base to keep from becoming a projectile himself.

A crimson bolt of crackling energy erupted from the surface of Saros' Swamp. A geyser of muddy swamp water shot into the air in its wake as the bolt etched a path toward the black clouds and blasted a hole through the dome, exposing the sun.

Soul Forge

The winds subsided and the driving rain diminished but the reprieve was short lived. The dome regenerated itself and the sun disappeared. The winds intensified. Driving rain fell heavier than before.

Rook lay helpless in the mud, unable to stand. Shrubs and larger vegetation flew over his head, touching down at random intervals and bounding away.

Saros' Swamp spilled its banks, pushing a wall of churning muck before it as another crimson blast shot skyward, followed by two more in rapid succession. Thunderous detonations reverberated overhead, shaking the ground. With each successive blast, the dome regenerated faster. It wasn't long before the blasts did nothing but rock the land and empty the swamp.

The parade of crimson bolts ceased.

A strange sensation flooded through him, dulling his senses.

A massive fireball hurtled skyward, totally emptying the swamp. The resulting explosion pulverized the unearthly dome and black ash rained upon the ruined land.

A wave of mud sloshed over Rook. Through the fog that had taken over his mind, he sensed that he no longer grasped the hut's stanchion. His body slid away from Saros' Swamp, entombed within a sliding wall of sludge.

The rain had stopped. Hurricane winds were replaced by stray gusts that stirred eddies of black ash around the Innerworld. Sunshine warmed the devastated landscape, revealing the extent of the destruction. Great branches littered the landscape—trees splintered and broken all the way to the horizon. Saros' golden aura hadn't returned.

A set of crimson eyes broke the plane of brackish water, nestled atop a large reptilian head. Seafarer emerged from the murky depths, rising to his full height upon the edge to survey the damage.

Rook lay twenty feet from the banks of Saros' Swamp. Muddy water swirled about him, the blackened sludge sliding back to the crater it had been blasted from.

59

Soul Forge

Silence gripped the land buried beneath a carpet of black ash.

Rook stirred. He lay within the embrace of a soft bush, although he had no idea how he had gotten there.

The smell of wet rot and charred flesh told him that all wasn't as it should be. Overhead, the sun drifted between puffy, white clouds.

Clouds!

Images of the unearthly storm bombarded him. He remembered the black dome and the wind storm that had annihilated his home.

Rolling free of the bush, he fell to his knees upon what had recently been the floor of his hut. Beside him lay his bow and quiver. He was instantly attuned to the fact that the golden aura no longer enshrouded Saros' Swamp. The little shrine he had constructed two decades earlier was gone.

A loud pop from a nearby fire alerted him to the fact that he wasn't alone. On the far side of the uprooted bush, a bonfire sent plumes of black smoke into the air. What shocked him most, however, was the sight of a friend he hadn't seen in a long time.

"Seafarer?"

The reptilian had gathered the dead swamp denizens strewn around the area and fed them into the fire. Dropping a twisted carcass onto the pyre, he said, "Rook Bowman. Welcome back to the living. It appears I have arrived too late."

Standing, Rook took a few moments to gain his equilibrium. Grabbing his bow and arrows he stumbled around the bush and embraced the towering creature.

Stepping back, he asked, "Who did this?"

"I fear you know the answer to that, my good friend."

"Helleden?"

The reptilian closed his eyes.

Rook turned a slow circle, expecting to see the vile sorcerer.

Soul Forge

"We don't know where he is, nor how he cast such a spell. The latest reports had him entrenched in the Altirius Mountains. He certainly never stepped foot inside the Innerworld."

Rook's arms flailed about helplessly, "But…" He couldn't find the words.

"We don't know how to explain it."

"We?"

"Saros and I. Saros was in dire straits when I received his summons. He had been battling Helleden long before either you or I were aware anything was amiss. Together, we shattered the dome Helleden conjured, but the battle is far from over."

Rook hung his head. How many creatures had died?

"There is more to the story you need to know."

Rook swallowed.

"First things first. Sit and eat. You will require all your strength and then some, real soon."

A short while later, Rook sat before the fire with a steaming bowl of broth cupped in his hands. Where Seafarer had found the bowl and the food within, he had no idea, nor was he sure he wanted to know. He picked at his meal, surveying the absolute destruction surrounding him.

Lying on his stomach beside him, Seafarer said, "You will be interested in this. I attended the Mountain Pools before coming here. Investigating a report of someone slaughtering wolves. You'll never guess who was responsible."

Rook looked up.

"Alhena Sirrus, a messenger from the Chamber of the Wise."

Rook grunted. He had never heard of him.

"He didn't know me. In fact, he was put off by my appearance."

"Imagine that," Rook muttered.

"His companion, however, knew me well. I thought him long dead, so this time it was me who was surprised."

Seafarer paused, causing Rook to stare at him.

"Who should walk out from beneath the waterfall? Silurian Mintaka!"

Rook choked, spitting a mouthful of food into the fire. Gruel drooled down his chin.

Soul Forge

"Aye, the one and only. Mind you, he looks rough. He is on his way to meet with the Gritian council. Anyway, before I get sidetracked, Saros asked me to explain the meaning of the thirteen eyes…"

Rook tuned him out, his brain stuck on the mention of Silurian. He should be elated, but instead it seemed like a weight had been loaded upon his shoulders.

Seafarer sprang to his four hind legs. Without explanation, he made his way to the banks of Saros' Swamp and slipped beneath the surface.

Rook followed, stopping at the water's edge. The water's surface stilled for only a moment before it bubbled again, marking Seafarer's return.

The large creature crawled from the water, dripping with flotsam.

"You must leave at once," Seafarer declared. "Saros and I will do what we can to ensure your safe passage to the Mid Savannah. You must leave now."

"What are you talking about?" Rook threw his hands up, slowly spinning around to include everything in sight. What had they just been talking about? Something about the thirteen eyes. "I can't leave. Not now. The Innerworld needs me."

"Rook, hear me. Saros falters. His hold upon our world draws nigh. He foresees the Innerworld's destruction. He can no longer prevent it."

"What are you talking about? The Innerworld's destruction? That's absurd."

"Nonetheless, the only thing left for you here is death. Saros and I have merely afforded us a temporary reprieve. When Helleden attacks again, the Innerworld will be obliterated. Do you recall what happened to Queen Quarrnaine's expedition a few years back?"

"Ya, but…Where is Helleden? Lead me to him. There must be something—"

"Rook!" Seafarer boomed. "Listen. Before it's too late. You need to leave. Now. Escape to the Mid Savannah. Silurian needs you."

Rook's next words caught in his throat.

"Aye, for Silurian do you listen. Heed my warning, Rook. Our hope, Zephyr's hope, depends on you two staying together. If you become separated, we may all be lost."

"Where will I find him? In Gritian?"

Soul Forge

Seafarer shook his head. "Saros has dispatched his disciple, Thetis, to rendezvous with you and Silurian at Madrigail Bay."

"Madrigail Bay? That's clear across Zephyr."

"Those are Saros' instructions. Now, you must make haste. If you can reach the Outerworld by high moon, you should be alright. We will try to afford you the time you need, but I'm thinking we'll be hard pressed."

The amphibian's red eyes shone brighter. Before Rook knew what happened, Seafarer enshrouded him within a translucent crimson aura—its cocoon-like properties bent and stretched with his every movement.

"How do we find this *Thesis*?" The world was cast in an eerie, reddish glow. Seafarer had done something to him. Turning his arms this way and that, mesmerized by the conforming force field around him, Rook asked, "And what the hell is *this*?"

"Thetis," Seafarer corrected. "You need not worry yourself about that. Thetis will find you." He glanced at the sky with concern. "You're wrapped within a protective barrier that will protect you as you flee and help you run faster, but it won't last long. You must go."

Seafarer had found Rook's old, leather rucksack and packed it with provisions. He held it out for Rook to shrug into. "Grab your bow and arrows. It's time to go."

Thunder rolled ominously in the distance.

Rook took a few tentative steps to the west. He hesitated. Seafarer was already making his way into the water. He wondered if he would ever see his old friend again.

Seafarer's great head swiveled upon his scaly shoulders. "You must go. Run!"

Whether it was the crimson aura tainting his vision or because of the energy Seafarer had spent in generating it, the reptilian looked haggard.

Rook wanted to ask him if he was going to be okay but Seafarer had already slipped beneath the surface.

Soul Forge

God is Dead

The translucent aura Seafarer had cast upon Rook turned his world crimson. He crashed headlong across the devastated marshland, marvelling at how fast he moved over the rubble-strewn landscape—not tiring in the slightest. He recalled their rushed conversation. *If you can reach the Outerworld by high moon, you should be alright.*

By Rook's calculations, even at his newfound pace, he wouldn't reach the border in time.

He struggled with what his flight meant. He was abandoning the creatures who had sheltered him through his darkest hours. He should be standing shoulder to shoulder with them in the face of this danger, not running away from it. Seafarer's warning echoed in his mind. *You are wrapped within a protective barrier that will not only protect you as you flee but will also help you run faster. It won't last long.* But fleeing while his friends were about to be destroyed went against every tenet he had lived his life by. He felt like a coward.

He stopped his headlong progress and attempted to turn around and return to Saros' Swamp, but the aura prevented him. He stepped forward and sideways without difficulty, but he couldn't step backward.

"Damn you, Seafarer."

Thunder rumbled in the distance. A cold shiver gripped him. It had begun and Seafarer had claimed he and Saros weren't strong enough to thwart the attack a second time.

With a despondent look over his shoulder, he sprinted faster than he had before. At this speed, his momentum carried him over smaller bogs and ponds in a single bound. He leaped giant boulders and downed trees. He almost thought he could fly.

Soul Forge

As he ran, the signs of destruction from Helleden's previous onslaught lessened.

The sky darkened. Tendrils of black cloud converged above him, coalescing into a low ceiling of impending doom.

Beneath his springing feet another swamp flew by. All he could do was run. Seafarer had seen to that. He must reach the border before Seafarer and Saros…what? Died? They would fight to their last breath if it meant he reached safety. Perhaps if he ran faster, they might find time to escape themselves.

A large, uprooted willow passed beneath his feet. Then a boulder, and a wide, stagnant river. On he ran, faster than the wind that blew in his face.

The Innerworld darkened. The light cast by the cocoon's aura allowed him to see, but his jumps became trickier in the diminished light.

Bounding ever westward toward freedom, he couldn't rid himself of the gut-wrenching knowledge that he abandoned his home and the creatures that had harboured him all these years. The beauty. The vegetation. The geographical anomalies that made the Innerworld so diverse. Everything he had come to love was on the verge of extinction, and he could do nothing to prevent it.

The wind increased to a gale.

He wanted to stop and shed the crimson aura so he could go back, but he didn't know how. Seafarer's words kept his legs churning: *the only thing left for you here is death.*

So? What was the point of living if everyone he cared for died?

Escape to the Mid Savannah. Silurian needs you. That last sentence echoed in his mind.

A heavy rain began to fall.

Silurian needs you.

He barely managed to avert his run and skirt along the shores of a large bog, its other side not visible in the aura's meagre light.

The black sky pulsed in several places, pushing aside the darkness, heralding the creation of great orbs of fire. Sickening whines tracked their earthward course. He looked up and almost lost his footing.

He resigned himself to the fact that he was powerless to alter the events set into motion, but by the gods' good grace he vowed to do

65

everything within his means to meet up with Silurian and set things right. Together, they would exact a dire toll for the Innerworld's injustice, and finish what they thought they had done years ago.

The earth shook. He picked up his pace as the first fireball detonated somewhere behind him, shaking the ground.

Resounding explosions heaved the landscape. Animals bolted from their burrows, scurrying about frantically, not knowing which way to flee. Rook cried out for them to follow, but they couldn't match his pace.

He ran and ran, amazed at his ability to maintain such speed, magically assisted or not. His tormented mind wandered from sadness to anger and back again in rapid, delirious succession. Vaguely aware of lapses in the onslaught, as Saros and Seafarer fought back, provided him little solace. They could not win.

He didn't know how long he ran. Occasionally the sky lightened, the wind dropped, and the rain lessened, but inevitably, Helleden overcame the powers opposing him.

A tremendous blast, many leagues away, threw Rook to the ground. He careened uncontrollably to a stop. The bogginess of his landing spot, together with the protection offered by the aura, kept him from serious harm.

He lay stunned at the edge of a slough. The air was still. The rain had ceased and the wind had died. The constant drone of plummeting fireballs was absent. He struggled to his knees, shrugged his rucksack into place, and unsteadily gained his feet. Nothing moved within the limited vision cast by the crimson glow. Had Saros and Seafarer found a way to make a difference?

Far to the east, a red wave rippled along the horizon. Another wave lit up the northern horizon, followed quickly by one to the south, and finally, one close to where he stood—the dome's eastern wall pulsated. Dark red veins of lightning forked up from the base of the dome toward the blackened canopy.

Rook sucked in his breath. He had no idea what it meant, but it didn't take a great leap of faith to realize it wouldn't be good when the lightning converged. Wasting no time, he ran harder than before.

Approaching the dome's wall, he had no idea how to break through whatever substance comprised the evil shroud. He glanced down to judge the leap required to span a small bog in his path. Looking up again, he found himself staring into the malevolent glare of two massive, red beasts brandishing tridents as they reared up out of the darkness. To either side of the well-muscled demons, Innerworld creatures bolted by, frantically trying to escape the impending destruction—only to vapourize into puffs of black smoke as they impacted against the dome's surface.

Rook winced. His attempts to slow his headlong collision with Helleden's minions failed. The aura cocoon impelled him forward. Even if he sidestepped the demons, the prospect of running into the black wall didn't seem like a good idea.

Evil grins twitched the corners of the demons' mouths. They brought their weapons to bear and jabbed at him.

Rook's feet slipped from underneath him. Hitting the ground hard, he slid below the jagged barbs and slammed into the wall.

A deafening concussion consumed his being. The wall exploded outward, covering him in black ash.

Soul Forge

Into Hell but Never Through

Silurian and Alhena spent the next two days waiting for Seafarer's return. Sitting high above the world, braving the cold mountain air did wonders to help their bodies recover from the wounds inflicted by the wolves.

Silurian had just finished shaving with Soulbiter and was wiping the blade when the pool of water closest to their camp bubbled and frothed, announcing Seafarer's arrival.

Seafarer pulled himself from the frigid water and rose upon his hind legs. Reaching the fireside, he dropped onto his stomach, his face bleary and fatigued.

Silurian slid Soulbiter into its sheath and jammed it into his belt. "We were wondering whether you were coming back."

Seafarer's great head shook slightly. "I wondered that myself."

Silurian looked at him with concern. "Can we offer you anything to eat?"

"I'm in no mood to eat."

"What's happened?"

When Seafarer responded, Silurian and Alhena had to lean in close to hear.

"Helleden attacked."

Puzzled, Silurian looked at Alhena. This wasn't a revelation. It was why they were here in the first place.

"Saros is dead."

Their heads snapped back.

"The Innerworld is no more."

"The Forbidden Swamp?" Silurian mouthed.

"Destroyed. Obliterated. Gone. A huge part of it, at least." Seafarer looked away. "Everything. Everyone. Dead."

Soul Forge

A cold dread shot through Silurian.

Seafarer's massive head swung toward them. "I don't know how Helleden did it. The destruction is widespread. Maybe all the way to the Undying Wall."

A knot turned Silurian's stomach.

"Saros believed Helleden accomplished this without ever setting foot within the Innerworld. In fact, Saros believed Helleden did it from his encampment in the Altirius Mountains.

"That being said, there may be a bit of good news. When I left Saros to his fate, Rook Bowman was on his way out of the destruction zone. I have no way of knowing for sure, but he should have made it out before the sky fell in."

"Rook is still alive?"

"I truly hope so, for everyone's sake. If he survived, he's on his way to Madrigail Bay to meet up with you." Seafarer's eyes fell on Silurian.

"Madrigail Bay? That's half way across the world."

"Madrigail Bay?" Alhena echoed. "I don't speak for the Chamber, but I'm sure they have other plans for Silurian."

"Those were Saros' instructions. He dispatched his disciple to find you at the seaport," Seafarer said. "But first, of course, the Chamber must be informed. Then you must find your way to the lost Shrine of Saint Carmichael and retrieve the Sacred Sword Voil—*your* sword, before you head west."

Silurian recalled the tale of the queen's demise. "Wouldn't it be better if Rook grabbed the sword? He'll pass right by it."

Alhena shook his head. "Only one with royal blood may place the sword within its sheath. Or an anointed member of the king's inner circle. I imagine the same rule applies to anyone wishing to withdraw the sword. Anyone else might ruin the blade."

Seafarer nodded his great head.

"Correct me if I have misunderstood something," Silurian said, turning to Alhena. "I thought that when Jarr-nash sheathed the sword, its power was spent?"

"Aye, to the best of my knowledge, that is what High Bishop Uzziah inferred."

Soul Forge

"So, what's the point of retrieving it? It's a fine blade certainly, but people die as we speak. I fail to see how wasting time to recover it benefits our cause? For all we know, someone has already stolen it."

Seafarer cleared his throat. "Saros claimed the sword still lies beneath the chapel ruins." The reptilian tried to shrug. "Your bishop is right about the blade, but Saros told me of a way you might recapture its enchantment."

Silurian frowned. "Recapture its enchantment? Why not use any blade?"

"No other blade is capable of containing the power you will be attempting to collar."

"Why? Where am I going?"

"Not so fast, my friend. Getting there will not be easy. I argued with Saros about this very point, but with his disciple's assistance, he claimed it possible. I'm still not convinced that this is our best course of action but after witnessing the power at Helleden's command, I fear our options are running out."

Seafarer's voice softened, "Saros implored I tell you this. If for any reason you and Rook become separated, or one of you should die, our hope will die with you."

Silurian knitted his eyebrows.

"In order to re-establish the sword's ancient properties, it must be transported far across the Niad Ocean. In fact, it must be taken, how do I say this? *Below,* the ocean."

Alhena's features mirrored Silurian's concern.

"You will travel to a land known as the Under Realm. The land Helleden Misenthorpe calls home. Once there, you must locate a place Saros referred to as Soul Forge. A place of great power. From this forge flows a mystical river. It is in this river that you must immerse your blade."

Seafarer noted their skepticism. "Oh, it can be done. Rumour has it that many have made the transition to the Under Realm, but there is a minor detail I should bring to your attention. You may have heard this old saying, 'Into hell, but never through.'" He swallowed. "As far as I know, no one has ever come back."

Soul Forge

Farriers

Leaving the Undying Wall behind, Alhena and Silurian descended the last league of the mountain trail in silence. From their vantage point high above the treetops below, Redfire Path levelled out to be swallowed by the Central Woodland.

Silurian set a good pace even though his head ached like the mountain had fallen upon it. He sure could use a nip, but his liquor supply was exhausted. His dry mouth felt like it was full of sand.

Crusted blood on his right temple held fast a few strands of hair, but his concern lay with Alhena who winced with every other step.

"We should stop," Silurian suggested, wiping sweat from his brow. "You look like you're suffering."

"We have already lost too much time. The full moon passed us by up in the pass meaning that we have missed the scheduled meeting of the Chamber of the Wise," Alhena said through a tight smile. "I am hopeful that all will be forgiven when I return with the famous, Silurian Mintaka."

Silurian rolled his eyes. "Ya, real famous."

Beneath the Central Woodland canopy of soaring hardwoods, Redfire Path consisted of spongy, well-trodden black soil, soft beneath their boots. Aside from the trail itself, the forest floor appeared impassible, cluttered with brush both living and dead—entangled amongst itself in such a way that only small animals or a raging forest fire might penetrate.

The sun, far to the west, fell behind the Spine as they trudged into gloomy twilight, the second day out of the Undying Mountain Pools and their strange encounter with Seafarer. They travelled well into the night hoping to make up lost time. It was past high moon when they stopped.

71

Soul Forge

Silurian got little rest. His hands shook for no apparent reason as he dwelled on the fact that he hadn't had a sip of liquor all day. Nausea gripped his stomach. He wasn't sure whether that was a result of a lack of food, lack of Dragonbane, or his worry about Rook's safety and the eventuality of being reunited with him.

When he finally dropped off, a strange dream troubled his sleep. He faced-off against Seafarer, high above the world, upon a ten-foot slab of rock suspended thousands of feet above the Undying Wall. The reptile's eyes blazed red.

Silurian brandished the Sacred Sword Voil, the rune-covered blade shrouded in its former blue hue.

Seafarer's eyes shone brighter. Rays of red energy burst forth from the reptile's glare and blasted Silurian from the ledge.

He tumbled through the air, his sword spiraling out of control just beyond his reach. The wind rushed by him. Looking up, the platform never got any smaller. He fell and fell, but the world below never got any closer. Suspended high in the air, above the Undying Wall's jagged peaks, he fell for eternity.

Alhena opened his eyes the next morning to discover Silurian had left. He wondered aloud, "Now where do you suppose he's gotten to?"

Someone approached from the direction of distant Gritian—the muffled sound of snapping twigs came from the left of the trail. Early morning mist shrouded the person's approach.

As he waited, unconcerned, Alhena thought it strange that they hadn't seen anyone on the road since setting out.

Beside him, a small fire crackled—Silurian had been up early. Warming his hands above the meagre fire, the silhouette emerged from the mist.

"Welcome," Silurian offered, dropping branches by the fire. "Nice of you to finally join me."

Alhena ignored the barb. He rummaged through his sack. "I am out of food."

Soul Forge

Silurian grunted, building the fire up. "Me too. I gathered us some acorns. Bitter as hell, but—"

"You've eaten?"

"Aye. Help yourself."

Alhena glanced around. Dawn must've just broken before he had awoken. "Couldn't sleep?"

"Not well."

Redfire Path left the Central Woodland behind at midday in favour of the Gritian Hills—a rolling scrubland devoid of many trees.

With nary a wisp of cloud in the sky, it didn't take long for them to consume their dwindling water supply. As the sun dropped into the western sky they crossed a stone bridge in serious disrepair, spanning a sizable creek.

They drank their fill and washed the accumulated road grime from their hands and faces. Refilling their water skins, they set off with a renewed energy in their step.

Alhena attempted to make casual conversation, but Silurian felt more irritable than normal. He grunted and snarled until Alhena got the hint.

Cresting a hilltop, they came across a wall of loosely placed stones bordering a field on the western edge of the trail. The first sign of human habitation in almost a fortnight.

Far off in the field, several cows stood about a water hole, beneath a large stand of trees. In the distance beyond, a small building dotted the horizon.

Alhena shielded his eyes and pointed. "That is where we shall eat."

At once, Silurian's anxiety rose. There would be people in that house. He swallowed. Panic gripped him.

"Are you okay?" Alhena's voice made him jump.

"Huh? Uh, ya, I'll be fine." He inhaled deeply several times.

Alhena gave him a forced smile. "It will be okay. They are just ordinary people. We can stay here until you are ready."

Silurian appreciated the fact that Alhena understood his anxiety. Taking one last big breath, he said, "Okay, I'm good. I can do this."

Soul Forge

By the time they approached the cabin, the sun sat like a crimson dome upon the pastureland beyond the farmhouse.

Cords of wood, chopped and neatly stacked, surrounded three sides of a two-story log cabin, its windows fitted with open shutters.

Smoke billowed from a lone chimney, stringing the cabin to the darkening sky. Outside the only door, a shirtless man about Silurian's age split wood with a large axe. Sweat dripped from his nose as he watched their approach.

With one last mighty chop and a loud crack, wood splintered in all directions. The farmer hoisted the axe to his shoulder and spat on the ground. "Welcome, strangers. What can I do for you?"

Both men stopped out of axe swinging range. Alhena took a hesitant step forward. "Please pardon our trespass. We have travelled a long way and are in desperate need of food. May we impose upon your family a good meal in return for our humble services? Perhaps help you chop your winter wood?"

The farmer mulled over the offer, but instead of answering Alhena, he extended his dirty hand to Silurian. "Janus Farrier, blacksmith and cattle rancher. You two look like you could set into a good meal."

Silurian accepted the callused hand with a nod, and introduced himself, "Silurian." He paused, afraid of the reaction his last name might evoke. "Silurian Mintaka."

Janus smiled, the name not registering. "Welcome, Mr. Mintaka." He then offered his hand to Alhena, a wary look on his face.

Alhena accepted the farmer's hand. "Alhena Sirrus. Senior messenger to the Chamber of the Wise."

Janus nodded, his eyes growing wide. "Aye, I know you. At least my boys and I have seen you about up in Gritian. One never forgets seeing a wizard."

Silurian caught Alhena's attention and raised his eyebrows.

Alhena cleared his throat. "Um, yes. I assure you Janus, I am not a wizard."

"Hah!" Janus blurted out. He swung his axe into the large chopping block. "Whatever you say Mr. Sirrus. You can't fool me, but please, do come in. Asa is preparing a hearty meal. She'll be tickled to have guests."

Soul Forge

He opened the door, revealing a cluttered, one roomed interior, its walls adorned with bad artwork. "Living way out here, we don't get many guests. Tonight will be a real treat for the family. Wait 'til you meet my boys. They're off in the fields tending..." His voice disappeared into the dimly lit hut.

They were joined for supper by Janus' boys. Phellus, the youngest, an aspiring artist according to Asa, Loquax, the middle son and tallest, and Bregens, the huskiest, who had just returned from Gritian after completing his training in the Gritian militia.

After a delicious meal of steak and vegetables, the men sat around the large oak table sipping wine, while Asa busied herself cleaning up after the big meal.

Janus nodded toward his youngest son, his gaze taking in the entire cabin. "Phellus here is quite the budding artist, don'tcha reckon?"

Silurian didn't respond.

Alhena looked at the pictures hung about the cabin and lied, "Aye, he is, uh, talented."

Janus' chest puffed out. A huge smile split his rugged complexion. "That he is. We're proud of him, indeed."

An uncomfortable silence followed.

"So, what brings you two this way?" Janus asked, his gaze upon Silurian's tooled scabbard propped up by the door.

Alhena looked to Silurian, who shrugged back.

Alhena cleared his throat. "Have you not heard of the threat to Zephyr?"

"Helleden? Aye, Bregens told us last night." Janus said. "He is to return to Gritian in the morning to begin active duty."

Alhena noticed Asa stiffen as she worked away at the kitchen counter.

"Is it true, Master Alhena?" Janus asked. "I thought the sorcerer dead?"

"As did I when I drove my sword through his heart," Silurian muttered, but no one paid him any notice.

Soul Forge

Alhena shook his head, more because he saw Silurian indulging in the wine a little too heavily. He sighed and turned his attention on Janus. "Alas, he is not. Her majesty believed that by returning the Sacred Sword Voil to the Shrine of Saint Carmichael, the threat would be vanquished for good. It seems she was mistaken."

Asa wandered over to stand behind her husband and placed her hands upon his shoulders. "Sacred Sword what?"

Alhena gave her a sympathetic smile. The rural people were always the last to know. "Voil. It is a long story. Suffice it to say, Queen Quarrnaine gave her life to rid Zephyr of Helleden, and yet, here he is. Again."

The Farrier family placed their left hand over their heart and said together, "May the gods bless her."

Quiet settled over the hut as the Farriers digested the news. Finally, Janus said, "This is dire news indeed. Is there naught we can do?"

"Your family has already been more than helpful. If we can impose upon you in the morning to borrow two of your mounts."

Without hesitation, Janus replied, "By all means. Tell us when you wish to be away and the boys will have them ready."

"First light will be fine. The Chamber will be in your debt for allowing me to deliver my renowned companion here as quickly as possible."

All eyes followed Alhena's.

"It is obvious, Janus, that you and your family are unaware who sups at your table tonight."

The Farriers looked at each other, shaking their heads.

Alhena smiled. The Farriers had no inclination of who Silurian was. They should have. The Battle of Lugubrius stood out as one of the pivotal victories in Zephyr's storied history.

"Before you sits a member of the Group of Five."

Janus knit his brows.

"Former king's champion."

The men sat up straighter and comprehension transformed Bregens consternation to awe.

"The Liberator of Zephyr."

Bregens nodded with enthusiasm. "Silurian Mintaka. Of course!"

Janus' face dropped.

Soul Forge

Meeting his stare straight on, Alhena wasn't sure whether he saw hope or despair registered in Janus' eyes.

Soul Forge

Gritian

Breakfast was eaten by candlelight the next morning. Alhena insisted they fulfill their agreement to chop cordwood, but Janus wouldn't allow it. He was adamant that no one would ever say Janus Farrier had made *the* Silurian Mintaka chop wood.

Asa and Janus bid Bregens a tearful good-bye as their son left with them to take his place in the local militia. Before the sun broke across the eastern fields, four horses trotted northward along Redfire Path.

Loquax and Bregens rode side by side, a few horse lengths ahead of Alhena and Silurian.

Silurian gazed off into the mist shrouded hills to his right, thinking absently of the small charcoal sketch Phellus made for him the night before. Phellus' rendition of the moment Silurian had impaled Helleden with his magical sword was amateurish, but Silurian had been touched. He had placed the parchment in his rucksack, secretly wishing it was a bottle of the Farrier's wine.

Shortly after high noon they crested the edge of a small dale and Gritian came into view. Redfire Path opened up as they approached a lone sentry hut. The road dipped into a wide basin, its banks rising to form a trench of exposed rock that bisected the bowl-shaped glen. Heavy wooden doors, spaced sporadically along the trench-like walls, marked several entrances to the underground town of Gritian. The path rose again on the far side of the basin, lifting out of the trench and disappearing northward, beyond the only visible buildings—a barn, a large stable, and three outbuildings, half a league distant.

Two sentries left the southern guard hut and stepped onto the path. Seeing Alhena, they lowered their pikes, and waved them on.

Pulling up on his reins, Alhena spoke directly to the older guard, "Kindly locate the high bishop and have him attend us at once."

78

Soul Forge

The guard looked at him, aghast. "Nobody demands the high bishop's attendance. Especially not a lowly messenger, and most certainly, not at once."

Unperturbed, Alhena said, "Tell him Silurian Mintaka has been found."

Shock replaced the man's scowl.

Alhena smiled. "We shall wait here."

The guard mumbled a few incoherent words under his breath. He started to order his subordinate to fetch the high bishop, but must have thought better of it, and hurried down the path himself, leaving the younger guard gaping in Silurian's presence.

By the time they ate the picnic lunch Asa had sent along, a group of soldiers and robed dignitaries exited the only entranceway that boasted a hut in front of it and made their way up the path.

Alhena shook out the cloth that Asa had packed for them and handed it back to Loquax. "Thank your mother for us, son."

Loquax shook their hands. "The pleasure was ours, I assure you, Master Alhena. Sir Silurian." Seeing the approaching horde, he added, "I think I should go now." With that, he hugged his brother good-bye, mounted his horse and led the borrowed horses back over the bowl's lip and out of sight.

Bregens led his own horse toward the approaching group, standing respectfully aside as they passed. No one so much as glanced his way.

Silurian muttered under his breath, "So much for an easy life."

Alhena lifted his brow and they walked side by side into the gathering conglomeration.

The assembled group consisted of eleven chambermen, several foot soldiers, and fifteen mounted knights who had charged down from the stables; horses and riders resplendent in deep forest green surcoats emblazoned with a brilliant yellow picture of twelve high backed chairs surrounding a golden eye—the coat-of-arms of Gritian.

The leader strode confidently ahead of the throng, his long, red robe cinched tightly around his thin waist by a simple, black rope.

Soul Forge

Chambermaster High Bishop Abraham Uzziah sported a well-groomed white beard that ended in a subtle point where it touched his chest. His weathered face, complete with deep wrinkles upon a prominent forehead, framed faded blue eyes. Tight, flesh coloured lips, barely visible beneath his facial hair, became more distinct as he opened his arms to embrace Silurian. "Silurian Mintaka. Well met, my friend. I can't tell you what a relief it is to know you are safe. More importantly, you are back amongst us."

Abraham turned to address Alhena. "When you hadn't returned by the appointed time, we feared for you." He gave the messenger a thin smile. "As usual, we needn't have worried."

Alhena bowed his head and fell back. "Your Grace."

Turning back to Silurian, the chambermaster stated, "Of course, the Chamber has many questions for you, but I'm sure they can wait until you've had a chance to wash up and rest, hmm?"

Lifting his robed arms, Abraham raised his voice, "Come, my people. Let us afford our esteemed guest the best hospitality in the kingdom!" He placed a hand to the small of Silurian's back, and ushered him into the throng.

The people closed around them as they passed, following the wisemen down the path toward the Chamber residence doorway. Two enormous guardsmen stood at attention on either side of the entrance shed doors. They moved aside to allow Abraham and Silurian entry into the bowels of the Chamber complex. At a nod from the high bishop, the guards closed in behind them, barring access to everyone else.

Silurian had been in this complex many times before. The tunnel they walked in, hewn out of the bedrock, was wide enough for four men to walk abreast. Acrid, black smoke billowed from evenly spaced sconces along the passageway.

A short walk brought them to an intersection. Abraham led Silurian down the left fork. They were soon confronted by another split in the tunnels.

Abraham nodded down the left corridor. "Hungry?"

"No."

The chambermaster nodded and continued down the right tunnel. "We had given up hope. When Alhena failed to return by the full

80

moon, the Chamber turned to other measures to assist the king's efforts."

Silurian didn't respond.

"You know, many believe that our good queen gave her life unnecessarily. That, uh, other means, or people, should have been there for her." The accusation hung in the air as they passed several wooden doors standing open on either side of the passageway.

Passing the last open door, Silurian stopped to glare at the high bishop. "What are you trying to say?"

Abraham threw his hands up. "I'm just preparing you for the inevitable. Come, let's get you to your room."

The corridor passed through a closed door. On the other side, they found themselves in a short tunnel with six doors facing each other. Abraham ushered Silurian toward the last door on the left.

The room contained a screened, four-post bed, two cushioned, wingback chairs, and an oak desk littered with blank parchment. Candles of varying lengths, and a prie-dieu adorned with a red cushioned kneeler beneath a beautifully woven tapestry of a winged angel prostrated before a mystical glowing presence, completed the room. These rooms were reserved for royalty or high-ranking clergy.

"I trust the room is adequate."

Silurian dropped his pack beside the prie-dieu. "It'll do."

"Good, good." Abraham's smile fell as Silurian dropped into a chair. He opened a cabinet atop the desk and pulled out a flagon of wine and filled two goblets. Handing one to Silurian, he held out his goblet. "To better days."

Silurian ignored the toast and drank deeply.

"Silurian, my good friend, what troubles you? It saddens me deeply to see you like this."

Silurian dropped his gaze to the floor.

Abraham put his goblet down and clasped Silurian's free hand in both of his. "Perhaps we are amiss summoning you to a battle you no longer desire to fight. If you wish to walk away, I assure you the Chamber won't stand in your way. Say the word and I'll appoint an armed escort to take you wherever you want to go."

Soul Forge

Silurian bit his lower lip. *Like the one you sent with Alhena to bring me here?* He finished the contents of his goblet and gazed into the high bishop's eyes. "That won't be necessary, Your Eminence."

Abraham frowned, clasping Silurian's hands harder. "Come now, we share a friendship deeper than the bonds of duty. Call me Abraham."

Silurian looked away.

"Sil. Look at me."

Silurian did.

"My friend, whatever has happened, I want you to know I'm here for you. Time cannot tarnish our friendship." He squeezed Silurian's hand and released it so he could refill Silurian's goblet.

Silurian offered him a weak smile. "I'm sorry." He searched for the right words. "Not for my absence. That was necessary. I apologize for the way I treated your messenger, Alhena. A pleasant fellow."

"No apologies are necessary."

"Alhena has been nothing but kind to me. You have a true gem in that man. Even if he does look like a wizard."

Abraham smiled.

"Sharing his food, his fires, his patience. He saved my life up in the mountains. In return, I ignored him, yelled at him, and despised his company."

"I'm sure—"

Silurian held up his free hand. "For years I have hidden within my cabin, afraid of life. Afraid of people. Afraid of what I might do. After the Battle of Lugubrius, I went in search of my sister. I never found her."

"Ah yes, Melody," Abraham said. "Is she still alive?"

Silurian frowned. What a strange thing to ask. He had just said he had never found her. He got to his feet and paced around the room, ignoring the question. Bitterness filled his voice. "I returned home, to discover that while I was off protecting the realm, someone had murdered my family."

Abraham nodded knowingly.

Tears trickled down Silurian's cheek. He pointed a finger at the high bishop. "Who protected them? The Group of Five risked everything to save the kingdom. Three of us laid down our lives so the people of Zephyr could go on living in peace with their loved ones, but who

82

looked after mine? I find myself loathing the people I saved. I'm angry my family was killed while I risked everything to protect theirs."

He shook his head to curtail Abraham. "I know it's wrong. It isn't the people's fault, and yet, that's how I feel. I'm sorry, but that's what I've been reduced to."

He returned to his chair and said softly, "I was wrong." He took another big swallow, a silent rage evident in his eyes. "Alhena helped me realize the error of my thinking. He's proof that the world still has good people left in it. It's taken me over twenty years to realize that the people of Zephyr aren't to blame for my misery."

He wiped the tears from his face and got to his feet to stand before a painting on the wall of a white stallion leaping over a brook. He stared at it blankly, attempting to calm his breathing.

Abraham joined him and placed his hands on Silurian's shoulders. "Indeed, Alhena is a blessing."

Silurian spun about, breaking the bishop's hold. "You don't understand. Alhena is the only friend I've had in years, and I wanted to kill him."

Abraham offered a warm smile. "Trust me, my friend, I know Alhena better than most. He knows your grief and has already forgiven you."

Silurian walked to his chair and slumped down heavily, almost spilling his wine. "Well I haven't. Please, leave me now."

Outside the Chamber entrance shed, Alhena conversed with the remaining chambermen as the villagers dispersed and the mounted units trotted up the road toward the stables.

Eleven chambermen, eight men and three women, listened to Alhena recount his search for Silurian, amazed that he had succeeded when so many others had failed. By the time he finished, the guardsmen allowed them to enter the Chamber complex.

Alhena kept pace with the last chamberman, Vice Chambermaster Solomon Io. "What happened at the scheduled Chamber meeting?"

"We didn't accomplish much," Solomon informed him.

Soul Forge

The Vice Chambermaster was one of the few people on the council he felt comfortable confiding in.

"Master Uzziah adjourned the meeting to an unspecified date. With Mintaka turning up, I imagine it will reconvene as early as tonight." Solomon became quiet as they passed a tunnel on their right leading to the dungeons and the militia's living quarters.

"You should be commended for your accomplishment, Sirrus. You were right to object to sending a younger group of messengers. You knew the situation needed a delicate touch. By the looks of Silurian, I quite agree."

Passing by the eating halls on their left, they approached an intersection. The vice chambermaster put a hand on Alhena's shoulder, bringing him to a halt. He waited until the rest of the group was several paces ahead before whispering, "Beware, good messenger. These are strange times."

"How so?"

Together they watched the receding backs of the Chamber. Solomon spoke quickly, "It's hard to explain. Odd things are happening within the council. Bizarre even. Their thinking and actions of late. I can't put a finger on it, but I thought you should know. Make sure Mintaka knows this.

Alhena mulled over Solomon's words. He had had his own suspicions recently. It was troubling that someone else had been having the same misgivings.

"Tread softly, my friend," Solomon said, leaving Alhena at a fork in the tunnel that led to the servant's quarters.

After a much-needed nap, Silurian made his way to the Chamber's private dining hall. He grabbed a tray full of steaming food and sat across from High Bishop Abraham Uzziah.

Silurian was halfway through his meal when Alhena strolled into the room.

Abraham glanced up. "Welcome Alhena. Please, have a seat."

Silurian greeted Alhena with a faint smile.

Soul Forge

"I don't wish to interrupt," Alhena walked over to the kitchen window, and returned with a wooden plate loaded with vegetables and stew. Sitting one chair over from Abraham, he set in.

"Not at all. We were just talking about you."

Alhena grunted. Speaking around a mouthful of food he said, "Nothing too bad, I hope."

Abraham returned his gaze to Silurian, "As I was saying, that's why I ordered another search. I'm glad Alhena found you. We need to start making preparations for you to travel to the king's court."

Silurian glowered, picking at his meal. He had no intention of returning to King Malcolm's court. "When's the next Chamber meeting?"

"Tonight."

Silurian nodded, washing his food down with a mug of wine. He feared tonight would be the first stepping stone in a long ordeal dictated by the Chamber. If he returned to Castle Svelte, he would find himself surrounded by the deceased queen's family and peers. He'd rather be spared that scenario.

Abraham's earlier words shouted inside his head, *You know, many believe that our good queen gave her life unnecessarily. That, uh, other means, or people, should have been there for her.* He didn't think he would ever be able to look his good friend, King Malcolm, in the eye again.

Alhena wiped his lips with his cuff. "And who is to accompany Silurian to the castle?"

Abraham hesitated. "Personally, I'd recommend an armoured escort of mounted knights."

Alhena nodded and set into his stew.

"Silurian has requested your presence."

Alhena nodded, raising his eyes in resignation. He swallowed and lifted another spoonful of steaming broth to his lips.

"You. Alone."

Alhena spewed the stew back into his bowl.

"Oh, don't worry, it gets better."

Alhena dropped the spoon into his bowl, the contents slopping onto the table.

"Apparently he doesn't see the need to attend the king's court at all. In fact, it seems he is intent on travelling to Madrigail Bay—

85

unguarded! And get this, he has been told that he will meet up with the former leader of the defunct vigilante Group of Five, Rook Bowman no less."

"Actually," Silurian said quietly, "I will travel to the lost Shrine of Saint Carmichael first, to retrieve my sword."

Abraham's chair scraped the granite floor as he rose to his feet. "We've already been through this. The power in that sword is spent. The shrine is destroyed. The Chamber will not permit you travelling anywhere without proper protection. It's taken this long to finally find you. The king will be incensed if we lose you again."

Silurian struggled to keep the frustration from his voice. "I'm no use to the king without the magical properties of that sword. When I find Rook, we will attempt to locate its ancient power source. This cannot be accomplished quickly if I'm accompanied by a contingent of armed men."

Abraham's breathing grew heavier. "Neither the king, nor the Chamber, is going to allow you to go off on some maniacal quest given to you by a fantastical creature claiming to be a demi-god." Sarcasm dripped with every word. "Helleden is on our doorstep. For God's sake, Silurian, you must see the lunacy of your plan." He crossed himself in disgust.

"Even so, I will travel faster alone. As far as Seafarer goes, he never claimed to be a demi-god, Abraham, and you know it. He is instructed by Saros, the warder of the Innerworld."

"Oh great," Abraham threw his hands in the air. "This crocodile thing gets its commands from the lord of the frogs. Well, isn't that just swell?"

"This, *lord of the frogs*, has dispatched his disciple to meet up with us at Madrigail Bay and provide us guidance." Silurian glared, his hands visibly trembling. High bishop or not, how dare Abraham stand there so smugly, refuting his well-meant intentions.

Remembering the promise he made to himself that night at the entrance to the Undying Mountain Pool pass, Silurian bit back an angry response. With a mighty effort, he dropped his gaze, stood, and calmly pushed his chair in before walking out of the dining hall.

Abraham's words followed him, "It's gonna be a hell of a Chamber meeting."

Soul Forge

The Chamber Be Damned

Alhena went in search of Silurian, but he wasn't in his sleeping chambers. Exiting the Chamber complex, he stepped into the twilit evening and approached the southern guard hut to inquire of one of the young sentries on duty. The mail clad watchman pointed Alhena to a tree on the east side of Redfire path, beyond the crest in the road.

Alhena found Silurian sitting against an elm tree with his knees hugged to his chest, staring blankly at the sunset. A small brook burbled gaily a few feet farther into the wooded area.

Although Silurian didn't acknowledge his approach, Alhena sensed that Silurian was aware of everything going on around him. He had probably known of his approach long before Alhena had spoken with the sentry.

Rounding the tree, Alhena pulled his robes past his knees, and sat against the opposite side of the trunk.

They sat like that, saying nothing for a while. A cool breeze wafted over the hilly terrain, ruffling their hair. The sun's inevitable departure had them clutching their cloaks tighter as stars twinkled overhead.

Alhena absently toyed with his long, thin beard, and polished his walking staff with the edge of his cloak. He nearly leapt out of his robes when Silurian's voice broke the stillness of the night.

"I thank you for your company. I'm afraid I'm not much for small talk," Silurian said turning his head to face Alhena.

"I would never have guessed that," Alhena responded.

Silurian tilted his head and almost smiled.

"There is something I should tell you before the Chamber meeting."

Silurian raised his eyebrows.

"There are suspicions of something strange occurring within the council. A chamberman asked me to warn you."

Soul Forge

"Warn me? Of what?"

Alhena shrugged. "He did not say."

"Thanks. I'll keep my head up."

"For your thanks, there is no need. You are troubled, that I can see. I probably should not have said anything. Anyway, we can remain here as long as you wish, the Chamber be damned."

Silurian blinked.

Alhena looked away, abashed.

Silurian let his head thud against the trunk and smiled.

"Alhena Sirrus," an authoritative voice bellowed.

Alhena blinked his eyes open. A robed man sat high above him, his face cast in shadow.

Silurian stirred beside him.

Alhena knew the voice well. Abraham had come searching for them. By his tone, he wasn't happy.

"Is Silurian with you? Why aren't you at the Chamber meeting?"

Several horses thundered up the path to join the lone rider. Two Gritian militiamen dismounted and approached the tree with swords drawn.

Silurian got to his feet and reached down to assist Alhena.

Vice Chambermaster Solomon Io dismounted, a bejewelled scimitar in hand. He walked between the two militiamen, his eyes constantly searching the shadows.

Alhena was about to respond, but Silurian stepped forward. "The fault is mine, Your Eminence. Alhena tried to persuade me to come back with him, but I insisted we relax beneath this fine tree while I contemplate my future."

Abraham gazed at Alhena. "Is this true, senior messenger?"

"Are you calling me a liar?" Silurian asked.

Abraham stuttered, but before he gathered himself, Silurian pulled Alhena by the wrist. "Come on. Let's get this mummer's farce over with, shall we?" He rolled his eyes. "We mustn't keep the Chamber waiting."

Soul Forge

Alhena glanced over his shoulder, offering Abraham a shrug as he stumbled down the path, pulled along in Silurian's grasp.

Soul Forge

The Chamber of the Wise

"**Vice** Chambermaster Io!" a tall knight, resplendent in burnished plate, proclaimed in a commanding voice as he pulled open one of two finely tooled, oak doors leading into the great Chamber hall. "Sir Silurian Mintaka, and Alhena Sirrus, senior messenger to the Chamber, entering."

As the three men crossed the threshold, Silurian marvelled at the number of people crammed into the cavernous hall. The faces staring back at him didn't appear thankful that he had returned.

Majestic, cylindrical, grey marble pillars, wider than a man's arm span, and set upon massive rectangular bases of white marble, lined the lengthy expanse of the high vaulted chamber on either side of a great aisle. Spaced evenly, the columns supported a natural rock ceiling, barely visible in the shadows of thousands of flickering rush lights placed throughout the hall.

Keeping his eyes on the polished floor, Silurian followed Vice Chambermaster Io down the central aisle toward an immense rock platform spanning the width of the cavern's far end. He passed row upon row of densely packed wooden benches, sensing every eye in the hall upon him. He snatched a quick peek. Some of the faces were twisted in disgust, while others appeared curious.

He averted his gaze to examine the four-tiered platform carved out of the living stone. Each level rose three feet higher than the one below it—the top two tiers, lined by a continuous, stone bench spanning the breadth of the cavern, were full of militiamen.

The second tier, narrower than those above, housed ten high backed chairs, allocated for the Wise Council.

Four thronelike chairs adorned the central stage on the main level, their backs to the audience.

Soul Forge

Reaching the base of a short flight of exquisitely carved steps fronting the platform, Solomon held up a hand. "Wait here."

The vice chambermaster mounted the stairs with dignified grace and strode across the stage to take his place in the throne closest to the stairs.

If Silurian hadn't felt vulnerable before, he certainly did now. The noise in the chamber increased. The undertones of conversations he overheard weren't encouraging. He fought the urge to turn around and face the verbal daggers people slung his way.

"Vice Chambermistress Arzachel Gruss. High Warlord Clavius Archimedes. His Eminence, High Bishop Chambermaster Abraham Uzziah now entering," The Chamber steward announced, his deep voice rising above the clamour.

The hall thundered as everyone got to their feet. Conversation dropped to a hushed whisper as the dignitaries strolled down the aisle. Reaching the stage, the chambermaster was the only one to acknowledge Silurian's presence.

Abraham sat down next to Solomon, while the high warlord took his place in the other central seat. Vice Chambermistress Arzachel Gruss took her place on the far right.

The Chamber steward closed the large entrance door, locked it, and placed a huge golden key into the folds of his green tunic. With a regimented cadence, he strode crisply along the aisle, his boots clicking rhythmically. He mounted the dais, and ceremoniously strode to stand before the high warlord.

"The Chamber is secure, sir," the herald announced, loud enough to include the congregation. He withdrew the golden key and placed it into the high warlord's upturned palm. He snapped a quick salute, turned smartly, and marched over to sit on a wooden stool on the far side of the steps.

Silurian jumped when Alhena grabbed his wrist. "Deep breath, my friend. We'll get through this together."

Leaving Silurian alone at the base of the stage, Alhena mounted the steps and turned to face the crowd. With a loud voice, he commanded, "Be seated!"

The hall rumbled momentarily as everyone sat.

91

Soul Forge

"By the grace of King Malcolm Alexander Svelte, The Learned, the Chamber of the Wise is now in session." He walked across the stage and took up a place behind Abraham's throne, facing away from the crowd with his hands clasped behind the small of his back.

The high warlord leaned over to whisper something to Abraham.

The chambermaster nodded several times.

Silurian recalled Alhena's account of Queen Quarrnaine's demise. He had gotten the impression that Clavius and Abraham didn't think highly of each other. Seeing the two of them together now, one might be convinced otherwise.

Abraham got to his feet.

The crowd rose as one, out of deference to the high bishop.

Abraham took his time to adjust the way his robes fell, before he turned and motioned for the crowd to sit. He walked to the top of the steps, his voice booming, "First, I must apologize for our late start. Our guest of honour was delayed."

A murmur of discord rippled across the audience, but Abraham's stern look thwarted any outburst.

"Before we start, let me introduce to you the man we have gathered for." Abraham extended an open hand in Silurian's direction. "Silurian Mintaka, former king's champion and Liberator of Zephyr. Some may know of his past deeds."

Disgruntled words whispered throughout the hall. 'Coward' and 'Queen Killer' but a few of the more poignant ones.

"Some of us elders recall Zephyr's darkest days when Silurian fought alongside King Peter, may God preserve His Grace."

Silurian fidgeted.

The slurs continued from the crowd, "Where have you been, coward?" "Don't you think you've done enough damage?" "Whoreson." "You'll get your comeuppance."

The chambermaster droned on, but his words were lost on Silurian. The barbs from the crowd spiraled his thoughts into the dark recesses of his mind.

"I cannot tell you how it gladdens my heart to behold the face of a dear friend I thought never to see again."

Abraham gave Silurian a smile. "Get thyself up here. You need never be subservient to any, but the king."

Soul Forge

Silurian swallowed his misgivings. If what Abraham claimed was true, then why had he been left at the base of the stairs? He mounted the steps and accepted the chambermaster's outstretched hand. Abraham used his eyes to tell Silurian to turn and face the scowling crowd.

"Just before noon today, the Chamber was informed of Silurian's arrival, and our joyous hearts have yet to simmer. It grieves me to say that one of our first conversations ended in argument. I apologize for letting that happen."

Silurian pursed his lips, unable to look at anyone in the audience.

"We had discussed the need for a foray into the Mid Savannah, and the question regarding the size of the delegation *I felt* needed to accompany Silurian arose. Thus, our quarrel."

Silurian knew how the Chamber operated. If the chambermaster decreed something be done, it was done.

"After hearing from myself, and Silurian, I proclaim the council's decision final. For my part, I shall remain neutral."

Silurian's head snapped sideways. What was Abraham up to?

"I trust no one assembled tonight disputes this?" Abraham spread his arms and scanned the audience. No one spoke.

Of course not, Silurian thought. Few people in Gritian, or in all the kingdom for that matter, were brave enough to openly defy the High Bishop of Zephyr.

"Excellent," Abraham went on, "in the unlikely event of a standoff, High Warlord Clavius Archimedes shall make the final decision."

Silurian knew where the high warlord stood. He was probably the one lobbying for the armed escort in the first place.

Silurian squinted, trying to decipher what was different about Abraham. When they had last seen each other, Abraham had been a newly appointed bishop in Castle Svelte's clergy. Now, as the Prelate of Zephyr and chambermaster of the Chamber of the Wise, his decisions were the king's law. Sure, he looked much older, but that wasn't what niggled at Silurian. There was something else—subtle, but sinister. For the life of him, he couldn't put a name to his unease.

He stood in the middle of the platform, scrutinized by the people who had made their feelings about him clear, while Abraham droned on about how important his reemergence was to Zephyr's welfare.

About the Chamber's duty to provide him with protection. About how incensed the king would be if he were to follow his own agenda.

An elbow poked him in the ribs. Abraham had stopped speaking and commanded his attention.

"This is your opportunity to speak before the Chamber," the chambermaster said. Lowering his voice, he asked, "Are you alright?"

Silurian stared at the wizened face, searching for the man he thought he knew. Swallowing hard, his voice squeaked at first, "I understand," he cleared his throat. "I understand His Eminence's position. Were I in his place, I might advocate the same course of action." He forced himself to look into the crowd. "Chambermaster Uzziah believes I should undertake the quest under the watchful eye of the high warlord's men. I disagree. Dragging a sizable host across the Mid Savannah wasteland is not a great idea."

Several chambermen coughed. Murmurs rippled through the crowd.

Silurian ignored them. "My need for haste is paramount. A large host will slow me down. If the rumours concerning the Forbidden Swamp are true, the size of the host will be irrelevant. It will only serve to attract unwanted attention."

He wanted to add what Seafarer had told him about travelling to Madrigail Bay, not Castle Svelte—to meet up with Saros' disciple and rejoin Rook, who in most circles today, had already passed into legend. But he didn't. Forefront in his mind was Abraham's sarcastic recital to Alhena in the mess hall. *Oh great. This crocodile thing gets its commands from the lord of the frogs. Well, isn't that just swell?*

He took a long breath. "The only way to move quickly, without drawing attention, is to travel lightly. I beseech the Chamber, don't jeopardize my mission with a perfunctory guard."

Silurian studied the chambermen's faces. They didn't appear impressed. "If it makes a difference, I request the presence of one other person."

All present in the Chamber leaned forward in anticipation.

Alhena lowered his face into his hands, shaking his head.

Abraham folded his arms, a knowing smirk upturning his lips.

"I ask that Alhena Sirrus accompany me."

Incredulous guffaws sounded across the stage while the crowd exploded in outrage.

Soul Forge

Instead of quelling the uprising, Abraham let it run its course. With calculated patience, he gazed about, then nodded to the Chamber steward.

The steward's voice outstripped the clamour in the hall and the crowd ceased its chatter.

Solomon Io and Arzachel Gruss got to their feet and ascended another fancy stairway up to the second tier to converse with the Chamber body.

Silurian glanced at Alhena. The senior messenger's face was grim.

Solomon Io returned to the main stage, holding his hands out to silence small pockets of hushed conversation in the crowd. "Let the record show that the Chamber is unanimous. Silurian Mintaka's quest to the Mid Savannah, and then unto Castle Svelte, shall be undertaken with the full support of High Warlord Archimedes' men. Thus, it has been decreed, thus it shall be done."

Soul Forge

The Wiser Path

Rook had no idea how long he lay unconscious, utterly exhausted from his superhuman flight. After busting through the dome of terror he had never stopped to look back.

He stirred at the bottom of a small bluff, a full day after his body had shut down. The clump of sod he sat upon was covered in the same black soot staining his clothes. He pulled his filthy tunic tight to ward off the damp morning chill and squinted into the sunlight. Upon the eastern horizon, black smoke billowed skyward in large pockets. Even from where he sat, the smell of burnt wood, and worse, turned his nose.

Memories of his flight overwhelmed him. He envisioned the placid waters of Saros' Swamp and the eerie silence before the chaos had taken over. He reeled as a nauseating wave of damning guilt gripped him. He had abandoned the Innerworld and now Saros was gone.

Nothing stirred other than a swirling breeze. It seemed as if every creature living near the Mid Savannah border with the Innerworld had fled the region.

Without thinking, he ran toward the devastation. Toward the place Seafarer and Saros had risked their lives to deliver him from.

He needed to see it for himself. Needed to know if anything had survived.

The ground cover blackened the closer he got. Withered plant life dotted the landscape, marring the ground with blotches of foul blackness. The only visible signs of life were carrion birds circling over what had been the Innerworld.

His pace slackened. Nearing the destruction zone, his mind tried to reconcile what it took in. Shriveled grass crunched underfoot. Any hope of finding something alive faded with each bleak step. The

96

border of the Innerworld, where the edge of the dome had met with the land, was evidenced by a black smudge of barren earth, as if drawn by the hand of a giant.

He crossed over the threshold and stopped, ankle deep in black ash. Withered carcasses of blackened trees, plants, and the remains of a few of the larger inhabitants lay twisted in death.

He sank to his knees, tears smearing his soot covered face, and grieved all that was lost. It wasn't until the sun had travelled deep into the western sky that he dragged his listless body out of the ashes and slumped away from the only life he knew.

He made it as far as the scar left by the dome before he dropped to the scorched earth in a fetal position and shivered profusely—his mind numb.

During a long, sleepless night, he struggled to pull himself together. There was nothing left for him here. Seafarer's words fought to take root in his fleeting sanity, echoing hollowly around his shattered mind. *Saros has dispatched his disciple, Thetis, to rendezvous with you and Silurian at Madrigail Bay.*

What choice did he have? He wanted nothing more than to find Helleden and kill him, but he wasn't equal to the task. With Silurian by his side, though, they might stand a chance. Provided his friend didn't kill everyone else around him first.

A faint hope took root, deep down, buried beneath his grief. Everything had always seemed better when Silurian was involved— well, almost always.

Rook forced himself to smile, the first time in days. Just a small one, but it went a long way to lift his spirits enough to carry on. Whenever the two of them had fought together, no matter the odds, they always managed to come out on top. Whenever all seemed lost, Silurian had a knack of finding a way to win. Unfortunately, at the end of their time together, Silurian's methods had deteriorated to something less than scrupulous.

A tear trickled down his cheek. He smudged it away with his tunic sleeve, smearing the black filth coating his face. Hunger gnawed at him. For the first time since fleeing Saros' Swamp, he opened his rucksack. Inside, he discovered a bunch of vegetables Seafarer had packed for him. Choking a few down, he shrugged into his pack and set out with a heavy heart. Refusing to look back, he trudged into the Mid Savannah.

Without a horse, Madrigail Bay was a lifetime away. Castle Svelte lay several days to the northwest. Surely King Malcolm would know what to do. At Castle Svelte, he would be able to commandeer a horse. He thought about Gritian to the southwest, farther away than the castle, but that was where Seafarer had said Silurian was headed. Whichever way he decided, getting to Redfire Path was his priority.

The day proved pleasant upon the rolling plains. The sun rose into a clear sky, quickly dispersing the morning chill. The farther he walked, the more the telltale signs of life reasserted itself upon the land—evidenced by the annoying buzz and occasional insect bite.

As night descended, he stumbled upon a clear stream tumbling its way toward the devastation in the east. He tested the water for its drinkability before deciding to camp for the night. He briefly thought about how his proximity to a water source made him more vulnerable to whatever hunted in the darkness but decided to remain there anyway. If something *was* out there, he'd know it soon enough.

He sat down upon a flat rock at the stream's edge. Dropping his sack behind him, he removed his boots to enjoy the sensation of the cool breeze on his toes.

As he sat there dangling his feet in the cool water, he couldn't help thinking that Helleden had become too powerful for anyone to deal with. Given the substantial losses the Zephyr army had suffered over the last two decades, the king's forces would be hard pressed to thwart the sorcerer's advance. The realm had lost a king and a queen during Helleden's previous two sorties. If King Malcolm were to fall, the remainder of the known world would surely die with him.

Rook shuddered to think about the consequences the death of King Malcolm would have on Silurian.

Rook sighed with relief the next morning—he hadn't been attacked or killed in his sleep by the brigands and vagabonds the Mid Savannah was notorious for. Perhaps the Innerworld's destruction had driven

Soul Forge

their ilk westward, though that thought wasn't reassuring as it was west he was headed.

A few days later, he stood atop an outcropping of rock, trying to ascertain his location. Judging by the sun, he still travelled southwest. He must've passed close to the Forgotten Shrine during the morning of the previous day. He thought briefly of visiting the broken building, but he didn't want to waste the time it would require to actually find it.

It had been years since he'd travelled through Zephyr, but he knew the land well. He was pretty sure he now stood along the northern fringes of the Gritian Hills.

He took a steadying breath. The prospect of being surrounded by mankind again made him nervous.

Scanning the terrain for signs of predators or thieves, he laughed out loud. Thieves! With all the impending peril, thieves were the least of his worries. Other than his bow, and a scant collection of old arrows, what else did he have to offer? A broken wooden plate? A leaky wooden bowl? A moth eaten wool blanket? He shook his head at the ludicrousness of it all. Chuckling, he set off at a brisk pace.

As the day drew to an uneventful close, Redfire Path was nowhere in sight. He set up camp beneath a jag of rock, topped by long, drooping grass and a lone, scraggy, red maple. Close by, a slow running brook meandered southward.

While stowing his gear the following morning, beating wings grabbed his attention. A skinny goose landed upon the brook.

He grabbed his bow, and slithered an arrow from its quiver, careful not to make a noise. Crouching low, he waddled around the jag of rock, notched the arrow, eyed the target and let fly. He missed terribly.

The goose squawked its outrage and took flight.

He quickly loosed another arrow.

The bird emitted a mocking screech as the arrow fell short.

Watching the skinny bird grow smaller in the sky, Rook grimaced at the irony. The mighty Rook Bowman, leader of the Group of Five, and holder of five Royal Tournament archery championships, bested by a malnourished goose at close range. All while on a mission to deliver Zephyr from its ultimate bane, Helleden Misenthorpe.

Perhaps returning to the Innerworld and starting over might prove the wiser path.

99

$\mathfrak{Soul}$ $\mathfrak{Forge}$

Damn the Chamber

Alhena accompanied Silurian to his sleeping quarters in silence. Silurian ambled along dejectedly, shoulders slumped, and head hung low. The Chamber's decision, although expected, had taken whatever spirit he had out of him.

Silurian sunk into a chair and buried his face in his palms. The Chamber's shortsighted decision, had in all likelihood, set into motion the needless death of many people. Preventable deaths if they only appreciated the endgame. Surely the high warlord knew better. A small group of horsemen travelled faster and far less conspicuously than a large, armoured contingent.

"Damn the Chamber," Silurian grumbled into his hands.

Alhena stared at the troubled warrior. *Damn the Chamber?* He nodded, a mischievous glint in his eyes. *Aye. Damn the Chamber.*

Taking a deep breath, he said quietly, "What if we left tonight?"

Silurian became still.

"Just you and I."

Silurian peeked around his hands, a slow smile upturning the corners of his mouth.

Early morning dew glistened in the moonlight. The singsong of birds announced the imminent arrival of sunrise, still some time while away.

At the north end of Gritian, two figures darted about the stable yards, moving from shadow to shadow to avoid the posted guard—keeping to the eerie shadows cast by the waning moon. Scurrying

100

toward the main stable from the side of a large hay barn, Alhena and Silurian ducked behind a smaller structure to catch their breath.

Alhena bent low, peering around the corner of the utility shed. A solitary guard leaned against the stable doors, peering into the shadows. Alhena ducked back out of sight.

"Do you think they miss us yet?" Silurian whispered, glancing back at the large hay barn. If anyone wandered about the yard they would easily be spotted.

"I hope not," Alhena said, not taking his eyes from the corner of the building they hid against. He snuck another peek. The sentry was searching the shadows in the opposite direction.

Alhena motioned for Silurian to move and followed him to the stable's side wall. Together they peered around the corner. The sentry still leaned against the stable doors, his breath visible in the night air.

Silurian pulled back. "What now?"

Alhena studied the grounds around the utility shed, scanning the darker shadows that clung to the large hay barn. There were no other guards in sight. He leaned out to check on the sentry.

Something thudded loudly upon Redfire Path, skipped off a rock, and rolled into a patch of dry leaves.

The sentry froze.

Alhena pulled back, eyes wide. "What the hell was that?" he said louder than he meant to.

The sentry started toward Redfire Path, but Alhena's voice stopped him.

"Shhh," Silurian whispered, crouching low. Standing up again he held out another rock, smiling.

Alhena couldn't believe it. Silurian had probably put the entire compound on alert. He hazarded a peek around the corner. The sentry was slowly approaching their position with his sword drawn.

Alhena glared at Silurian. "Have you taken leave of your senses?"

Silurian ignored him, steadying himself for another throw. He pitched the rock high into the air. If he had been trying to send it over the stable, he missed terribly. The rock hit the side of the building with a hollow thud and fell back to the ground, nearly hitting Alhena.

"Shit," Silurian cried, and made to follow Alhena's dash toward the rear of the stable.

Soul Forge

The guard's hurried footsteps rounded the corner. "Hold!"

Alhena stopped and turned around. The sentry held a sword tip to Silurian's chest.

"C-come out of there," the sentry ordered, motioning for them to step out of the shadows.

Alhena feared Silurian might do something rash. A dead guard was the last thing they needed. Looking at the sentry's face, he almost choked. "Bregens?"

At the same moment, Bregens' eyes registered who stood at the point of his sword. Arguably the deadliest swordsman in Zephyr's history. Bregens' eyes almost popped from his head. Had the ground not caught the tip of his blade, he would've dropped it altogether.

"S-Sire Mintaka? What are you doing sneaking around in the shadows?"

Alhena held his hands up and walked into the moonlight. "Bregens, our good friend. We seek mounts to ride north."

"But the quest doesn't leave until sunrise."

"Aye, but hear me out. The Chamber has appointed a large contingent of armed men to accompany us on a perilous quest."

"Yes, so I was told." Bregens eyes darted from one man to the other.

"I bet they neglected to tell you Silurian opposed that decision."

"No, they never said anything like that."

"Well, Silurian and I believe the Chamber's decision is misguided. The warlord's men will place the quest in peril. Their presence will slow us down and needlessly risk their lives."

Bregens didn't appear any less confused.

"Silurian must leave tonight. Not to disobey the Chamber's wishes, certainly, but to *save* the lives of those appointed to protect him. Do you understand what I am saying? If we do not leave now, alone, the quest will fail."

Bregens chewed on his lower lip.

Alhena knew the young guard didn't have the authority to make such a weighty decision, but he persisted, "I ask you, knowing the lives of your peers are in the offing, to grant us this." He lowered his voice, sounding as grave as possible, "Should we fail, Zephyr will fall. I do not think you would want to be the one blamed for not acting when you had the chance to make a difference. In the name of freedom, it is imperative that you allow us to leave on our own."

"No, of course I wouldn't want that. It's just...I just don't know. The Chamber has entrusted me with the security of the stables. High Warlord Archimedes will flay me alive."

"You have been entrusted by the Chamber to protect its citizens. That is exactly what you will be doing. Bregens, hear me. Many lives hang in the balance." He gave Bregens the most serious face he could muster. "If you fear the warlord, you may accompany us."

Silurian glared at him.

Alhena ignored it. "We will respect your decision, but you must decide quickly."

Bregens closed his eyes tight, visibly shaking. Opening them, he looked sheepishly at Silurian. "You are Silurian Mintaka. I would love nothing more than to honour what you ask, but I can't go against the high warlord's order." His scrunched expression denoted the moral dilemma he fought—he appeared to be on the verge of crying. He said loudly to no one in particular, "Why me? This is my first official duty!" He closed his eyes and shook his head.

Alhena nodded knowingly at Silurian.

Bregens slapped his forehead with both palms. Dropping them to his sides, he muttered, "Okay."

Alhena didn't hear him. "I am sorry. What?"

"I said okay but make it quick." Casting a glance around the yards, Bregens pulled the double stable doors open and motioned them inside. He scanned the shadows once more, took a heavy breath and followed on their heels, wagging his finger. "Don't even *think* about taking Archimedes' mount."

Soul Forge

Kraidics!

The sun sank low upon the western horizon, tucking in for the night. Rook kept walking in the ample light provided by a three-quarter moon.

Peculiar and unnerving sounds drew his attention to the deep shadows, some he recognized, others he didn't. Imagining things lurking just out of sight, his pace slowed. He kept looking to the overcast sky, expecting the clouds to blacken.

He stopped and listened. An unnatural hoot sounded in the distance to the south. Whatever it was, it didn't repeat itself.

He shook his head. His mind was playing tricks on him. And then he smelled it—the aroma of burning wood upon a breeze. It seemed to be coming from the south as well. Taking great care, he made his way up a steep knoll and scrambled down its far side.

Deep voices reached him upon the breeze. He stopped, fearing he had been spotted, but nothing moved. Creeping up the side of the adjoining rise, he peered over its top and froze. The unmistakable glow of a campfire flickered beyond the next hill, illuminating the trees along the ridge.

He scrambled down the slope and crept up the far hill, thankful for the thicket near its top.

If not for the sudden sound of trickling water from the other side of the brambles he crept through, he would've been spotted.

Espying the silhouette of a man much larger than himself, he held his breath.

Groaning with satisfaction, the man relieved himself. Once finished, he adjusted his garments, spun about, and walked over the crest of the hill, but before he disappeared from view, he stopped to inspect the thicket, as if sensing something.

Soul Forge

The man stared right at him, but after a tense moment, he continued into the valley.

Daring to breathe, Rook fought to still his racing heart. He counted to a hundred before inching his way to the base of a large pine near the top of the hill. Crawling beneath the low hanging boughs he peered down at a large campsite.

A band of heavily armoured, wildly bearded men milled about a bonfire in the shallow ravine.

At first glance, Rook had no idea who these men were. They definitely weren't the king's men. Judging by their apparel, they weren't Gritian militia either.

He tried to make out their conversations but could only hear unintelligible snatches. He started to slither from beneath the branches for a closer look.

Someone stepped away from the fire and pointed up the hill, shouting in a language he didn't understand.

A loud voice shouted back, sounding like it was right on top of him. On the far side of the tree, a sentry stepped from the shadows and descended into the ravine.

Rook crept back beneath the pine's prickly confines, careful not to disturb the bough scratching the back of his head.

The original man who had shouted met the other man halfway, exchanged a few words, and walked toward the pine—apparently, a changing of the guard.

The man walked up to where Rook lay—so close that Rook could reach out and grab his thick ankles. He followed the sentry's progress around the tree, more by sound than by sight. The man's footsteps drifted away, crunching and crackling into the distance down the far side of the slope behind him. It was a wonder he hadn't been spotted earlier.

Satisfied the sentry hadn't seen him, Rook crept to the edge of his cover and studied the men's fur skinned garments, their long hair, and unkempt beards. One man in particular bent near the fire to retrieve a massive battle-axe. Everyone jumped to their feet as he circled the fire and disappeared into the only visible tent.

They all carried the same types of weapons. Axes and hammers. Rook's eyes grew wide. The significance struck him as if he had been hit by one of their warhammers. Below him, deep in the heart of Zephyr, sat an encampment of Kraidic warriors. A savage race bent on pillaging, killing, and raping everything in sight. How they had gotten this far inland without opposition?

Perhaps they were in league with Helleden Misenthorpe. That made sense. Forming an alliance with the Kraidic Empire, the strongest nation north of Zephyr, Helleden's army would be unstoppable.

Unsure of where the sentries might be posted, he lay beneath the relative safety of the pine throughout the night. He must have dozed off because when he opened his eyes again, the horizon was lightening in the east. It wouldn't be long before the sun drove the gloom from the valley. When it did, the Kraidic warriors would have no trouble spotting him.

Soul Forge

Companion Lost

Galloping three abreast, Silurian glanced across Alhena to where the young Farrier boy rode on the opposite side of the path. As the sun's reddish glow lightened the eastern horizon, Silurian stewed over their inclusion of Bregens.

The day passed in silence; each man lost in their own thoughts while their mounts churned league after league of Redfire Path's turf.

Silurian was thankful that the horses Bregens had recommended were performing better than they had a right to expect. They stopped twice at streams they encountered to water the horses and allow them to crop at the vegetation along the banks.

With the daylight fading, Silurian was surprised when they approached a road on their right that led southeast to the Forbidden Pass. They had covered a lot of ground in their effort to distance themselves from the inevitable pursuit.

If they wished to stop for the night, they needed to get off the roadway. Silurian was sure that High Warlord Clavius would drive his men mercilessly until they caught up with them.

Without warning, Silurian said, "Follow me," and led them into a hilly forested area east of Redfire Path.

A short while later they approached a tributary of the Calder River. Silurian located a shallow stretch of river and led them across to the eastern bank.

Bregens walked his horse free of the stream and joined Alhena. Waiting for the horses to drink, he looked to the east. "Master Alhena? Why do they call it the Forbidden Swamp?"

Silurian overheard the question. His shoulders tensed.

Alhena's colourless eyes studied the farm boy. "Two reasons, really. The inhabitants of the Forbidden Swamp are not people, they are

Soul Forge

animals. Animals that have, I don't know, uh, banded together to form a community, you might say."

"Banded together?"

"Aye. Well, not just like that, but anyway, as a community, the swamp denizens do not take kindly to outside interference. People, especially, are forbidden within their domain."

"That's weird."

"Yes, I guess, but knowing what people are capable of, I cannot blame them."

"Why do you say that?"

"Heh-heh, that is something you will learn."

"You said there were two reasons."

"Aye. The second one, as far as Zephyr is concerned, is more important. The Forbidden Swamp acts as a buffer between Zephyr and the Wilds."

Silurian still sat upon his mount. He drank from his waterskin and listened.

"A buffer? For what?" Bregens asked.

Alhena drew a long breath. "Let us just say, there are things that inhabit the Wilds that are better off left there."

"Things? Like what? People?"

Silurian pulled up on his reins, directing his horse away from the stream. His harsh voice startled them. "You talk too much, kid. Give it a rest. Mount up and let's be off."

They rode deep into the Gritian Hills—a tactic that was unlikely to throw off the warlord's bloodhounds for long, but it might buy them the time they needed to rest for the night. None of them had slept much since the previous morning at the Farrier homestead.

It was Alhena who finally called their flight to a halt, well into the night. "The horses need rest. We are lucky they have lasted this long. It will not do to drive them into the ground."

Locating a deep hollow to set up for the night, it took a great deal of coaxing to lead their mounts into it. Lost in the shadows at the bottom of the depression lay a stagnant pool of water—green and smelling of rot.

Soul Forge

Choking down a cold meal, Silurian disappeared back up the steep embankment to assume first watch. A cool wind greeted him as he crested the top. The first signs of a storm rolled in from the west.

Alhena and Bregens huddled beneath rough wool blankets Bregens had secured from the militia stores in the barn. Trying to find a spot level enough to lie on wasn't easy.

Alhena sensed Bregens facing him, wide awake. "How fair you, young Bregens?"

"I'm not sure. I don't rightly know how to express my feelings to one as experienced in the ways of fighting men as you are."

Alhena frowned but allowed Bregens to continue.

"I'm afraid of the punishment awaiting me should Clavius catch us."

Alhena nodded. "Aye, Clavius will not be pleased. I am sure his anger will fall upon myself and Silurian, however. You are not to blame."

"You can't say that. I gave you the horses. We're in this together and that's what really troubles me."

"How so?"

"Sir Silurian. He despises me. He hasn't spoken a word all day except to tell me to shut up. I shouldn't have come."

"Do not say that. You could not remain behind. Like you say, Archimedes would have flogged you for allowing us to depart without his protection. He might have handed you over to his dog, the Enervator. I pity anyone suffering that fate."

Bregens gulped. "I guess, but I'm the reason Sir Silurian is uneasy."

"I am not sure I follow you."

Bregens elaborated, "Silurian's not happy I'm here. He probably thinks I'm useless in a fight."

Silence fell over the bottom of the hollow. Alhena sensed Bregens had more to say so he bided his time listening to cricket chatter and the throaty croaks of frogs inhabiting the stagnant water.

"I might be young, but I can handle myself. I just think he'd be happier come morning if I were gone far away from here."

Soul Forge

"Tsk. Do not talk like that. I have travelled many leagues with Sire Mintaka. Believe me when I say he is not a social beast at the best of times."

"There's more to it than that. Not speaking often is one thing, but not saying anything all day except to chew me out, is quite another."

Alhena had only known Silurian for a short while, but he had gotten to know the man better than anyone else had for the last two decades. "Sir Silurian is a troubled man. The weight of Zephyr rests upon his shoulders and I do not think he believes he is up to the task the kingdom expects. Your presence is a variable he had not planned for."

"Exactly. He feels responsible for me."

Alhena raised his eyebrows. The kid was right.

"I hope I get to prove my worthiness to Sir Silurian. He needn't worry. I can handle a sword."

Alhena grimaced at Bregens' bravado. He hadn't yet learned that one should be careful what they wished for. "Fret not. He will come around. Believe me, you will know when he accepts you. When that day comes, he will angrily warn you to stop calling him Sir. Only then will he consider you a friend."

Morning came quickly, grey and cold, laden with a light rain. Bregens had taken last watch. When the day had brightened enough to see by, he slipped down the slick grass into the depression to wake Silurian and Alhena, but they were already up—sleep impossible in the chilly drizzle.

Silurian led his mount up the steep banks, pulling hard on the reins, mindful of the footing to reduce the risk of his horse slipping. Bregens and Alhena struggled in single file behind him. Cresting the rim of the hole, he was ill prepared for the sight awaiting them.

A tall knight astride a large, black stallion watched them lead their horses out of the hollow—his face hidden beneath a dull grey, flat topped helm.

Soul Forge

The knight and his mount were draped in forest green surcoats. Emblazoned upon a field of yellow sat twelve high backed chairs surrounding a golden eye in the middle.

Silurian's heart sank, recognizing the Chamber of the Wise coat-of-arms. He looked around, expecting to be surrounded by the warlord's men, but the knight appeared to be alone.

No one had heard him approach, not even Silurian. For all they knew, the knight had lain in wait for them all night.

The man pulled off his helm and placed it on his saddle horn, a smug smile parting his black goatee. A two-handed crossbow, loaded with a barbed quarrel, sat casually upon his lap.

Silurian noted the golden knot of office on the man's shoulder. The badge of the Enervator. The Chamber's whip.

Alhena jumped, while Bregens noticeably paled.

Before either one of them had time to fully appreciate the ramifications of the knight's presence, a metallic hiss announced Silurian's sword escaping the shoulder baldric he preferred to carry it in while riding.

The knight pointed the crossbow at him. "Ah, the Queen Killer. How quaint. Tempt me, I beg you."

Alhena stepped between them, motioning for Silurian to lower his sword. "Come now, Thwart, even *you* wouldn't dare loose that bolt on Silurian Mintaka."

Thwart's eyes darted toward Bregens.

Alhena frowned. "Really, Avarick? Harm a young militia man? He's barely older than a boy. We forced him to come against his will."

The Enervator regarded Alhena with contempt. Suddenly his foot shot out, clipping Alhena on the shoulder. Alhena's staff flew from his hands as he tumbled to the ground.

Silurian advanced upon the knight.

"Halt, Queen Killer. Make no mistake. I *will* kill you."

Silurian winced at the unfair honourific that had been bestowed upon him by an ungrateful people—he had heard it spoken often enough by the cowards who had attended the Chamber meeting. He debated his options as he faced the business end of the barbed quarrel pointed between his eyes.

111

Soul Forge

If he had been twenty years younger, the impertinent Enervator would already be dead. He stepped back a pace, never taking his eyes from the crossbow.

"Who is this horse's arse?" Silurian asked, frustrated at his inability to deal with him.

Bregens answered in a wavering voice. "The Enervator of Gritian." He attempted to look the man in the face but when Avarick glanced his way, he dropped his gaze to the ground, muttering, "A very powerful and deadly man."

Silurian already knew that. He studied the Enervator, taking his measure, searching for a weakness to exploit. He knew all about Enervators. The hand that meted out the Chamber's justice. Hired assassins, really. Silurian had been out of the public eye for a long time, but there was something familiar about this one.

Stepping back to stand beside Alhena, Silurian recalled the name Alhena had mentioned. Avarick. He had heard that name before. A long time ago.

Avarick addressed Bregens, "Yes, Bregens Farrier. When old man Archimedes said you deserted your post, I wasn't surprised."

Bregens scowled.

"I can smell cowards like you a league away."

Bregens withdrew his sword and started toward the horseman. Alhena grabbed him by the elbow and pulled him back.

"I shan't hesitate to dispatch a deserter. As far as old man Archimedes is concerned, your life is already forfeited. I can hardly wait until he hands you over to me," Avarick said raising his eyebrows twice in quick succession.

Alhena stepped in front of the boy, his staff back in hand. "You'll have to go through me."

The Enervator snorted. "Your frail corpse will do little to impede my quarrel. You're nothing but an old man who carries useless bits of paper around. You've no more standing than the coward."

Silurian nodded to himself, gaining the perspective he needed to deal with the insolent man. He walked confidently up to the Enervator, who instantly trained the crossbow on him.

"Halt, Queen Killer."

Soul Forge

Ignoring the threat, Silurian slapped the man's leather boot from its stirrup and yanked him from his saddle. The quarrel fell harmlessly away as Avarick threw his arms out to break his fall.

Silurian stood over him. "But you won't harm me. I'm needed."

The Enervator glared at him. He scrambled to his knees. Locating the errant bolt, he reloaded the crossbow upon an upraised knee.

"If you so much as lay a hand on either one of them again, make no mistake, *I* will kill *you*," Silurian snarled.

Avarick spat his disgust and lowered the crossbow. He got to his feet and squared to face him. Less than a whisker separated their faces.

"No, Queen Killer, *you* make no mistake. When this business is over, you are mine."

Alhena's voice cut the tension, "Quiver your quarrel and begone, Thwart. You hold no jurisdiction here."

"You forget your station old man. My office has no bounds." The man sneered, gathering his reins and adjusting his saddle.

Thwart? The name triggered something in Silurian's distant memory. *Alhena had called him Avarick. Avarick Thwart. Could he be the same man?*

The Enervator appeared about the same age. Now that he thought more about it, the man bore the same heraldic symbols that he had worn back then. Suddenly, Silurian recalled the conversation he had overheard in the king's box all those years ago between the then, Prince Malcolm, and his younger brother, Prince Nicholas. *'Headstrong, that one,'* had been Malcolm's words. It made sense.

"The Royal Tournament," Silurian said.

Avarick didn't pay him any attention. He put his left boot into the near stirrup.

"Twenty-seven years ago. In, Millsford, I believe. Yes, Millsford."

Leather creaked and tack jingled as Avarick mounted. Adjusting his posture and finding the other stirrup, he ignored Silurian's odd ramblings.

"I believe the tournament was supposed to have been held in Ember Breath that year, but for some reason I can't recall, it was moved. A flood or a storm or something?"

Avarick snarled, "What are you on about?"

Silurian sheathed his sword behind his back, walked toward his own horse and checked the cinch. Adjusting his pack, he made sure his gear was securely bound to the saddle. Satisfied, he walked his mount closer to Avarick. "That's where I've seen you before."

"So."

"You were headstrong even then. A hotshot, if I recall King Malcolm's sentiments correctly. Of course, Malcolm was just a prince then."

The Enervator's brows drew together in a scowl. "Watch yourself, Queen Killer."

"You were one of the favourites to win the tournament, but you drew the local entrant—a farm boy, no less." He paused to look pointedly at Bregens. "And you were beaten. Soundly," Silurian finished, offering the Enervator a smug smile of his own.

Avarick Thwart glared at him for a long while, recollection evident in his eyes. Silurian could tell that that particular tournament still held a raw edge in the Enervator's mind, even after all these years.

"Bah! The kid got lucky." He pulled hard on his horse's bit, stopping the mount from grazing at Silurian's feet.

"Lucky?" Silurian laughed. "That farm boy was Javen Milford."

The Enervator shrugged.

"He went on to become a member of the Group of Five."

Avarick yawned. He turned to Alhena. "Don't think I'm leaving you, old man. My job is to bring traitors to justice." He turned back and spat, nearly hitting Silurian. "As for you, Queen Killer, mark my words. When this is over, when the king no longer needs you, I shall deliver unto you my own justice."

Thunder sounded in the distance. A bad storm was rolling in.

Lightning lashed the landscape as four drenched horsemen rode northward over the rolling Gritian Hills in silent misery. It rained steadily all morning, growing heavier as the day wore on. At one point their path was blocked by the wide course of the Calder River. The swollen river ran swift, sweeping storm debris northward where it eventually crossed Redfire Path on its way around the Muse to join the mighty Madrigail River at Millsford. It took them a long time to find a section shallow enough for the horses to cross. When they did, they had to dismount and lead them.

By mid-afternoon, Silurian second guessed his sense of direction. Their course took them up the side of a high embankment—the ground between the rise and the river, an impassable marshland.

Cresting the top of the lofty berm, they carried on, wary of an ominous drop-off to their right.

All heads turned skyward despite the drenching rainfall as the sky darkened further. Horizontally flying rain stung their eyes in the face of the wind. Complete concentration was required to maintain control of the terrified horses and keep them moving forward.

Jagged bolts of lightning zigzagged every which way. Thunder detonated and shook the ground, causing the frightened animals to rear up on their hind legs. The poor visibility made it hard for them to stick together. They needed to find a place to shelter, but exposed high upon the berm, there was no place to hide.

They approached a lone elm bent incredibly by the wind; rooted precariously to the eastern face of the hill. Silurian coaxed his roan past the whip like tree, followed loosely by Bregens, Avarick and Alhena.

The sky lit up with a blinding flash. The hair on Silurian's body stood on end as lightning arced to the tree he had just passed—an electric zap filling the air. His horse tried to throw him.

By the time he reasserted a measure of control over his mount, the elm tree had disappeared—dropping over a hundred feet into the gloom below. He struggled to coerce his mount toward the smoking remnants. He glanced to the east and shivered. Was this how the Forbidden Swamp had been destroyed?

Bregens and Avarick were off their horses, fighting hard to keep them in check.

Silurian pulled up short of the impact area—his mount refusing to get any closer. The lightning strike had not only taken the tree over the edge, but a large section of the cliff side as well.

His blood ran cold.

Of Alhena, there was no sign.

Soul Forge

Strange Irony

Rook wasn't sure how the sentry hadn't spotted him when the Kraidic war band broke camp. Perhaps the impending storm blowing in from the west triggered the oversight.

When the last of the warriors disappeared over the next rise, he had trouble moving. He remained stock still, buried beneath the bottom boughs of the lofty pine and afraid to breathe, for the entire night. Cramped muscles, an aching back, and scratched skin had him feeling like he'd been punched repeatedly by a cactus.

He followed the Kraidic warriors southward, a course paralleling Redfire Path somewhere to the west. Thunder rolled in and before long the first droplets of rain rang off their armour.

Rook trailed their progress from a ridge line, staying well back, checking and rechecking that no one followed him. It wasn't long before the storm kicked into full force. Torrential rain and buffeting winds assaulted everyone travelling the Gritian Hills.

Tailing the enemy force, Rook pondered their destination. If they had travelled this far south of Castle Svelte, their intended target must be Gritian and the Chamber of the Wise. He debated the merits of trying to get ahead of them and warn the Gritian militia, against the cost of losing track of them in case he was wrong.

Wherever they were headed, they were a well-disciplined troop, maintaining tight formations as they ran even with the geographical and environmental issues they were forced to deal with in the untamed Gritian Hills.

The band never stopped to eat the whole day. When a cold wind blew in and the overcast sky opened up, Rook estimated it to be mid-afternoon.

Soul Forge

Forked lightning flashed continuously, followed by booming thunder that rumbled in from every direction. He lost sight of the band more than once in the incessant deluge and had to scramble to find them again—their forced march barely slowed by of the storm.

A jagged lightning bolt struck a high embankment to the southwest—the ensuing thunderclap rocked the land. From that point on, the storm receded to the east. After another hour, the wind moved on, taking the cold rain with it.

At first Rook had thought the storm's cessation was a good thing but the Kraidic warriors picked up their pace. He had to practically run to keep from losing them. It was impressive how fast the heavily armoured, pack and weapon laden men were able to move, especially after slogging through the severe weather. If Gritian was their target, the Chamber was in serious peril.

When night fell, the skies cleared. The Kraidic warriors pitched camp at the bottom of a deep ravine. Rook figured they wouldn't move again until dawn so he backtracked a safe distance away and located a relatively dry spot tucked beneath a rocky overhang, two gullies west of the band's position.

He had no sooner shrugged off his pack and laid his bow and quiver aside when the small hairs on the back of his neck stood up. He could still hear the occasional ruckus coming from the Kraidic encampment, but he sensed someone, or something, approaching his shelter from the opposite direction.

He froze and listened. Other than the sound of the breeze through the trees shaking loose water droplets that pattered on the sodden ground, nothing stirred. He hadn't slept for two days. Perhaps his bleary mind was imagining things. It had been a long day.

A soft footfall sounded atop the ledge he sheltered beneath.

He almost yelled out in fright. He was relieved to be beneath the cover of the crag, but he had no way of telling if whatever stood above him was aware of his presence. He moved to the edge of his concealment and slowly leaned out, risking a peek at the ridge fifteen feet above.

The half-moon's light filtered eerily throughout the treed hills. At first, only the silhouettes of trees, bushes and a large rock met his gaze.

117

Soul Forge

He was about to lean out farther when another footfall sounded upon the crag of rock jutting out directly overhead.

He saw the outline of a person with long flowing hair, stooped upon the edge. A woman? Out here in the dark?

Whoever it was, they appeared to be looking eastward toward the Kraidic encampment. The silhouette didn't appear anything like the bulky Kraidic Warriors. He squinted, not believing what the poor light revealed. The shadow's arms ended in long, claw-like fingers.

Rook ducked beneath the ledge and scrabbled for his bow and quiver. He cursed himself as the arrows rattled together.

He hazarded a look up to determine if the creature had heard him. Sure enough, it was crouched low. It looked straight at him, its crazed eyes catching the moonlight.

Rook loosed a hastily strung arrow. The missile's flight nicked the side of the rock face and ricocheted harmlessly into the night.

The creature pulled back from the brink, out of sight.

Rook cursed his rotten luck. *Now what?* He cowered deeper into the shadows as a strong voice broke the still of the night, "Please, I mean you no harm."

Sure you don't, Rook thought. *Out here, in the middle of nowhere at night, with a Kraidic warband camped nearby.* He strung another arrow. Keeping his back against the rock he wondered which side the creature would come at him.

"I am but a lone traveller, on my way to Gritian."

Sure you are. Rook searched the shadows to his left, then to his right. It was likely trying to get him to drop his guard.

He felt trapped. If he bolted, he risked being pounced upon. If he didn't, he risked being pinned underneath the ledge. Not knowing what to do, he said, "Show yourself. What kind of creature are you?"

The scrape of metal on rock announced the creature's movements as it scrambled down the side of the rock face.

"I am human, I assure you. Perhaps not as alive as I would like, but…" The voice trailed off.

It sounded human.

"How do you explain your hands?"

The sound of metal scraping metal made Rook flinch.

"You mean my knucklettes? They are weapons I wear on my hands."

Soul Forge

Rook frowned. "Knucklettes? Never heard of them."

"Not many people have. They come from a land far away."

Rook regripped his bow. "What are you doing in Zephyr then?"

"In Zephyr? I live here. Fear not, for I am Alhena Sirrus, senior messenger to the Chamber of the Wise. I am on my way to the Mid Savannah, to uh, bear witness to the unfortunate demise of the Forbidden Swamp."

Rook swallowed. So, the Chamber already knew about the firestorm. That was good news *if* the creature could be trusted.

Other than the gentle gusts playing in the trees, silence settled over the forest. He almost squeaked when an old man slid down the bank on his right and faced him, arms held high—a pair of spiked weapons in one hand and a tall staff in the other.

Rook brought his bow to bear. *Oh, great. A wizard.*

"I mean you no harm," Alhena pleaded. "I was travelling with others when we were caught in that awful storm. I got separated." He shivered. "I lost my horse and most of my provisions."

It had been many years since Rook had actually had contact with real people. The old man appeared harmless enough but relying on appearances was a sure way to end up dead. He had encountered many crafty magic users in his time.

"Who are the people you travel with? Where are they now? How come they aren't looking for you?"

Alhena shrugged. "I do not rightly know."

Rook frowned at the evasive answer and the strange way the man spoke every word. If not for his bizarre eyes, Rook might have lowered his guard—they seemed like they had rolled up into his head. He kept an eye on the man's hands. If they started to make strange movements, he wouldn't hesitate to bury an arrow into the old man's chest.

"A representative of the Chamber travelling to the Innerworld and you don't know with whom you travel? I find that hard to believe."

"And who might you be, my archer friend?"

"You haven't answered my question yet?"

"Aye, but I have given you my name. Surely, I deserve to know with whom I speak."

Rook studied the man's staff, looking for a sign that it was anything but a stick. "Fair enough. I am Rook Bowman..." He stopped.

Soul Forge

The old man's mouth dropped open. He staggered backward, his foot finding nothing but air.

Rook scrambled forward to catch the old man before he tumbled into the ravine.

Soul Forge

Sacred Sword Voil

Avarick paced his horse a few yards behind Silurian and Bregens, not caring to join in any conversation, not that there was any to be had.

They rode beneath a clear evening sky, their mounts slopping through wet grassland. They had searched all afternoon for Alhena but were unable to find any trace of him. It had taken a long time to get to the base of the rockslide. They had dug through the debris with little success. The broken tree lay half buried beneath chunks of stone bigger than the three of them could ever hope to move.

Silurian rode with his head hung low. He had lost his only friend in the world. A friend he hadn't deserved—a friendship he hadn't earned. The kindly old man had stuck by him even after Silurian had threatened to kill him. He had mocked him, laughed at him, yelled at him, and Alhena barely said anything to the contrary. Alhena had truly been a once in a lifetime find and Silurian had led him to his death.

Every so often he caught himself looking over his shoulder, hoping to see a grey bearded wizard following them. Each time he was greeted by Avarick's uninviting scowl.

The evening stretched on until it proved too dangerous to keep riding. Avarick suggested they stop for the night. Silurian agreed.

Tethering his mount to a small maple, Silurian rummaged through his saddlebags and withdrew a bottle of wine he had taken from his room in Gritian. He worried the cork free with the tip of Soulbiter and sat against the far side of the maple.

Draining the bottle, he fell, exhausted, onto his left shoulder, fast asleep.

Soul Forge

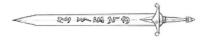

By mid-morning, the sun burned brightly in a clear sky. Silurian sat upon his mount atop a high ridge. Far below, the sun sparkled upon the glassy surface of the Calder as it turned sharply westward, making its way toward Redfire Path.

With a final glance over his shoulder, more to espy the imminent pursuit than to catch sight of Alhena anymore, Silurian heeled his horse eastward.

The Gritian Hills grudgingly gave way to the Mid Savannah; a brown grassed, barren landscape that supported few trees and even less water—the land of the legendary Shrine of Saint Carmichael.

Silurian was apprehensive about what he might find when he reached the shrine. After the tale Alhena had spun about Quarrnaine's ill-fated quest, he was skeptical he would find anything at all.

The following day, with the sun losing its grip on the land, Silurian altered their course, due south. Bregens glanced at Avarick who merely shrugged.

The land they travelled through seemed to wither the farther east they went. Soon, telltale signs of the firestorm that had ravaged the region four years ago became apparent. The larger trees dotting the landscape were little more than charred skeletons. They were getting close.

Shadows lengthened into twilight as a dark mound rose up in the distance through a haze of ground fog. Silurian knew at once they had reached their destination. The unnatural rock formation was comprised of large, broken sections of stone wall. Walls that had once supported the granite roof of the Shrine of Saint Carmichael.

Trotting his horse closer, Silurian studied the remnants of the large statue that had once stood over the shrine's entrance. The monument and doorway were blasted beyond recognition. A pair of large granite boots straddled the remains of a small flight of stairs that led into the shrine. All around, blackened clumps of broken trees stood ghastly vigil about the ruined chapel. The surreal sight sent shivers up his spine. Zephyr's queen had died here.

A cool breeze stirred the grasses around the shattered walls, swirling the ethereal mist that clung to the rubble within. It was as if those who had died here wanted to make their presence known.

Silurian tethered his horse to the remains of a charred tree trunk near the entrance and reverently approached the ruins. He had been here twice before. Once, as a squire on patrol with Prince Malcolm, they had stumbled upon it during one of the region's notorious snowstorms and taken refuge within its hallowed walls. The second time was with the Group of Five, just days before the ill-fated Battle of Lugubrius.

There had been a powerful presence within the chapel all those years ago, but Silurian couldn't sense it anymore.

"Hey Queen Killer, over here," Avarick Thwart's petulant voice cut through his reverie. The Enervator had picked his way over the rubble on the opposite end of the devastated building. He was several paces inside the back wall and bent over, pulling up weeds. "I think I've found it!" The man's enthusiasm made him sound twenty-five years younger.

Silurian walked around the shrine's perimeter, carefully making his way through the vegetation growing rampant amongst the ruins. Stopping beside the Chamber's whip, he followed Avarick's outstretched arms.

The Enervator pulled with all his might on what appeared to be the pommel of a great sword. Sweat formed on his reddening brow, but try as he might, he couldn't wiggle the sword free. He stood and stretched his lower back, examining the marble slab lying upon the stubborn blade. "It won't budge. The stone's crushing it. It'll be worthless."

"Let me try."

Avarick shot him an incredulous look. "I just told you, I can't budge it. It's stuck." With a sigh, he stepped aside.

Silurian moved into the gap between the thick growth and the edge of what appeared to be a broken statue. Grimy and weathered as it was, there was no mistaking the rusty pommel of his infamous sword.

Soul Forge

He reached down, only able to properly grab it with his right hand, but as his fingers wrapped around the cracked leather encasing the hilt, he smiled. This was *his* sword.

Avarick sized up a large, charred limb, buried in the long grass, wondering if they could generate enough leverage with it to move the slab.

He spun around at the sound of metal scraping on stone as the mystical blade slid effortlessly from its marble sheath and rang joyously in the evening air. He gaped at the sight of the Queen-Killer hoisting the venerable weapon high above his head in triumph.

He shook his head. If the sword possessed any of its ancient enchantment, Silurian was going to be hard to deal with when the time came for him to mete out his justice.

Bregens, tending the horses at the far end of the ruins, stopped what he was doing and followed Avarick's gaze.

The legendary Sacred Sword Voil glinted brilliantly in the last vestiges of daylight. Elaborate scrollwork surrounded ten magnificently crafted runes etched along its length; five on each side.

Soul Forge

Flight

Alhena couldn't believe his good fortune. Zephyr had lamented the disappearance of their last two heroes for over two decades, and here he sat, recently separated from one, only to find the other.

Beside him, hidden within a shallow depression upon a ledge, Rook Bowman slept. They had spoken at great length before Rook had given in to his need for rest.

Alhena's bruised and battered body kept him awake. He wasn't sure if he had broken a rib or two on his left side. When the lightning struck the edge of the embankment and spilled him and his horse over the edge, everything had happened in quick succession. He vaguely remembered a sizzling light that split a tree beside where he had been riding. The rapid events of the fall itself were a blur. He had been trapped in his stirrups and his horse had fallen on its side as they slid amongst the grinding debris. The next thing he knew, his horse had somehow sprung free of the slide just before they hit the ground below and had bolted away, taking him with it. It wasn't until a short while later when his horse stumbled and dropped to its knees that he became aware of the fatal wound it had incurred in the fall—a thick sliver of the blasted tree had driven itself deep into the animal's chest.

He winced at the recollection and mulled over what Rook had said about his own harrowing flight from the chaos unleashed on the Innerworld. Perhaps even more concerning was the news about the roving band of Kraidic warriors. If the Kraidic empire had joined with Helleden Misenthorpe, as Rook suggested, Zephyr's fate was already sealed.

A cold feeling of despair washed over him. High Warlord Clavius Archimedes had taken the Gritian militia in search of Silurian. They would be deep in the Mid Savannah by now. Gritian was unprotected.

Soul Forge

Alhena woke Rook before sunrise. "Sire Bowman. We need to be free of here. We must warn the Chamber."

Rook rubbed the sleep from his eyes. He didn't disagree. He had thought the same thing. "Aye, you're right, though we'll be hard pressed to get ahead of them."

After a hurried breakfast, they descended into the ravine and made their way over the next two ridgelines as stealthily as possible, hoping to confirm the warband's direction of travel, before setting off ahead of them.

Creeping to the top of a hillock overlooking the breaking camp, Alhena gaped. He pulled back from the rim and tugged on Rook's tunic for him to follow.

"Not good. Not good at all."

"No, it's not. Those guys are huge. That's why I use a bow," Rook mumbled, backing down the hill a little before he stood. "Come on. If we're lucky we can pass them before they start moving."

They had only taken a few steps at the bottom of the ravine when an arrow zipped by their heads. The missile disappeared into a thick layer of brush beside them.

Rook pushed Alhena behind the nearest tree. He grasped the trunk and poked his head out. A Kraidic archer looked right at him, aiming. Rook ducked back as bark exploded into splinters where his head had just been, the arrow ricocheting harmlessly into the foliage beyond.

The archer hollered to his unseen brethren.

It wouldn't be long before the hill teemed with Kraidic warriors.

Rook gave Alhena a worried glance. The old man stared wide-eyed back at him. They had but a few moments before all was lost. With the archer pinning them down, they were stuck. They couldn't risk running into the open, but neither could they remain where they were.

Rook took a couple of steadying breaths. He reached behind his shoulder and withdrew three arrows. Selecting the one he thought would fly truest, he notched it, and was about to peer around the tree when Alhena jumped into the open and then back again. The sound of an arrow's flight crackled through the undergrowth below them.

Rook smiled and nodded. The archer would have to reload.

He stepped calmly out from behind the tree, hopeful there was only one archer. He drew his bow string taught, sighted the warrior atop the hill, allowed for gravity and the sporadic breeze, and let fly.

The arrow took the Kraidic archer below his collarbone, burying itself deep. The man's strung arrow flew harmlessly into the air.

Rook lowered his bow and grabbed the two arrows on the ground. "Run!"

He started past the tree, intending on running south toward Gritian, but before he took a dozen steps he stopped short.

Alhena almost ran over him.

Two large men scrambled down the embankment ahead of them, shouting in their native tongue.

Rook grabbed Alhena's robes and tugged him back. In the short time it took them to pass the tree they had hidden behind, several Kraidic warriors had crested the top of the hill.

Rook and Alhena scrambled away, running so fast they barely kept from tripping over the thick undergrowth.

The ravine ascended toward a spot less than a half a league away, where the opposite embankments converged. Nearing the apex, they were disheartened to hear an angry voice shout after them from the opposite hilltop. Taking his eyes off the ground in front of him, Rook stumbled over a rock.

The large man kept pace. As they reached the crest of the slope, the warrior angled in on them, whooping and hollering.

Rook and Alhena veered left, across the path of the men chasing them along the western embankment, still a score of paces behind.

Rook cursed at how fast these men ran. He was equally amazed at how Alhena, easily twenty years his senior, ran faster, especially in those robes.

They slowly outpaced the pursuit but weren't able to shake it.

They fled slightly northward, but steadily west. Cresting a prominent escarpment, the broad expanse of the Calder River appeared far below, glistening in the morning sun and disappearing into the southern hills.

Soul Forge

Rook contemplated running southward along the river bank, maybe losing the pursuit in the bush, but he had no idea how many Kraidic warriors gave chase. He didn't care to be pinned against the river if the Kraidic warriors had spread out.

Scrambling down a steep embankment, they reached the river's edge and stopped long enough to replenish their water. They had barely dipped the waterskins in the river when the first of their pursuers slid down the side of the forested hill.

Rook kept his skin filling as he tried to ascertain where the Kraidics were coming at them from. A movement to the south decided their course. Taking a steadying breath, he corked his waterskin and led Alhena north.

Well into the insufferable heat of the afternoon, the Calder River veered west. Every so often an arrow splashed into the river nearby as one of the warriors caught sight of them and started whooping. The sound jarred Rook's senses.

In the distance, a stone structure rose above the river—an impressive monolith connecting Redfire Path from north to south.

They were forced to skirt a marshy area along the eastern bank before they could head toward the bridge directly.

Alpheus' Arch was by far the most ornate bridge in all of Zephyr. Towering corner stones of rearing horses flailed over the water. Instead of low walls along the sides of the flat stone bridge deck, over a hundred, child-sized gargoyles, depicting anything from naked people, to angry dogs, to axe wielding dwarves, lined its edges. At the bridge's midpoint, two identical, godlike figures stood facing each other with arms folded, as if passing judgment over anyone who dared pass between them.

Rook and Alhena stopped at the footing of the northeastern cornerstone to refill their waterskins, relishing the brief respite from the sun that the bridge's mass provided. Stepping quickly up to the bridge deck, they spared no time admiring the stone masons' craft.

Passing between the central deities, Alhena stopped and pointed toward the south bank.

Three Kraidic warriors marched toward them from over a rise in the road south of the bridge.

Soul Forge

Alhena and Rook spun about but the first of many warriors had already made their way around the wetland and were climbing the embankment below the cornerstone.

Rook thought briefly about jumping into the Calder to let the current carry them away, but aside from the real possibility of drowning in the swift moving water, they would risk becoming easy prey for the Kraidic archers.

Grabbing Alhena by the wrist, he ran south, across the remainder of Alpheus' Arch, the distance between themselves and the fast-approaching warriors on Redfire Path, rapidly diminishing.

The Kraidic warriors approaching from the south were neither archers, nor fleet of foot, but they were still almost upon them as Rook and Alhena left the bridge deck.

Only one direction remained open to them now. West, across the Gritian Hills toward the Midland Grasslands. In the distance, the lofty heights of The Muse rose stark against the sky, their peaks highlighted in the afternoon sun.

Rook led them toward a hill southwest of their position. If they reached the Midland Grasslands above the Torpid Marsh, they might yet lose their pursuers. He almost laughed out loud. If they led the Kraidic band *into* the Torpid Marsh, that might help finish them off. The only problem with that idea was that they, too, would be susceptible to the creatures that lurked there. He'd rather turn and face the Kraidic warband.

The sound of heavy boots thudding across Alpheus' Arch caused Rook to pick up his pace. Looking back, Alhena remained right behind him, the man's white beard flowing over his shoulder while his black cloak and voluminous robes fluttered in his wake.

Rook relished a chance to send a few arrows at the dogged pursuit but didn't think it wise to waste his meagre arrow supply on chance shots.

It wasn't until darkness had enveloped the land that the rolling hills gave way to lush grasslands skirting the southeastern foothills of the Muse. Rook's hope of using the tall grass as cover was dashed when he realized that their trail was clearly marked by the trodden foliage they left behind.

Soul Forge

Their pace had dropped to a fast walk, and then a bleary stumble through the night. Every so often an errant arrow prompted them to move faster.

They had risked stopping to rest during the wee hours of the morning, but at the first sound of pursuit, they were off again, driven toward the foothills. When daylight pushed aside the night, an oppressive heat washed over the land.

They tried deviating southward, but the Kraidic warband had fanned out across the grassy plain and forced them deeper into the tough terrain abutting the base of the Muse. As the morning wore on, it became evident they were being herded toward the base of a cliff.

Soul Forge

Hammer Fall

Silurian mounted up first the next morning. His black stallion stomped about, not the least bit impressed by their proximity to the mystical chapel—it had been a long night for the animals. Something about the desecrated shrine spooked them, but when sunlight broke across the Mid Savannah, nothing untoward had happened. It promised to be another sweltering day.

The Sacred Sword Voil now in hand, Silurian turned his mind to Madrigail Bay, knowing full well Avarick Thwart wasn't happy that he'd actually retrieved his sword.

With sweat dripping off them and glistening on the horse's flanks, they rode west, hopeful to reach Redfire Path by midday tomorrow. As sluggish as their pace was, their passage still kicked up a trail of dust.

By high sun the next day they came across a tributary feeding the Calder. Redfire wasn't far off. The horses didn't have to be urged into its gently flowing waters.

Avarick broke his usual silence, eyeing the hilt of the Sacred Sword Voil peeking over Silurian's shoulder. "What did you do with your other sword."

"I replaced this one with it."

Avarick frowned. "You left it at the shrine?"

"Ya, I put it in the stone sheath I pulled this one out of." Silurian offered the Enervator a smirk. "Should provide some interesting conversation if anyone else goes searching for this one, don't you think?"

Avarick laughed, despite his apparent dislike of Silurian.

Bregens dismounted with a splash in the middle of the stream, nearly losing his footing. He caught his balance and went to grab the horse's reins but stopped short.

Soul Forge

Silurian caught himself smiling at Bregens' antics until he saw the boy's face turn ashen. He swiveled in his saddle. "Shit. Mount up!"

Avarick jockeyed his horse to face the near bank, and grinned.

A wide swath of dust approached them, merging with a smaller one from the south and another from the north.

Silurian waited for Bregens to mount before urging his horse across the wide stream. Bregens followed, but Avarick spun his mount around and galloped toward the rapidly advancing dust cloud.

Halting on the river's far side, Silurian shook his head as the Enervator disappeared behind his own cloud of dust. The pace the high warlord must have driven his men was incredible.

Avarick, almost unrecognizable in the distance, made an abrupt turn, and charged back toward the stream ahead of the main group.

Bregens slowed beside Silurian, his eyes wild.

Silurian sighed. He didn't have time for this. "Let's move." He kicked hard, not waiting for Bregens to respond.

"Sir Silurian, wait. Those aren't the warlord's men." Bregens called out in a high-pitched voice.

Silurian reined in his horse and turned to face the river. Bregens still sat upon his horse in the centre of the stream as Avarick's black stallion charged up to the far bank.

Before he hit the water, Avarick spun around, brandishing his serrated, black sword at a dozen strangely armoured horsemen who thundered up and circled him.

A long chain struck out from the end of a scorpion flail, ensnaring Avarick's sword arm above the wrist. The man on the other end pulled the Enervator to the ground.

Silurian steadied his shying horse. "That's not good." He heeled his horse into action and plunged across the stream.

Bregens didn't follow.

Two riders rode in from the north, while two more approached from the south, veering into the stream to engage Bregens.

Silurian ignored them, his focus on the man holding Avarick's sword arm fast at the end of a long chain. He directed his horse out of the river and was on Avarick's attacker in moments—the Sacred Sword Voil in hand. It felt oddly comforting to wield his old sword again.

The man holding the chain turned at the sound of his approach.

Soul Forge

Avarick took advantage of the distraction—gripping the chain with his free hand and yanking for all he was worth.

The marauder fought to stay in his saddle.

Silurian never slowed. His sword arced through the air, lopping off the hand holding the flail.

Avarick stumbled backward as the chain went slack.

The injured man attempted to throw himself from his horse but Silurian's sword took his head from his shoulders.

Silurian attacked so fast, the other horsemen didn't have time to react. Old fighting instincts, practiced over and over again as a young man, came back to him in a rush. His control over his mount was masterful. He dodged around the fallen man's horse and engaged the next marauder in line.

The man turned in time to see the bloodied tip of Silurian's sword dive for the gap between his plate armoured shoulders and metal helm. As he fell from his saddle, trying to stem the blood spurting from a fatal wound, his left leg entangled itself in its stirrup. His frightened horse bolted upstream, dragging him away.

Before Avarick had a chance to exchange blows with those nearest him, Silurian manoeuvred his horse between them. He couldn't fight everybody on horseback at once, and Avarick certainly didn't stand a chance fighting them from the ground, so Silurian quickly evened the odds. Instead of engaging the horsemen moving in on the Enervator, Silurian hamstrung and stabbed the three horses closest to Avarick. The injured animals reared up, or fell to their knees, rendering their riders helpless as they fell hard to the ground.

It pained Silurian to resort to such tactics but he only knew one way to fight, and that was to win.

Avarick wasted no time taking advantage of the brief reprieve. Before the three unhorsed men had time to recover, his jagged black sword had dispatched them.

The remaining seven marauders surrounded Silurian, jockeying for a turn to take a swing at him.

Silurian parried their advances like a madman, deflecting three separate weapons in quick succession.

Soul Forge

Seeing Silurian's fighting skills first hand, Avarick gained a grudging level of respect for the Queen Killer.

A marauder on a horse behind Silurian cocked a quarrel into a heavy crossbow balanced in his lap. He clicked the shaft home and levelled the cumbersome weapon at Silurian's back.

Avarick's hand suddenly held a throwing knife, procured from the folds of his sleeves. Faster than a cobra strike, the knife flew true to its mark, imbedding itself into the horse's flank—the razor-sharp blade cutting deep.

The horse reared, and the bolt fired harmlessly away. The man flew from his saddle, hit the ground, and lost his breath. Before he took another, a second throwing knife embedded itself in his throat.

Avarick covered the distance separating them to ensure the man was dead. He spun in time to parry a spike-studded mace swinging at his head. He followed the block with a dagger stab to the passing horse's haunch.

The horse whinnied in pain and charged blindly into another mounted man who had locked swords with Silurian. Both horses collapsed to their knees and fell onto their shoulders.

The original rider jumped free of his mount but was immediately stamped to death beneath the startled horse next to him. The second rider remained trapped beneath his collapsing mount, fighting to free himself from the floundering animal's crushing weight. His eyes grew wide as Avarick's black blade plunged in for the kill.

The next man in Silurian's path made the mistake of watching Avarick dispatch the trapped man. He looked up to see the heel of Silurian's leather boot kick him in the ribs. He fell screaming to the fate awaiting him on the ground.

The two remaining marauders broke off their attack and spurred their horses out of Silurian's reach. They broke into a hard gallop and headed back the way they had come—a cloud of dust in their wake.

Silurian gave chase, but Avarick stopped him. "The boy!"

Soul Forge

In the middle of the stream, two riders circled Bregens. The rider behind Bregens swung a warhammer at his head, knocking him from his saddle.

Before Silurian could respond, Bregens lay face down in the slow current, his limp body scudding along the gravel stream bed, following two other lifeless bodies that the farm boy had done battle with.

The two marauders responsible took one look at the carnage on the riverbank, met Silurian's deadly glare as he charged his horse toward the riverbank, and spun their mounts around. They tore off upstream through the shallow water, before cutting a trail eastward, following the receding cloud of their now distant companions.

Silurian jumped from his saddle at the water's edge and stumbled to his knees. Dropping the Sacred Sword Voil on the bank, he plunged into the river. He grabbed Bregens' shoulder armour and pulled the boy's bloody face from the water.

Avarick bent to gather Silurian's discarded blade—the revered talisman, soiled, nicked and bloodied. He held it absently in his left hand, his own sword hanging forgotten in his right. Now was his chance to take the Queen Killer into custody and drag the wretch back to Gritian. For some reason he hesitated.

If he didn't know better, he might have been able to convince himself that he watched the two in the river with empathy.

Soul Forge

Leap of Faith

Kraidic warriors were everywhere. Though Rook couldn't see them from their vantage point on the rocky plateau, high above the grassland, he tracked their progress through the tall grasses by following the multiple lines of trampled foliage converging upon their position.

Behind Rook and Alhena, a spur of the Muse shot straight up, the peak of its accompanying mountain lost behind a dark cliff. Overhead, massive white clouds dominated the sky, creating great shadow ships that undulated across the grassland.

Alhena slumped to the ground and tried to squeeze a few drops of water from his empty waterskin. Rummaging through his tattered sack, he retrieved his knucklettes. "I guess this spot is as good as any to make a stand."

Rook knelt at the edge of the steep embankment, clutching his loosely loaded bow. Several arrows were set into the ground around him.

He scanned the cliff face over his shoulder, his eyes coming to rest on a high ledge. He gauged the sheerness of the climb and made up his mind. He pulled his array of arrows from the ground and put them back in his quiver. "No, my friend, we're not done yet."

Alhena stopped adjusting the first set of knucklettes and followed Rook's gaze to the heights. His opaque eyes darted from ledge to crevice to shale rockslide. "You are crazy, you know that?"

Soul Forge

If Rook thought the first half-hour of climbing was next to impossible, he was ill prepared for what awaited them. Clinging desperately to the crumbling shale cliff face, he looked past his feet, far below, to a group of Kraidic warriors launching arrows at them from the plateau.

The volleys fell short, but one of the arrows embedded itself into the thigh of a Kraidic warrior who climbed after them. The man cried out, clutching the protruding shaft, and tumbled down the steep incline. On his way down, he took out a man ascending below.

Creeping his way higher, Rook wondered for the countless time how the Kraidic warriors, large as they were, and with all the equipment they carried, kept up the pace they did. They were relentless. The only thing preventing them from overtaking himself and Alhena on the crumbling rock face was the cascade of debris their passing precipitated.

Sweat rolled off Alhena's nose in a stream. His wispy hair disheveled, his fingers dirty and bleeding, he never once complained. He just kept on doing whatever needed to be done. Every time Rook contemplated giving up, he drew strength from Alhena's silent fortitude.

A pointed ledge on their left, about thirty feet above, gave Rook hope. He pointed it out, but Alhena, too exhausted to reply, just nodded and searched for a way to clamber over to it. How he kept that walking stick in his hand while he climbed, Rook had no idea.

The Kraidic chieftain watched one of his crossbowmen climb within range of their elusive quarry, but before he got a shot off, the two men disappeared over a pointed ledge.

The chieftain made the daunting climb, following the rest of his patrol over the ledge. He had expected to be met with resistance but the two men were nowhere to be seen.

He grunted his disdain and surveyed the rugged mountainside. They stood at the foot of a gap between two high peaks. There was no way up the side of either cliff. The only way forward was through the gap—the trail rising steeply toward the upper reaches of the mountain.

Soul Forge

The chieftain urged his men forward. Passing over a crest between the opposing cliff faces, the trail sloped steeply downward into the deep shadows of a narrow crevice that curved left and out of sight. The warriors scrambled into the crevice, navigating the remnants of several rockslides, but stopped short as they rounded the last bend in the trail.

Sunlight burst into the fissure from its far end. Shrouded in angelic light at the end of the pass stood a white-haired man bearing a staff and his green clad companion with bow raised.

An arrow zipped by the chieftain's shoulder, claiming the man directly behind him. Before the Kraidic warriors were able to take evasive action, another man fell, clutching at an arrow protruding from his stomach.

The Kraidic patrol fell back to the curve in the pass to regroup. With shields held before them, bowstrings taut, crossbows cocked and javelins at the ready, the chieftain signaled their charge into the sunlight, but the wizard and the bowman were gone.

The Kraidic troop sprinted down the pass, fully expecting the path to veer left or right as there appeared to be nothing but a sheer drop straight ahead.

The warriors stopped a heartbeat away from the edge of a cliff—the trail terminated at the brink of a colossal drop. Far below, the turquoise waters of a great lake greeted them, its perimeter lined by the distant peaks of the northern Muse.

The Kraidic band searched all about, expecting arrows to rain down on them, but all they saw were the sheer cliffs on either side of the trail. Short of growing wings, there was no way anyone could have left this end of the trail.

Frustrated, the chieftain grabbed a crossbowman and flung him over the edge. "Find them!"

The flailing man's scream marked his inevitable demise. He plunged head over heels out of sight beneath the curve of the cliff, his death cry punctuated by the impact of his heavily armoured body as it struck the blue waters far below.

Soul Forge

Death of a Friend

Deep within the Chamber of the Wise catacombs, Bregens lay beneath a heavy woollen blanket, close to death—the right side of his head, crushed.

A sputtering candle on the edge of a stained, bedside table, cast the room in flickering light. The table was the only furniture in the gloomy room other than the bed. Incense burned within a tarnished thurible set beside the stubby candle, its white vapour thick in the stale air, smelling faintly of sandalwood.

Vice Chambermaster Solomon Io, himself a bishop, knelt upon the cold stone floor, his elbows propped on the edge of the straw mattress. A shiny gold chain wrapped tightly about his gnarled fingers gave him something to fiddle with as he offered the dying man absolution.

Standing in a shadowed corner, Silurian observed the ritual, barely visible in the flickering light. If Bregens hadn't fended off the four horsemen in the stream, he and Avarick might not have fared so well. The boy, the farmer, the green hand newly enlisted with the Gritian militia, had slain two experienced thugs, and detained the other two long enough to allow he and Avarick to deal with the rest.

Silurian leaned against the stone wall, his face cupped in his hands. Traces of dried tears streaked his grimy face. He wasn't prone to crying. He'd seen many gruesome things in his time. Lost many a good friend, but for some reason, Bregens' injuries affected him more than he wished to admit.

Back at the stream, Avarick had taken one look at the stricken boy and said it didn't matter if a healer were right there with them, but Silurian wouldn't hear of leaving the boy to die in the wilderness. He had plucked Bregens from the stream and tied him upon the boy's horse.

139

Soul Forge

Avarick had located his own horse not far away, and together they galloped back to Gritian in search of a healer.

They had ridden into town near sunrise the following morning. Upon Silurian's insistence, Avarick dispatched a rider to alert the Farriers. Another had been sent north to inform the high warlord of Silurian's return. As of yet, neither had returned.

It was now past suppertime and Silurian wore the same clothes he had on when they had trotted into town. He had practically fallen from his horse when a stable boy took the reins from him. Others rushed to offer him aid before realizing who they were dealing with.

He had shrugged off their scorn and staggered after the litter bearing the Farrier boy. A few of the braver men conspired to take Silurian into custody, but the Enervator intervened and sent them away.

The candlelight in the dim chamber flickered more than usual. Silurian looked up.

The head healer had entered the room. Shooing the bishop aside, he examined the motionless body. It wasn't long before he rose and shook his head.

"He's beyond my ken. It won't be long," the healer whispered, brushing past Solomon into the hall.

Solomon glanced at Silurian and swallowed. With a sigh, he knelt at the bedside to finish administering the boy's last rites.

Silurian listened absently to the bishop's ministrations. When the final words were spoken, Silurian stepped from the shadows and squeezed into the tight space beside the bed, taking Bregens' hand in his own.

He grimaced at the bruised face, squished beneath a heavy swath of blood-soaked bandages. The young man who had faithfully followed him to his death was unrecognizable. This wouldn't have happened if he hadn't gone against the council's wishes.

He dropped to one knee upon the cold, stone floor, banging his baldric against the wall. He couldn't get the images of Bregens' parents from his mind. Proud Janus and sweet Asa. They were going to be crushed. He tightened his grip on Bregens' lifeless hand. As cold as his hands were, Bregens' were colder. He closed his eyes and wept.

He had no idea how long he knelt that way, but he became aware of the absolute silence that had settled over the chamber. He opened his eyes to see Solomon shrouded in the last vestiges of sputtering candlelight, the bishop's eyes closed. Silurian nearly leapt from his skin when he glanced at Bregens.

The boy's eyes were open. One more so than the other. Beneath all those wrappings, despite the excruciating pain, Bregens tried to smile.

Silurian smiled back, choking out a laugh. Tears rolled unabashedly off his face.

"We beat them, Sire?"

Bregens' pathetic voice made Silurian's throat constrict. He could barely draw a breath. He nodded as his vision blurred. He grabbed the stained sheet to wipe his eyes and clasped the boy's hand to his chest.

"I knew we would, Sire. You are Sir Silurian, king's champion, and Zephyr's saviour."

Silurian fought the urge to cry even harder. "We couldn't have done it without you. Avarick and I owe you our lives." He raised his voice, "Now stop calling me Sir!"

The bishop jerked backward, stunned by his sudden loud voice.

A tear welled in Bregens' good eye and rolled down his cheek. Delirious, he rambled, his voice sounding far off, "Alhena was right. He said to me, 'you will know when he accepts you. When that day comes, he will angrily warn you to stop calling him Sir. Only then will he consider you a friend.'"

Silurian bit his lips and nodded, unsuccessfully trying to smile.

Another tear followed Bregens' first. "Aww…" He coughed. His body convulsed. Brutal pain twisted his face. When the coughing fit passed, another agonizing pain took hold of him. His grip on Silurian's hand was incredible.

The spasm passed.

Bregens turned his head to look Silurian squarely in the eye. "Bregens is Silurian's friend?"

Silurian nodded again, his throat too tight to speak—his vision blinded by tears.

Bregens' hand clenched Silurian's once more before he released his death grip. His eyes became vacant and his shallow chest rises came no more.

Soul Forge

The Edge of the World

Waterfalls! The sound of thousands of gallons of water plunging over a precipice reached Alhena's ears as he and Rook clung to the side of a mountain, submerged up to their necks in water. A gentle current propelled them westward.

They had been in the water for hours. Ever since their leap of faith from the terminus of the gorge trail they had fled down. Their capacity to think straight or move effectively was slowly diminishing in the surprisingly warm waters of Madrigail Lake. Neither man had been able to stop their teeth from chattering since the direct sunlight had disappeared behind the western mountain peak.

They pulled their way around the edge of the lake by using natural handholds along the otherwise unclimbable rock face that shot up from the depths of the bottomless water body.

Alhena had been upon Lake Madrigail twice before. In a boat. If he had his bearings right, they were near the end of the lake where the majestic Splendoor Falls spilled the lake's contents thousands of feet to the mainland below.

He recalled a small platform, hewn out of solid rock, on one side of the monstrous falls. He hoped it was this side.

Rook glanced at him, his hair dripping—every so often the roll of the surface water slapped against the cliff wall, splashing them in the face.

Alhena forced a grim smile. "It is the pull of Splendoor Falls we feel." Alhena picked up his pace, forcing Rook to pull himself along faster to remain ahead.

Rook's voice trembled through chattering teeth. "The pull of Splendoor Falls? You mean…"

142

Soul Forge

"Aye, we are close to the brink of the waterfall. If we are lucky, there will be a platform where we can pull ourselves free of the lake." Despite the cold seeping into his bones, Alhena's pace increased further. They had to get out of the water.

A gap in the unbroken ring of mountains materialized a few hundred feet ahead of them.

The current increased. It wasn't long before they were struggling to slow their progress along the slippery periphery of the lake, desperately trying to hang onto the rock face and not be pulled away.

Alhena's trepidation mounted. He couldn't see the platform he sought. He had a clearer view of the far side of the gap and couldn't see the platform there either, but that did little to alleviate his concern. If the water level had risen or dropped, the rock ledge he sought might be too high above, or submerged uselessly beneath, the water's surface.

"Uh, Alhena," Rook's voice reached him over the rising crescendo of rushing water. The worry in his eyes told Alhena that he had come to realize their dilemma as he slipped along the algae covered rock face, fighting his forward momentum.

Alhena, bobbing along behind, bumped into him, and he lost his purchase.

"This can't be good." Rook glanced back at him, fear evident in his eyes.

Less than a hundred feet separated them from a drop they couldn't survive. The incessant current pulled them along, their handholds slipping through bloodied fingers.

Puffs of white clouds appeared between the gap in the mountains, the land beyond appearing far away.

The water churned into a froth as it flowed toward the brink, funnelling around a protrusion of flat rock just before the drop.

"That's it!" Alhena cried out. "Grab the chains!"

"Chains? What chains?" Rook searched the rock face.

The din of cascading water rose to a deafening roar.

Alhena held his breath. Rook floundered ahead of him, his long hair whipping about as he searched for the chains.

There were two sets, rusted and thick, attached to large, metal eyelets driven into the rock face below the lip of a small ledge carved into the mountainside.

Soul Forge

Rook missed the first set. Scrabbling frantically to keep from being pulled away from the edge and around the outcropping of rock, he reached out for the second chain, brushed it with an outstretched hand, and missed. He floundered helplessly toward the outcropping.

Alhena let the current pull him past the first chain. He threw his staff over the lip of the platform, snatched the second chain and grabbed hold of the back of Rook's green suede tunic.

Panicking, Rook nearly pulled Alhena's one-handed grip free of the chain.

"Stop struggling! Grab my arm!"

Rook's eyes were wild.

Alhena hung on to him, dangling precariously from the chain, the struggle evident in his pained features.

Rook reached around and grasped Alhena's outstretched arm with both hands and allowed Alhena to pull him free of the stronger current.

The water's tug wasn't as severe snuggled up against the massive chain. Using the thick links as hand holds, Rook pulled himself onto the granite platform. Utterly exhausted, he rolled over and helped pull Alhena to safety.

They sat upon a slab of granite measuring no more than a few hundred square feet. Behind them, the mountain rose outward, its peak lost in the clouds. Beyond the current of the falls, Madrigail Lake rolled toward the distant mountains surrounding its perimeter.

Both men removed their sodden clothing in stages and rang them out, the lake breeze making them shiver profusely.

Fully dressed again, Rook crept on his hands and knees to the edge of the shelf rock abutting the falls. He had seen Splendoor Falls from a distance on several occasions, but he wasn't prepared for how great the drop actually was. And the view! Far below, lost for the most part behind a veil of mist, Splendoor Falls' catch basin frothed and churned, giving birth to the mighty Madrigail River, Zephyr's largest waterway. He followed the river's course, shimmering splendidly beneath the setting sun, cutting a northwestward swath through dense forestland. Its blue ribbon entered Lake Refrain, many leagues away, before continuing its journey toward the lofty heights of the Spine; the mountains dark and visible upon the western horizon.

"Quite a sight, isn't it?" Alhena shouted over the roar of the falls.

One of Rook's hands slipped over the brink. He caught himself by falling flat on his stomach. He crept backward and turned to sit up, his heart hammering in his chest. He hadn't heard Alhena come up to him.

"You scared the wits out of me. I almost jumped over the falls!"

"That would be the quickest way down!"

He gave Alhena a sour look and scooched away from the edge. Making his way to the middle of the platform, he sat with his back firmly placed against the cliff face and hugged his arms around himself in a vain effort to get warm.

Alhena stood on the edge of the shelf. Thousands upon thousands of gallons of water thundered past his feet. Leaning against the stone wall on his left, he gazed out across the land. The wind whistled through the mountain gap and whipped his wet hair and robes about.

Rook kept an eye on him, not happy at how close to the edge he stood. As if reading his thoughts, Alhena turned and walked close to where he sat. He followed Alhena's gaze to the several rusted eyelets anchored along the water's edge, obviously used to moor boats. Who in their right mind would risk bringing a boat this close to the falls? Yet, at the moment, a boat was the only means off this godforsaken platform.

Alhena stopped before an eyelet set apart from the rest, closer to the middle of the shelf. He studied the rusted iron ring and slowly scanned the rock between himself and Rook. His gaze met Rook's.

Rook forced a smile past his chattering teeth. "What are we going to do now?"

Alhena smiled. "We obviously cannot swim the lake, so…"

Hearing the crazy old man's next words, Rook almost fainted.

"We will descend the falls."

Soul Forge

Chamber of Chaos

Leaving Bregens' death bed in the capable hands of the good bishop, Silurian strode with purpose toward High Bishop Abraham Uzziah's personal chambers.

Avarick, who had kept watch on Silurian from outside of Bregens' chamber, followed closely on his heels, unsure, and more than a little concerned about what the troubled warrior had in mind. Avarick had long since shrugged out of his filthy riding cloak and now wore his usual tan suede tunic bearing the twisted golden knot of rope on his left shoulder. He stroked his well kempt, black goatee. After witnessing Silurian in action, he didn't relish crossing swords with him as much as he had wanted to when they first met.

They continued past the fork leading to the regular sleeping chambers and carried on beyond the eating halls. At the next crossroad, they turned left down a narrow corridor. The passage veered right several yards in and ended at a large, iron strapped, wooden door. Two burly pike men stood at attention, but they moved aside at the Enervator's approach.

Silurian pushed down on the brass door lever and entered the private passageway housing the Chamber council.

Twelve doors faced each other, matching the one they had come through, six on either side of the short tunnel. Sconces flickered between the doors, illuminating exquisite battle scenes and religious ceremonies, intricately carved into the granite walls. At the tunnel's end, another door, strapped with bronze and inlaid with silver and gilded metalwork, stood before them.

Avarick stepped in front of Silurian. Glancing a warning at the grim-faced man, he rapped loudly.

Soul Forge

Before Avarick's knuckles had struck three times, the large door swung noiselessly inward. Both men jumped. The forbidding countenance of the chambermaster glared back at them, mantled in his red robe of office. It was as if they had been expected.

Without waiting for an invitation, Silurian brushed by Abraham into the warmth of his lushly appointed chambers.

Abraham grimaced as Silurian trod across his priceless rug in dirty riding boots and plunked his filthy self onto the end of a plush, leather couch.

Avarick felt the high bishop's scowl follow him across the rug as he joined Silurian beside the couch. The door shut harder than usual.

He respectfully allowed the high bishop to take his seat in front of an ornate, ivory topped table across from Silurian, before he joined Silurian on the settee.

Abraham steepled his fingers, waiting, his face an unnatural shade of red.

Avarick glanced from one powerful man to the other. He could've cut the tension with his sword. Breaking the awkward silence, he said, "If I may?"

The chambermaster blinked. Averting his glare from Silurian, he nodded.

"I have returned Silurian Mintaka to your justice."

Silurian slowly turned to face him. "Returned me to justice? I came back to save Bregens."

Avarick ignored him. Instead, he related the retrieval of the Scared Sword Voil at the Forgotten Shrine. He failed to mention that he had been unable to remove the blade himself. He spoke of the subsequent battle at the river, which had precipitated their return to Gritian with the unrealistic hope of saving the farm boy. Not once during Avarick's tale did he belittle Bregens as a coward or a traitor.

The high bishop nodded, but it was obvious by his expression, or lack of one, that he already knew all of this.

Avarick paused to gather himself. He hadn't realized until now how much the young man's death had affected him. As the Enervator of Gritian, he wasn't accustomed to these feelings. Death didn't bother him. He dealt with it almost every day. More often than not, he was the instrument of it. But now, standing before the stone-faced

147

chambermaster, inexplicably, Bregens' demise cut him to the core of his being.

The most telling revelation struck him as he related to the chambermaster, the *high bishop* no less, about Bregens succumbing to his injuries. The prelate of Zephyr listened with what could only be perceived as feigned interest. In fact, if someone asked how the high bishop had taken the news, Avarick would have said their spiritual leader appeared bored.

As if Avarick hadn't spoken a word, the high bishop returned Silurian's icy gaze. "What of the blade? Is it still enchanted?"

Silurian glared at the callous man. Had he not heard? A young man had died. Needlessly. If the Chamber hadn't voted the way it had, he wouldn't have had to sneak away in the middle of the night. Bregens would still be alive, performing his duties upon the stable grounds. Not waiting to be interred beneath them.

Fighting an urge to vent on the heartless high bishop, Silurian shook his head ever so slightly, seething.

The chambermaster stared back at him for a few moments before gaining his feet. Without preamble, he declared, "I'm convening a private meeting of the Chamber."

Silurian stood up just as quickly. "Why? My mind is already made up. I only came back to save the boy. I'll be leaving for Madrigail Bay with or without the Chamber's sanction." Silurian glanced at Avarick, about to say something to him as well, but decided not to. Instead, he stormed from the chambermaster's living quarters, the door closing firmly behind him.

Avarick followed Silurian from the room—the door closed more respectfully in his wake.

In the passageway, Avarick called out, "Mintaka! Wait!"

Silurian's shoulders stiffened. If Avarick intended on stopping him, it would be his last action as Enervator of Gritian.

Avarick caught him at the corridor's far end, his weapons clinking and clanging loudly in the tunnel, still in their holders.

Soul Forge

Silurian spun about, almost taking Avarick's left eye out with a pointed finger. "Don't even think about it, Thwart. I'll not warn you again."

Avarick stepped back, arms out, palms up. "Easy, Queen Killer, I didn't come to stop you."

Avarick's unexpected words gave him pause.

"I came to join you."

The abruptness of the revelation stunned him. "Stay outta my way, *Enervator*. You're the last person I want help from. If you hadn't engaged those men in the first place…" He left the rest unsaid and turned to face the heavy door.

Grasping the brass lever, he pushed down. Nothing happened. He pulled up. Nothing happened. Grabbing the handle with both hands he pushed up and down on the handle, pushing and pulling on the door, his movements becoming more animated—the door was locked.

"Damn!" He pounded the oak with the side of his fist. "Guard! Open the door. Guard!"

"Only the chambermaster can unlock that door," Avarick muttered.

Abraham's door opened at the opposite end of the hallway.

Avarick and Silurian turned as one.

The red clad high bishop leaned against his doorjamb and raised his eyebrows.

Silurian stomped back down the corridor, Avarick hard on his heels.

"I shall assemble the Chamber at once," Abraham declared. "I cannot allow you to leave without a full understanding of your intentions."

That said he disappeared into his quarters and latched the door.

Silurian stopped. He stared helplessly at the Enervator.

Avarick shrugged.

Within half an hour, the chambermaster managed to convene a private session of the Chamber of the Wise. A contingent of armed men liberated Avarick and Silurian from the locked tunnel and escorted them to the Chamber.

Soul Forge

No one waited at the double doors of the vast meeting hall to announce their arrival. There would be no pomp and ceremony tonight.

Once inside the Chamber, the escorting guards stopped to close the large doors. Two remained in the outer tunnel while four more took up a position just inside.

Silurian strode down the marble aisle, through the symmetrical array of grey marble pillars. He had accepted that the meeting of the Chamber, a sham though it promised to be, was at this point unavoidable. The sooner they got it over with, the sooner he'd be on his way.

Avarick walked silently beside him.

Approaching the carved steps at the far end of the Chamber, it became apparent that the majority of the chambermen were absent as well. It struck Silurian as odd, but nothing about how the eclectic group of policy makers conducted their business fazed him anymore. Solomon had warned them.

Coupled with the angst he felt toward the council, he considered what role the Enervator had to play in this whole charade. Uncanny as usual, the Chamber whip gave him a smug grin and raised his eyebrows.

Silurian sighed and concentrated on ascending the stage.

Chambermaster Abraham Uzziah, Vice Chambermaster Solomon Io and Vice Chambermistress Arzachel Gruss were already seated. Three more grey bearded chambermen stood beside Gruss, but Silurian had never seen them before, other than briefly at the last council.

Avarick remained by his side as he stopped before Abraham.

The chambermaster was involved in a heated, yet hushed discussion with Vice Chambermaster Solomon Io. When he finally pulled himself away, he gave Silurian and Avarick a knowing smirk, not bothering to welcome them.

Silurian glared at the high bishop. "Let's get this over with."

"Very well," Abraham said, loud enough to include the few in attendance. "I have convened an emergency meeting of the Chamber—"

Silurian frowned. "Convened the Chamber? Only half the ruling body is here."

150

Soul Forge

Abraham ignored him. "—to discuss Sire Mintaka's intention of travelling to Madrigail Bay." He paused.

As if on cue, the three chambermen Silurian didn't recognize piped up. "Why, that is mere folly." "You should be heading north to Carillon." "The king needs every available sword. What good will you be out on the coast when Helleden comes at us from the north?"

Abraham entertained the dialogue for a short time before holding his hands up. "According to Silurian, Madrigail Bay is where he will be of greatest service to the king. On the far side of the realm. A talking crocodile has beseeched him to ignore the wisdom of your counsel and set off on a reckless journey at the whim of the Lord of the Frogs, no less. Silurian believes he must embark upon a hair-brained foray in search of a mystical realm straight out of a child's nightmare. The Under Realm, no less. He aims to immerse his sword in the waters of a magical stream, thus restoring the enchantment to that cold piece of steel strapped across his back."

Silurian's cheeks flamed hot. His armpits moistened and his breathing quickened. Listening to the high bishop tell it, he started to doubt the merits of his plan. It did seem like an irresponsible course of action if he thought about it.

The massive Chamber doors flew open, interrupting his self-recrimination. Abraham and the others jumped to their feet.

A ragged, middle-aged warrior scuffled up the aisle, his colours depicting him as one of Archimedes' men. His torn and stained attire attested that he had recently seen action.

Two of the guardsmen posted inside the Chamber doors flanked him as he struggled to make his way to the stage. With their assistance he mounted the steps and stumbled to a tenuous halt before the assembled group.

"My lords," he wheezed, coughing up bloody mucus. He wiped the spittle upon a filthy cuff. "Forgive me, my lords…" He coughed again. He would've fallen had the two guardsmen not held him by the elbows.

"Damn it man, spit it out!" Avarick shouted at the teetering militiaman.

Gulping a few deep breaths, he tried again, "Sires," he gasped, but did not cough. "The high warlord has been gravely injured."

151

Soul Forge

"What are you on about?" Abraham demanded.

The man didn't respond. His eyes rolled back in his head.

Avarick grabbed the front of his torn cloak and shook the frazzled man. "How?"

The militiaman wheezed, his head lolling to either side, "While searching for…" His head rolled in Silurian's direction. His eyes narrowed. "Him! Lord Archimedes took a quarrel in the back because of *him*."

Avarick released the man. The high warlord's duties would fall upon his shoulders, at least temporarily, should Archimedes succumb to his injuries.

If not for the guardsmen, the militiaman would've fallen to the floor. Without prompting, the man said, "We were attacked south of Alpheus' Arch by a roving band of Kraidic warriors."

"Kraidic warriors? That's impossible," Solomon declared.

The man gasped. "I was sent ahead to warn the Chamber of its imminent peril."

Everybody turned to the high bishop for direction. When Abraham didn't respond quickly enough, Solomon nodded toward Avarick, and the Enervator bolted from the Chamber. With the high warlord incapacitated, the defense of Gritian was now in Avarick's hands.

Vice Chambermistress Arzachel got up and strolled to the nearest guard supporting the militiaman. She whispered into his ear. The large man nodded. Leaving the responsibility of the wounded man to his companion, he turned crisply and marched from the stage. The Chamber doors remained open long enough for him to follow the departed Enervator.

Abraham glared at the floundering man, beseeching him to continue.

The militiaman spoke in short spurts, "We were besieged by an intense storm." He cast Silurian an angry stare. "It washed away all traces of him."

"We scouted east, toward the Forgotten Shrine. Nobody knew where to find it, so we headed back to Alpheus' Arch, hoping to catch this man on his way west." He coughed up phlegm. "At the Arch, we found traces of people passing south into the Muse."

The man fell silent, on the brink of unconsciousness. The guard shook him.

152

Soul Forge

The man's eyes opened, unable to focus on anyone in particular. "We were ambushed by a Kraidic warband. They must've realized Archimedes was our leader. He was the first to fall." He broke into a coughing fit. "The brutes came from everywhere at once. We took to fighting them, but there were too many. A few of us were sent ahead with the injured high warlord, while the rest were ordered to remain behind and slow the Kraidic advance."

He shut his eyes tight, fighting through his pain. When he opened them again, a profound fear replaced their earlier intensity.

"Scouts were sent out to ward our flanks. They never returned. We found the grisly remains of our forward scouts." He coughed and his eyes misted up. "Their heads and limbs torn from their bodies. They hadn't even drawn their weapons."

Everyone looked at each other, confused.

The militiaman steadied himself long enough to find Abraham's stare. "I don't think the Kraidics killed them, Your Eminence. Nor any man, for that matter…" He trailed off, wracked by pain. His eyes rolled back into his head and he slumped into the guard's arms, unconscious.

"Enough!" Silurian declared. Too much time had already been squandered. The militiaman's tale drove that sentiment home. If a Kraidic warband had ventured this deeply into Zephyr, unopposed, the kingdom was in worse shape than he thought. He stormed from the stage.

An irate voice chased him from the platform. It came again, shriller, but Silurian chose not to hear it. It thundered a third time and the Chamber opened to admit the two guards stationed outside, joining their two comrades already brandishing their weapons.

Silurian stopped in the middle of the cavern. Surely Abraham didn't mean to forcefully detain him. Strange things were indeed happening within the Chamber but Silurian didn't have time to figure out what.

Abraham pointed. "Seize him!"

The high bishop had gone mad. That was the only explanation for his bizarre behaviour.

Silurian shook his head and strode with purpose toward the Chamber exit. The huge men standing at the exit, bladed their stances, their heavily muscled bodies tense. They meant to fight him!

Soul Forge

Silurian raised his eyebrows. So be it.

Despite their toughness, the four battle-hardened Chamber guards flinched when Silurian reached over his shoulder and unsheathed the Sacred Sword Voil. The guards had never witnessed Silurian in a fight, but he could tell by the wary look in their eyes that they had heard tales of his exploits. He also knew, that as members of the Chamber's elite guard, they were sworn to uphold the chambermaster's orders.

Silurian stopped out of their reach and gestured for them to step aside. "Come on guys. Let me pass."

The men stood defiant.

He sighed. "Look, I don't want any trouble, but I will only say this once. I'm leaving here, and I'm leaving now."

The guards shuffled uneasily but didn't step aside.

Surely, they wouldn't cause him injury. Wasn't he their supposed saviour?

"You leave me no choice." Silurian raised his sword, unconsciously finding its balance. He narrowed his eyes and focused on what he needed to do. Emitting a low growl, he said, "This isn't personal."

Before the last word reached their ears, his sword had engaged the two men directly before him. The sound of metal blades coming together resonated throughout the Chamber. Faster than thought, Silurian forced the two men back against the door. The guards on either side rushed in to grab him, only to collide with each other as Silurian gracefully dropped low and backstepped, coming up behind them.

Before the large men recovered, Silurian smacked the flat edge of his sword off the back of the largest man's head.

The guard fell against his partner, who turned in time to see the butt end of Silurian's sword coming for his temple. He never saw anything else.

A commotion arose from the stage. The sound of heavy footfalls descending the steps and charging up the aisle echoed within the Chamber.

He needed to be away quickly lest they overwhelm him. The last thing he wanted to do was kill a Chamber guard, but if he didn't get moving fast, they would detain him, and that he couldn't allow.

154

Soul Forge

The two guards against the door did their best to delay him, allowing the remaining guard and the chambermen charging down the aisle, time to assist with his apprehension.

Silurian threw himself at the guards barring the door, his sword a blur. He unarmed the guard on his left, while parrying the other's sword as it swept at him. With deft footwork, he manoeuvred the armed guard away from the door. A feigned killing stroke forced the man to lose his balance and stumble backward into the guard arriving at the head of the chambermen.

Unlatching the right door with his left hand, Silurian threw his shoulder at it and the massive door swung outward.

Nimbly stepping through, he pushed the door closed and hurtled down the tunnel—the inevitable pursuit echoed in the passageway behind him.

Dashing by the chambermen's dining area, several chambermen were enjoying their dinner, apparently oblivious to the fact that a meeting had been convened.

Approaching the fork in the tunnel that led to Alhena's quarters, he contemplated ducking into the side tunnel to see if his friend had made it home, but that would leave him with no egress from the Chamber complex.

The guards giving chase rounded the bend by the dining hall and spotted him motionless in the intersection.

"Halt, Silurian Mintaka. By order of His Eminence." One of the guards ordered.

Jumping into a dead run, Silurian gained the outside exit quickly. As fast as he ran, the younger guards, even burdened by the weight of their chainmail, were able to run faster.

Passing through the wooden shack housing the exit door, he heard the approach of hoof beats from the direction of the stables.

The evening sunlight blinded him as he stepped onto Redfire Path. Squinting, he looked up to see a tall man sitting astride a black warhorse, blocking his passage.

The Enervator!

Soul Forge

Splendoor Catacombs

Daft. The only way to describe the old man was daft. Unless Rook had missed seeing a hidden ledge, or a stairway of some sort, or perhaps even, the gods forbid, a rope, there was no possible way to descend the falls. Not if one wanted to be alive when they reached the bottom. The old man had better be carrying a set of wings in that weathered bag of tricks of his or their descent would prove to be a quick one.

Rook crawled back to the lip of the shelf. On hands and knees, he leaned out farther than he was comfortable. He didn't see any way to even *begin* descending the falls.

He glanced over his shoulder, trying to spot Alhena. The vertigo instilled by such a simple action almost had him rolling over the brink. He pulled back quickly, dropping to his chest and hugging the shelf rock. There was no way in hell he was descending that. He would sit here and starve to death first.

He crept backward until he felt safe enough to turn around.

Alhena stood calmly in the centre of the rock shelf, ignoring him. What the heck was the old man up to?

Alhena bent at the knees and grasped a thick, rusted iron ring between his feet and yanked.

Nothing seemed to happen at first, but astonishingly to Rook, the platform rumbled beneath him.

A granite hatchway swung upward in Alhena's hands, its squeaky hinges swinging upon a counterweight hidden beneath the platform.

Rook approached the hole in wonder. An old wooden ladder, lashed together with frayed mariner rope, stretched several feet down to the floor of a tunnel.

Soul Forge

Alhena offered him an impish grin and descended the ladder. He retrieved a blackened torch from a rusted iron basket at the base of the ladder and struck a spark to it. The torch flared into a fist-sized flame, flickering wildly in the draft created by the open hatchway.

Rook shouldered his sack and swung his legs over the hole. When he stepped free of the bottom rung, Alhena pushed the torch into his hand and climbed the ladder. Grabbing a loop of rope attached to the hatch's underside, he shut out the daylight with an eerie scraping of rock upon rock.

Rook shivered. Even in the decent light of the calmly burning torch, it took a few moments for his eyes to adjust. Other than the ladder creaking beneath Alhena's weight as he descended to join him, and the torch's soft hiss, no other sound reached their ears—the silence deafening after being subjected to the howling roar of the falls.

Alhena grabbed three more unlit torches from a rusted iron basket sitting beside the ladder, leaving a couple for the next person who might come this way. He handed one to Rook and raised his eyebrows as he brushed past him into the darkness ahead. "Well, here goes nothing."

Rook called after him, "You've been this way before?"

Alhena stopped at the edge of the torch light and turned halfway around. "Aye, a couple of times."

"Then you know where you're going?"

Alhena gave him a half smile. "I would not say that, exactly."

"You wouldn't say that, *exactly*? Great."

"Those torches will not last forever." Alhena set off down the roughly hewn tunnel.

Rook swallowed and started after him. As he strode to catch up, he strained to hear Alhena's shaky voice muted by the closeness of the passage walls.

"We'll be lucky to find our way out of these catacombs as it is. I don't envy trying to do so in the dark."

Rook stopped short, not sure he was meant to hear that. He swallowed again and scampered after the wizened old man.

The tunnel swerved back and forth, always descending, seemingly winding underneath itself. It wasn't until after they had lit their third torch that a distant roar sounded ahead of them. A damp breeze buffeted their hair, and the rock surface became increasingly slippery underfoot. The noise sounded like the roar of the falls.

Neither man had spoken much since entering the catacombs, wrapped in their fear that escaping the labyrinth might prove to be a serious issue, but the thunderous noise of falling water and its accompanying wind boosted their spirits.

Rounding a sharp left bend, the roar of Splendoor Falls assaulted them in the tunnel's close confines. Natural light, muted by thousands of gallons of plummeting water, illuminated the tunnel from a gap in the right wall. The tunnel passed directly behind the falls.

Farther ahead, the tunnel snaked left again, out of sight—a faint glow emanating from beyond the bend.

They held onto each other as they made their way along the slimy passageway, keeping close to the back wall for fear of slipping through the gap.

The floor levelled beyond the hole in the wall and began a slight ascent. Ahead of them, daylight infused the tunnel's end. Passing beyond the break in the wall, their pace picked up.

At the tunnel's end, Rook reeled as vertigo threatened to topple him. They stood upon a ledge, a thousand feet above a lush green landscape that stretched off into the distance, terminating at the foothills of the iron-grey monoliths of the Spine. He dropped into a shaky crouch and steadied himself against the wall. He pulled back into the dimness and safety of the tunnel. Trying to catch his breath, he frowned at Alhena who lowered himself against the adjacent wall.

The old man appeared flummoxed. They had travelled for most of the day, expended three of their four torches and hadn't passed a single passageway. "My memory seems to have slipped me," Alhena said casually. He pushed aside the scraggly wet hair from his dripping forehead and attempted to dry his staff with the hem of his sleeve. "These passageways were engineered to thwart an attack on Songsbirth."

"You don't say?" Rook muttered. "The town of Songsbirth? Nestled somewhere safe, high in the Muse?"

"Aye, that is the one." Alhena unsteadily gained his feet, readjusted his shoulder sack and walked back into the mountain, protecting their last flaming torch as he approached the hole in the rock.

Soul Forge

Rook jumped to his feet, conscious of the open ledge beside him. Adjusting his gear, he scrabbled after Alhena, trying to keep the fading glow of the torch in sight.

Alhena waited for him on the far side of the fissure. "If I remember the intricacies of the catacombs correctly..." Alhena eyed the walls and reached out to touch irregularities in their surface. "There are many cleverly concealed exits along this first section of the tunnel." He poked and scraped at something.

Rook couldn't see anything but roughly hewn rock. "You're just remembering that now?"

Alhena broke a nail. He stuck his filthy finger into his mouth and spoke around the injured digit, "Some of the hidden tunnels lead higher into the mountain, while others will take us into the bowels of the earth. If I am not mistaken, there is only one tunnel that leads to the valley below."

"Oh, great." Rook rolled his eyes. "A fine time to remember an insignificant piece of information like that."

Twinges of anxiety crept into Rook's psyche. How were they going to find their way out? They had one torch left and were still a long way from the bottom of the falls. He inspected the wall opposite Alhena, not sure what he was looking for. What if the plunge into the lake had made Alhena delusional? It had been a long time since they actually had any rest, or for that matter, decent food. Thinking about everything they had just experienced, it was a miracle they were alive at all.

Panic prickled his skin. The last thing he wanted was to die here. It felt as if he had been buried alive. He wasn't claustrophobic, but the deeper they ventured, the more he imagined the weight of the mountain pressing down on him. Just when he thought he couldn't stand it any longer, he heard a 'snick.'

Farther up the tunnel, Alhena exclaimed, "Aha."

The sound of rock scraping upon rock reverberated through the tunnel. It stopped, and then started again. The sound made Rook's teeth ache. He rushed up to Alhena.

Alhena looked pleased with himself. "I found a hidden nook in the wall." He had triggered a small section of the wall to open, and then

159

closed it again. He placed his fingers within a hidden crevice. "There is a small lever in here. Try it."

Rook probed the nook with his fingers. Sure enough, he felt a lever the size of his little finger. "Humph."

Alhena pushed on the wall.

At first nothing happened, and then a small, circular section of heavy stone receded inward. Alhena paused long enough to raise his eyebrows and stepped into the breach.

Rook followed him through and moved out of the way as the portal slowly sealed itself, leaving behind no trace of its existence. They were in a tunnel no different from the one they had just left.

The tunnel appeared to travel in the same direction as the previous one. Gone was the distant roar of Splendoor Falls from the breach in the tunnel wall—the atmosphere replaced by colder, stale smelling air. He didn't know if that was a good thing or not. What he did know was that he needed to get out of the mountain as quickly as possible. Alhena's puzzled expression did little to alleviate his anxiety.

"Which way?"

Alhena shrugged his stooped shoulders and started right, following the tunnel's downward slope. It made sense. In the previous tunnel, this direction would have taken them to the cliff edge.

A short while later the tunnel ended.

Rook's shoulders slumped. Standing face-to-face with the dead end, he dropped his belongings to the ground, turned about, and slid his back down the granite barrier. They were going to die trying to unravel the mystery of the labyrinth. Perhaps they should locate the trap door that had led them to this tunnel and head back to the lake?

Alhena stared at the rock face behind him. "Well, I guess it is not this way."

Rook studied him. "Do you honestly have a clue how to get us out of this forsaken hole?" When Alhena didn't reply quickly enough, Rook shouted, "Do you?"

Alhena dropped his eyes to the ground. Unkempt wisps of thin grey hair dangled in front of his face.

"I'm sorry, Alhena. Please…" Rook said, angry with himself. He stared at the ground in shame. "I have no right to take this out on you. Forgive me."

Soul Forge

An awkward silence settled between them. Alhena's gentle voice in the dead stillness nearly gave Rook a stroke, "I have travelled to Songsbirth but twice in my life. Both times were with a Songsbirthian guide, and both times were a long time ago. However, with each wrong path we choose, I am slowly recalling the route." With a grim smile, he added, "And this is not it."

Rook forced a smile. He couldn't help but notice their last torch was more than half spent. "No, probably not." He accepted Alhena's hand and got to his feet.

"I am afraid it is going to take a lot of trial and error," Alhena said, waiting for Rook to gather his stuff. "Hear me not wrong. There are small signs along the passages that show those in the know what to search out. All I know for certain is they are not in this direction." He offered Rook a sad smile and walked up the tunnel.

A short while later, Alhena discovered one of those signs, but when the circular slab of granite slid inward, they were greeted by the distant sound of Splendoor Falls. They had found the original tunnel. They discussed going back to the surface, but with Alhena's assurances, decided against it.

Time slipped by, marked by the lessening of their torch's life. The only thing they had managed to achieve so far was to stub, scrape and rub their fingers raw as they probed the imperfect rock surfaces. Weariness and hunger had them swaying on their feet, addling their thoughts.

Rook was about to give up when a small stalactite caught his eye. Stretching on tiptoe, he reached up to grab it. He couldn't believe his luck. He wiggled it and a small crack appeared in the granite roof—the sound of sucking air caused them to catch their breath.

Alhena pushed up on the ceiling with his staff and a small oval section disappeared into the tunnel above.

Grabbing hold of the edges, Rook pulled himself into the hole. Once through, he turned upon his stomach and hoisted Alhena's belongings and the sputtering torch through the gap. With some effort, he hauled the frail man after him.

Winded, he asked, "Do you remember coming this way?"

Alhena picked up the torch and waved it about, searching the darkness. "Honestly? I do not know."

161

Soul Forge

"How can you not recall dropping through a floor?" Rook asked, trying not to let his frustration get the better of him.

Alhena sighed. "It was so long ago. I am sure we must have."

Rook glared at him but said no more.

The third passageway was no different than the previous two in appearance, but a strong smell of stagnant water reached their nostrils. Instead of pushing the ceiling slab back into place, they left it open in case they were forced to return topside.

The passage sloped down to their left and up to their right, both ways disappearing into impenetrable blackness beyond the wavering torchlight. Down was the way they wished to travel, so they set off left, both men conscious of the little life remaining to their torch.

Soon afterward, they left the stale air of the narrow passage and stepped into an enormous cavern, its height and depth imperceptible in the limited light of their dying brand.

Alhena stopped and cursed. "I don't remember passing through a cavern this size."

Rook's shoulders slumped. He didn't have to ask. They had gone the wrong way and wasted their last torch.

Alhena dropped his provision sack to the floor, the sound echoing off cavern walls unseen. He sat on the dank ground and released the butt end of the torch before it burned his hand.

The licking flames sputtered briefly, hissing loudly in the all-consuming silence. As the faint glow collapsed in upon itself, they came to realize the grim reality of their fate—lost and alone, in the absolute darkness of their living tomb.

Soul Forge

Treacher's Gorge

Thwart! Of all people, Avarick Thwart was the last person Silurian wished to bump into at the moment.

He hadn't asked for this. Nor did he care to shed the blood of a knight, but if the Chamber thought they were going to deny him his freedom, they had another think coming. If the Enervator itched for a fight, Silurian was prepared to give him one.

Surprisingly, Avarick manoeuvred his horse sideways, giving Silurian space.

He admired the beauty of Avarick's majestic animal; a finer horse he had never seen. It would be a shame to harm such an exquisite beast. Stepping free of the Chamber entrance shed, he kept his back against the wall lining Redfire Path, his sword poised to defend himself.

The Enervator's visor was down, his eyes unreadable in the shadow of his helm. As cocky as ever, he hadn't even drawn his serrated, black sword—nor was that nasty crossbow in his employ.

A whinny on his right took his focus away from the dangerous man. Tethered to an iron eyelet, fully outfitted with a black saddle matching the Enervator's, and complete with black leather provision bags, another black destrier pulled restlessly at the lead restraining it.

Avarick's throaty growl puzzled Silurian.

"I'm thinking we don't have all day, Queen Killer." Avarick nodded toward the riderless horse.

Pounding footsteps and clanking armour sounded from within the entrance shed. The high bishop's angry voice barked orders to stop Silurian at any cost.

Silurian cast Avarick a bewildered glance.

"Any time now, would be good."

163

Soul Forge

Not taking his eyes off the Enervator, Silurian slashed the leather thong restraining the second horse. He slid his sword into the baldric strapped across his back and mounted the large animal. "What are you up to, Avarick?"

Shouts rose up from the stables. The barnyard crawled with militiamen scrambling to respond to the crisis.

Avarick positioned his mount in front of the entry shed's door, preventing the soldiers from exiting. "Just shut up and ride."

Silurian pulled hard on his horse's reins and heeled his mount into a gallop, heading southward toward the Undying Wall—away from Madrigail Bay.

As soon as he passed Avarick, the Enervator spurred his own horse in his wake, its pounding hooves churning up chunks of Redfire Path.

Approaching Gritian's southern rim, the two guardsmen stationed there stepped out to confront them but leapt out of the way when Avarick yelled at them to move.

The sound of pursuit was lost to them after cresting the rim. The only sounds left in their world were the pounding cadence of their horse's hooves and the jangle of equipment flopping rhythmically about their saddles.

Twilight cast Redfire Path in long shadows. Flashes of orangey-red light made it hard to see in the dimness of the forest as the setting sun flickered through the trees.

Silurian functioned on adrenaline alone. He hadn't slept in two days. As far as he knew, neither had Avarick.

He eyed Avarick from time to time. The Enervator had removed his helm and pulled level with him shortly after departing Gritian. He rode silently alongside him, his expression unreadable, his dark eyes focused on the lengthening shadows ahead.

He wondered at the man's motivation. The Enervator had left the secret Chamber meeting at a signal from Solomon, presumably to marshal the militia to defend the town and to ensure the high warlord made it home. Avarick was supposed to be looking after the defense of

164

Gritian. Why had he helped him escape? There had to be other forces at play here. Perhaps he acted under the secret orders of the high bishop.

They travelled in the wrong direction. Was that also by the high bishop's design? Whatever the reason for Avarick's actions, Silurian was grateful to be free of the accursed council and out upon the open hills where he could look after himself.

Trying to keep his weariness at bay, Silurian pondered how to get where he needed to be. There weren't any good routes to Madrigail Bay this far south. Doubling back along Redfire, or attempting to skirt Gritian to the east, risked capture by the warlord's men, or running across the rumoured Kraidic warriors—neither scenario desirable. To track west toward the Torpid Marsh and hazard the creatures lurking there wasn't a great idea either.

There were southern routes to consider, but they all had their own drawbacks. He knew of a mountain trail, high above the world on the shoulders of the Undying Wall, winding its way westward to the Spine where it picked its way along Niad's Course all the way to Madrigail Bay. That certainly wouldn't be his first choice as Treacher's Gorge lay along that route. Once experienced, Treacher's Gorge was best left forgotten.

He could travel beyond the Undying Wall and take the Nordic Byway through the Gulch, but that was another place he'd prefer to avoid if given the choice.

As they passed the Farrier homestead, he briefly thought about holing up there for some much-needed rest, but the thought of facing Mr. and Mrs. Farrier was too much for him to bear.

They pushed on into the night. The Undying Mountain Pools were too far away to reach before daylight, but the more leagues they put behind them, the safer Silurian felt. He surmised the pursuit would only last so long given their knowledge of the Kraidic warband's approach. Gritian's lack of a military leader, with the warlord injured and Avarick gone, left the militia in a bad way.

If they reached the foothills of the Undying Pass, they should be okay, but the rocky crags were still a long way off.

Soul Forge

The moon had descended into the early morning sky before they trotted into the fringes of the Undying Wall—its great peaks black against the predawn sky.

They stopped beside a small brook well east of Redfire Path, utterly exhausted. Not bothering to post a watch, they took only enough time to tend their horses before collapsing into the bedrolls Avarick had packed.

They awoke before sunrise, their breath visible in the predawn light. They had only slept for a couple of hours, but it was enough to shake the bleariness from their minds.

Mountainous clouds scudded swiftly across a greying sky. A storm front swirled in from the north, promising unsettled weather. With the proximity of both mountain chains serving to pen in low-lying cloud cover, weather patterns in this part of Zephyr had the occasion to be severe. With any luck, the storm wouldn't be as bad as the one they had lost Alhena in.

Silurian sat astride his new horse, the animal not showing any lasting effects of having raced halfway through the night.

A cool northerly wind whipped the hem of Avarick's forest green surcoat about his legs. The coat of arms emblazoned upon his cloak was barely recognizable beneath the layers of dirt and other unspeakable filth he had picked up since locating Silurian and the others. He mounted his destrier and prodded the beast into action, following Silurian beneath the thinning tree cover.

Back on Redfire Path, they urged their mounts to a gallop, heading into the lofty reaches of the Undying Wall, the grey heights lost in brooding storm clouds.

They rode through the afternoon at a more sustainable pace for the horses, thankful the clouds had decided to hoard their moisture. The path continued its course south, rising ever higher toward the saddle of Mountain Pool Pass.

Soul Forge

They stopped beside a racing watercourse that plunged from an unknown height and disappeared into a black fissure on the edge of the trail.

Avarick sat upon an outcropping of rock commanding a good view of the way they had come. Surveying the roadway snaking its way northward, he said, "Doesn't seem like they followed us. Clavius' men would have caught us by now if they had."

Silurian placed a wooden bowl of water before his horse and joined the Enervator, aware of how vulnerable he was standing here alone with the Chamber's assassin. If Avarick wished to follow through with the threat he had issued a few days before, Silurian couldn't think of a better place to do it.

He didn't know what to think where the Enervator was concerned. The man obviously wasn't ready to follow through with his threat. Avarick had all the opportunity he needed when they had stopped for a quick sleep, and yet, he hadn't made a move. Something must be holding him back. Even so, Silurian gave him a wide berth on the outcropping and followed his gaze. To the north, the land below was lost in the approaching front.

Studying the terrain, he sensed Avarick watching him. Things would be much simpler if he could be rid of the Enervator's company.

"So, what now?" Avarick asked.

Silurian shrugged. "I have to get to Madrigail Bay."

"Right." Avarick spat over the lip of the promontory. "Gonna be tough getting there if we continue this way."

Keeping a watchful eye on his travelling companion, Silurian sat on a log near the edge of the outcropping and listlessly chewed at a bruised apple. If he remembered correctly, the entrance to the goat path that would take him along the treacherous heights of the Undying Wall should be close. Hopefully they hadn't passed it. The path, if still passable after all these years, might take longer than travelling all the way to the Nordic Wood, but it was preferable to travelling through the Gulch. Besides, he didn't want to go anywhere near his old home.

"I'm considering Treacher's Gorge."

Whatever Avarick had been doing, he stopped and shot Silurian an incredulous look. "The Gorge? You *are* as mad as they say."

Soul Forge

Silurian didn't know who *they* were. Nor did he care. "You'd prefer the Gulch?"

"Over the Gorge? In a heartbeat. At least I'd have a say on how I died."

Silurian gave him a wry smile.

"It's been over five years since I last crossed Treacher's Gorge," Avarick said. "It was sketchy then. The gods only know whether the bridge still stands. We might travel all that way for nothing. If the bridge isn't there, there's no other way around."

"Who said anything about *we?*"

Avarick glared at him.

"There's nothing holding you with me anymore." Silurian looked the Enervator directly in the eyes. "Is there?"

Avarick held his gaze for a moment, before looking north again. "No."

Silurian stared hard at Avarick, contemplating his words. Should he chance the goat path with the hope of saving a few days, but risk mishap, especially where the horses were concerned, only to have to turn back should the Gorge prove impassable? To be forced to travel the Nordic Byway anyway?

He raised his eyebrows—he could always travel south to Ember Breath and take the Ocean Way, but that would cost him another week. Ember Breath was the safest way left to him but urgency predicated he take a more dangerous, direct route.

Standing up and stashing his apple core into a pocket, a habit he had learned as an orphan, Silurian walked off the outcropping.

Readying his horse, he watched from the corner of his eye as Avarick attended to his own mount. That was one thing the Enervator took great pains at doing—seeing to the welfare of his horse. He had to admire the man for that.

He sighed. It wouldn't hurt to have a riding companion, especially if he were to encounter trouble along the way. The Enervator's sword would prove a welcome ally in that case. Unless, of course, his riding companion *was* the trouble.

"I'm going to Treacher's Gorge. You can accompany me or not."

Avarick stiffened. Without meeting Silurian's questioning stare, he muttered, "May as well. I got nothing left here."

168

Soul Forge

The rain held off until they stepped onto the goat path and then assaulted them mercilessly for the remainder of that first day away from Redfire Path.

It took them four days to reach Treacher's Gorge, a deep divide between four abutting mountains where the Spine intersected the Undying Wall. The crumbling ledge they traversed curved around the latter's windswept peak, circling its southwest face until it dropped into a fourteen-thousand-foot gorge.

If not for the existence of the bridge, Silurian would have believed they were the only people ever to have witnessed the sight, so desolate was the region. He had stood upon this brink twice before, but the sheer depth of the yawning abyss still rendered him breathless. Never had he travelled this way with a horse. No one in their right mind would ever contemplate doing so, and yet, here he was.

Soul Forge

Before them, a rickety wood and rope bridge stretched clear across to the centre of the breach between four jagged peaks. The death-defying structure was bisected by a platform at its midpoint. From where they stood, the bridge had originally split off into three other directions, radiating out from the platform, but the left span had since collapsed. A large section of the broken bridge swirled about below the platform.

The bridge deck consisted of oak planks supported by thick ropes. A thick hawser, suspended a few feet above the decking, traced the bridge's length on either side, providing unstable handrails. The entrance to the derelict span lay between two sickly trees perched on the brink of the abyss, the left tree, nothing more than a broken stump. The ropes supporting the bridge were anchored around these tree trunks. The handrail hawsers looped from the trees, through iron eyelets atop thick iron posts, driven into the bedrock.

A strong wind buffeted the bridge, its separate spans undulating toward the central platform—the picket bridge decks swinging wildly back and forth. Frayed ropes held the entire structure together, creaking in the wind with the promise of failure.

How anyone had built the bridge was a mystery. It traversed a thousand feet of open air to the centre, and again that far to the three facing peaks.

Silurian and Avarick fought for all they were worth to keep their mounts from stepping away from the precipice. Any slip upon the crumbling ledge would surely prove fatal.

Silurian had no idea how he was going to coax his mount onto the derelict structure. Nor did he know how he was going to convince himself.

Avarick slid from his saddle, keeping a firm hold on his horse. Maintaining control of his frightened animal, he grabbed Silurian's reins.

"Well?" Silurian dismounted, the bitter wind whipping his unkempt hair. "Who's first?"

"A gentleman like myself must respectfully defer!" Avarick gestured with a slight bow and an outstretched hand. "I insist! After you!"

Silurian swallowed. He scanned Avarick from head to toe. "You weigh less!"

Soul Forge

Avarick raised his eyebrows, studying what remained of the bridge. "If it bears itself, will it not bear us?"

Silurian didn't acknowledge the remark. He couldn't wrest his eyes from the broken section of bridge swirling about beneath the central platform. How it hadn't dragged the rest of the decrepit structure down with it, he had no idea.

"Perhaps try it by yourself first, without the horse?" Avarick suggested.

"Cross it twice? And you think *I'm* mad?"

Silurian struggled to keep his horse from pulling away from the brink. It had been his idea to come this way. He was the one who needed to reach Madrigail Bay. The Enervator was likely only along to keep an eye on him—to rein him in should he decide to abandon the kingdom again.

Seeing no other way around it, Silurian studied his shying horse. They couldn't leave the animals up here on their own. He undid the lashing securing the flap on his saddlebag and pulled out a small blanket. The wind attempted to snatch it from his grasp. With difficulty, he cinched it over his horse's face, effectively blinding it, all the while patting its neck and speaking softly to soothe the animal.

Taking a deep breath, he tugged on the reins. The horse balked at first, but finally it stepped forward.

Silurian tapped the first plank with an outstretched foot. The bridge's motion beneath his probing boot did little to reassure him of the sanity of his decision to come this way. Nor did the grisly sight of the broken stump securing half of this section of the bridge.

Grabbing the thrumming hawser handrail with his free hand, he closed his eyes and stepped out over the chasm. Amazed the planks actually supported him, he opened his eyes. Seeing the gorge yawning below, he froze.

"Don't look down!" Avarick's voice sounded above the wind.

"Thanks," Silurian grunted. Gathering his courage, he took another small step and stopped again to breathe. This was going to take a while and he still had to coax his horse onto the swaying bridge.

Soul Forge

A light sleet lashed at them, dampening the bridge deck.

Wide eyed, Avarick couldn't find his breath. He expected at any moment to bear witness to the death of Zephyr's supposed saviour. To watch helplessly as their hope plunged thousands upon thousands of feet to an unmarked grave. He should have taken the initiative himself.

Seeing Silurian struggle with his mount, the man's demise didn't seem far off. At least that would save him the trouble of killing Silurian when this business was done.

Silurian's mount balked as the bridge moved beneath its hooves, but once on the bridge, two remarkable things happened in quick succession. The bridge, with the considerable amount of extra weight added to it, instead of sagging further into the abyss, became tauter. The second was the reaction of Silurian's horse. The frightened beast had only one thought in mind—get off the shaking surface as quickly as possible. It began stepping so quickly that Silurian struggled to keep far enough ahead of it to prevent from being trod upon. Should the horse overtake him on the narrow span, or misstep sideways, they were both lost.

Avarick was amazed. Silurian was actually doing it. Against all that made sense, the man had reached the junction and yet, the bridge still held.

He almost screeched when Silurian slipped on the slick boards of the central platform and fell to his knees.

Throwing his arms out, Silurian grabbed the far hand rope and pulled himself upright, and then they were off again, man and horse, swaying toward the northern peak.

Before long, far too soon for Avarick's liking, it was his turn to cross. Silurian and his horse waited safely on the far side of Treacher's Gorge.

Avarick almost turned back. Almost. For some reason, he had developed a strange affinity for the wretch awaiting him on the far side of the fourteen-thousand-foot chasm. Was he developing feelings for the man he had so recently condemned? Perhaps Zephyr had hope after all. Perhaps, but the only way to find out for sure was to see the journey through and that meant crossing the bridge. If he lost the legendary man now, he might never find him again.

Wiping the sleet from his cheeks, he followed Silurian's example and hooded his horse. With a heavy swallow, he stepped out over the yawning abyss—the cataract at its base lost in the mist far below.

As the tiny figures of the Enervator and his horse entered the far end of the rickety span, Silurian examined the fraying ropes that secured the bridge. His eyes flicked to the sheath upon his belt holding his fancy dagger. It would be too easy.

Soul Forge

Songsbirth

Sleep never came. Lost in the darkness of the cavern, Rook and Alhena lay shivering in the silence of their subterranean tomb. An occasional plip-plop of dripping water sounded from deeper within. Despite his weariness, Rook decided to locate the water source.

Alhena joined him as he advanced slowly through the stygian pitch, crawling upon hands and knees lest they hit a rock wall or topple into an unseen crevice. By sound alone, they closed in on the source of the sporadic drip.

Rook reached out in the darkness and touched Alhena's robes, assuring himself they were still close together. "There must be a pool of water up ahead."

Bits of loose scree covered the floor, digging into their palms and knees. Before long, the floor deteriorated into a slimy, damp softness beneath their fingertips.

"We are getting closer," Alhena commented. "The cavern probably fills during a storm."

Rook nodded. A natural reaction. Realizing Alhena had no way of seeing him, he grunted, "Probably."

They started forward again. The floor sloped away at a sharper angle, but before it became unmanageable, it levelled off.

The plip-plop sounded close. The slime covered floor soaked through his breeches. Rook could only imagine what a sopping mess Alhena's robes were.

Creeping forward, he was surprised when the floor abutted a wall. When the next drop fell, the noise came from directly above.

Groping blindly overhead, Rook attempted to get a sense of the slimy wall beneath its slippery coating. He couldn't be certain, but it felt as if the wall was constructed of cut stone. Rising to his toes, he located what seemed to be a recess in the rock face overhead. Further inspection told him it was indeed a ledge that curved away to either side of where he stood.

"There's a ledge up here." His voice sounded hollow in the darkness. Struggling to maintain his footing in the muck, he searched for a handhold. "Here, give me a boost."

Alhena located Rook's foot. Cupping his hands, he helped Rook scramble up the wall.

Upon the ledge, Rook cautiously rose to his feet, careful to hold his hands above him to avoid whacking his head. Unable to feel anything higher, he dropped back to a crouch, suddenly conscious of the fact that he had no idea where the edges of the shelf were.

The next drip sounded directly beside him, but before he had time to investigate, the dripping became a trickle, splashing him in the face.

The trickle turned into a deluge, the sudden gush of water threatened to wash him off the ledge.

"What did you do?" Alhena's voice sounded above the noise of the rushing water. "I am drowning down here!"

Rook had no idea what had just happened. In the all-encompassing darkness he couldn't see the nose on his face. He dropped to his stomach, extending his arms over the edge of the wall as a steady flow of water spilled over him. "Grab my hands!"

Alhena held his staff over his head for Rook to grab. With a great deal of effort, he pulled Alhena up.

A dozen torches flared to life above them, driving away the darkness. At the same time, the cavern rumbled and a large section of wall opened up, admitting armed men and women who immediately spread out to either side with torches in hand.

Rook squinted, looking up to see that the torrent of water cascaded through a fissure in the ceiling. It plunged into the mouth of a large stone well, erected in the centre of the cylindrical dais he and Alhena lay upon—the well overflowing into a lakebed below.

Alhena reached for his pack but Rook stayed his hand, pointing with his eyes to archers kneeling on wooden platforms that encircled the many stalactites hanging from the cavern's roof.

One of the archers issued a command and the fissure closed in upon itself with a grating tremor, curtailing the flow of water.

Soul Forge

A man standing in the breach in the wall stepped forward. "What business do you have here?"

Rook couldn't distinguish the man's uniform from such a distance in the flickering torchlight. He certainly wasn't a Kraidic warrior. Grasping the lip of the well, he pulled himself to his feet.

"It is okay. They will be the Splendoor Catacombs Guard." Alhena said, joining him.

Together they put their hands in the air. The sound of bowstrings drawing taut was disconcerting. Everyone in the cavern ducked.

"Lower your staff!" The man at the breach ordered.

Alhena lowered his staff slowly, and said, "We come in peace. We seek only to leave this mountain labyrinth and continue our journey to Madrigail Bay."

The apparent leader held a hand up to stay the archers. "Madrigail Bay? You've chosen a strange route to get there."

"Indeed. It is a long story."

The leader crossed his arms.

Alhena cleared his throat. "We ascended the Muse far to the south. Running from men intent on killing us. They forced us into the lake." He swallowed, glancing up to the archers in the heights. "We made our way to the brink of Splendoor Falls and have been attempting to reach the mainland ever since."

The leader glanced at a large man towering over him and declared, "I'm not believing you. Enlighten me, where have you come from?"

"We are on a quest to find Silurian Mintaka."

The leader and the large man looked at each other.

Alhena improvised, "We have been dispatched by the Gritian Council."

"The Chamber? Who are you, then?"

"Alhena Sirrus, senior messenger to the Chamber of the Wise." He pointed to Rook. "My esteemed colleague here is none other than Rook Bowman. The leader of the Group of Five."

An excited murmur sounded throughout the cavern.

The leader took a moment to mull over Alhena's words. He conversed with a second man standing beside the taller one. The second man nodded and disappeared behind the wall.

Soul Forge

The leader pointed his sword at them. "This had better not be a trick!" He directed his gaze to someone unseen in the heights. "Drain the well!"

A gurgling noise rose from behind Alhena and Rook. The water in the well bubbled and dropped away.

"Descend the interior of the well," the leader ordered. "Heed my words. Any treachery will be met with instant death."

With the archers still poised above them, Rook followed Alhena's lead over the lip of the well and climbed down a set of rusted iron rungs embedded in the well's interior wall.

Darkness filled the well as they descended to a shallow puddle at its bottom. The smell of damp stone mixed with the odour of their wet clothing was suffocating in the close confines of the well's interior.

A small portion of the well's wall swung outward, flooding them with light.

Rook squinted in the brightness, nearly stumbling through the gap.

An unarmed man beckoned them to step forward into the room. Behind him, four marksmen trained their crossbows on the well.

Rook stepped uncertainly into the room and turned to assist Alhena who held his free hand before his eyes.

The room was small in comparison to the cavern above, but it was large enough to hold fifty men. Benches and open chests brimmed with a wide variety of bristling weaponry around the room's perimeter. Shields of all sizes and design were piled in two corners. A large, stone table dominated the centre of the granite floor, bearing scrolls stacked in a wooden crib. The edge of the crib held down a large, aged map. Dusty tomes littered the table's surface. Several thick candles, burnt to varying heights, illuminated the room with flickering light. Apart from the well shaft traversing the height of the room, there was only one way into the chamber.

The spokesman from the cavern burst into the room. Eyeing Rook's bow and Alhena's staff, he motioned for the crossbowmen to stand down.

One of the tallest men Rook had ever laid eyes upon, followed the leader into the room—the giant's hammered brass cuirass reflecting the flickering torch light. Rook thought of his deceased friend, Helvius Pyxis. He doubted even Helvius matched this man's height.

Soul Forge

The leader introduced himself. "I am Johnnes Holmann, captain of the Splendoor Catacombs' guard."

Rook and Alhena shook his hand.

"This is Guardell Caulder, my second in command." Captain Holmann nodded at a short man with broad shoulders and powerful forearms. They accepted his handshake.

"And this," Captain Holmann stepped back to introduce the goliath of a man, "is Pollard Banebridge."

Rook extended his hand, but Pollard merely stared back at him. In the uncomfortable moment that ensued, Rook couldn't help but notice the massive weapon the man held casually at his side. The hilt alone was longer than Rook's forearm, but it was the fact that the unique weapon consisted of two, full-length, broadsword blades, joined at the hilt that made him take notice.

The captain interrupted his admiration of Pollard's sword. "So. Is that the famous bow of Rook Bowman?"

Pollard folded his massive arms and raised his bushy red eyebrows.

When Rook didn't respond right away, the captain persisted, "From the exploits I've heard tell of Rook Bowman and his band of vigilantes, I was expecting a fiercer looking sort than you."

A mocking guffaw escaped Pollard.

"From what I know," the captain continued, "Rook Bowman would never have been taken as easily as we took you this day."

Pollard nodded.

"I don't believe you are who you claim to be…"

Great, Rook thought.

"…but that's not for me to judge."

Rook couldn't help staring at Pollard's mocking grimace. Making a conscious effort, he locked eyes with the captain. "It's been…" His voice dropped to a whisper, "a long time."

He snatched a glance at Pollard, despite his attempts not to. Pollard seemed like he wanted to smash him.

"I've only recently returned to Zephyr. It's been many years since the Group of Five fell. As to how easily we were taken…"

The rattling of arrows jostling about in quivers interrupted him, announcing the arrival of two female archers clad in the same slate coloured, loose fitting clothing the rest of the men and women wore.

Soul Forge

The shorter archer brushed aside a stray wisp of auburn hair from her freckled face. "The cavern is clear, sir."

"Excellent, Sadyra. We'll be sailing to the Birth shortly."

"Understood." Sadyra bowed slightly in deference, her storm-grey eyes taking in the two captives. "We'll head topside and ready the boat."

Captain Holmann nodded and the two female archers left without a sound.

The captain said to Rook, "May I see your bow?"

Rook frowned, taking a step back. One look at Pollard drove home the fact that he really didn't have much choice in the matter. Reluctantly, he handed it over.

Holding the bow up to the torchlight, the captain studied the intricate runes running the length of the well-used bow. It wasn't long enough to be a longbow, yet it was longer than any of the bows his own archers employed.

"A magnificent bow. I'll give you that." The captain gripped it in his left hand and tested the draw. "I don't believe I've seen its equal."

Eyeing the bow from top to bottom, the captain frowned. "Legend states that only Silurian Mintaka's blade lost its enchantment at the Battle of Lugubrius. If I recall, every member of the Group of Five carried a magically imbued weapon. I see no golden hue about this bow."

Rook sighed. They were wasting time, yet nothing he could say would allay the captain's suspicions. "It's a long story," he said, his voice barely perceptible.

"Aye. Seems like all your stories are. And tall, perhaps, hmm?"

The captain handed the bow to Guardell. He gestured for Alhena to hand over his staff.

"And you claim to be a messenger from the Chamber?"

Alhena nodded and handed his staff to Pollard.

"I wasn't aware the Chamber employed wizards," the captain said, folding his arms across his chest, and gazing into Alhena's colourless eyes. "Seems to me the religious values of the Wise Council contravene those of magic users. I assure you, I have all the time in the world to hear what you have to say," his gaze flicked to Rook and then back, "in case your explanation is a long one."

179

Soul Forge

Alhena shrugged and held his palms up.

Everyone standing close to Alhena flinched.

Alhena let his hands fall and sighed. "I assure you, Captain Holmann, I am not a wizard. I use that staff as a walking stick. Nothing more."

The captain gave Alhena a hard stare, not appearing to believe him, but he turned his gaze back to Rook. "Enlighten me. How *is* such power lost?"

Rook resigned himself. If the captain wanted to hear the story, he was going to hear it from the beginning. He started with the events following the Battle of Lugubrius. Of how he had left the king's court in search of his missing wife, Melody. Of how the trail he followed had led him to the border of the Forbidden Swamp where he was ambushed, beaten, and left for dead—if not for the intervention of a band of swamp denizens. They took his broken body back to a place known as Deneabola, a mystical swamp many leagues into the harsh marshland. For months, the creatures tended his wounds and nursed him back to health. While in their care he learned their strange language, but his need to find Melody eventually saw him bid them farewell.

Back in the Mid Savannah, he lost the trail he had been following and with it, all traces of his wife's disappearance.

Roaming the wilderness in ever widening circles, despair settled in. Late one night, he stumbled upon an encampment of miscreants who had captured nine swamp creatures. Four of the creatures were already roasting over a cookfire while the other five had been bound by twine and hung alive from a tree limb in preparation for upcoming meals.

Rook ingratiated his way into the marauders' company, claiming he wished to join their band. A demonstration of his magical bow had won them over, their leader voicing many great things they were going to be able to accomplish with his gift. That same night, he set fire to the camp, wreaked havoc amongst the marauders and freed the remaining creatures.

During their flight back to the Forbidden Swamp, he took an arrow in his right hip and another through his left forearm. Crossing into the marshlands, creatures from the swamp rose up, and with the help of an old friend, fell upon the band and destroyed them.

Soul Forge

For the second time in less than a year, the swamp creatures nursed him back to health. While he recuperated, a deranged Silurian Mintaka remained with him on the banks of Saros' Swamp.

When he was fit enough to travel, he followed Silurian on a whirlwind foray into the Wilds, searching for those responsible for murdering Silurian's family.

Rook refused to elaborate on what happened within the Wilds, other than to say that he had given up his bow's power in a desperate move to save his best friend's life.

Scanning those nearest him, he could tell they didn't believe a word he said. He couldn't blame them—he hadn't actually explained what had happened to his bow's power. Undaunted, he informed the Splendoor Catacombs Guard about the recent events involving Helleden's firestorm.

Captain Holmann and the rest of those gathered around listened with rapt attention, their faces aghast at the revelation of the Forbidden Swamp's destruction.

He related his subsequent flight toward Gritian, meeting up with Alhena, and their harried escape from the Kraidic warband.

"And that, captain, is how we came to be hopelessly lost within your catacombs. Now, if you don't mind, we must be on our way."

"I see." Captain Holmann nodded, his mind clearly elsewhere. "I see." He motioned Guardell and Pollard to follow him out of earshot to confer.

Captain Holmann returned and declared, "Most of your story cannot be confirmed…"

Rook's eyes narrowed.

"…nor denied. The historians lost touch with Rook Bowman, *you*, if we are to believe your wild tale, soon after Lugubrius. I hear the conviction in your voice, but I have neither the knowledge nor the authority to take you at your word. In my opinion, your story is nothing short of bizarre." He nodded toward Rook's bow, now in Pollard's hand. "Your bow alone should distinguish you as the leader of the Group of Five, but without its power…" He shrugged.

The captain's gaze acknowledged Alhena's presence. "As for you. You claim to be not just *a* messenger, but *the senior messenger* to Zephyr's illustrious wise council. At your age, I think your place would be beside the chambermaster, not running about the land. I cannot help but suspect there's more to you than you admit."

"Fool yourself not, *young* captain," Alhena shot back, lifting his chin. "The only restraint accompanying age lies within the soul of the individual. I assure you, my heart beats as strong as any person here. It has been my experience that the will driving the person determines their ability, not the misguided perception of the ignorant. As to my magical ability?" He shrugged.

Guardell chimed in, "There's nothing left for us to do here. I say we parade them before the Songsbirthian council. The elders will ferret out their true intent."

"Aye. Songsbirth it is." Captain Holmann motioned for Rook and Alhena to step past him into the hallway, but Alhena didn't move.

"Do Faustus and Allyx still sit on the council?" Alhena asked.

Captain Holmann narrowed his eyes. "Aye, they do."

"And Master Pul? Does he still kick?"

Captain Holmann raised his eyebrows at Guardell. "Aye, he does."

Alhena stepped into the passageway. "Then lead on, good captain. It will be good to see the old codger again."

Rook caught up to Alhena and tugged at his sleeve, leaning close to his ear as they walked. "We don't have time for this."

Alhena winked. "I do not believe we have a choice."

Mid-morning sunshine crested the tips of the eastern Muse, a welcome relief to the two captives shivering within their damp clothing. A clear sky stretched across the lofty mountains all around them. Two snow covered peaks stood silent vigil directly in their wake, one on either side of Splendoor Falls.

Accompanying Alhena and Rook in the bow of a large skiff were Captain Holmann and Guardell Caulder. Amidships, two female archers pulled at the oars, while Pollard's bulk dominated the stern. A cool breeze swept down from the heights at their back, aiding the boat's journey toward the northeastern edge of the gently rolling lake.

Soul Forge

Approaching the small hamlet of Songsbirth, nestled at the base of a cliff, Rook admired the harmony the builders had created with the flowing designs of the stone and wooden buildings fronting the sliver of shoreline.

As the boat scraped the shore, Pollard jumped knee-deep into the water and pulled the heavy boat halfway onto a stony beach. Rook and Alhena followed Guardell and the captain over the gunwales and crunched across the gravel beach.

Rook looked around in wonder as they made their way into the heart of the sleepy village of Songsbirth. They passed eclectic buildings painted in a kaleidoscope of colour, their faces dotted with countless bird's nests. The singsong of avian wildlife drew their attention upward to hidden aeries in the cliffs high overhead.

They were led through an iron studded door set into the face of the cliff, following Captain Holmann into a well-lit passageway beyond. Pollard had caught up to them in the streets and entered behind them, ducking, even though the arched ceiling comfortably cleared the top of his head.

The short corridor housed several doors on either wall. Arriving at the last door on the left, the captain knocked and slid inside, leaving the others in the cool passageway. Before long, the door swung inward again. A stooped, grey-haired, wisp of a man greeted them with a toothless grin as he shuffled into the corridor with the assistance of a gnarled walking stick.

Leaning forward and squinting his eyes, the shaky man eyed Rook and then Alhena. He gave Alhena's smiling face a long stare. "Alhena? Alhena Sirrus? May the gods be blessed." He threw open his gangly arms to embrace Alhena.

Alhena returned the hug, a huge smile on his dirty face.

The older man released Alhena and held him at arm's length. "What in tarnation brings you all the way from Gritian unannounced?"

"Easy Pul, you old codger. You are going to give yourself a stroke," Alhena laughed.

"Bah, me? If I only live to be half your age, eh?" Master Pul cackled. "Come, come. You look a mess. Let's get you and Rook Bowman cleaned up." Stooped over his cane he squinted at Rook. "Rook Bowman eh? The gods favour us once again."

Soul Forge

Captain Holmann exited the room, respectfully sliding past the two older men, and stood beside Guardell.

"Well I'll be." He spoke to Pollard, indicating Alhena and Rook with a tip of his head. "They're fine. Fetch Alhena's staff and make sure Larina sees to Rook's bow."

Pollard nodded and walked away as Master Pul ushered Alhena and Rook through the doorway into his private chambers.

Alhena and Rook spent the next four days recuperating from their long ordeal. Rook had been adamant that they couldn't afford to waste any more time, but Master Pul had insisted.

Alhena had smiled the following morning when Rook shuffled up to him like an old man, his body aching miserably from head to toe. He admitted to Alhena that perhaps Master Pul was correct in his assessment that a few days rest would go a long way to expediting their journey in the long run.

Alhena walked beside Rook as they followed Master Pul through the cobbled streets, the fourth night since being rescued from the catacombs.

Master Pul led them into the Songsbirthian Chamber hall, set deep beneath the mountain. The hall, more an elaborate cave than a proper room, was already full of curious people when they entered—most of them looking older than Alhena. A stone table dominated the hall's far end, every seat occupied except three chairs at the head of the table.

Without any pomp, Master Pul introduced his esteemed guests and bid them to relate their story.

Alhena informed the council about his quest to find Silurian Mintaka, pausing to let the audience digest the revelation that the Liberator of Zephyr had not only been found, but was alive and well. At least he had been when they were separated.

When Rook spoke, the chamber became deadly silent. Shock registered on everyone's face. Horrified by the news of the Innerworld's demise. He expressed his view that something must be thwarting Helleden's use of the power because Zephyr still stood.

Soul Forge

Whatever hampered the sorcerer, Rook stressed it was only a matter of time before Helleden overcame it. They needed to act swiftly.

Master Pul absorbed it all. After listening to the suppositions of the council go around in circles, he grasped the edge of the table and shakily pulled himself to his feet. All discussion ceased.

"The cause of Helleden's bane requires a more informed deliberation than we can give it. Sir Rook's revelation concerning the Forbidden Swamp, and the fact that good King Malcolm's forces are unable to drive Helleden from his stronghold in the Altirius Mountains, tells me that our kingdom's theurgists and apprentice conjurers are not sufficient to curb this threat."

Alhena remembered Master Pul during Helleden's campaign twenty-three years ago. The man had been old even then.

"Sir Rook has informed me of his plan to travel to Madrigail Bay where he hopes to be reunited with Sir Silurian."

Another aged man rose to take the floor. "Surely, King Malcolm will be better served if they attend Castle Svelte and consult with His Majesty before travelling all the way to Madrigail Bay."

Many fists pounded the table, the council erupting into a new round of debate.

Master Pul let the discussion run its course before asserting his position. "I hear the wisdom of the council, but as Master of this Chamber, and someone who has been involved with defeating Helleden in the past, I exercise my right to overrule. Sir Rook has an intimate history with Helleden. If he deems it's in Zephyr's best interest for him to journey to Madrigail Bay, who are we to gainsay the leader of the Group of Five? This council will honour his decision and offer any assistance he requires."

The hall became uncomfortably quiet as the wise men and women digested Master Pul's decree. Before long, the Chamber discussions resorted to revelling old tales of chivalry and derring-do.

As the evening wore on, Rook leaned close to Master Pul's ear, requesting permission to leave.

Master Pul offered him a warm, knowing smile, and nodded his consent.

Alhena, so engrossed in a discussion with the two men nearest him, never saw him leave.

Soul Forge

Exiting the cliffs, a cool breeze accosted Rook, tussling his unkempt hair. He strolled through the quiet town, acknowledging whomever he passed. The locals, well of aware of his presence by now, greeted him warmly, even if they did cast him a furtive glance after he passed. The sun had dropped behind the western peaks, bathing the town in lengthening shadows.

At one point, he crossed paths with the Father Cloth of Songsbirth. He stopped to chat with him for a short while before the Father blessed him and continued on his way. As darkness settled over the mountain hamlet, Rook made his way along the gravel beach.

A person sat atop a large rock, beside the skiff that had brought them across the lake. A small fire burned before one of the Splendoor Catacombs Guard—the taller brunette female that had propelled the skiff. His bow lay in her hands.

She didn't look up at his approach, but he sensed she had been aware of his presence long before he was of hers. He stopped across the crackling flames, appreciating the warmth, his stomach strangely aflutter.

She gazed up at him with large, brown eyes, and smiled. "I hope you don't mind, Sir Rook. I've been tasked with warding your belongings."

"Aye, so I've been told," Rook said trying to think of something clever to add. Anything. For some reason the words wouldn't come. His eyes flicked to his quiver sitting beside the rock. It was full of newly fletched arrows.

She took off her suede cap, shaking out long, thick, brown hair. "I hear we're leaving tomorrow."

Rook needed to sit down. He had been watching her for the last couple of days but hadn't been able to work up the nerve to engage her in conversation.

"I'm sorry if I overstep my authority, but I just had to admire your bow. The workmanship is exquisite." She trailed off, looking sheepishly at the rocks at her feet.

186

Soul Forge

"No," Rook squeaked. His cheeks flushed. Controlling his voice, he continued, "No. It's alright. In fact, I, uh, am glad you're taking care of it, um, for me. Thank you, uh…" For the life of him he didn't remember if anyone had mentioned her name. If they had, there was no way he was going to remember it now.

She saved him. "Larina."

"Larina. A pretty name." He felt foolish.

She gazed into his eyes.

He thought for sure his knees would give out.

The moonlight reflected off the lake, basking her in a halo. A touch of colour flushed her freckled cheeks.

Rook, embarrassed beyond belief, couldn't keep from gawking at her pretty face. He tried to break his stare, but instead, he just stood there like an oaf. In a desperate attempt to avert the awkward silence, he blurted out, "Will, uh, I-I mean, would you care for a drink?"

Wow. It had been so long since he had spoken to a woman this way. He felt like he was butchering the whole affair miserably.

She moved over to allow him to sit beside her, smiling shyly.

He all but fell into the fire.

Soul Forge

Up the Spine

Shivers tingled up Silurian's spine, rousing him from an unusually sound sleep. Eyes wide, he tried to locate whatever had woken him. Eerie. The only word to explain the feeling gripping him.

Silurian and Avarick had set up camp high in the crags of the Spine, two days south of Madrigail Bay. A three-quarter moon hung far out over the Niad Ocean, basking the mountain in a soft glow. Long, ghostly shadows stretched about their makeshift campsite. They had ridden hard along Niad's Course, over a week since crossing Treacher's Gorge, following a circuitous mountain trail northward, traversing the shoulder of one mountain after another, paralleling the impassable Niad Ocean shoreline far below.

Silurian wasn't happy about how long it had taken them to travel the mountain trail, but he was content that they had made the best time possible considering the terrain.

He propped himself up on his right elbow and scanned the darkness, his woollen blanket tumbling from his shoulder. Something was out there, watching. Something close. The goose flesh prickling his skin had little to do with the cold breeze buffeting the lofty heights.

Low lying fog obscured most of the mountainside. Their horses were tethered to a stand of pines off to his right, next to a babbling rill that glimmered through the mist in the silvery light of the moon.

He studied the animals, wondering if something they had done had caused him to waken. The visible vapour escaping their muzzles in regular intervals told him they hadn't sensed anything out of place.

He questioned his anxiety. The fact that he travelled alone with an assassin who had openly professed his desire to kill him, might give him cause to worry, but he knew that wasn't it. The Enervator, other than being gruff, had actually been cordial with him so far. Who was *he* to gainsay anyone for being gruff?

A sudden loud snore on his left proved Avarick didn't share his unease. Silurian studied the man for a time. What *were* his motives?

He scanned Niad's Course. The path passed below their camp and disappeared into the shadows and mist in both directions.

Trolls? He didn't think so. Trolls weren't as prevalent along this section of the Spine. At least they weren't the last time he had travelled this way. They preferred the northern climes, specifically the Altirius Mountains.

He shook his head.

He often felt this way after a disturbing dream, but he hadn't had one for some time. Since the day after he and Alhena had met with Seafarer at the Mountain Pools. That seemed like such a long time ago. What had it been? Over four weeks? He'd lost track. He took another slow look around before settling under the scant warmth of his blanket. Lying on his back with his hands cupped behind his head, it took him a long time to drift off again.

Silurian's eyes snapped open. Something *was* out there. And it was close. Something watched their camp. More specifically, it watched him.

Wide, luminescent green eyes stared down at him from the darkness directly above.

He stared back. There weren't many times in his life that he'd been truly afraid, but he was spooked now. He hadn't felt this way since the days he and Melody lived on the slopes of Mount Cinder, far to the north, chased from cave to cave by a troll they had affectionately referred to as Hairy.

He needed to gain his feet and prepare to face whatever lay behind those eyes, but to his horror, he froze. A cold sweat washed over him. He closed his eyes for a moment and opened them again.

He wasn't imagining it. The eyes shone brightly in the moonlight.

Soul Forge

He garnered the nerve to turn his head sideways. Avarick slept soundly, oblivious to the imminent threat. He should wake him.

A guttural growl brought his attention back to the set of eyes floating in the black nothingness. The creature must be peering at him from the ledge high above their campsite.

The descending moon drifted behind a cloud. The clearing darkened and the glowing eyes disappeared.

Silurian jumped to his feet and stumbled sideways, his feet entangled in his bedroll.

"Thwart!" Kicking his feet back and forth in a panic, he found his voice, "Get up, man!" He kicked the sheets into the night and scrambled sideways, searching for those damned eyes.

"What the..." The Enervator stirred. "Silurian?"

"Shhh!" Silurian hissed. "Something's up there. On the ledge." He backed away from the ridge, stumbling blindly over a small rock, onto the path. He caught his balance but when the horses gave a sudden start, he nearly backed over the cliff on the far side of the trail.

"What are you doing?" Avarick's disembodied voice called to him.

Before Silurian could answer, the growl sounded beside his left leg. He froze and looked into a pair of haunting, green eyes. At his feet, a mountain cat hunkered down, poised to strike.

His breath caught in his throat. His weapons lay by the discarded bedroll, lost in the darkness. They may as well have been on the other side of the mountain.

The horses whinnied and stamped, straining against their ropes.

As the waning moonlight faded toward the darkest part of night, deep growls rose up around the camp. The horses pulled at their leads trying to break free.

Silurian thought he saw Avarick backing away from two huge forms lumbering out of the shadows.

Movement near the horses caught his attention. Two of his childhood nightmares loped toward him—two pairs of yellow eyes refracting the dim moonlight.

He grimaced. So much for his theory about the scarcity of trolls this far south. He contemplated his chances of retrieving his weapons. Even if he was fast enough to elude the trolls' advance, surely the cat would be on him before he took his first step.

Soul Forge

The cat emitted a low growl and hunkered down.

Silurian braced himself for the worst. If he was quick enough to dodge out of its way, the cat might leap over the edge of the cliff. He admonished himself. He was panicking.

He flinched as the cat took two powerful strides and lunged into the air, taking the nearest troll in the throat and forcing it to the ground.

He bolted for his bedroll. On hands and knees, he located his discarded blanket, but not his sword.

Off to the side, Avarick battled two enormous trolls in the poor light.

Silurian didn't have much time. The third troll, the one not engaged by the mountain cat, loped after him. He slapped at the ground in a frenzy as a shadow fell over him.

The troll emitted a ferocious howl, lifting its hairy arms out wide.

Silurian's left hand made contact with a familiar object. Jumping to his feet, he spun to face the threat, his left hand discarding an empty sheath behind him. His sword swung out wide, opening a long gash across the troll's matted chest—a high-pitched scream escaped its lips.

In his heightened state of awareness, fueled by raging adrenaline, Silurian was acutely aware of everything around him.

The trolls closing on Avarick had lost their focus for only a moment, but that was all it took for Avarick to gut the nearest beast. Before the second troll had time to react, its severed head bounced with a hollow thud off a small boulder and careened down the sloping edge of the encampment and across the path to where it disappeared over the brink of a three-thousand-foot cliff.

The horses pulled violently upon their ropes, whinnying louder than before.

Barely visible from where Silurian stood panting, the last troll had gained the upper hand on the cat, but what the cat gave away in size it made up for with speed and agility. Unfortunately for the cat, a troll's thick hide made it difficult to maim.

The cat shrieked, snapping, twisting, and clawing faster than Silurian's eyes were able to follow as the troll fell on it, craning its neck to tear the cat's throat out.

Silurian's blade took the beast below its rib cage, its razor-sharp edge scraping up the beast's spine and exiting its neck. He shoved at its

191

Soul Forge

heavy corpse with the bottom of his boot and promptly slipped on the blood left behind by its gory wound.

His foot slid out from underneath him so fast he didn't have time to catch himself. His head bounced off the rocky ground with a crack—a white light flashed inside his head.

Stunned, blackness began to narrow his vision. The shimmering moon set upon the distant horizon, slipping out from behind a storm cloud, its light dimming as his consciousness dwindled.

A low growl sounded above his face. Luminescent green eyes stared down at him.

Soul Forge

The Mighty Madrigail

Madrigail Lake rolled softly in the early morning breeze, the slight chop breaking upon the gravel shore fronting Songsbirth. Grey clouds roiled overhead as Alhena approached the stern of the large rowboat they had arrived in a few days before. He lugged two heavily laden, burlap sacks, supplies given to him by the council of elders. He felt groggy after the copious amount of spirits he had imbibed the night before in the company of his old friends. Bemoaning his foolish decision to partake in the spirits, he silently cursed the prospect of rain as his wispy hair whipped about his face.

The beach bustled with fishermen and warriors preparing for the day. Before Alhena reached the boat, the sound of gravel crunching beneath rapidly moving feet announced the arrival of the massive Songsbirthian guardsman.

Pollard's deep voice sounded with respect, a nice change from the haughtiness he had exhibited when they first met, "Let me take those for you, Senior Messenger." Without waiting for a response, Pollard relieved him of his burden, hoisting the bulging sacks like they were empty, and placing them into the skiff.

"My thanks, Pollard…?"

"Banebridge. Pollard Banebridge, son of Thoril of Stormsend."

"Banebridge, that is right. My memory is not what it used to be." Alhena cupped his chin in thought. "Stormsend, eh? Thoril, the Kraidic Crusher?"

"Heh." The large man's smile was scary. "That would be my grandfather."

"Right, right…" Alhena rubbed at his bearded chin, and then, as if he needed something to say while he mulled over long lost memories, he asked, "How tall *are* you? You must be well over seven feet."

193

Soul Forge

"Eight-foot three."

"Eight-foot three, eh? Yes," Alhena said absently. Opening his eyes wide, he took in Pollard's stature, as if seeing him for the first time. The hand cupping his chin shot out as he snapped his fingers. "Your family is from Stormsend!"

Pollard nodded.

"Your grandsire is Thoril, the Kraidic Crusher…"

Pollard raised his eyebrows.

"And your father is Thoril! Named after your grandfather," Alhena said with conviction.

"Aye."

"Thoril of Stormsend…He is an elder."

"Master of Stormsend, actually."

"Right, right…right." Alhena ran his tongue over the front of his teeth. "Your father is missing the last two fingers on his left hand."

"How do you—?"

"He lost them defending the old king, Peter Malcolm Svelte, at the Battle of Lugubrius."

"That's right. You knew him?"

"Knew him? Knew him? Of course, I knew him. He and I trained in the King's Guard together."

Pollard shook his head. "You were in the King's Guard?"

"Hmm? Me? No. Well, not exactly," Alhena said, trying to remember where he was going with his thought. "Oh yes, your father. Poor man. He never recovered from the guilt of not being able to save the king, did he?"

Pollard bowed his head. "No, he hasn't. He still feels responsible to this day."

"Bah!" Alhena wagged his finger, his white eyes intense. "Do not believe that. Your father was a great warrior. Is still, I bet. If they only knew how many demons he cut down before our position was overrun. Shy of slaying the entire minion horde, there was nothing your father could have done to alter that fateful day. I should know."

Alhena's voice dropped to a reverent hush. "I was the king's personal aide. I was with him when he fell. Your father…" Alhena's eyes moistened, "…saved me that day. He stood bravely over His Grace's body, dealing death to any who got near. Slaying beast after

194

demonic beast with such fury that we survived to witness the Group of Five ride in and change the tide of battle." As an afterthought, he mumbled, "If only they had gotten there sooner."

Pollard gave him a sympathetic grin and patted him on the shoulder. "I thank you for that, messenger Alhena." He turned quietly and walked back toward the gathering town elders standing upon the edge of the shelf rock fronting the gravel beach.

Alhena heaved a heavy sigh. Watching Pollard crunch away from him, his attention was drawn to the far side of the boat. Two figures sat beside each other on a rock only big enough for one. Rook sat with his back to him, engrossed in a conversation with one of the female archers—Lena, or something like that.

Captain Holmann of the Splendoor Catacombs guard, and Guardell Caulder, interrupted Alhena's observation of the two archers, as they stepped free of the elders, each carrying a small crate of supplies.

Pollard put his fingers to his lips and whistled.

Larina gave Rook a quick peck on the cheek and jumped into action. She rushed over to relieve the captain of his burden and lugged it to one of the larger boats anchored nearby, waist deep, in the choppy water.

Alhena noted the other female archer, Sadyra—he thought he had heard her called that in passing—with the auburn hair, also helping load supplies for the return leg.

Sure enough, the rain held...until they were halfway across the lake. The skies opened up in a blinding deluge of icy darts, lashing their faces and soaking them through, even with tarpaulins clutched tightly about them.

The usual hour-long trip across the mountain lake took them over two. By the time the noise of Splendoor Falls reached them above the raging storm, those not paddling were sore from bailing.

Larina and Sadyra paddled wide of the enormous pull of the falls and butted the craft against the same shelf Alhena and Rook had used to pull themselves out of the lake a few days ago.

Soul Forge

Larina had pled to accompany the quest to Madrigail Bay, but the council of elders had only appointed Sadyra and Pollard. Standing forlornly on the ledge, shivering in her wet suede uniform, she gave Rook a sad wave as he followed the others through the stone hatch and into the depths of the Splendoor Catacombs.

The rain had stopped and the sun shone through a break in the clouds. Beside her, through the gap in the mountains, a majestic rainbow arced brilliantly over the vibrant land.

Late in the afternoon, the company exited the catacombs several hundred yards south of the base of the falls. Even from this distance the noise and wind generated by Splendoor Falls was incredible—if somebody spoke, they had to shout. Luckily, a wind ushered the vast column of mist shrouding the valley to the northeast, leaving the company relatively dry.

Pollard and Sadyra led them along a steep path through heavy forest—the rocky descent making for tough travel. It was early evening before the lush trail left the foothills and wound its way to the banks of the mighty Madrigail, leagues downriver from the falls. Even this far from the plunge, the river raced by, churning through great chutes of massive boulders.

Night fell fast in the Madrigail Basin. In the morning, they would travel beyond the rapids, to where a boat awaited their arrival.

The Songsbirthian contingent pushed their way into the swift moving water, aboard a fair-sized riverboat—the *S'gull*. The river flowed swiftly for the better part of the afternoon. The oarsman seated below decks were primarily employed to assist the tiller in keeping *S'gull* in the centre of the frothy course. As the sun set, the oarsmen guided the riverboat into a sandy cove on the north shore.

Before the sun crested the Muse the following day, the *S'gull* had already put a few good hours of sailing behind her.

Nearing sundown, the oarsmen put their backs into propelling the boat as the mighty Madrigail widened and slowed to a lazy crawl.

Rook joined Alhena on the prow. The steady cadence of oars slapping the water made the *S'gull* jump forward, lull, jump forward and lull.

Deep in thought, Alhena didn't look up at the bowman's approach.

"I trust I'm not bothering you?" Rook asked, resting his elbows on the weathered railing.

Alhena offered him a slight smile and turned his gaze back to the passing waters. "You are never a bother, Sir Rook. I was just thinking about Gritian."

Rook nodded.

"I hope the town is okay," Alhena said more to the river than to Rook.

Rook patted his arm. "Aye, I'm sure they're fine. High Warlord Clavius will dispatch the Kraidic patrol in short order. I daresay, after the heroic chase we put the Kraidics through, they'll be hard-pressed to lock swords with the Gritian militia anytime soon."

Soul Forge

Alhena raised his eyebrows. "What if the band we stumbled upon is an advance scouting party? What if there are more bands creeping through the deep countryside? The vanguard of an invading host? With the king preoccupied battling Helleden's forces in the Altirius Mountains, it would not be hard for the Kraidic empire to launch an offensive of its own."

"Ya, I've been wondering that too. Krakus the Kraken covets Zephyr."

Alhena's face turned sour at the mention of the Kraidic Empire's emperor. "I cannot help thinking about what you said a while back. What if they *are* working together?"

"The Kraken and Helleden. Pfft. They'd kill each other."

A cold tingle washed over Alhena. Helleden and Emperor Krakus, together. Hearing it spoken aloud seemed to add validity to the chance it might be true. Zephyr was surely doomed if the two leaders found a way to align their forces without killing each other.

Rook settled in next to him. Alhena sensed his apprehension. "Something is bothering you."

Rook swallowed, his eyes appearing on the verge of tears.

"What is it?"

Rook studied the river. His breathing became heavier. "Silurian."

"Silurian? What about him?"

Rook shook his head. "I don't know. Silly stuff I guess. I find myself constantly wondering, what he's like now after all these years. Will he remember me?"

Alhena gave him an incredulous look.

"Ya, I know he'll remember me. That's not what I meant. I mean, how will he react when he sees me again?"

"I suspect he will be happy. Why would he not?"

Rook dropped his gaze and swallowed again. "You don't understand. You don't know Silurian like I do. It's hard to explain."

Alhena cast his gaze around the forested riverbank on either side of them. "It just so happens I have an abundance of time. Enlighten me."

"It's not important."

"Perhaps not, but it certainly seems to be bothering you. If you do not wish to speak of it, I understand." Alhena purposely paused and then added, "It is my experience that talking lightens burdens."

Soul Forge

Rook slapped the railing with his palms and spun to walk away.

Alhena kept his eyes forward.

Rook came back to the railing, grinding his lips together. "Silurian Mintaka was orphaned in his teens—"

"I am familiar with his family history. He was taken under the wing of the benevolent King Peter."

"Yes!" Rook blurted. He calmed his voice. "King Peter took him into his household as a reward for saving Prince Malcolm. Anyway, you may know the history but the tales of Silurian don't touch on the kind of person he used to be."

"I knew him as a polite, chivalrous knight in King Peter's employ. Everyone at Castle Svelte liked him."

Rook shook his head. "He was *so* much more than that. He was bigger than life. Always able to see the good in a person no matter how badly they treated him. He had the ability to remain calm during times of great stress. While everyone else panicked, he patiently figured out ways to overcome whatever dire event was happening. During our years with the Group of Five, Silurian was our rock. Aye, I was the leader, but if truth be told, he *was* our leader. Albeit, a silent one. It was his shining soul that elevated the Group of Five's deeds into legend."

Alhena frowned. "Hmm. I don't think I am understanding."

"That's because that was before his fall."

"His fall?"

"Aye, his descent into darkness. Life changed for him after the Battle of Lugubrius."

Alhena nodded knowingly. "His family."

Rook stared at him, his eyes red and puffy. "His family was the catalyst, there is no doubt, but even then, after losing Melody and discovering his family murdered, he found me in the depths of despair and convinced me that I wanted to live again. Yes! As incredible as that seems, it was Silurian who had kept the faith. Together we continued the search for Melody and an answer to who had been responsible for his family's murder. He needed closure. *We* needed closure.

"We picked up on a faint trail that led us into the Wilds. Foolishly, we followed it. I will spare you the details, but it was during this time that his fortitude, his ever-positive attitude began to crack. I was oblivious at first. Thinking back, I believe I purposely ignored the signs. We're talking about Silurian Mintaka, the Liberator of Zephyr. How could one such as he falter? I turned a blind eye to his struggle, until it was too late. Suffice it to say, Silurian's mind descended into a place of such darkness that I was powerless to pull him back."

Alhena offered him a sympathetic look, respectfully waiting for him to collect himself.

"In the end I was forced to make a decision. Either kill him to save him from himself or just let him go. Obviously, I chose the latter. I couldn't bring myself to end the life of the one person whose beautiful soul had once enriched the lives of everyone who knew him. King, queen, knight, steward, peasant or beggar. It didn't matter. Silurian always took the time to appreciate a person's merit, no matter their station. He would treat a scullery maid or a chamber pot boy with the same respect he offered a nobleman—probably more so. He had that rare ability to see and appreciate each person for who they were, not how the chance of birth had placed them. And yet, in the end, what did *I* do? I abandoned him to his fate."

Alhena's chest tightened hearing Rook's grief. He spoke past the lump in his throat. "That must have been hard."

Rook pursed his lips, tears dripping off his cheeks, his words barely audible, "You have no idea. I left my best friend to die. He would never have done that to me."

The river slipped by, gently gurgling as it broke against *S'gull's* prow. Birds burst from the trees as they passed. Alhena took it all in. The wonders of life. Finally, he put an arm over Rook's hunched shoulders. "That was many years ago, and Silurian is still alive. Perhaps your action saved him in the end."

Rook nodded. He wiped his cheeks on his shoulder and appeared to force a smile. "I wish that were so. Anyway, I'm not sure I can face him again."

There was no way for Alhena to alleviate Rook's guilt. Deserting a friend during their darkest hour was a tough thing to live with. All he could do for the moment was to stand beside Rook and offer whatever comfort his presence provided.

Together, they stared into the murky brown waters ahead of the sloop, lost in their own private thoughts, lurching back and forth with the rhythmic slap of the oars.

Soul Forge

Mourning Lynx to Madrigail Bay

Silurian woke to a rough tongue lapping his left cheek. A soft rumbling accompanied the administration. The stench of stale breath accosted his nostrils. He lay on his back in a congealing pool of blood. A briny scent hung in the air, wafting up from the sea, or emanating from whatever stood over him—he wasn't sure. He winced at his throbbing headache. The lightening sky meant that he'd been unconscious for a while.

The tongue licked at him again. Haunting green eyes stared at him between a set of brown, fur tufted ears. As his senses came back to him, he opened his eyes and jerked his head back.

"About time you came around," Avarick's voice sounded from somewhere close by.

Silurian attempted to scooch away from the large mountain cat purring beside him, its keen eyes following his every move. To his chagrin the lynx scrabbled its massive paws forward, keeping pace. When he stopped, the black striped feline nuzzled its forehead into his side. Dried blood matted the fur on the side of its face.

"It's a good thing it likes you," Avarick said, approaching him. "Every time I try to check on you, the damned thing snarls at me."

On cue, the cat growled.

"See?" Avarick stopped, throwing his hands up. "Between the damned thing alternating between licking itself and you, you haven't missed much." The Enervator grunted. "Anyway, you appeared to be breathing so I left well enough alone."

Silurian's strained look shot from the cat to Avarick and back again. "Um...nice kitty?"

The lynx watched for a moment longer before settling back into Silurian's side, purring softly.

Soul Forge

Silurian was at loss. Where had the bond with the lynx come from? Perhaps the fight with the trolls had garnered its respect. The cat had surely displayed no love for the vermin, but still, this was a wild animal.

He held out his left hand.

The lynx stopped purring, backing its head away from the proffered hand.

Silurian held his hand as still as his nerve permitted.

The lynx tilted its head to one side and sniffed at the air. Slowly it stretched forward and sniffed Silurian's fingertips, before pulling away. It got to its feet and casually pawed toward the horses.

Silurian sat up, watching it saunter away. It was the largest cat he had ever seen—probably weighing more than fifty pounds. He marvelled at how such a relatively small creature had attacked a troll and survived.

The lynx stopped before it passed out of sight beyond the horses, staring at him, before it moved beyond the stand of pines and leapt up to a ledge, four feet off the ground.

It stopped and stared again. Did it expect him to follow it?

He walked over the where it waited, a sudden pain pounding in the back of his head. He clambered onto the shelf and followed the lynx as it padded up the scree-scattered trail that led above their campsite.

Avarick's voice called up to him, "Where are you going?"

Silurian paused long enough to shrug.

Rounding a bend, the ledge terminated at a fissure in the rock face. The trail narrowed to little more than a few inches wide before it disappeared altogether. Without pause, the lynx sprang into the gap and was lost to sight.

Silurian turned to face the cliff's irregular contours, trying to locate suitable hand holds to prevent him from falling to his death. What the heck was he doing following a mountain cat along a perilous ledge?

Reaching his right hand into the crevice, his left foot slipped out from underneath him. With a decisive pull, he slipped into the dark confines of a narrow cleft that disappeared into unfathomable depths, fully expecting to be attacked by the lynx.

The only thing to hit him was a strong wind that howled through the gap, ruffling his hair. It took a little while for his vision to adjust to the entrance shadows and the gloom beyond. He picked out a set of sad eyes. The lynx watched him from just ahead. A faint whine reached him, but he wasn't sure whether it had escaped the large cat or was just the wind blowing across the cliff face.

Slowly, he took a few probing steps. Something lay at the lynx's feet. Three somethings. The lynx let out a sad mewl and everything became clear. His heart caught in his throat as the mother cat groomed the fur of two dead kittens. The third kitten didn't appear to be too much longer for the world.

Silurian knelt down, placing his left hand against the wall to steady himself. Light filtered into the cave allowing him to see the cause of the cubs' deaths. They appeared to have been mauled. Most likely by a troll.

The lynx pushed the nearest kitten toward him with her nose. The kitten's eyes opened and emitted a weak mew.

Staring dumbly at the little ball of bloody fur, he swallowed. The kitten would be better off dead. Troll inflicted wounds usually led to nasty infections.

A lump formed in his throat. This was silly. They were cats. He'd faced much worse than this during his troubled life, and yet, tears blurred his vision.

The sun shone high over the Niad Ocean by the time Silurian carried the two dead kittens down the poor excuse of a ledge. The mother lynx followed him back to the camp carrying her injured kitten by the scruff of its little neck.

Under the watchful eye of their mother, he buried the tiny bodies beneath the stand of pines.

To his credit, the Enervator never once voiced his displeasure at having to wait. He merely shook his head and went about cleaning up the grisly campsite.

While Silurian ministered to the cats, Avarick busied himself hauling the troll carcasses to the edge of the cliff and pushed them over the brink.

Silurian hoped the dead trolls fell into the ocean and not on some poor sap travelling along the desolate shore road, far below. He was skeptical the bodies would make it that far down the cliff face, but at least they weren't polluting the ridge trail.

Avarick grunted as he returned from the edge after pushing the last troll into oblivion. "I thought about burning them but didn't think we had the time. Had I known you were going to play healer to a furball, I probably could have."

As they mounted their horses and set off along the narrow trail, Silurian glanced back at the heart-rending scene of the mother lynx curled around her baby, licking its bloodied fur.

He swallowed. Life was cruel.

Two full days of steady riding along the Ocean Way brought the travel weary men to a crossroads. A trail from Madrigail Bay rose to meet Niad's Course. Only a couple more hours remained in their journey.

A slight drizzle stuck Avarick's hair to his face. "Well, Queen Killer. Let's be done with this."

Silurian tensed, but the Enervator spurred his horse down the steep, rubble strewn path.

Silurian paused a moment longer, wondering for the hundredth time why Avarick had chosen to accompany him? The man had held a high-ranking position within the Zephyr military hierarchy. Perhaps he still did, and this was all a ruse, but it didn't make sense. He watched Avarick's straight back as he trotted his horse down the path.

Somewhere down there, unseen at the bottom of the trail, awaited the man Silurian had once considered his best friend. A man he hadn't seen in a very long time. His lost sister's husband. The man he had practically led to his death.

He almost started along the other fork. It veered east, emptying out along the Madrigail River, a day's ride from the large farming town of The Forke. He was undecided how he felt about meeting up with Rook. He didn't think their relationship could ever be the same. His past actions had seen to that.

Soul Forge

He sighed and heeled his mount into action. Whatever the outcome, his life was about to change immeasurably. For better or worse, only time would tell.

Soul Forge

Wharf's Retreat

Not surprisingly, Pollard saw the distant spires of Madrigail Bay through the misty treetops and light rain before anyone else. The *S'gull* rounded a long, lazy bend in the river, the watercourse meandering through a wide valley as it cut its way through the Spine. The river emptied into a long bay that flowed out to meet the distant shores of the Niad Ocean. The great city of Madrigail Bay lay sprawled along either side of the lengthy inlet.

Emerging from a deep gorge, the *S'gull* sailed up to the massive iron portcullis dominating the river gate bridge. Guards watched their progress from the towers flanking the opening as the sloop's masts slipped easily beneath the raised gate into the heart of the city.

Madrigail Bay's northern shore was littered with odd shaped buildings varying in size—some built of mud and brick, others from wood. The more spectacular edifices rose predominantly upon the hills of the south shore, beyond the grey warehouses lining the wharfs. Large blocks of sculpted granite and polished marble were built into the side the mountain.

In all of Zephyr, the bay city, especially the south shore, was only outshone by Carillon, the kingdom's capital at Castle Svelte.

The *S'gull's* captain piloted the craft north of the estuary and berthed her against a reserved pier, amongst a tangle of busy docks.

The company disembarked onto the weathered dock and pulled their sodden overcoats tight to ward off the drizzle.

Rook said to Alhena, "You probably know this place better than I. Where do we start?"

Alhena cinched his sack to his back. "I was wondering the same thing. Perhaps the baron has news of Silurian's arrival."

Soul Forge

A hunchbacked, ragged man materialized from behind a stack of old crates, his face mostly hidden beneath a cowl. He appeared harmless enough as he hobbled up to Alhena. "May I be of assistance, m'lord?"

Alhena regarded the sodden creature with pity. "Thank you, but I am sure we are fine."

The creature ambled over to stand in front of Rook. He made a movement to grab the sack sitting at Rook's feet.

Rook snatched up the bag before the beggar had a chance. "Be gone. We don't need your help."

The grizzled man glared at Rook, his wart-covered face, bent nose and angular chin gave Rook the shivers.

"Ach, you comed in from the Songsbirth, eh?"

"Mm," Rook grunted, clearly annoyed.

"What did ya say yer name be?"

"I didn't."

Without another word, the beggar nodded and shuffled away, cackling to himself. He disappeared amongst a collection of broken ships pulled up onto the shore.

Rook and Alhena waited for Pollard and Sadyra, before setting off through the warehouse district on their way to the baron's estate which was nestled all the way across the bay.

A few leagues distant, Avarick led Silurian down the last trace of mountain track into the lower southwest end of Madrigail Bay. Rain splattered noisily upon the muddied trail as the horses clopped through the mire. Smog clung to the air above the cityscape. The pungent aroma of burning wood, coal, and dung permeated their nostrils.

Approaching the southern gatehouse, they came up against a twelve-foot-high wall of spiked tree trunks lashed together and were briefly detained from entering the cobblestoned streets until the guards realized Avarick Thwart, the Enervator of Gritian, stood before them.

Walking along the main road toward the docks, Silurian was riddled with mixed emotions. There weren't many people out and about due to the poor weather, but he studied everyone they passed. Upon reaching the main cross street fronting the bay, he shook his head. He couldn't expect to just bump into Rook in a city of this size.

They strolled along the waterfront, the houses and specialty shops giving way to large mercantile warehouses and dockage facilities. Between gaps in the buildings on their left, the piers crawled with activity as crews bustled about like ants, loading and unloading cargo. The aroma from cook fires along the quay had their stomachs rumbling for a decent meal.

Avarick led them to a tavern nestled against the water between two rundown warehouses. They dismounted and tethered their horses beside several others along a rail and walked beneath a weathered sign dripping with rain: *Wharf's Retreat*.

The tavern doors swung inward with an annoying peal, announcing their entrance. All eyes inside the dingy bar fell upon them momentarily before swinging away with disinterest. Acrid smoke hung in the air, overpowered by the waft of strong mead. It was stifling hot inside compared to the chill outside but the biggest attack on their senses came from the raucous din of bawdy patrons. All the tables were full to overflowing. Drunken sailors and dock hands exchanged tales of adventure or bet upon games of chance: cards, rocks, bones, and others Silurian had never seen before.

Huge thugs stood at random places throughout the tavern, muscled arms crossed over beefy chests, observing the patron's comings and goings.

Silurian unconsciously clenched and unclenched his sword hand as they pushed between tables and through rowdy groups gathered around in tight clutches. A few no-nonsense women sat amongst the men, carrying on as badly as, if not worse than, their male counterparts. The only other women present were the scantily clad barmaids, and the even scantier clad women plying their trade.

Avarick smiled when Silurian muttered, "Nice place."

The Enervator approached the massive, oak bar running the length of the back wall. All the bar stools were occupied by at least one person, with more people standing in between. He stopped behind a surly brute hunched over a tankard of ale.

While Avarick attempted to catch the bartender's eye, Silurian scanned the crowd, not relishing the thought of being recognized.

Soul Forge

He cringed when Avarick spun slowly about, garnering the attention of everyone in the tavern. "This here is Silurian Mintaka."

Ensuring everyone knew exactly to whom he referred, Avarick added, "Aye, *the* very man who stared Helleden in the eye and slew him!"

All eyes fell on Silurian.

Silurian felt two inches tall. He wanted to crawl under the battered woodwork of the bar and disappear. He glared at Avarick. What was he thinking?

The group of people sitting and standing near the surly man at the bar eyed Avarick and Silurian skeptically, but when Avarick shrugged out of his rain-soaked cloak, revealing the golden knot of rope upon his left shoulder, whispers of 'Enervator,' and 'Gritian,' and 'assassin' sounded around the bar area. The men in front of Avarick vacated their stool, slipping respectfully around the two newcomers and disappeared into the crowd.

Avarick gestured to the first stool with open palms.

Silurian wanted to leave Wharf's Retreat but he accepted the proffered seat, hoping that by doing so, Avarick might cease making a scene.

On the next stool, a curious patron stared at them. One look from the Enervator sent him scurrying into the crowd.

Avarick addressed the barkeep, who was, without a doubt, one of the largest men in the building. "Two barleys, and two platters of whatever slop you're cooking."

The bald-headed bartender regarded them with hard eyes spaced wide on either side of an oft-broken nose. His gruff words, spoken through thick, bare lips that clenched a well-worked toothpick, surprised Silurian. "And who's to pay this time, Thwart? Last time you came through here I was shut for more'n a week." He crossed forearms bigger than Silurian's thighs over his chest, glaring disdain at Avarick, obviously caring little for his rank.

Avarick offered him a disarming smile. "Come now, Keepy, don't be like that. I know the Chamber looked after you."

Avarick glanced at Silurian. "Keepy here can lift a horse with one arm while he shakes your hand with the other."

Soul Forge

The barkeep glowered. When he stepped forward to lean against the bar, the saloon became deathly still. He stared hard at the arrogant Enervator.

Silurian prepared himself for the worst, but to his credit, Avarick calmly returned the barkeep's stare.

"Ack!" Keepy spat the tattered toothpick to the floor. Producing a dirty rag from a worn apron string around his waist, he wiped his hands. Without another word, he dispensed two bowls of the best tasting stew either man had eaten in quite a while.

The noise in the Wharf's Retreat rose again, but not to its previous level.

Although Silurian was famished and the food delicious, he struggled to eat it—conscious of the gawking people talking behind cupped hands.

Avarick, on the other hand, was well into his second bowl when the faint verse of a song Silurian hadn't heard in years sounded behind them. His neck hairs stood on end. The deep voice wasn't professional, but it held the tune of the ballad well enough.

> "Again, he masters the beasts,
> Wrought from the fires of hell underneath.
> Decade intervals mark his passing,
> sailing forth, wave after wave,
> minion hordes, our death they crave.
> Oh, where have all our heroes gone?"

Silurian nearly choked on a spoonful of broth.

> "Our warriors armed, their swords a-gleamin',
> valiant their efforts, but his might's unseemin'.
> Maimed warriors, home never coming,
> battled afore 'n suffered great harm,
> e'er stronger, n' swifter at arm.
> Oh, where have all our heroes gone?"

Soul Forge

Avarick pushed his bowl aside, wiping his mouth on the cuff of his tunic. He whirled about on his stool, searching for the man behind the voice.

With every line the man sang, the more the people joined in the long-forgotten verse—a song written shortly after the Group of Five had been shattered upon the plains of Lugubrius.

> "Sadly bereft, our legendary arms,
> the Group of Five have faded to yarns.
> Decades pass, nigh upon two.
> We hold faint hope, for what has been,
> he came again and took our Queen.
> Oh, where have all our heroes gone?"

Silurian dropped his spoon into the bowl, its contents sloshing onto the bar. He hadn't heard the verse sung that way before. The previous verses were well-known, sung in the dark, dank places he had frequented during a period in his life best left forgotten. His shoulders tensed. Goosebumps prickled his skin.

Hauntingly, the entire bar joined in.

> "The Altirians are slain, their squaws molested,
> children tortured by beasts detested.
> As Altirians pass into legend,
> Zephyr's peril comes again, we pray, oh please.
> Hordes rain down, borne upon a malignant breeze.
> Oh, where have all our heroes gone?"

Silurian swallowed hard and turned slowly on his stool. All eyes were upon him. He forced himself to look at the people, abashed by the raw emotions reflected there. In some faces he found hope. In others, pain. For the most part, he saw only loathing.

The tavern became deathly still. An uncomfortable silence gripped the room. Just when he thought the tension was about to erupt, the original singer picked up the verse again, this time by himself,

211

Soul Forge

"Zephyr falls upon bloodied knees,
oaken strength breaks on minion breeze.
Oh, what have ye done?
Rumours have surfaced, two still do thrive.
Forth arise the wayward, two of five.
Oh, from where have our heroes come?"

Detested swordsman and bowman deserted,
forsaking the people—magic departed.
Oh, what have ye done?
Zephyr succumbs to the minion horde,
our fate now sealed by the Stygian Lord.
Oh, what have our heroes done?"

The singer's last note dissipated eerily over the crowd.

Silurian swallowed harder.

Avarick's eyes darted about, the earlier smugness no longer prevalent on his face.

The place was a powder keg. Silurian's presence, the spark.

Off to the side where the mysterious singer's voice had originated, a fully armed and armoured man, big as the barkeep but lacking an ounce of fat, parted the crowd. A shallow, two-horned helm sat askew upon his black mane—the helmet more of a decoration than a means of protection. Judging by the size of the bushy bearded hulk, he required little protecting.

The man walked up to Avarick, and before the Enervator knew what happened, he flew from his bar stool into the crowd. The look of surprise on his face as he crashed atop a table full of half drank flagons and wooden bowls of stew was one to be reminisced upon a future date, but at the moment, they needed to escape the ensuing riot.

Avarick took the table over with him, disappearing amongst the angered mob. The golden knot on the Enervator's shoulder no longer held weight with this crowd.

Soul Forge

Wooden chairs scraped across hardwood planks, followed closely by fists crunching faces as the tavern exploded into mayhem. Many patrons didn't know why they fought but were more than happy to oblige.

The hinges of the saloon's swinging doors squealed, announcing the untimely exit of one of Wharf's Retreat's customers—unceremoniously launched into the muddy street by the taverns hired thugs, but there was little the burly men could do to thwart the full-scale melee.

Silurian went for his weapon.

The brute was faster. One huge meat hook clamped Silurian's right wrist before he unsheathed the Sacred Sword Voil from its baldric. Another hand clamped around his throat.

"Hold!" The pandemonium paused at Keepy's urgent plea. He reached over the bar quicker than anyone would believe, and grabbed the brute's wrists, preventing him from tossing Silurian as well. "I'll not have their blood shed in here!"

Avarick's head poked up from behind the upturned table, shrugging off the many hands clutching him.

Silurian gave Keepy a thankful look.

"Finish this outside," Keepy growled.

Silurian did a double take.

Before the large man holding Silurian hoisted him from his stool, however, a flailing body flew out of the crowd and sailed past them, clearing the bar with plenty of room to spare. Barely missing the disheartened barkeep, the human missile slammed into the liquor shelves upon the back wall. Glass shattered and wood splintered as the man smashed more than himself before he fell out of sight beneath the subsequent avalanche of debris.

Keepy winced as the entire place erupted anew. He shook his head, stepped back over the inert man, and muttered, "Every time that damned Enervator comes a-calling."

The saloon doors swung outward, another man flew into the evening air, but before they swung back again, a shadow fell across the waning rays of daylight filtering through the entranceway.

The chaos came to a bizarre halt. All eyes, at least those not beaten shut, fixated upon the beast blocking the only public exit in Wharf's Retreat.

Soul Forge

The biggest man Silurian had ever seen, stood hunched in the doorway, brandishing a colossal weapon. It seemed to be the day of big men.

When the monster of a man cleared the threshold, straightening to his full height, his head brushed the cobwebs decorating the log ceiling.

Sliding quickly through the doors and sidling up on either side of the mountainous brute were a middle-aged man garbed in green suede, bearing an intricately carved bow, and a striking female archer with a polished dark wood bow in hand. As the three newcomers advanced toward the bar, a figure cloaked in black, and bearing a staff, slipped into the tavern behind them.

The man with the bow pointed at Silurian and the behemoth made his way through the gawking throng. Everyone in his path scrambled to get out of his way.

"Unhand him," the newcomer growled at the brute who still clutched Silurian. "Now!"

The two archers notched arrows, scanning the crowd with bows partially drawn. For all the toughness in the bar, not a soul stirred.

The large sailor gave the newcomer a once over, taking measure of the golden plated giant. His eyes narrowed as he took note of the archers warding the crowd.

After what seemed an interminable amount of time to Silurian, the sailor relinquished his iron grip and sneered at the newcomer—his eyes never leaving the gleaming, double broadsword blades suspended in the air between them. He touched the large hilt of his own great sword but thought better of it when his opponent's corded forearms flexed in anticipation. With a glare full of promised malice, the sailor sidestepped around the newcomer, snarling, "I'll see you again."

The newcomer's eyes narrowed. "I look forward to it."

Without a backward glance, the sailor swaggered out of Wharf's Retreat, lumbering between the two archers who stepped sideways to avoid being trampled.

Silurian barely noticed his rescuer—his attention solely upon the male archer. Was it really him? After all these years?

His breathing quickened—the vision before him surreal. One of the few men he had ever respected stood looking back at him. Someone who, up until a few weeks ago, he never thought to see again. The former leader of the Group of Five. His best friend once upon a time. A man he would have willingly died for. Rook Bowman.

A faint smile upturned the corners of his usually somber mouth. He stopped within reaching distance of his friend, unable to do anything but stare—unsure what to do next. He sensed his friend's apprehension. No doubt, well-deserved.

Close by, Avarick freed himself from the men pinning him. He had dispatched two of them when the colossus had entered ahead of Rook. He still gripped the third man. A rivulet of blood leaked from the Enervator's left nostril.

Visible in the way the bar patrons straightened themselves, the crowd had overcome its initial fear of the huge newcomer and his companions.

The newcomer stepped past Avarick on his way back to the exit, his double-bladed weapon held threateningly before him—each blade longer than a short man was tall. He paused beside Avarick, long enough to say under his breath, "If you are with Silurian, I'm thinking we should make our exit."

Avarick nodded once. He pulled the man he held toward him with his left hand and laid him out cold with his right. The man's limp body fell into the brooding throng.

Avarick shook the pain out of his fist as pandemonium exploded throughout the tavern. If the newcomer with the double sword hadn't hurled a few large tables at the enraged mob, Silurian didn't think they would have made it out alive.

As they scrambled up the street, another patron flew from Wharf's Retreat, his crashing body taking one of the swinging doors with him.

A few of the braver, or drunker, men gave Silurian's group chase, but their numbers thinned the farther they pursued. It wasn't long before their numbers dwindled and the chase lost its bravado.

Soul Forge

Resurrection

"**We've** lost them," Avarick said as they rounded a corner between two dilapidated warehouses fronting the shoreline. He peered around the building's corner, down the mist shrouded, cobblestoned street. "They must've given up. I'll sneak back and grab our horses."

Silurian heard Avarick speak, but the words didn't register. He struggled to catch his breath. Not from running away from those intent on killing him, but because of the sight standing next to him. Seeing Rook again in Wharf's Retreat, after all these years, had been a wondrous event, but it was the man clutching the staff that took his breath away. Alhena Sirrus stood alive and well, bent over next to a massive man in a brass cuirass and a female archer clad in wet grey suede. He had never met those two, but he recognized the female's outfit as befitting someone employed by the Songsbirthian Guard.

He didn't know who to look at first. Rook, a friend who had put his life on the line many times to save his own sorry hide, or Alhena, a man he had just come to know, but one who in all respects, had reached through his self-loathing and resurrected his soul.

Sadyra broke the strange tension. "Well, are you guys gonna just stare at each other like a couple of dullards or are you going to hug and get this over with?" She glanced up at Pollard and rolled her eyes.

"Aye," Pollard chimed in, "it's not like we have anything pressing to get to. Like getting a roof over our heads and a meal in our bellies."

Silurian looked between Alhena and Rook, absolutely at a loss. His heart felt like it was going to explode. He gritted his teeth, but there was nothing he could do to stem the tears that broke loose and dripped from his cheeks. He rubbed at his throat, not certain if it was

216

the grasp the brute in Wharf's Retreat had had on him, or the emotions flooding through him, that threatened to cut off his airway.

He had lost much of his will to carry on, especially after losing Bregens and the subsequent way the Chamber had treated him. He was beginning to question the point of it all. Seeing Rook and Alhena fortified his resolve. There were people left in his world that deserved preserving. Helleden hadn't taken everything from him. Now that Rook and Alhena stood in front of him, catching their breath in the darkness and rain, he still had something left to fight for.

Alhena nodded at Rook and stepped toward Silurian with open arms. Rook emulated the wise old messenger. Time seemed to stand still as the three men shared a group hug, unabashedly letting their emotions run wild.

Standing restlessly upon the deserted street, between two disgustingly smelling buildings, Avarick sighed. He absently studied the fingers on his battered hands. The rain picked up, soaking them all through. "Well, I don't know about the rest of you," he said to no one in particular, "but unless I grow gills sometime soon, I'm thinking there's a good chance I might drown."

Soul Forge

Soul Forge

"Olmar," a bandy-legged, giant seaman replied when asked his name. He thumbed his chest proudly. "And that there ship, y' can just make out anchored astern of yer *S'gull*, way out in d' bay, is me own ship. *Gerrymander*, we calls 'er." He scratched his unkempt red-grey beard with one hand and pointed across the bay with his other. "I's told yer needing a," he winked at them conspiratorially, "special transport across the Niad."

The early morning hours had dawned clear and cool, promising a pleasant day in Madrigail Bay—nary a wisp of cloud marred the sky.

Avarick and Pollard had been sent out together, the day after the bar brawl, to roam the streets and inquire about the one known as Thetis. They had scoured the southern shore without success, and now walked near the piers along the northern shoreline. Other than the curious stares they received, nothing particularly exciting had happened during their trek until now.

Avarick sized up the giant sailor, comparing him to his newfound friend, Pollard, and not discreetly so. Just when Avarick thought he'd never meet another man taller than his companion, along comes this unusual individual. He wondered whether Olmar's bowed legs were a result of his ample stomach.

Olmar stood with slumped shoulders, probably due to his massive girth. Were he to stand straight, he would certainly eclipse Pollard in height.

Avarick mused about how big people were in the bay area. No wonder they sailed in such large boats.

Beside him, Pollard straightened his posture, giving Olmar a once over, clearly put out by the man's presence.

Soul Forge

Avarick's brow came together at the man's words, however, annoyed at the presumption. "That's news only we should be knowing. Who told you this...uh, captain?"

Olmar laughed. "Cap'n? Nay, not I. I steers the ol' gal, is all." He scratched his beard. "Ain't exactly sure who she were that told me, t' be honest wit' ya..."

"She?"

"Aye, most 'suredly." He raised his eyebrows twice in quick succession. "Some perty waif, an' that's sure. Come a-callin' our ship last night, she did. Said me *Gerrymander's* the only vessel suitin' yer needs." His chest puffed out.

Pollard gave Avarick a, 'what the heck is this crazy man talking about?' look.

Avarick shrugged. Though irked at Olmar's knowledge of their quest, Avarick was enjoying the undeclared rivalry Pollard exhibited toward the tall sailor.

Pollard straightened his spine and pulled his shoulders back, stretching his neck higher.

Avarick half expected to see him rise to his toes. "This lady. She spoke with you? Out there? She told you we were looking for a sea going vessel, did she?"

Olmar looked at him as if he were daft. He returned Avarick's question with a blank face, blinking repeatedly. "I 'as just be tellin' ya that, ain't I?"

"She didn't happen to have auburn hair and carry a bow, did she?"

Olmar laughed, "Nay. T'was blonder than yon snow-capped peak."

Avarick glanced at Pollard. Blowing out a breath, he said, "Okay. Sure. We'll keep that in mind...Elmer?"

Pollard snickered.

"Olmar's me name." He tipped his battered leather, sailor's cap. "I shall inform me cap'n we've 'ad words. We await yer bidding." With that, the bowlegged mountain waddled away.

Pollard raised his heavy eyebrows at Avarick as the strange man shuffled off. It took a long while before the busy wharf side crowd swallowed his bulk.

"Right," Avarick drawled. "Come on then, not so big guy, I'm thinking I'm parched."

Soul Forge

Pollard glared at his receding backside.

The sun rose above the break between the mountains leading into the Madrigail valley. Avarick and Pollard walked along the docks with renewed purpose—Wharf's Retreat visible in the distance.

When Pollard's frame dimmed the light in the tavern, the dreary eyed barkeep spun around angrily and stormed over to head them off. "I'll no have the likes of you in here again, wrecking me place and busting up me clientele!"

Avarick pushed past Pollard.

A large vein on Keepy's temple pulsed profusely. "Oh no. Oh no, no! Not you again, Thwart." He stopped and turned to a skinny teenaged boy sweeping up debris in the poorly lit room. "Boy, fetch the Watch."

The dirty faced boy gave him a dumb stare.

"Now!"

The boy's eyes grew twice their size. His worn broom fell with a clatter as he hurried through the remaining swinging door.

Avarick threw his hands up. "Easy, Keepy." Surveying the damage from the previous day, he tried to mollify the angry proprietor, "You know the Chamber always looks after you."

The large man stepped toward the Enervator, bumping him back a step and pointing a thick arm toward the door. "Out!" He grabbed Avarick by the shoulder and turned him about. "I don't care a horse shit about the Chamber. I want you out, and I want you out now!"

Pollard stepped between the two, the large barkeep visibly surprised by how easily he was knocked aside by the giant man. He wasn't used to being pushed around.

Pollard gave Keepy a no-nonsense look. "We're in need of a place to organize our business, and your fine establishment here," he said, beholding the gutted venue, "is the ideal location for us to accomplish this."

"Over my—"

"Hear me out, Mr....?"

Soul Forge

Keepy just glared.

"Keepy, then. All we require from you, *Keepy*, is privacy, food, and drink, and a place to stay."

Avarick stepped to the side, grinning smugly at the bartender.

Keepy tried to interject but Pollard raised his voice.

"For which, of course, you shall be handsomely compensated."

"I don't want your money."

"Ah, ah, ah." Pollard wagged a warning finger at him. "You shall assist us nonetheless, by the baron's decree." Pollard produced a thin scroll from a pouch attached to the broad leather belt cinched about his waist. He handed it to the speechless barkeep.

Keepy stared at the embossed, white wax seal of the baron of Madrigail Bay. He turned the scroll around in his thick fingers before inhaling deeply and shattering the seal. Unraveling the writ, his face reddened further. He glared at Pollard, mad enough to spit. He shook his head and stomped away in disgust.

Pollard gave the grinning Enervator a stern look and called after Keepy, "Let us know where to start cleaning up."

Keepy took a few more steps before stopping at the end of the bar.

The smirk slid from Avarick's face.

Keepy turned to face them.

"While we wait, we will clean and repair the damage."

Avarick's face reddened.

Keepy strolled behind the bar, a smug grin on his face.

Wharf's Retreat remained closed to the public while Pollard and his entourage cleared, cleaned, repaired, and replaced much of the bar furniture and the structure itself. When they had finished, the bar was a brighter and cheerier place than it had been before the brawl.

Keepy stood with his back to the newly hung, swinging doors with arms crossed, surveying his establishment with pride. He had lost two days' business, but he could hardly complain. The free restorations were mostly completed by the adept giant and his female cohort,

Soul Forge

Sadyra, along with the assistance of Avarick Thwart, the disgruntled Enervator of Gritian.

Alhena holed himself up during the daylight hours in the baron's residence going over the ancient tomes that Baron Lychman kept squirreled away in his private library. He returned each day to Wharf's retreat to eat supper and to the rooms above the saloon to sleep.

With more than a little convincing, Avarick and Pollard, with the financial backing of Baron Lychman, had persuaded Keepy to give them exclusive use of the several small guest rooms above the tavern for as long as they remained in Madrigail Bay. The baron had offered them a place at his manor, but they wanted to remain available in case Saros' disciple showed up during the night.

Rook and Silurian spent the days wandering the streets and alleyways of Madrigail Bay searching for the one called Thetis. They visited every bar and mercantile in the bay area, questioning the locals as to whether anyone had inquired about them, and left instructions that they could be found at Wharf's Retreat. So far, nobody had heard of Thetis.

More importantly, Rook and Silurian spent the time catching up on each other's lives. They should have enjoyed their time together more than they did, but the dark years searching for Melody, and those responsible for the slaughter of Silurian's family, had placed a serious damper on their relationship.

Wandering about Madrigail Bay, uncertain of where their course lay, did little to alleviate their unspoken animosity.

They were discussing whether Thetis may have become lost, or worse, when someone called out from a dark alleyway.

Silurian stopped to peer into the shadows.

A haggard old woman sat amongst a pile of rubbish, her filthy hands palm up. Another figure, half buried in the refuse, lay unmoving behind an old wooden crate.

"Pleas-s-s-e good s-s-sir. Anything to help an old lady make it through another day?" She lisped with her one good tooth.

Rook followed Silurian's gaze, a look of revulsion on his face. The alley reeked of vomit, urine and other human waste. He backed away a step. "Come on Sil, let's go."

Disgusted as he was, Silurian couldn't bring himself to leave. He knew what it was like to starve. He and Melody were once beggars themselves, eking out an existence in a town far seedier than Madrigail Bay. He knew about despair. About how cruel it was to watch the more affluent strut around with full bellies and a hearth to go home to, while he had nothing.

He opened the money pouch lashed to his belt and emptied its meagre contents into his palm.

He could tell Rook didn't want anything to do with it. "Come on. Surely, she needs the coin more than us. What happened to the caring Rook Bowman of days gone by?"

Rolling his eyes, Rook withdrew a few coins given him by the Songsbirthian council and handed it to him.

Silurian took a deep breath and held it. He stepped into the alleyway and knelt low enough to place the coins into the scabbed hands of the one-toothed hag. Forcing a smile for her benefit, he straightened up and began to walk away.

Clutching the coins to her bosom, the hag gave him a lopsided grin and cackled, "One good turn, son, begets another. Get yourself to the Retreat. Grans will see to you."

Silurian had no idea what she was on about. He turned to peer back into the gloom. Goosebumps prickled his skin. The motionless figure still lay amongst the garbage. Of the hag, there was no sign.

That afternoon, with the newly constructed Wharf's Retreat bustling with business, Silurian and Rook made their way to the back corner of the murky saloon where Sadyra, Avarick, Alhena, and Pollard settled into their second tankard of mead.

Pollard stood long enough to allow them access to the back bench—ensuring that he and Avarick were the first line of defense should trouble arise.

They no sooner sat down when trouble arose.

An enchanting woman strutted through the newly hung saloon doors. The noise level in the bar dropped considerably, all eyes followed the woman as she sauntered toward the freshly polished bar.

Soul Forge

The men gathered about the nearby tables whistled and offered her a litany of crude remarks.

To her credit, she merely smiled at those nearest her, obviously used to such treatment.

Perhaps the presence of Keepy's thugs held the hounds at bay. Perhaps it was the men's fear of offending the blonde-haired lady and turning her attention away from them, but no one made a move to slow her advance.

She gazed into Keepy's softening eyes and with the twitch of a delicate finger, motioned for him to bend his ear close.

Pollard, like every other warm-blooded male in the bar, raised his eyebrows as the stunning lady put her full lips close to Keepy's ear.

Pollard was shocked when the smile on Keepy's face became a scowl. Keepy searched the crowd and pointed directly at Avarick, clearly not pleased at directing her attention their way. His frown softened as she kissed his cheek before she bounced back into the crowd.

Pollard studied her approach with more than curiosity. They hadn't ordered entertainment. He admired how well her rose coloured, soft skinned shirt and leggings clung to her womanly attributes. He raised a tankard of ale to his lips, taking a deep swallow. He nearly choked on it when a man stood up and approached her from another table.

The mysterious woman sauntered through the crowd, ignoring the leers and jeers she received, but as the sailor jumped in front of her and went to grab her, she physically threw him out of her path.

The man, bigger than either Silurian or Rook, hit the table nearest him hard. The patrons gathered around the table hoisted their drinking vessels high into the air to avoid them being spilled.

The entire tavern howled.

Spurned, the sailor angrily caught himself on the table's edge. His lust filled eyes became slits. He pulled himself upright, and lurched after her, shouting incoherently and grabbing at her shoulder before Keepy's nearest thug had time to react.

The woman appeared oblivious to the threat. His eyes widened when she spun around, grasped him by the shoulders, and slammed her knee into his crotch.

Everyone in Wharf's Retreat roared.

Soul Forge

The incredulous man bent over in pain only long enough for the woman to lay him out cold with a vicious downward elbow to the back of the neck. If he wasn't unconscious before he fell, his head bouncing off the hardwood floor made sure of it.

Anyone else with similar ideas returned their eyes to their ale.

Stopping in front of the group from Songsbirth, the woman assessed everyone at the table. She raised her eyebrows briefly at Sadyra, before demanding in a honey sweet voice, "Who among you claims to be the Lord of the Innerworld?"

All eyes turned to Rook.

Rook glanced at Silurian, and then at Pollard. With a shrug he said, "That would be me. Who wants to know?"

She scrutinized Rook, her eyes examining his bow and quiver sitting next to him. Ignoring his question, she said, "Aye. Saros has spoken of you."

Her eyes lingered a moment longer on Rook's bow before Pollard reiterated Rook's question, "You heard the man. Who're you?"

Her piercing eyes narrowed. "Depends on who's asking?"

"Pollard Banebridge, third in command of the Songsbirthian Guard, entrusted with the protection of Sir Rook Bowman," he declared proudly.

She appeared weaponless. She certainly couldn't hide much within her tightly fitting attire. Her legs disappeared into knee-high, black leather boots. If she carried a blade, it would be hidden there.

He gripped the huge two-handed hilt of his double-bladed broadsword, each blade sheathed within a separate scabbard.

The movement wasn't lost on the woman.

He rose to his full eight-foot three height.

Everyone tensed.

Instead of flinching, the woman stepped back, allowing herself to observe him without straining her neck.

"That's some blade you carry. I bet few men around here are strong enough to lift it, let alone wield it."

Pollard watched her closely. She'd have to go through him to reach the table.

Alhena spoke up, "May I ask, young Miss, why you seek the Lord of the Innerworld? He obviously has no idea whom you are."

"I'm thinking he knows more than he lets on," she crossed her arms beneath her small breasts.

Everyone turned back on Rook.

Rook ignored them. "How do you know Saros?"

"I'm here at his request." She paused to let that wash over the group. "And Silurian Mintaka? It's believed he's also on his way. Has he arrived?"

She scanned each face, disregarding Sadyra and Alhena. Her gaze fell on Avarick. "You must be the one they call, Helleden's Bane?"

Avarick glared. "Pfft. Hardly."

Her eyes followed Avarick's outstretched finger and met Silurian's stare. Disappointment reflected in her eyes, but a furtive smile creased her face, if only for a moment. "I thought you'd be more...uh...formidable."

Avarick rose, his chair scraping the floorboards. "State your business, woman, and be gone."

Rook squeezed out of his own seat and wiggled past Pollard.

Pollard attempted to block his progress.

"It's okay, big guy."

Pollard wasn't happy. She had a clear shot at the bowman should she prove false.

"Thetis, I presume," Rook said matter-of-factly.

She offered the table a cunning smile. Before them stood Saros' disciple. The person sent to assist Rook and Silurian on their journey. It took Pollard a moment to comprehend the fact that all this time it was a woman they had been searching for.

They remained in Wharf's Retreat for the remainder of the day, even allowing Thetis to sit, albeit with Pollard on one side of her and Avarick on the other.

The group shared their separate accounts of the journeys that had brought them to this point.

When it was her turn, Thetis provided vague details about where she came from and how she arrived in the bay area. She had been travelling the Wilds, east of the Innerworld, when Saros issued an urgent summons for her to attend Madrigail Bay in search of the last two members of the Group of Five.

Many tankards of ale later did little to loosen her tongue, but when her tone adopted a more serious timbre, the group gave her their undivided attention.

"We cannot afford delay. With Saros' demise, it may already be too late to save Zephyr. The longer we tarry, the more entrenched the Stygian Lord's army becomes. I have it on good authority that King Malcolm's forces are withdrawing back to Castle Svelte to make their final stand. It's only a matter of time before Helleden unleashes another firestorm upon the land."

Stygian Lord? Stygian Lord? Silurian mulled over the name. Where had he heard it before? She obviously referred to Helleden Misenthorpe.

Alhena's voice broke through his thoughts. "Seafarer claimed you are not powerful enough to stand before Helleden."

Thetis shook her head, "No, I am not. Thus, we need Mintaka and Bowman to step up."

"I fail to see how Rook and Silurian can stand against Helleden without enchanted weapons. If, as you claim, the king's forces are withdrawing, they will have little chance to get close to the sorcerer. If you are indeed a disciple of Saros, you must be more powerful than the entire group seated here."

Avarick and Pollard shot the old man a dirty look.

"Aye, you speak wisely, Alhena. I possess a power none of you comprehend, but it isn't what's required against the Stygian Lord."

Everyone spoke at once.

She offered an upraised hand. "Only by redeeming the lost magic the Group of Five once possessed shall we have any hope of defeating him."

"Silurian slew him years ago, or so we thought. Queen Quarrnaine banished him again, four years ago," Rook cut in emphatically. "In the end, even Saros wasn't strong enough to stop him." His voice dropped off, "Our power came from Saros, and now he's dead."

Thetis nodded. "Saros' magic proved insufficient to repel the Stygian Lord this time..." She paused, likely out of respect to the fallen lord.

Soul Forge

"Before he died, he entrusted me with the location of the source of his power."

Everyone started muttering again, but when Thetis spoke, they became quiet. "Years ago, Saros deemed five people capable of wielding this power safely. Alas, three are long dead, leaving..." She indicated Rook and Silurian with a nod.

"I must warn you. Saros said the endeavour he proposes may actually serve to expedite your demise."

Pollard and Avarick stiffened.

"Saros instructed me to deliver you across the breadth of the Niad Ocean to a portal...Well, not really across, but, um, under..."

Seafarer said something similar at the Undying Mountain Pools, but the relevance had been lost upon Silurian.

"...unto the Under Realm."

Silurian stared at her like her hair was on fire as the reality of her suggested destination registered. He had thought Seafarer had been exaggerating about where they needed to travel to. Everyone knew the Under Realm only existed in fables and religious idiom. It was a term used to instil fear in small children, nothing more. One didn't travel to a myth.

"Oh, it gets better, I assure you. *If* we survive the transition," she breathed deeply, "and make landfall in the Under Realm, we are to head straight for," she paused, drawing her captive audience in even further, "Soul Forge."

Soul Forge

Gerrymander

Midnight found the strange group from Wharf's Retreat standing on the end of a rickety jetty. The moon glinted off the bay as it drifted amongst wispy blotches of cloud. Gentle waves slapped against the pier supports beneath them, every so often spraying their legs through gaps in the decking. A thick mist settled across the entire bay area, bringing with it a permeating dampness. Driftwood bobbed about within patches of flotsam, drifting first one way and then back again, inexorably making its way toward the river gate bridge to join the endless eddies that milled about the mouth of the mighty Madrigail River. Hawsers from nearby vessels creaked in eternal protest, the noise more profound now that the majority of the port had retired for the night.

Six burlap sacks stuffed with supplies lay slumped before the group. To a person, they fretted over the destination of their upcoming voyage. Soul Forge was a place visited in nightmares—a mystical realm found in legends or ancient tomes. No one had believed it to be an actual place.

Avarick and Pollard's bizarre encounter with the bandy-legged character had proven prophetic as they huddled in the chill night air awaiting the arrival of a skiff to ferry them to the tall ship anchored in the deeper waters of the harbour—the *Gerrymander*.

The group fell silent at the sound of oars breaking water. Shortly, a large rowboat materialized out of the mist. A solitary figure sat amidships, far too big for the craft, pulling for all he was worth.

The sketchy boat bumped against a wooden ladder leading up to the pier deck. The same man who had contacted Avarick and Pollard a few days ago beamed up at them, his face dripping with sweat.

Soul Forge

"Ahoy, lads 'n lassies." Olmar tipped his ragged sailor's cap. "Hand yer stuff t' ol' Olmar and we shall be on our way, right?"

Avarick creased his brow, giving Pollard a wry smile. There was barely enough room in the boat for Olmar's bulk. There had to be another boat coming. He squinted into the night, only to be greeted by the mist.

Pollard shrugged and lowered the two biggest sacks to the helmsman of the *Gerrymander*.

Olmar took each bag in turn with little effort and placed them into the stern of his wide craft.

As the last of the baggage was stowed, Avarick craned his neck over the edge of the pier. "We'll wait 'til you get back."

Olmar laughed, "Nay, man, yer to accompany me now. Tide's a-pullin'. Make haste, unless yer hankerin' t' swim?"

Everybody squeezed themselves precariously within the barely afloat vessel. Sadyra, Avarick and Pollard sat high atop the pile of burlap sacks trying their best not to fall off the back of the boat.

Olmar lent his considerable back to the oars to propel the craft into the fog, his great bulk rubbing against those stuffed around him.

After what seemed an interminable amount of time in the overloaded skiff, the cloud cover broke. Moonlight cut through the mist before them, illuminating the hulk of a tall ship.

"Ahoy!" Olmar called into the night, rowing the craft alongside *Gerrymander's* bulk.

Answering cries reached them from the deck of the ocean-going vessel. A thick rope ladder dropped over the port rail and splashed into the bay.

The ship, bedecked with three tall masts and a sizable aftermast, rested with her sailcloth wrapped in thick furls upon great, upper and lower yard arms. The intricate rigging bustled with rough men and tough women scurrying about the taut shrouds like spiders on a web. Large iron block and tackle sets creaked under the strain as the great sheets began to unfurl. Wooden shuttles scooted about the myriad of lines, criss-crossing between spars, sheets, yard arms, and back again. *Gerrymander* prepared to set sail.

Gaining the lantern-lit deck, the small company took in the intricacies and scope of the vessel.

Soul Forge

Their attention was drawn aft, to a well-dressed man descending a wide staircase that led down from the quarter deck. Clad in a silken red blouse, cinched tight at the wrists, and piped with golden thread, the man's cream-coloured doublons snapped about his thighs in the cool wind. It was obvious this was the captain of the fine vessel beneath their feet. A pair of gangly sailors followed in the captain's wake.

Stopping before the assembled group, the captain introduced himself, "Welcome aboard *Gerrymander*. I'm Captain Thorr Sandborne." His square cut, tanned visage, weathered about the eyes, measured each and every person standing before him. The wind ruffled his well kempt, black hair, greying about the temples. "I understand we are to undertake a perilous journey to regions unknown. I've been told it'll prove to be a long journey so I suggest that from this point forward we dispense with formality. These fine men, Ithnan and Ithaman," he gestured to the lanky, young men flanking him, "shall see you below decks and get you settled. The hour is early, but by the time the sun crests the mountains, I aim to be well underway."

The captain dipped his chin, spun on well-polished boots, and walked smartly away, disappearing up the stairs.

Gaining the quarterdeck, Silurian squinted into the rising sun where the mountainous Zephyr coastline should have been. Instead, all he saw was water stretching to every horizon. *Gerrymander* was indeed as fast as the helmsman had boasted.

The mighty aftsail fluttered and snapped, straining at the spar above the afterdeck as it harnessed the prevailing northwest wind.

Silurian considered his steps in an effort to remain balanced as the ship bobbed momentarily atop a tall swell before falling smoothly into a deep trench in the heavy seas. Every so often, remnants of ocean spray drifted far enough back to make itself felt. Goosebumps riddled his uncovered skin—it was much cooler above deck.

A short, steep flight of open faced wooden steps brought him onto the smaller afterdeck, the highest, rearmost deck on the ship. The smiling visage of bandy-legged Olmar greeted him. Standing behind a

Soul Forge

spoked wheel, his massive hands gently urged the oak helm to and fro, piloting *Gerrymander* across the swells. He wondered whether Olmar ever slept.

Standing beside Olmar, behind a dark wood map table, the captain engaged Pollard and Avarick in an animated conversation.

"Ah, Sire Mintaka, welcome," Captain Thorr offered. "We were just discussing our destination. Or, more specifically, our roles when we get there."

Silurian nodded in greeting.

Gerrymander crested a higher than usual wave and hurtled into its adjoining trough. All present braced themselves for the inevitable jolt when the bow cut into the next riser—all except Olmar, whose peculiar stance made him seem part of the ship. Lurching into the next wave, a wall of spray shot over the rails.

Olmar's cheery voice squeaked above the noise of the billowing sails, "A touch of nausea, Sire?" He laughed.

Silurian nodded slightly and addressed the captain. "I assume Thetis has consulted with you?"

"Aye, she has. We travel slightly northwest. She went over the charts with Olmar last night before heaving anchor."

"And you know of this, uh, portal?"

"Never heard of it. Our charts take us hundreds of leagues west of Zephyr. What's after that, only the sea gods know."

Silurian mulled that over. "Has Thetis been there, herself?"

"She didn't say. She assured me she can guide us to the transition area, whatever that means."

"Doesn't that concern you? Not knowing where you're going? Not knowing what your ship might face?"

"Aye, bothers the salt outta me, but what am I to do? You're unusual cargo. I daren't go against the edicts of the Chamber."

Silurian thought that ironic. That was exactly how he came to be on board. *Defying* the Chamber. Alhena had convinced Baron Lychman that the Chamber of the Wise had condoned their expedition and the baron had issued an edict to that effect.

Two figures appeared above deck, aft of the mainmast. One sported a green tunic, the other a mane of blonde hair. They initially started aft,

Soul Forge

but turned and made their way toward the bow, disappearing beyond the mess hall that sat amidships between the central masts.

Silurian felt a twinge of jealously. He and Rook had been together for almost a week now, but it was apparent to both of them that a large rift still separated them. Too many things were left unsaid about the years following the Battle of Lugubrius. It shocked him to realize how raw the wounds remained. Perhaps his demons were determined to follow him to his grave. If he didn't reconcile the gulf between himself and Rook, that prospect might not be too far off.

After three days of steady sailing, the winds diminished to nary a breeze. The great sheets hung listless upon their yardarms—the nauseating swells of the heavy seas an unpleasant memory to those not used to sailing.

With the ship becalmed, Pollard, Avarick, Rook and Silurian were called upon to take shifts manning the oars alongside the crew. The captain refrained from asking Alhena or the women of the quest to help propel the ship, but the messenger and Sadyra did their part. Thetis did not.

Gerrymander boasted twenty oars, properly manned by two oarsmen each. It was unusual for such a big ship to contain oar banks, but *Gerrymander* had been uniquely constructed to accommodate the oar deck, providing her with added agility should she need it.

Though not all the oar banks were utilized, experienced rowers took up positions fore and aft, while Silurian and Alhena manned one of the middle banks on the port side of the ship.

Across a wide, dingy aisle, Pollard and Avarick sat together, the top of Pollard's head threatening to scrape the exposed timber ceiling in the close confines. Sadyra pulled alongside a weathered sailor none of them had met before. Of Rook, there was no sign.

They were well into their rotation when Rook ventured into the long rowing chamber to replace Sadyra's partner, relieving the man to perform some other pressing duty.

"Welcome," Sadyra offered.

Soul Forge

Rook struggled to match the cadence set by the coxswain sitting at the head of the oar chamber. "Sadyra." He took in the other members of the quest. "I appear to be a wee bit late."

Nobody said anything. They were busy sweating, doing their best to maintain the monotonous sweep of their long oars; each rower mindlessly concentrating on the coxswain's droning voice. Pull. Push down. Push forward. Lift. Pull. Over and over as the members of the quest tried to ignore the blisters forming on their palms.

Rook's voice broke through their drudgery, "She's quite a woman, that Thetis. I can't believe how much she has taught me about the wider world. Especially about the Wilds."

Nobody paid him any attention.

"The Chamber would do well to sit down with her when we return. With the Forbidden Swamp gone, the creatures from the Wilds will surely find their way to Zephyr."

A prickly anxiety niggled at Silurian. Memories assaulted him from his dark years. He was thankful when Rook stopped talking about the Wilds.

"Aye, quite a woman indeed," Rook directed his voice at Silurian. "Reminds me of Melody."

Silurian went cold.

"Her looks, her personality, even her sense of humour. She's, different than most women…"

Why don't you just shut up, Silurian caught himself thinking, and then felt angry with himself.

"…loves to travel to different realms, experience diverse cultures. Does she not remind you of your sister, Sil? I mean, *really* remind you?"

Silurian grunted.

"I knew it! If I didn't know better, I'd swear they were sisters. It's uncanny how similar she is." His exuberant voice dropped into melancholy, "By the gods, I miss her so."

Silurian sighed.

234

Soul Forge

Alhena noted Silurian's miserable expression. It didn't take much for the old messenger to read between the lines. He was pretty sure Silurian didn't think too highly of this Thetis woman. He hardly knew her, but through no fault of her own, she stood between Silurian and Rook.

Pulling back on the end of the oar, and pushing down and outward again, Alhena recalled the look of wonder on Silurian's face when he had first learned he might be reunited with his long-lost friend. The same day Alhena had first noticed a spark of life return to Silurian's eyes. The meeting with Seafarer had breathed life into Silurian and put a skip in his beleaguered step. The mention of Rook had quite simply given Silurian the will to live again.

Even though Rook was congenial with his old friend, there was an obvious, underlying issue paralyzing their relationship. Whatever had transpired between them refused to allow them to move on.

As the days wore on, Rook spent more and more time with Thetis. He no longer shared a berth with Silurian at night—preferring to retire in Thetis' cabin at the end of the day.

With a sigh, Alhena wiped the sweat from the tip of his nose and pulled on his oar.

Long days stretched into a dreary week. The relationship between Silurian and Rook deteriorated to an occasional passing hello as they went their separate ways. Rook with Thetis constantly at his ear. Silurian in the company of whomever happened to be around at the time.

Concerned about their relationship, but even more mindful of Seafarer's insistence that they needed to act together if they wished to complete their quest, Alhena took Rook aside in an empty hallway, near the galley.

"Can you not see how your apparent lack of interest affects him?"

Rook shrugged.

"Really? Silurian means that little to you? I find that hard to believe."

Soul Forge

Rook sighed. "Look. I don't know what he told you, but I suspect, knowing him, it's very little."

"About what?"

"Aye, I didn't think so. You don't know the whole story. Silurian and I have our differences."

Alhena leaned on his staff. "That much is obvious, but it does not make sense. You have already touched on the troubles you two had, but that was twenty years ago. What could possibly be so bad that time has not been able to mend it?"

Rook raised his eyebrows. He blew out a long breath and offered Alhena a fake smile. "I don't wish to discuss it. Let's just say we had a fundamental disagreement of irreconcilable proportions."

"A fundamental disagreement of—what?" Alhena shook his head. "Whatever happened, you need to realize that to confront Helleden and survive, you must be united. If you two are not operating like you did while part of the Group of Five, I fear our journey to whatever this Soul Forge is will be for naught."

Rook lowered his gaze. "You don't understand."

"Oh, I understand alright. I understand that if you cannot see past whatever bad feelings you harbour for each other, this quest is meaningless. You, of all people, should appreciate what you are up against."

Rook looked Alhena in the eyes, his own red and watery. "Don't you think I know that? The firestorm Helleden unleashed on the Innerworld is the last thing I see before I go to sleep at night." He looked away. "It's the last thing I see before I wake up again."

A galley cook entered the passageway and made his way past them. An awkward silence settled in.

When the cook disappeared through the door at the end of the hall, Alhena placed a hand on Rook's shoulder. "You do not need to explain it to me, or to anyone else for that matter. Whatever the cause of this disparity, it is between you two. No one has a right to demand an explanation. *But,* if we are to have *any* hope of saving the realm, it is time to put these differences aside. I also lived through a firestorm. I know the damage Helleden is capable of. I beseech you, Rook Bowman, see past your personal conflict. If you don't, Zephyr is lost."

Soul Forge

Rook remained quiet. Another cook entered the passageway. When she had gone, Rook wiped his eyes on his sleeve and offered Alhena a weak smile. "Okay. You're right, my wise friend. I will do what I can." He swallowed and his voice turned bitter, "I only hope he doesn't kill us all before we get the chance to make a difference." He pushed past Alhena and left the passageway.

Alhena frowned at his receding back. *Kill us all?*

The next few days aboard the *Gerrymander* found Rook spending most of his waking hours in Silurian's company, whether rowing together or simply standing about the helm, discussing what little they knew to expect if they ever reached the Under Realm.

The effect on Silurian wasn't lost on Alhena. He saw it in Silurian's facial mannerism—melancholy no longer Silurian's primary look.

Unfortunately, it became apparent that Rook also wanted to spend time with Thetis. The blonde-haired woman confronted him more than once, pulling him aside and engaging him in heated discussions.

Rook's first step back to Thetis was his last toward Silurian.

The following morning, Silurian waited patiently in the galley for Rook. When noon hour came, he ate his midday meal alone. He spent the afternoon below decks in the sweeps galley, sweating alongside the other quest members. All except Rook and Thetis. By the time the late day meal sat untouched before him, Silurian was halfway into a bottle of spirits.

When not manning the oars, those aboard *Gerrymander* attempted to keep busy fishing and sparring. Many of the fiercer sailors took particular joy locking swords with Pollard, trying to defend his massive, two-bladed weapon. They teamed up in groups of two or three just to see how long they could last against the behemoth. They also looked forward to seeing a fellow crewman, or quest member, get pummeled by the big man. The only ones to hold their own against Pollard were Avarick, Silurian, and Olmar with his mighty warhammer, but most on board whispered that Pollard probably took it easy on Silurian.

Soul Forge

The crew enjoyed competing with Avarick and Sadyra as the two attempted to outshoot each other. Avarick's deadly aim with his crossbow was a sight to behold, while Sadyra, who notably shot left-handed, was equally proficient with her bow. On the days she bested the Enervator, Pollard was sure to let him know about it. Only once had Rook joined in the competition. Avarick and Sadyra, as skilful as they were, were no match for the former leader of the Group of Five once he got his aim back.

Silurian, for his part, spent the rest of his free time above deck, learning from grizzled tars how to man the rigging—should a breeze ever decide to grace them again. He spent hours crossing swords with Olmar, Avarick and Pollard, appreciating the challenge these seasoned fighters gave him, going to bed every night with sore muscles and fresh bruises. He was finally beginning to feel like his old self again.

A beefy female sailor, Tara, enjoyed watching the sword play, and locked blades with the best of them. She was no match for Silurian, or Avarick, or indeed the mighty Pollard, but her skills proved far superior to most of the warriors Silurian had engaged with over the years.

Tara and Silurian started to spend a lot of time together. He taught her some of the finer ways to defend herself with dagger and sword, while she instructed him in the nuances of scrambling about the shrouds, adjusting the block and tackle in such a way that *Gerrymander*, when under full sail, achieved her best speed.

Alhena stood off to the side, grimly watching Silurian and Rook drift further apart. The success of their mission, and their very lives, depended on the two men working together. Whatever enchantment Saros' disciple had on Rook, Alhena was powerless to break its hold. A sense of foreboding filled him.

When the day came that the sheets filled with wind, instead of being a joyful event, it instilled the quest with the dread of being pushed inexorably toward an unknown fate.

Soul Forge

Captain Thorr topped the steps to the afterdeck after overseeing the raising of *Gerrymander's* great sails. The warship leapt gazelle-like over the increasing swells, taking everyone onboard closer to wherever this mysterious portal awaited.

Approaching the weathered leather map pinned to the chart table, the captain nodded to Olmar at the wheel, and Alhena who spent most of his time hanging out with the helmsman.

Off to the right side of the featureless section of map sat a polished, triangular, white marble marker showing *Gerrymander's* position. They sailed through unchartered waters, somewhere in the middle of the vast Niad Ocean. According to their incomplete map, there wasn't a sign of land anywhere.

"I've never sailed this far west before," the captain commented out of hand. "In fact, I don't know anyone who has sailed this far and been heard from again. According to the charts, there's nothing to sail to."

Alhena adjusted his grip on his staff. "Are we on the right course?"

"Aye, according to Thetis we are. Ask me not where she takes us, but she's confident we sail true. She claims the portal is near."

"Are Sire Mintaka and Sire Bowman aware of this?"

The captain shrugged. "I would imagine Rook is, surely. Silurian? Who knows?"

"We must gather the quest. Thetis needs to explain what we are about to face," Alhena stated. "Do either of you know where I can find Sire Mintaka?"

"Aye." All eyes followed Olmar's sausage-sized finger. "'e spends his free time aloft in the foremast crow's nest, if'n he ain't bein' dragged about the riggin' by Tara. Me thinks 'e's lookin' for the end of the world."

239

Soul Forge

Be Wary

$\mathfrak{Silurian}$ stepped from the last rung of the rigging, swinging onto the deck like a seasoned hand. He wore a heavy woollen, grey sweater given to him by Tara. It was cool upon the open deck, but it was considerably colder in the ship's forward aerie. He walked aft, acknowledging and mock saluting every sailor he passed, wondering why the captain had sent for him. He hadn't spotted anything on the horizon.

Climbing to the helm's deck, more people than just the captain and Olmar awaited his arrival. The prevailing winds played havoc with Alhena's grey hair and tossed Thetis' blonde mane all about. Pollard's great bulk towered over Rook and Sadyra. Beside them, an impatient Enervator and several of *Gerrymander's* officers watched his arrival.

Must be important, if she is here, he mused and came to a stop in front of the chart table. He glanced at Alhena, then Avarick, Pollard, Sadyra, Olmar, and finally Thorr. He purposely avoided Rook and Saros' disciple.

When nobody spoke, he raised his eyebrows at the captain, but it was Alhena's voice that rose above the wind and creaking rigging.

"I summoned the quest together so Thetis can explain what to expect when we reach the portal."

Without preamble, she said, "According to Thorr's charts, the portal approaches nigh."

Silurian cast a furtive glance at the useless charts. They were blank.

"Though these eyes have never witnessed the event, Saros's words were explicit. The portal's mystical properties will attempt to numb your mind. If it gets into your head, it will steal your soul."

Everyone around the chart table fidgeted.

240

Soul Forge

"According to Saros, if you are not strong enough, you will be sucked into its vortex and be forever lost. Your soul will fuel the eye of its power, so, be wary."

Be wary? Silurian almost choked on the absurdity of the statement. He also felt a pang of emotion for his long-deceased friend and Group of Five member, Alcyonne. Be wary used to be his catch phrase, although in his native tongue, it was, 'yaw bre.'

"I cannot stress this enough. Whatever you do, *do not* gaze into the mist that will invade the ship when the portal takes hold. Do not give into the insatiable desire that will try to wrest control of your thoughts. It will seduce you into gazing into its fury. No matter what voices you believe you hear, do not be deceived. Should you ignore this warning, you will be lost to us."

"What of my ship?" Captain Thorr asked.

"Of that, I cannot say. Be assured, however, there is a reason I chose *Gerrymander*. Pray it's strong enough to withstand the portal's fury, else we're all lost."

Captain Thorr cast his eyes over the bow, to the great expanse of rolling sea. Swallowing, he turned to Olmar. "When we reach the portal, I want you at the helm. You must keep us safe."

"Aye, sir," Olmar responded without hesitation.

"Once in the portal's grip," Thetis interjected, "you'll have no need of tiller, nor sail. The sheets must be lowered the moment we feel the first sign of transition."

The captain looked indignant. "*Gerrymander* will not be left unguided."

Alhena interrupted, "This transition. What are we to expect?"

Thetis turned her indigo eyes on Alhena. "Saros didn't elaborate any more than I have said, except, perhaps, that the seductiveness of the transition maelstrom is more intense at night."

Thorr bristled. "What does that mean?"

"The colours of the vortex are more definitive during darkness?" Thetis shrugged. "I don't know."

"Vortex? We be 'avin' a choice when t' enter the blasted thing?" Olmar asked.

Thetis shrugged again.

An uneasy silence settled over the helm's deck.

241

Soul Forge

Finally, Thorr said, "Unless there is anything else to add?" He glanced at Thetis who said nothing. "Then we are done here."

The captain pulled Ithnan and Ithaman aside. "Make sure the entire crew knows what to expect. I'd rather frighten them now than lose them later."

As the sun dropped low in the western sky, a violent spasm shook the *Gerrymander*.

Soul Forge

The Portal

By the time Alhena returned to the helm's deck after supper, the captain, Silurian, and Olmar were already standing against the aft railing, scanning the darkening horizon.

At first, he didn't detect the change in the atmosphere, but the unmanned wheel, the sails furled upon their shroud arms, and the fact that the ship leapt across the waves at a fair clip, informed him something strange was afoot. *Gerrymander* sped along, caught in the grip of the portal.

The ship veered slightly south of its own volition, the sudden change in direction causing everyone to brace themselves.

An ethereal bank of mist had materialized upon the horizon ahead of them, shrouding the setting sun.

Captain Thorr ordered the decks clear of all but essential personnel while Olmar approached the great wheel, ready to wrest control should *Gerrymander* get herself into trouble. The helmsman's warhammer was strapped across his back.

When Ithnan, Ithaman, Avarick and Pollard appeared on the afterdeck to report the ship was secure, Thorr said, "Excellent. And what of Thetis?"

"We know not, captain." Pollard said, eyeing the wall of mist. The last of the natural light had faded from the world, leaving the *Gerrymander* illuminated eerily by the faint, orange haze.

The ship moved through the waves faster than it had ever sailed before. Thankfully, the swells had fallen away, leaving the ocean's surface still.

Alhena's hair whipped about his head. Staring intently, he recalled Thetis' warning not to look at the mist. The others were doing

243

likewise, sheltering their eyes behind raised arms—the impinging mist approaching fast. He fought the urge to snatch a quick peek.

Realizing that this was but the beginning of their worries, he shouted into the wind created by the ship's passage, "Everyone, below deck. Our curiosity is our doom." He stumbled toward the stairs, struggling not to glance at the coming maelstrom.

No one followed his lead.

He walked back a couple of steps, "Do you forget Thetis' warning?" He pointed at the empty masts. "There is nothing you can do out here. The sails and tiller are useless."

Thorr raised his thick eyebrows. "As captain of this ship, I need to be ready the moment *Gerrymander* steals free of the portal."

"I'm t' see our course true," Olmar piped in. "I remain alongside cap'n 'til the storm, or I, perish."

No one else spoke.

Exasperated, Alhena's gaze beseeched Pollard for assistance with Silurian.

Pollard shook his massive head. "I have been entrusted by the Songsbirthian council with the welfare of Sire Mintaka and Sire Bowman. My duty is to stand before them in the face of peril. I will remain above deck if Silurian chooses to stay."

Avarick, standing beside the big man, crossed his arms.

Alhena considered the stubborn men as the first tendrils of orange mist crept across the foredeck. He threw his hands in the air and descended the port staircase. *Fools.*

By the time he reached the rear galley door, an orange fog washed across his face—the mist sweet on his lips. The eerie feeling wasn't unpleasant. He closed his eyes as a blissful sensation crawled across his skin. Strange whispers called out to him—entreating him to open his eyes. He desired nothing more than to lie down and enjoy the seductive sensations infusing his body.

Gerrymander's prow sent twin geysers of spray aft as it altered its course, soaking him from overtop of the galley roof. It startled him back to reality.

He sat against the outside wall of the galley, licking the sweet ichor from his lips. He glanced around in horror. The invasive mist had enveloped the entire ship, most of it lost to sight. What was he doing?

Soul Forge

He closed his eyes again and stood up, fumbling to open the door. Voices whispered ever so softly, calling to him, pleading with him.

He struggled with the latch. It shouldn't be this hard to open the door. It seemed as if he watched himself through a dream, his movements sluggish and exaggerated. When the door gave way he almost didn't have the capacity to step through. Concentrating as much as his faraway thoughts would permit, he closed the door behind him.

He placed his back against the door and slid to the floor. If he could only shut out the voices echoing within his head.

Silurian faced the stern as the feathery caress of the orange fog tickled his cheeks. He stood defiantly with the others who had opted to weather the portal's fury. The mist crept over him, massaging the tenseness from his taut muscles. It beaded upon his lips, sickly sweet. Curiosity turned him to face the bow. *Gerrymander* was obscured by the strange haze.

"Sire," came Avarick's muted voice. The man had been standing right beside him a moment ago.

"Avarick?" Silurian slowly turned in circles, unable to see anyone through the fog.

The sweet mist enticed him to lick his lips. He tried to stop himself, but as soon as the thought entered his mind, it was gone again. His tongue lapped at the sweet nectar.

Dammit. He caught himself. He stopped turning in circles. Without appreciating the movement, he vaguely understood that he was sitting on the deck.

Deep down he was aware that *Gerrymander* had lost speed. A soft, melodic humming permeated his flailing thoughts, distracting him further. Unbeknownst to him, he fell over sideways and sprawled onto his back. Eyes closed, the ethereal mist numbed his mind.

He let forth a shout and sat bolt upright, his breath coming in spurts. This was wrong. He searched the mist, seeing nothing but the impenetrable orange blanket.

Soul Forge

Voices echoed along the fringes of his consciousness. Was that Pollard?

His eyelids grew heavy. He sensed he was on the verge of lying down again. With a determined effort, he garnered enough wherewithal to shake his head but the pervasive song—yes, that's what the voices were, a song—dominated his thoughts. Tendrils of mist massaged his body. His tongue ran across his lips.

Alarms cried out from the deepest recesses of his mind.

The ocean had stopped rolling. *Gerrymander* had stopped moving.

The enchanting melody soothed away the last traces of his wit. Sweat soaked his clothing, and yet, his body shivered profusely. He fought to remain lucid but he couldn't stop himself from slipping further into the trance intent on claiming him. He had to stop this. He had to stop the portal from latching onto his soul.

Without warning, the song stopped. The mist no longer tasted sweet. The fog ceased to massage his weary body. He jumped to his feet and unsheathed the Sacred Sword Voil. Holding it with both hands, turning first one way and then the other, he had no idea how he was going to battle mist with his sword.

Seeing nothing but an opaque, orange haze, he blinked his eyes several times to rid his lashes of the moisture that had settled upon them. He wasn't prepared for what stood before him when he blinked the last time.

The imposing form of Seafarer loomed over him. The reptilian creature faced him from atop a large slab of granite that they *both* stood upon. All signs of the *Gerrymander* were gone.

Silurian closed his eyes and shook his head. The mist was playing tricks on him. Daring to open his eyes again, fearful of what he would see, the creature's burning red eyes glared back at him.

"Seafarer?"

The creature didn't answer.

The runes etched into the Sacred Sword Voil sword emitted a light blue glow. He must be dreaming. He'd had this dream before.

Seafarer started toward him.

Silurian stepped back. "Seafarer. It's me, Silurian."

When the first crimson blasts shot forth from Seafarer's eyes, he deflected them with his sword.

Soul Forge

"Seafarer. What are you doing?" He parried another blast.

Seafarer stopped his advance. For no discernable reason, his massive head twisted and began to melt.

Silurian wanted to scream but the shock of what he was seeing prevented him from doing so. What kind of devilry was this?

Green flesh and twisted bone fell to the rock platform they hovered upon, sizzling and disappearing in a puff of smoke. As disgusting as the vision was, he wasn't prepared for what stared back at him.

Buried deep within the gore that had been Seafarer's head, Silurian detected a piece of broken glass. Long, bloodied hair grew from the carnage.

Silurian looked on in horror. He dropped his sword with a clang. "No," he managed to whimper.

Seafarer's head transformed into the last image Silurian had of his beautiful wife, Siaph—the base of a broken vase driven into her ruined face. To either side of the vase, her terrified eyes beseeched him to help her.

Silurian dropped to his knees, the strength sapped from him. His chest convulsed with wracking sobs. He had to help her. He reached out to grab his suffering wife.

The revolting thing before him emitted a hideous laugh.

Recoiling, he retrieved his sword—the bluish glow gone.

Bloody hands reached for him. A gruesome gurgle escaped his wife's throat, her broken jaw attempting to close on the broken vase.

"No!" His anguished scream hurt his throat. Adrenaline he hadn't experienced in many years gripped him. He hefted his sword above his head.

Long claws reached out and clutched him by the front of the woollen sweater Tara had given him, pulling him into its grasp.

He stepped backward to break the creature's hold. Shredded pieces of the grey sweater Tara had given him were held within the abomination's ghoulish grasp. He drove his sword into the middle of the gory vision.

The air ignited in a blinding flash, shattering the platform. The concussion lifted him from his feet and hurtled him through the ethereal orange mist.

Soul Forge

If not for the bulk of the central mast, Silurian would have been thrown overboard. His body broke upon the unyielding pole.

Soul Forge

Hell's Stew

Gerrymander carved through light seas of her own accord, the air cool upon the rolling waters. Her sails strained against their ropes, propelling the ship with considerable speed, though peculiarly, without the aid of a discernable wind. It had been three days since the eye of the portal had abruptly released her.

Thorr stood before the chart table with Rook and Alhena with a look of frustration. "These charts are useless. We have no idea where we are, if we've gone anywhere. Nor do we know where we're headed."

Rook didn't know what to say. There was no sign of land anywhere but they must have gone somewhere. He followed the bleary-eyed captain's gaze to the horizon ahead of them. The most peculiar part of the whole experience since being released by the portal was the absence of the sun, the moon, and the stars. Above the *Gerrymander*, the unblemished sky seemed no different than any other, except for the fact that it lacked a sun.

The days consisted of regular intervals of daylight and darkness, but where the light came from, no one had any idea. When the night did fall, it did so without warning. One moment it was light, the next it was pitch black. No moon or stars illuminated the night sky.

The captain lifted his hat and combed his hair with his fingers. "I can't believe we lost three men during the transition through the portal. Where'd they go?"

If the question wasn't rhetorical, nobody answered.

Rook glanced up at Olmar's sad face as the helmsman kept the wheel steady. How did he know where to steer?

Seeing the worry on Alhena's face, he placed his hands on his shoulders. "Fear not, my friend. Silurian will recover from his hurts."

Soul Forge

Alhena shrugged free of his grasp. "Hell damn you, Bowman! Where were you when the portal hit?"

Everyone around them gave a start.

Undeterred, Alhena persisted, "You cannot possibly know if Silurian will recover. What if he does not? The only one capable of warding Silurian properly is you."

They had been over this ground before, but Alhena wouldn't let it go. Rook patiently allowed him to vent.

"Three men lost their lives. Had the main mast not interrupted Silurian's flight, it might have been four. Where would we be then?"

Rook couldn't look Alhena in the eye. "I figured he was well taken care of."

"Is that so? Well..." Alhena was beside himself. "The success of this mission depends on the two of you—not one, *two*. If we lose one of you," he motioned for Rook to look around. "We will have sailed to this godforsaken place for nothing. Hellfire, we do not even know if we can get back. According to what Seafarer told us, our chances are not good. If Silurian had died while you were putting your..." Alhena's face shook. "Everyone will have put their lives on the line for what?" He didn't wait for an answer. "Absolutely nothing, that is what."

"You're right."

"Right? Of course, I am right. We have been over this before. He should mean more to you than that woman. More to you than all of Zephyr combined. How do you fail to see that?"

Rook shrugged.

"Thetis is a beautiful woman, without a doubt, and critical to our cause, but without your total devotion to Silurian, our quest is meaningless."

Rook's cheeks burned. He didn't know how to explain his deep-rooted emotions, both for Silurian and Thetis.

Alhena threw his hands up in disgust and stormed from the helm's deck.

Rook thought he heard him mutter as he descended the stairs, "We may as well lay down our arms and save Helleden the bother."

250

Soul Forge

"I care not for this place." Captain Thorr said to no one in particular. The sails hung slack the morning after Alhena's confrontation with Rook.

The captain stood in his usual spot behind the chart table. Olmar manned the helm, his great bulk making the large wheel seem like a child's toy in his grasp. Alhena had joined them at daybreak.

"Cap'n?" Olmar asked.

The captain stared over the port rail, his distracted response barely audible, "No sun. No moon. No stars. No clouds, nor wind." He studied the unfathomable water skimming past the gunwale. "Who knows what unearthly creatures lie in wait below."

Neither man disagreed with his misgivings.

Thorr scanned the horizon for any sign of land.

Olmar did likewise. "I 'ope blondie made a proper choice o' course. I'm thinkin' she ain't rightly sure 'erself where this Under Realm lies."

"If these waters aren't the Under Realm itself," Alhena mumbled.

Thorr wrested his gaze from the peculiar sky. "You think so?"

Alhena shrugged. "No, not really. I hope not anyway. Not many of us have been gifted with gills."

Thorr squinted at Alhena for a moment and then smiled for the first time in days.

"Master Alhena!" Pollard's voice reached them. "Master Alhena!" The large man strode with purpose across the lower deck.

Alhena raised his eyebrows at his two companions and hurried to the top of the steps.

"Master Alhena, Silurian has come to."

Reaching the healer's cabin, Pollard opened the creaky door wide, allowing Alhena to enter first. The room was cloaked in a thick pall of pipe smoke.

Soul Forge

Nashon Oakes, the ship's healer, sat huddled over a small desk, scribbling notes on a worn parchment. He clutched a crudely carved wooden pipe between a set of imperfect, yellowed teeth.

A bed dominated the cabin's back wall with Silurian sprawled beneath a lump of woollen blankets. Sporadic, rasping breaths escaped his lips. As his head turned slowly to regard his visitors, his gaze focused on Alhena. He smiled ever so slightly, before slipping back into unconsciousness—his wheezing exhalations eased noticeably.

Alhena couldn't see. Tears of thankfulness dripped into the wisps of his grey beard. The trials that Silurian had continuously endured in order to save the people of Zephyr from Helleden overwhelmed him.

The healer checked his pipe's contents before placing it in the only adornment in the room that didn't appear ratty—a finely carved pipe holder depicting a mermaid lounging upon a bed of rocks. He rose from his desk. "That is the first time he has focused on anything…A good sign."

Alhena rubbed at his eyes. "How are his injuries?"

"'Tis hard to say. He shan't die from them."

"But?"

"Time will tell. He isn't young anymore." The healer retrieved his pipe and lifted it to his lips, his tone making it obvious he had left something unsaid.

Pollard went to stand by Silurian, concern written on his face.

Mulling over Nashon's statement Alhena prompted, "Go on."

Nashon ran his fingers through his wavy hair. "I'm concerned with his mental state. He mutters incoherently, speaking disjointed words like, Guardian, Melody, Sye-af? I believe that's the word he uses."

"That would be his deceased wife, Siaph."

"Ah."

"Does he eat?"

"Aye, and drink, when we put it to his lips."

Silence fell over the cabin.

The healer resumed his seat and glanced over his notes. When his deep voice broke the serenity, Alhena jumped. "Something poisons his thoughts, of that I am certain."

Pollard looked up at that, a great sadness on his face.

Soul Forge

"Your presence seems to have brought him a measure of peace," Nashon said solemnly. "Perhaps he will be alright after all."

Alhena felt nauseous.

"Fret not, my friend," Captain Thorr's voice sounded behind him. "You've said he's a stubborn man. From what I know of him, he won't give up easily. He's just gathering his strength to deal with what lies ahead."

Alhena turned to acknowledge the captain, but Thetis' sudden entrance caught him off guard.

She stopped in her tracks and frowned at him.

Alhena pushed past her in disgust and left the cabin.

"What's with the old man?" Thetis asked no one in particular.

Pollard eyed her with disdain.

"We should reach the Under Realm within a couple of days," she said, ignoring the look. She spun on Nashon. "How does he fare? We'll need him shortly."

Nashon gave her a cold stare. "I wouldn't count on him doing anything anytime soon, unless you plan on killing him."

She stared at the healer, frowning, and then paced to the bedside, almost bowling Pollard out of the way. She bent low over Silurian's face.

Pollard glared at her, but she either didn't notice, or didn't care.

He restrained the urge to wrap his hands about her thin waist and throw her from the room.

Thetis gathered Silurian's limp hands in her own and whispered into his ear. Her incoherent words sounded like a soft chant.

Without a word, she let Silurian's hands fall limp to the bed and spun about, walking quickly from the room.

Pollard exchanged puzzled looks with the men left in the room. He glanced back at Silurian, shocked to discover him totally at ease. No sound escaped his lips. In fact, he didn't appear to be breathing at all.

Soul Forge

The next two days passed strangely. Rain fell from a barren sky while *Gerrymander* moved along at incredible speeds in the absence of a discernable wind. Day suddenly became night, and night day.

Oarsmen were constantly on standby. The billowing sails would suddenly hang slack and then, just as quickly, fill with air again.

Olmar manned the helm more often than he didn't, always accompanied by Captain Thorr.

Alhena, Avarick and Pollard took to rotating watches at Silurian's bedside.

Rook seldom appeared above deck, except for the occasional foray aft to check on the ship's progress, or to stand with Thetis on the bow.

Alhena watched her appear above deck with mixed feelings. *Gerrymander* had already lost a few good people to something they had no control over. Judging by the bizarre environment they now sailed in, things weren't about to improve any time soon. Where had she taken the ship? He was still mulling this over when Rook appeared on deck.

The bowman approached the helm, pulling his weatherproof cloak tightly around himself as rain suddenly lashed the deck, though not a cloud dotted the sky. The ship's spars creaked under the strain of the billowing sails. He nodded to those assembled around the wheel, making a point to avoid Alhena's scrutiny.

The always cheery Olmar smiled. "Greet'n Master Bowman. Why so glum?"

"Ah, nothing…just tired."

Alhena bit back the bitter words on the tip of his tongue, pretending to study the map pinned on the chart table. Three sand dials sat upon the blank map, filtering time at various rates. Olmar had made a crude inscription upon the chart, representing the body of water they sailed upon, and labelled it, 'Hell's Stew.'

Pollard elbowed Alhena and pointed with his chin.

Soul Forge

Thetis appeared on the afterdeck. She stopped beside Rook and without so much as a greeting said, "Mintaka fares much better this day."

When no one responded, she added, "Must be comforting news to the quest."

Alhena scrutinized the odd woman. There was something not quite right with her.

"Now the quest can pick up where it left off," her sweet lilt washed over the assembled men. "If my instincts hold true, the Under Realm lies just over the horizon. If the sails continue to hold wind, we should make anchor this afternoon."

All eyes widened at that. If what she said was true, the quest would soon be leaving *Gerrymander's* relative safety and setting foot on foreign soil. Not just any alien land, but the Under Realm itself, in search of the Soul Forge.

Before anyone responded, Thetis grabbed Rook's hand and pulled him toward the stairs.

"Land ho!" came the cry from the mainmast crow's nest later that afternoon. All hands not required elsewhere made their way to the prow. With the ship skimming the low rolls at great speed, those assembled along the bow rail were mesmerized as the dark blur upon the horizon grew into bluish-purple crags.

The captain ordered the mainsails furled to slow *Gerrymander's* approach. The last thing they needed was to break upon an unseen reef. He stood aft with Olmar, checking the sand dials' progress. Ever since their first day upon Hell's Stew, when it became apparent that the light abruptly winked out and left them floundering in absolute darkness, Olmar had set up the sand dials. With the aid of his three-different time measuring devices, he had discovered that the time between daylight and darkness remained constant.

Captain Thorr lifted the middle hourglass, its grains almost spent. He gave the order to unweigh the anchor.

Soul Forge

Shortly after the great anchor broke the water's surface, the light simply vanished.

By following the acrid smoke, anyone could find their way to the healer's cabin blindfolded. Squealing hinges announced Alhena's entrance into the hazy, ill-lit room.

Nashon sat at his desk, two flickering tapers spilling wax onto the tabletop. Placing his pipe within the mermaid's embrace, he stood and shook Alhena's hand.

"How does he fare?"

The healer nodded several times, as they observed Silurian sleeping. "Well…quite well, actually."

"You sound surprised."

Nashon kept nodding, biting at his bottom lip. "He's doing better than he should be."

Alhena frowned.

Nashon shook his head. "I knew he would recover from his physical ailments, but not this fast."

Alhena squinted through the pipe smoke haze at his resting friend.

"And yet, by some miracle, he is pretty much healed."

"And that is unusual?"

"I'd say. Very much so." The healer lowered his voice, "If you ask me, I think that Thetis woman had something to do with it."

"Thetis? How?"

Nashon shrugged and sat at his desk. He struck a flint stone over his pipe bowl and drew deeply. Once the contents smoldered, he gave Alhena a perplexed look, and turned to pick up a quill to carry on with the notes he had been working on. He apparently had nothing else he wished to say on the matter.

Soul Forge

Debacle Lurch

$\mathfrak{S}$ometime after the light of day had switched on to dispel the darkness, men and women gathered upon the ship's prow, gazing up at a blue-grey cliff rising out of the murky waters over three hundred feet high. Gnarly trees twisted out of hidden crevices along the imposing rock wall. Below the cliffs, stretches of water-pocked stone rose like sentinels along the shoreline, awash in ocean spray. Attempting a landing was out of the question. According to Thetis, they had arrived at the Under Realm.

Unfamiliar black birds swirled along the daunting cliff face, following *Gerrymander's* progress, as if watching them.

To their right, the cliffs went on for leagues before bending out of sight. On their left, however, the cliff face shot out toward them like a barrier, sheltering what appeared to be the inlet of a wide fjord.

Captain Thorr stood at the forefront of the conglomeration, laced with conflicting emotions. He was proud of his crew. They had safely delivered the quest to the shores of a place no one had believed even existed—albeit, not entirely without harm. He sighed, thinking of the sailors they lost at the portal.

Thetis had provided him with no further input as to which way to sail from here. He studied the imposing shoreline before informing the crew to sail left, around the promontory, and into the fjord. With a little luck, the inlet might lead to a river mouth. With a bit more luck, that river might take them to the Soul Forge. He nodded hopefully and ordered the sails to remain furled, preferring to propel the ship by oar this close to land in the unchartered waters.

Shortly after entering the fjord, they were pelted by rain.

Soul Forge

Around midafternoon, according to the helmsman's reckoning, *Gerrymander* was well into the channel. Through the constant rain, the captain observed the opposite shorelines were gradually converging.

Rounding a bend in the channel, a distant rumble sounded from beyond a wall of roiling mist. The ship's pace slowed as the oarsmen battled to move *Gerrymander* along in the face of a strengthening current.

Captain Thorr consulted his time pieces and gave the order to drop anchor. Whatever lay beyond the strange mist, it was prudent to keep the ship back from the bank of swirling fog when night fell. The fjord walls, the mist, and the swift current told him they sailed toward the base of a sizable waterfall but given the peculiar weather trends and celestial absences in the Under Realm, he wasn't taking a chance on which way the waterfall actually flowed. *There is no way in hell,* he smiled at the irony, *I am going to allow* Gerrymander *to sail over the brink of an unseen waterfall.*

When the light disappeared, thankfully, so did the rain.

Captain Thorr ordered a ten-man watch to ward the decks, and dispatched an unusual sailor known as Blindsight to the main crow's nest. Blindsight's vision rivaled that of a cat, but in the absolute darkness, even his sight was insufficient to see very far.

Gerrymander strained at her fetters in the strong current. To many aboard, the high cliffs, unseen in the darkness, felt like they closed in on them. More than one sailor clung to the deck rail like his life depended on it.

Satisfied that the ship was as secure as possible, Thorr and Olmar wearily entered the galley to break their fast. Olmar ducked low to avoid cracking his head, squeezing his girth through the door frame. They joined Alhena, Pollard, Sadyra, Avarick and a few others already sitting about the central table.

Halfway through their meal, Nashon entered the galley with Silurian in tow.

Everybody aboard *Gerrymander* suffered from a lack of sleep, but with Silurian's arrival, those seated at the central table passed away the dark hours partaking of the ship's dwindling wine stores.

Soul Forge

Late the next morning, three skiffs paddled into the turbulent waters toward the wall of mist.

Something about the ethereal shroud gave the captain a cause for alarm. No matter how thick, they should be able to glimpse the falls behind the mist. For a waterfall to create that much moisture, it had to fall from an enormous height, but from where he stood against the stern's port rail, the only things visible beneath the ghastly pale heavens were the water, the encroaching cliffs, and the mist itself.

The captain forbade the original quest members from taking part in the reconnaissance foray. It was his ship and until they were on solid ground, he insisted it was his call.

Pollard was noticeably unhappy about being left out, Avarick somewhat less so. Both were responsible for Rook and Silurian, and there was no way Silurian was going to be given leave.

Rook thought about tagging along, but Thetis had privately advised him not to.

Ithaman and Ithnan each piloted a skiff with two other sailors as they followed in the wake of a third boat. The two oarsmen in each craft struggled to hold their course steady in the strong current. Traversing the fjord at an angle, and cutting back again, the skiffs made their way into the roiling mist.

Everyone aboard *Gerrymander* watched the launches flounder against the current and then abruptly disappear through the wall of mist. The boats weren't heard from again that day.

At supper, Olmar lobbied vehemently to launch another craft to go after them, but the captain wouldn't hear of it. When darkness blinked out the light, all thought of pursuit was quashed. Before retiring to his cabin, the captain ordered *Gerrymander* on high alert, and the night dragged on.

Soul Forge

By Captain Thorr's reckoning, midday approached, when, against his better judgment, he organized another crew to take to the water in search of the lost boats. If his worst fears were realized, the original vessels had gone over the brink of a waterfall.

Before the boat hit the water, an excited shout reached him from high up in the rigging.

"There! Boat to starboard!"

All heads snapped to where the right cliff face emerged from behind the veil. A skiff rowed vigorously toward them.

The ashen faces of the harried sailors in the boat made the hair on the back of the captain's neck stand on end.

Almost as soon as they sighted the first boat, another one popped out of the mist, near the middle of the river. The men in the second boat propelled their craft away from the mist at a frantic pace.

"Anchors aweigh!" Captain Thorr barked. "Man the ballista! Hold our position!"

Gerrymander became a maelstrom of activity. Two teams of brawny sailors furiously cranked up the heavy anchors. The vessel lurched in the current, but her drift was prevented when the oar banks shipped out of the wash-strake and slapped the water.

Anxious eyes sought out the third boat. It wasn't until the first two were safely aboard that the lookout in the foremast brought everyone's attention to the wall of mist. The last skiff slipped free of the haze, swirling in the current, drifting toward their position. Empty.

The captain stared at the slowly spinning boat floating past and heading out to sea. He immediately thought the craft had capsized in the turbulent water, but as it drifted by, it became apparent that all the gear lay dry and untouched in the bottom of the boat.

"Captain, permission to launch an' find them?" Olmar shouted. He stood alongside Tara, who had already grabbed the davit to lower a launch.

"Negative. Make all haste to retrieve the third boat." The captain shouted.

Olmar stood gaping in disbelief.

When the oarsmen hadn't spun *Gerrymander* about fast enough, the captain yelled, "Now!"

Soul Forge

The men manning the ballista swivelled it around to remain fixed on the wall of mist as *Gerrymander* manoeuvred into position to snag the empty skiff. As soon as the boat was on deck, the captain ordered the sails raised.

Olmar scrambled to assume his place at the helm, while Tara made her way into the rigging.

Gerrymander sped down the fjord toward Hell's Stew.

Soul Forge

'Ware the Sentinel!

Upon hearing about the events concerning the boats within the mist, Alhena sought out Thetis for an explanation.

The sailors who made it back reported that as soon as they had entered the mist, the turbulent current they fought against had changed direction and spirited them forward. Enshrouded by mist, they could barely see the water beside them.

Against everything that made sense, they believed they were being pulled toward the brink of an enormous drop. They immediately began to row against the reversed current, but no amount of effort was able to stop their forward momentum.

They prepared to abandon the skiffs at the first sign of a waterfall's edge, only to be stunned when they broke free of the thick mists. Looming high overhead, cascaded the largest waterfall any of them had ever seen. Not nearly as high as Splendoor Falls, but much wider, its far ends lost to sight as the fjord walls opened up into a wide basin.

Instead of being relieved, the sailors panicked. They discovered, to their horror, that their skiffs were being dragged toward a massive whirlpool at the base of the falls. It took everything they had in them to break free of its pull.

After recovering their collective breath, they ventured along the base of the waterfall, hounded by its natural mists and the terrific wind the cascading water generated. Their progress proved slow as they traversed first one end of the fjord beyond the falls and then the other, all the while cognizant of the sucking vortex tugging at their boats. At no time were they able to find a way to the land above.

Exhausted, they started back to the *Gerrymander*, keeping close to the northern wall. Entering the unnatural wall of mist, they were buffeted by crosscurrents and pulled away from the cliffs. Not long afterward, the daylight vanished, leaving them floundering with no sense of direction.

Ithnan and Ithaman kept their boats together, but they lost contact with the last boat. Unsure of their direction, the vortex became their biggest fear, until, out of nowhere, muffled voices spoke to them from within the fog.

They had no idea where the voices came from, but they were certain they hadn't originated from the lost skiff. Disembodied, mournful sounds whispered to them, sounding like they were pleading for something. Snatches of words were almost intelligible—the same guttural grunting uttered over and over again.

When the tortuous darkness lifted, the voices became silent. The beleaguered skiffs that had stayed together found themselves twirling aimlessly within the safety of a small shoreline cavern.

It took them the entire morning to make their way safely around the vortex and into the mist.

Thetis had no explanation.

By midafternoon, according to the helm's deck, *Gerrymander* broke free of the fjord under full sail.

After conferring with Thetis and Olmar, Captain Thorr ordered *Gerrymander* to veer portside and follow the left shoreline.

When night fell, *Gerrymander* unweighed anchor. Everyone not required to man the ship retired to their berths. Few had trouble sleeping, excepting the captain, Olmar and those unfortunate enough to have ventured beyond the mist.

Rook had just lain down with Thetis when a strange sensation turned his stomach. Something wasn't right. He laid in the dark, listening. Beside him, Thetis slept undisturbed. Curious, he slipped from their berth and padded softly from the cabin.

The ship's interior was quiet, save for the occasional snore and the creaking of the wooden ship as it pulled at its anchors.

Soul Forge

The soft roll of the waves gave him a little trouble navigating the faintly lit passageway. The greasy smell of burning lantern oil made his nostrils twitch.

He set out for the deck, but passing the healer's quarters, he paused at the open doorway and peered in. Nashon snored unevenly, his head sprawled at an awkward angle upon folded arms, amongst the clutter of his desk. The aroma of stale pipe smoke permeated the cabin. The sound of Pollard, slumped at the foot of Silurian's berth, grunting awake, startled him.

The large man got to his feet, bending low to avoid bashing his head on the low ceiling, and joined Rook in the passageway. Without a word, he pulled the bowman along the corridor so as not to disturb Silurian.

"How does he fare?" Rook said in a hushed voice.

Pollard attempted to lower his voice but he may as well have spared himself. His hushed, throaty voice was louder than his normal speaking voice. "Nashon says he's doing better than he has a right to."

"How come he still sleeps in the healer's cabin?"

Pollard shrugged, an awkward movement as hunched over as he was. "Dunno. Precaution, maybe. Seems he and Nashon get along."

Rook thought he heard something unspoken in the big man's voice. He swallowed. It should be him that Silurian got along with.

Two women appeared at the far end of the passageway, refueling the lanterns that were mounted infrequently along the walls. The dirty faced women made their way toward them, nodding as they passed by.

After the women disappeared around the next corner, Pollard asked, "What brings you to walk the ship this late?"

Rook thought of telling Pollard about his unease but decided not to. "Just restless, I guess. I can't help wondering what happened to those sailors at the falls," he partially lied.

"Aye. A strange business, that."

Not knowing what else to say, Rook bade Pollard goodnight and watched the big man disappear into the healer's cabin. Standing within the relative silence of the flickering passageway, he tried to put a name to his unease, but whatever had bothered him was gone. With a resigned sigh, he returned to the cabin he shared with Thetis.

Soul Forge

The following morning, he bumped into Alhena on his way up to the mess hall. A chill crept into his feet and sent shivers up his spine, confirming the absurd rumour circulating the cabins of ice encrusting the ship's decks.

Before locating a table, they opened the rear door of the mess hall to satisfy their curiosity, much to the dismay of everyone huddled over their breakfast. The deck was covered by a thin layer of snow—the shrouds visible to them, laden with ice. A brisk wind blew swirling snow into their faces.

Angry snarls sounded from around the mess hall.

Rook pushed against the howling wind, slamming the door shut to a chorus of sarcastic cheers. Stunned, he followed Alhena to a spot on the end of one of the tables while the scowling faces around them returned to their porridge.

The next two and a half days passed with no change to the cliffs on their left, and Hell's Stew's boundless vista everywhere else. They passed many rocky crags in the waters between themselves and the shoreline, but none of them appeared remotely inhabitable, let alone reachable without fear of wrecking.

Other than a brief rite for the lost sailors, nothing broke the tension and monotony of the voyage.

Around the middle of the third day since fleeing the fjord, the cliff wall veered west, following a gradual southwest tack. The coast, however, remained too dangerous to consider launching a landing craft. The bizarre cold snap had stuck around for the remainder of that first day but had since been replaced by an oppressive heat.

A lookout spotted the estuary of a great river tumbling its way down the broken heights of an imposing cliff. All aboard wondered whether they were looking at the river they searched for, but short of flying, there was no way to reach it.

The following morning, the coast dropped away southward around the head of a great peninsula.

Soul Forge

Olmar guided the ship into the relative calm of a large bay southwest of the promontory.

Captain Thorr took stock of the rugged shoreline and gave the order to drop anchor. Given the coastline they had encountered up to this point, this might be the only spot on the forsaken mainland to put ashore. As the anchors unweighed, he ordered everyone not required to run the ship to meet within the mess hall.

Thorr sat between Alhena and Olmar at the head of the central table. Rook, Silurian and Sadyra sat beside the messenger. Pollard opted to stand behind Silurian with muscled forearms folded across his chest. Avarick stood at the far end of the table, his dour glare dissuading any bold enough to catch his eye.

Thorr addressed the crowd, "We were tasked with delivering Rook Bowman and Silurian Mintaka to a mythical land known only in legend as the Under Realm. I am not ashamed to admit that when the prospect was first presented to me by Thetis, I balked at the notion of such an absurd undertaking."

He paused, scanning the crowd. Thetis wasn't present.

"She convinced me Zephyr's fate hung in the balance, so we were honour bound to assist two of Zephyr's greatest heroes. I must add that the stipend provided by Baron Lychman helped persuade me as well."

That garnered a few laughs from his crew.

"Even so, I never once dreamt I would actually be standing before you, off the shore of what many consider Hell itself, discussing preparations for a landing party. As crazy as all that sounds, here we are."

He purposely looked each of his crew in the eyes, proud of their unwavering loyalty.

"Under Baron Lychman's accord, our duty is now done." He took a drink from a wooden mug. "What I'm about to ask goes beyond what's expected of my crew. Should you rather not participate, I ask that you remain aboard *Gerrymander*, keeping her safe and prepared for our return."

Murmurs shot through the crowd.

Thorr held up his hands. "That duty is paramount to our success. The time draws nigh that our paths shall part. Alhena and I have worked extensively the last few days putting together a formidable landing party."

He could sense the tension in the room grow.

"I cannot, in good conscience, allow Rook and Silurian to march unprotected into the Under Realm. I *cannot.*"

He nodded toward Pollard, Avarick and Sadyra. "Aye, they are well guarded, but there is greater strength in numbers.

"*Gerrymander* shall be in the capable hands of Sytesong." The captain indicated a man with braided, waist-length, blonde hair framing a long, angular face.

Sytesong nodded.

"He is instructed to keep *Gerrymander* close in the event we need to make a rapid escape, but his ultimate responsibility is the good ship's safekeeping. If danger presents itself, *Gerrymander* will make for open water where her full might can be brought to bear."

He paused to drain his wine. "Our journey may be filled with perils unknown, but we shall meet them the way we meet every challenge. With strong arms, and clever minds. Woe betide any who stand against us."

A busy morning followed a restless night for the men and women entrusted to guard the quest. At daybreak, five skiffs paddled away from *Gerrymander* into the crashing surf. It took three trips to ferry the landing party of sixty-six, and their gear, to the gravelly shore. Only one craft capsized during the exercise, the loss of much needed provisions the sole casualty.

Once ashore, Thorr overheard Alhena admonishing one of the crew.

"Nay. I shall bear my own burden, thank you. You will be sorry help to us should you exhaust yourself carrying my gear as well."

Soul Forge

Alhena gave the abashed sailor a haughty, "harrumph," and snatched his satchel from the stricken man's hands. He struggled briefly to hoist the bulging sack over his stooped shoulder before he stormed off, giving Thorr a wink on his way past.

Thorr smiled and shook his head as the oldest member of the quest stomped after the lead members of the company who were in turn following the direction Thetis had set out. How she knew which way to go, he had no idea. Alhena's fortitude was the least of his worries. Indeed, Alhena continually proved to be an asset—his wisdom, their counsel, his determination, their inspiration.

Thorr ordered the gangly Ithnan and Ithaman to scout the company's flanks and sent the other brothers, Longsight and Blindsight ahead to search out the best route forward. Longsight was the sailor often seen perched high in the main crow's nest—the man possessed uncanny vision.

The large party travelled southward, making their way around jagged tors into the Under Realm's interior. Leaving Hell's Stew behind, the rugged terrain gave way to a rolling, lush green landscape, similar to that of the Gritian Hills.

Longsight marked their trail with strips of cloth tied to various plants or held by rocks. Olmar and Tara tracked the scout's progress, collecting every other marker they came across, leaving the others to assist them on their return leg. Occasionally, the bandy-legged giant and the brawny female missed one, forcing the rest of the quest to assist in the search.

They traversed grassy knolls and descended into lush valleys bursting with exotic vegetation that were alive with alien insect life. This was the last type of environment they had expected. Their only hardships were aching feet and a nasty insect sting one sailor received while relieving himself in a thick patch of fragrant flowers; much to the delight of his peers.

Without the aid of Olmar's timepieces, darkness caught them unaware. They hurriedly set up camp under torch light and settled into an uneasy night. Several sentries were dispatched to ward their perimeter, but with the exception of Blindsight, no one was able to see beyond the flickering torchlight.

268

Soul Forge

Before daylight broke, Blindsight led Longsight out into the pitch to begin searching the new day's route.

Near the end of the third day since disembarking *Gerrymander*, the quest halted. Longsight and Blindsight ran toward them, bearing the cloths they had previously set out.

Blindsight rarely spoke, so Longsight addressed the captain, "Our path ahead is blocked by a gorge."

"What lies beyond?"

Longsight hesitated. He glanced at his brother, but Blindsight's impassive face didn't help. "A river, of sorts."

Captain Thorr furrowed his brow.

"The river appeared as, um…the best way to describe it would be, uh, flowing milk."

"Flowing milk?"

"Aye sir, and smelly."

"Seems bizarre."

"Aye sir, but wait, it gets better."

"I'm listening."

"Well sir, I'm not sure how to describe what we heard."

"Heard?"

"Aye sir." Longsight paused, but the captain said nothing, awaiting his next words. "Well, we, Blindsight and myself, we heard voices. Many voices."

All gathered looked around, remembering the story from days earlier when three of their shipmates were lost at the great waterfall.

Thorr frowned deeper. "Voices?"

"Aye sir. And peculiar sounding too, eh Blind?"

Blindsight nodded slightly, biting his lower lip, staring at the ground.

"What did they say, these voices? Where did they come from?"

"Well that's the rub, isn't it? We don't rightly know. We looked everywhere."

"And?"

"That's just it. They came from everywhere."

Soul Forge

"I believe you. Pray, do go on."

"That's about all, sir. We searched for over an hour. Nothing."

"What did they say? Did they speak an alien tongue?"

"No, sir," Longsight answered slowly. "That's the weirdest part. They spoke our language. It's strange, but…I can't explain it. Eerie like."

The captain raised his eyebrows. He was about to confer with Thetis, who had slipped in beside him.

Longsight's voice stopped him. "By the urgency in their voices, I believe they're trying to warn us of something." He grimaced. "Actually, we did make out one phrase."

Everybody pressed closer.

"'Ware the Sentinel."

Blindsight nodded vigorously.

Alhena clutched at Thorr's shoulder in an effort to remain standing.

270

Soul Forge

Seated around the perimeter of the central campfire, Alhena and Thorr ate in silence. Silurian, Pollard, Avarick and Sadyra sat with them, engrossed in their own thoughts.

Alhena was troubled. Longsight's message bothered him more than it should have.

Thorr looked up from his wooden bowl. "What are you thinking?"

Alhena ignored the question and continued to gaze into the fire.

Longsight and his twin appeared out of the darkness from the direction of the distant bluff where they had encountered the strange voices, and joined the group, nodding to everyone in turn.

Sadyra shuffled over to make room on the fallen tree trunk she shared with Pollard.

Rook appeared shortly afterward. Everyone looked behind him, expecting to see his shadow, but Thetis wasn't there.

Avarick gestured for Rook to join him on the large rock he sat upon.

Rook nodded at the group and took a place beside the Enervator. He removed the awkward sword given to him by the *Gerrymander's* stores master and placed it next to Avarick's crossbow before turning his attention to polishing his bow.

The evening grew late as the group discussed the recent turn of events. They spoke of old yarns and myths, trying to unearth the significance of the warning, ''ware the Sentinel.'

Rook and Avarick spoke quietly beside Longsight and Pollard who were engaged in an animated discussion with Sadyra.

Everyone stopped in midsentence to stare at Alhena—a stunned revelation had twisted his features.

"What is it?" Thorr asked.

"Hell. The Under Realm. They are the same thing."

271

Soul Forge

Thorr frowned. "What are you talking about?"

"I know where it comes from," Alhena whispered.

"Where what comes from?"

Alhena shot back a frown of his own. The captain wasn't usually this daft. "The warning, 'ware the Sentinel.'"

Everyone leaned closer.

"I knew I had heard that phrase at some time in my life but I could not place it." His voice dropped off as he thought about what he said.

"And?" Thorr prodded.

A lengthy silence ensued before Alhena nodded to himself. "A long time ago, long before I started running for the Chamber, I was an archivist in the royal library under Castle Svelte." He drifted off.

Suddenly he pointed at no one in particular. "Yes. Yes! That is it!" He carried on a private conversation with himself. "The scroll. That is where I have seen it before."

"The scroll? What scroll?"

Alhena gazed into Thorr's eyes, but his focus lay elsewhere, far beyond.

When he spoke, his words came in spurts as memories slammed into him. "It was an old scroll. Ancient. Brittle. We almost were not able to preserve it long enough to read it…Yes. Carmichael's scroll. That is it!" He laughed a little insanely. "That is what *we* called it, anyway."

No one knew who *we* were.

"Saint Carmichael's scroll, actually. At least we believe he wrote it." Alhena sat back on the rock, pleased with himself.

When he didn't offer anything further, those around him looked at one another, rolling their eyes.

Thorr spoke through clenched teeth, "And what, pray tell, did this scroll say?"

"Huh? Oh. Well, it is more of a song than a story. Do not expect me to sing it, though. Hmm? Let me see…if I remember…"

Just when the group believed he wasn't going to say anything more, he did, "To the best of my recollection, mind you it has been fifty odd years at least, the scroll read something like this:

> When the shadow stabs,
> the life-giving sun,

272

Soul Forge

forth shall he ride,
leaving nothing but ruin."

He paused, staring vacantly past all those watching him, trying to recall the verse correctly.

"Freedom will be denied,
to those who fall,
within his shadow;
death dealt to all.

Upon naive waves,
he unfurls his sail.
Fear ye who live,
for only he shall prevail.

We live now only to await,
our life blood courses nigh.
The Stygian Lord comes again,
blighting the land, razing the sky.

Only one hope remains,
for those foolish enough to pursue.
Onto the Under Realm,
into hell, but never through.

Venture forth to unknown power,
a cradle of evil disgorge.
A quest of unspeakable terror,
at journey's end, Soul Forge.

For those who search,
death shall follow.

𝖘𝖔𝖚𝖑 𝖋𝖔𝖗𝖌𝖊

For those who persist,
shall be riven hollow.

As does the Innerworld,
also does hell.
A drinker of souls,
'ware the Sentinel!"

An eerie silence gripped the group. Everyone attempted to peer beyond the reach of the fire's glow, half expecting this 'Sentinel' to claim them right then and there.

They waited for him to elaborate.

Alhena looked directly at each member of the quest seated about the fire. To a person, their eyes displayed a wariness not present before.

"Perhaps I should not have mentioned it." He dropped his gaze to the flames, his voice falling to a whisper. "Probably has nothing to do with us."

After everyone left for their tents, Thorr requested Thetis' presence within his own.

She shrugged when he mentioned Alhena's story, feigning indifference. She was adamant they continue their present course. If the members of the quest were uneasy about continuing toward the gorge, she suggested they skirt around it, eastward.

"You believe that will keep us from harm?" Thorr asked.

"I don't, but it might allay their fear."

"What if that is the river we seek?"

"It's not."

"And our destiny lies this way?"

"I am certain of it, good captain."

"For someone who has never been here before, you know a fair bit about this land. I'm thinking you know more than you let on."

Thetis smiled sweetly and disappeared into the night.

Soul Forge

With Ithnan and Ithaman scouting their northern flank, and Longsight and Blindsight searching out the best route southeastward, all with the purpose of avoiding the canyon and whatever this Sentinel thing was, the quest trudged onward. Two brawny sailors were sent south to further investigate the voices.

As the day wore on, the trees gave way to barren rock, and before night fell, to hard-packed, hot sand. Thanks to good planning, camp was set up before darkness dropped upon them like a cudgel.

Alhena made his way to the captain's fire and sat down to eat. As he dug into his meagre fare, Longsight stopped by to report there was nothing but sand to the north as far as he could see.

After Longsight left, Ithaman and his brother strolled into the firelight to report the same held true in the east, where the sand became softer, making it harder to walk. The land reportedly rolled with small dunes that grew to greater heights farther east.

Of the brawny sailors who had ventured south, there was no word.

Pollard, Sadyra and Avarick followed on Rook and Silurian's heels to join the captain's campfire with meals in hand. To everyone's surprise, Thetis accompanied them.

Alhena studied her as she engaged the captain in private conversation. She hadn't brought along anything to eat. There was something strange about that one, but he couldn't put a name to his misgivings. Saros had appointed her to guide them, and she hadn't led them astray yet. She had led them to the portal, and successfully guided them through it. She had navigated Hell's Stew and brought them to what she claimed was the Under Realm. Yet, she hadn't prevented the loss of three crewmen at the waterfalls she referred to as, Debacle Lurch. How she knew the falls' name was a mystery.

Thorr's gruff voice cut through his reverie, "We are faced with an unfavourable decision. Turn back and head toward the cliffs with the voices or continue along our present course and brave an increasingly inhospitable landscape." He nodded toward Thetis. "Thetis claims either route leads us to where we need to go."

Soul Forge

Everyone stopped eating, but no one responded.

"Our southernmost scouts have yet to return, and that concerns me. It is my humble opinion that we turn back and brave whatever creatures inhabit the canyon region, if for no other reason than to locate our men. I'm thinking that if these creatures meant us harm, they would've done so by now. To forge deeper into the desert screams to me of disaster, but I will defer the decision to Rook and Silurian."

Silurian, staring off into some other world, became aware the attention had swung his way. He shrugged indifference. "Unless the creatures are protecting something and have left us alone because we no longer prove to be a threat."

Thorr nodded.

"I don't relish walking through this desert any longer than I have to. If it is a river we seek, the cliffs seem like the place to start," Rook offered. "Not a desert."

Silurian put his meal aside. "That makes sense. As the captain said, there is also the matter of the missing scouts. We cannot carry on east until we know that they are safe. I say we head to the cliffs." He got up and stepped into the night, his supper abandoned.

The following morning passed quietly as the contingent from *Gerrymander* reversed their route out of the desert. The rocky, windswept terrain, devoid of all but the hardiest scraps of scraggy vegetation, began wearing at the group's demeanour.

After the midday meal, Alhena walked alongside Thorr. "I should not have mentioned that story the other night."

Thorr frowned.

"Look at them." Alhena indicated the men and women trudging along in silence and glancing over their shoulders as if something followed in their wake.

"Fear not. We all bear the burden of the task before us. Aye, they don't relish the mystery of what lies ahead, but know for certain that when the time comes, my people will account for themselves admirably." The captain slapped him on the shoulder. "And if what you said is but a child's tale, then all's the better, eh? If nothing else, you have them considering worst-case scenarios. I'm sure you'll agree, most of our darkest fears ferment in the unspoken parts of our mind. Rarely do they match our anxiety."

Alhena offered a half-hearted smile. "Aye, but do your people journey willingly, or do they simply respect your command?"

"Bah. Their spirits will lift again, you watch. I know them well. Handpicked each one. You'll see." Thorr stopped and grabbed Alhena by the wrists, causing those behind to shuffle around them. He stared into Alhena's colourless eyes. "Forth we go toward an unknown destiny. We travel as one, mighty and strong. Woe betide any who hinder us."

Before Alhena responded, a murmur rippled through the ranks. A lone runner had made her way back to them.

Sadyra pulled up before Thorr, out of breath. "Sir, Olmar and I believe we've located the scouts' tracks along the edge of the gorge."

Soul Forge

Harbinger

Bandy-legged Olmar fought to catch his breath. He had scouted ahead with Sadyra and dispatched her a few hours earlier to inform the quest of their discovery. While waiting for her return, he followed the tracks along the cliff's edge, his warhammer in hand.

The double set of prints led him eastward. Not even Longsight or Blindsight had travelled this far south. The tracks led him to a spot where the scouts' trail descended down the faint traces of a ledge cut into the face of the sandstone cliff.

Thorr watched the awkward, loping gait of Olmar's approach as the quest came within sight of a colossal landfall.

"I were to be after the lads, but I came across another set of prints an' it be givin' me pause," Olmar said without preamble.

Thorr ordered the quest to a halt. "Another set? Ours?"

"Nay, cap'n, and there's the crux." The giant man squatted, still taller than Thorr, and scanned their immediate area conspiratorially, causing the captain angst.

When Olmar spoke again in a harsh whisper, Thorr nearly leapt from his boots. "The tracks, they was strange. Different sized feet, some ending in claws. I didnae wish to leave the lads to their fate, but I couldnae have ye walking into a trap."

"Clawed tracks?"

"Aye."

Soul Forge

Thorr rubbed his bearded chin. He sensed that his giant helmsman itched to get back to the cliff. "Take Sadyra and a couple others on ahead. Wait for us at the top."

Olmar snapped a crisp salute. "Aye, cap'n." He spun around, about to leave.

Thorr stopped him. "You must be tired. Let me send someone else."

The helmsman stopped, shoulders tensing. He spun his massive head about. "Not on your life, cap'n."

Without waiting for an argument, Olmar lumbered away.

The company joined Olmar, Sadyra, and the two other sailors that had accompanied them, on the brink of the windswept cliff. The land fell away to a dizzying depth. A canyon scarred the land as far as they could see in both directions. In the centre of the gorge flowed a milky white river.

Thorr sensed the darkness wasn't far off so he ordered camp to be set up, well away from the yawning abyss.

Shortly after darkness fell, the voices began. Softly at first—mistaken by most as the wind. The gentle murmurings grew perceptibly, like a muffled whisper rising into a chorus.

Having been told what the voices said, the catchphrase was obvious. "'Ware the Sentinel. 'Ware the Sentinel. 'Ware the Sentinel." It repeated itself, over and over again, in ghostlike whispers. Not in any particular cadence, but regularly enough that the quest wasn't able to sleep well. Search as they might, with the aid of torches and Blindsight's innate nocturnal vision, they were unable to locate the source. It was as if the cliffs, themselves, lamented their presence.

To a person, the men and women of the quest were geared up and ready to go as soon as the light switched on, ready to face whatever awaited them at the bottom of the gorge.

Thorr stood at the trailhead leading into the defile. He addressed Thetis, Alhena, Rook, Silurian, and the ever-present Pollard and Avarick who were rarely more than a sword's reach from Silurian. "Mayhap we've found the mystic river." His gaze took in the peculiar

279

coloured waterway. Beyond its far banks, the land rose straight up again.

Thetis shook her head. "As I told you before, that's not the river we seek."

All eyes turned on her.

"That putrid river is known as the Marrow Wash. Deadly to any who touch its diseased waters. It will eat your flesh and dissolve your bones in moments, so stay clear. Take heart, though. It's the byproduct of the river we seek. Should we live long enough, we shall find the Soul Forge at its source."

Take heart? After that statement? Thorr frowned and studied the white river. "It's acidic?"

"Very. The Marrow Wash gets its colour, and name, from the discarded corpses fed into the Forge."

Everyone involuntarily took a step back from the cliff's edge.

Thorr stared at the mysterious woman. Odd that she knew these details. He needed to have a more complete, private conversation with her.

Thetis added, "Follow the Marrow Wash upstream and we locate the river we seek."

Before anyone said anything further, Silurian separated himself from the gathering and stepped onto the thin trail ledge.

Avarick, his crossbow loaded, and Pollard, double sword in hand, followed closely upon his heels.

Thorr ordered the company to follow Silurian's lead.

Soon, the entire quest was stretched out along the precarious trail, unsure of what they were descending into.

Twisted hulks of dead trees clung to crevices along the cliff face. After circumventing an outcropping of windswept sandstone, the trail widened into a series of short steps, carved into harder rock underneath. Where the stairs were blown clear of the drifting sand, runes and primitive pictures of unknown beasts were etched into the bedrock steps. Though they hadn't seen anything yet that bespoke of intelligent life in the Under Realm, the primitive engravings testified otherwise.

It took until midday for the lead members to step from the last stair into the river basin of sand blown rock. The company milled about the base of the thousand-step stairway, trying not to gag on the suffocating smell of rot.

Thorr, Silurian, and his two shadows broke away from the crowd, following the lost scouts' footprints to the river's edge—the slow-moving water, a thick, white sludge.

"Smells like a dead body," Thorr said, scrunching his face. He located a small stick and hurled it into the middle of the Marrow Wash. The stick impacted the river's surface with a 'thlop' but instead of floating away, it hissed and crackled—slowly absorbed by the white ooze.

Ithnan had been sent ahead to scout upstream. He came back to stand beside the captain and watched the river devour the stick. "Captain. You need to see this," was all he said before charging off.

Thorr caught up to Ithnan. He knelt on one knee, examining something on the ground. There were three sets of footprints now, two human—the third more sinister.

"And look at these." Ithnan pointed toward the cliffs. In the areas where sand had drifted over the bedrock, many more strange footprints led toward the river, matching those Olmar had found. "They join the trail we follow."

Thorr stopped to examine the new footprints. Some resembled bird tracks, while others appeared as pawprints. Perhaps the most surprising ones were those akin to human footprints. Who in their right mind would choose to live here? To confuse matters further, most pairs of prints didn't seem to match each other.

"Do they lead anywhere?"

Longsight's shout echoed from farther up the canyon, interrupting their conversation, "Captain. Over here." The man's distant form waved frantically.

Swords slid free of their sheaths.

Approaching Longsight's position, Silurian's eyes grew wide. "No."

The scouts moved aside, revealing a large body on the ground. The creature resembled a large crocodile with four back legs, its body maimed almost beyond recognition. Small pools of blood were evident around its mangled body.

Silurian sheathed his sword and knelt beside the creature's head. Rook came up behind him and dropped to a knee, shaking his head.

"Seafarer. You poor thing," Silurian whispered to the unmoving creature. He nearly jumped into the Marrow Wash when Seafarer opened a blood-filled, unseeing eye.

Horrified at the gurgling rasp from Seafarer's throat as the creature tried to speak, Silurian bent close, tears dripping down his cheeks, but no sound escaped Seafarer's lips.

"Seafarer. It's me, Silurian. Rook and I are with you."

Seafarer emitted a burbling cough.

"Seafarer. It's Rook. Who did this to you?"

Just when Silurian thought their reptilian friend had succumbed to his injuries, Seafarer rasped, "The Sentinel, but that is not your biggest concern..."

Silurian glanced at Rook with alarm.

Seafarer spat up a wad of blood. A spasm trembled the great creature's body. He clenched his eyes tight. As the spasm eased, Seafarer struggled to speak, "I came to warn you...You are in grave danger..." Another spasm took hold of him. When he spoke again, his words were so faint, Silurian almost bumped Rook's forehead with his own as he leaned closer. "Do not...trust...th..." And then he was gone.

Silurian frowned. The shock of Seafarer's death sent his thoughts spinning. "Do not trust who?"

Rook shrugged and stepped away, obviously in shock himself.

More disturbing to the rest of the quest were the dismembered bodies of their missing scouts, lying in their own gore, a little farther up the riverbank.

Pollard and Avarick ran to inspect the sailor's remains. At once, they turned, bristling their weapons toward the cliffs.

"You won't find whoever, or more likely, *whatever* is responsible over there." Ithaman crouched low and examined the ground near the sailors' remains. "See this?"

Soul Forge

A large set of tracks led away from the gory scene. They didn't originate from the cliffs. They came from, and led back into, the Marrow Wash.

Soul Forge

Misshapen

Under the glow of a great fire, along the banks of the oozing Marrow Wash, Silurian placed the last rock atop a makeshift cairn they had built for Seafarer and the slain sailors.

Captain Thorr gave a brief eulogy on behalf of his men, and Alhena, after only meeting Seafarer once, spoke eloquently about the reptilian creature that no one, other than Rook and Silurian, had ever heard of before. Except perhaps for Thetis, but as was her usual wont, she remained unfazed by the current events.

"He deserved better than this," Silurian muttered, after everyone else walked away. He drove his sword into the sand beside the mound. With a heavy heart, he joined the others around the central fire.

Pollard took it upon himself to stand guard over the Sacred Sword Voil, keeping a wary eye on the malodourous river slogging by.

With the coming of darkness, so came the voices—drifting down from the heights, whispering, "'Ware the Sentinel."

It promised to be another long night.

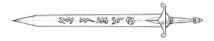

Morning dawned cool—the company's mood, grim. No one slept well, their minds rife with fear of the creature responsible for slaying Seafarer and two seasoned fighters. Most disconcerting, however, was the fact that the creature had slipped back into the acidic waters of the Marrow Wash from whence it came.

Silurian sat with his arms wrapped about his knees beside his implanted sword, staring vacantly at the mound of rocks before him. He couldn't escape the anxiety seeping into him. It was happening

284

again. Every time he set out to correct a wrong in his life, people died. Five sailors, Seafarer, Bregens. And then there was the Gritian militia who had set out under High Warlord Archimedes command. The gods only knew if they had survived their ill-fated attempt to bring him in—hopefully they made it back to Gritian before the Kraidic warband had fallen upon the city. There were even the wolves and the trolls. None of them would be dead if not for his actions.

Alhena's voice cut through his turmoil of emotions, "Come, my friend. We must flee this place ere we meet the same fate."

Silurian hadn't spent a lot of time in Seafarer's company over the years, but on the few occasions they had met, he sensed a binding purpose between them. During his darkest years, Seafarer had been one of the few guiding lights instrumental in pulling him away from the brink.

A pall of vengeance darkened his thoughts. He cringed. That was how it had started before. Helleden's machinations were drawing him in. Again. But why? Nothing made sense. Reflecting back, it never had. What was it that drove Helleden's hatred for Zephyr?

Rage simmered behind his icy stare. He wanted Alhena to leave him alone—hadn't the wise, old man figured out that being around him was dangerous?

Ignoring Alhena's hand, he jumped to his feet and yanked his sword from the earth. Absently wiping the blade on his tattered breeches, he stormed away from the burial cairn. Thinking of Seafarer, he promised himself to live long enough to return to Zephyr one last time. No matter what the consequences were, he vowed to finish this business with Helleden once and for all.

The company made their way upriver for the remainder of the day, the scenery changing little. The rank waters of the Marrow Wash oozed by on their right, while the sandy cliffs, dotted with ugly tree skeletons, paralleled their left flank. The heights rose ever higher as the dreary afternoon wore on.

Soul Forge

Before darkness fell, Alhena assisted the company to make camp and set into his evening meal, his mind on the tentative plan Captain Thorr had shared with him about catching whoever was responsible for the voices. He looked around the several small cooking fires. He could tell the rest of the quest were anxiously waiting to spring the trap.

Surprisingly, the voices didn't wait for darkness. As the quest ate, keeping its concentration on the Marrow Wash, the voices started up. Alhena had to hand it to Thorr's men and women. On cue, they jumped to their feet and scrambled to present their weapons.

The voices went quiet.

With a nod from the captain, Longsight and Blindsight sprinted toward the base of the cliffs and ducked out of sight. The captain quietly ordered the company to put away their weapons and return to their meals.

The voices came again but this time they were accompanied by a high-pitched squeal that echoed down the canyon.

Two flailing objects caught Alhena's attention as they plummeted from a hidden crevice, a dozen feet above the canyon floor, and fell behind the large boulder Longsight hid behind.

Blindsight appeared above Longsight, clinging to the cliff face. He proceeded to scale back down and disappeared behind the boulder.

Before anyone had a chance to provide them assistance, the brothers strode toward the camp, each holding aloft a creature half their size, wiggling and squirming, emitting high-pitched screams.

Stopping within a circle formed by the company, Longsight said to his captive, "Settle yourself, little one. We mean you no harm."

The human looking creature hissed, and chomped on the lanky sailor's forearm, causing Longsight to throw it to the ground.

The creature hunkered down, its eyes wild, searching for an escape route.

The company tightened the circle, their swords drawn and arrows notched.

Blindsight set his wriggling captive down.

It joined its companion in the centre of the ring, preparing to bolt. Patchy grey fur covered its exposed body parts—neither creature over three feet tall. Despite the fur, their faces were human in appearance— the taller one more so than the other. Stranger still, were their appendages. The taller creature sported human feet, but its arms ended in shaggy paws. The smaller creature boasted three entirely different appendages—a human left foot and left hand, a right paw to stand on and a right arm that ended in talons.

Alhena moved toward the frightened creatures but stepped back when the shorter one hissed and feigned an attack. He held his hands in the air. "Fear not, little ones. Can you understand me?"

The captives didn't respond but they noticeably calmed down.

"We are strangers to your land. We search for a place known to us as Soul Forge—"

The creatures dropped to the ground, cowering.

"Yes, you know of it. Soul Forge," Alhena persisted.

The creatures squealed, searching desperately for an escape route.

"You understand me. I can see it in your eyes. We seek the power of the river."

The creatures' eyes grew wide, focusing upon his staff.

"Mustn't go there," the taller creature squeaked. "Only death there. No good, Soul Forge. Must not go."

Alhena tried to smile. "We appreciate the warning, little friend. Is that where the Sentinel is?"

The creatures slumped low, fidgeting, searching for a way to break through the wall of men and women.

Thorr stepped forward. The creatures backed away from him. Realizing they neared the edge of the circle, they skittered back into the centre, keeping the captain directly in front of them.

"Weapons down," the captain ordered.

Thorr crouched. "Yes, that's right. The Soul Forge. You know where it is, don't you?"

The creatures shuddered.

"We travel with one who needs to harness the river's power. We've been told Soul Forge is the place to do that."

The misshapen creatures shook their heads. The taller one said, "You must not. The Stygian Lord will get you. Take you and bend you, yes. Make you like us, or worse." The rambling creature's voice rose to a hysterical shriek, "Ware the Sentinel."

On impulse, Alhena looked at the Marrow Wash.

Soul Forge

Thorr persisted, "Who exactly are you, little people? I don't understand what you mean. Who will make us like you?"

The misfits studied each other. When the taller one nodded, they responded together, lyrically, their voices squeaky but extraordinarily pretty.

> "Boring into solid stone,
> within these cliffs, we make our home.
> Cast from ships that lost their helm,
> taken as bricks, into this realm.
>
> To the dungeons were we sent,
> our minds were twisted, our bodies bent.
> Some were trained, and gilded in gleam,
> the likes of us, cast into the stream.
>
> Considered useless, a waste of time,
> deemed as no good, no body, no mind.
> Discard us did they, left us for dead.
> escape did we, an' 'ere have we fled.
>
> Now we dwell, our ancestry unknown,
> comprising a new race, we call this home.
> Offering refuge to those cast into hell,
> warning brave travellers, 'Ware the Sentinel.'"

There was that warning again. Pity welled up in Alhena's heart. The song's implications were clear. These were refugees who, like them, had travelled to the Under Realm. Seafarer's words at the Mountain Pools came back to him—*many have made the transition to the Under Realm, but there is a minor detail I should bring to your attention. You may have heard this old saying, 'Into hell, but never through' As far as I know, no one has ever come back.* He nodded. It was because they were still here.

Thorr's voice broke the eerie silence that had settled over the canyon floor, "What exactly is this Sentinel…thing?"

288

Soul Forge

The taller creature shuddered. "Big. Yes, huge. And bad. Oh yes, mean. *Very* mean."

"But what does it do, this big creature?"

"What does it do?" the creature sounded incredulous. "It guards the Wash."

Alhena interjected, "Can it be defeated?"

The two captives studied each other again, the smaller creature having to look up at his companion.

The taller one shrugged. "It is mighty, but…" He gazed at his smaller companion, who nodded. "It was nearly beaten yesterday." The squeaky creature's gaze settled on the ground before him—his dejected whisper barely heard, "Alas, it prevailed. We live in fear. Always fear."

The smaller creature patted his companion on the shoulder, his eyes darting around the wall of people. "You must come. Aye, come. Danger will arise from the Wash ere the day turns cinder. Yes, black. Darkness is the harbinger of death when the Sentinel is nigh. He cannot be seen in the dark. Nor heard. Forsooth, only one creature has lain eyes upon the Sentinel after light's demise. He lies buried by your own hands. We thought he was the warrior of legend sent to deliver us from our fate. Come, make haste."

The creature's companion smacked him in the shoulder, frowning.

"What? They cannot remain here. No. The Sentinel will come. They will be taken. More souls to feed the forge. No. They must follow. Into our home."

"What will Menthliot say?" the taller creature asked.

"Yes! We will let Menthliot decide," the squat creature said, turning his attention back to Thorr and Alhena. "Come. You must follow."

Alhena wasn't sure what to make of the invitation. They didn't know anything about these creatures. Who knew what treachery they were capable of? "I do not know. Master Rook? Silurian?"

Rook appeared uncomfortable about making a decision.

Silurian saved him. "We are honoured by your invitation. If there are free people living in this so-called hell, we should band together."

Alhena thought he saw Thetis tense.

The taller cave dweller saw it too and went stiff, his head snapping in Thetis' direction. He squinted and waved a finger at her. "She cannot enter. She is evil."

289

Soul Forge

Unconsciously, to a person, the company stepped away from her.

Standing on the far side of the circle, Silurian started toward her, remembering Seafarer's last words. *'I came to warn you...You are in grave danger...Do not...trust...th...'* The Sacred Sword Voil slid from its scabbard.

Thetis' eyes narrowed. She whispered something into Rook's ear, prompting the bowman to step in front of her. He pulled an arrow from his quiver, notched it, and aimed. The arrow pointed at Silurian.

Silurian stopped a dozen paces away, his sword gripped in both hands, holding the hilt at waist level.

"Sil, this is madness," Rook pleaded. His draw arm shook with the effort of keeping the bowstring taut. "Think about what you're doing. Thetis is on our side."

Nobody moved.

A voice cried out from the cliffs. "Kill it!"

From ledges hidden along the cliff face, dozens of the little cave denizens emerged, watching the bizarre scene unfolding below.

Years of pent up rage impelled Silurian forward, imploring release. His angst wasn't directed solely at the blonde-haired woman, however. His supposed friend had confronted him like this on another occasion, long ago.

A primal urge threatened to consume him. He struggled to contain the dark emotions clawing their way to the surface of his mind. If it came to blows, Rook would be the first to die.

Alhena stepped toward Silurian, his staff held out, pleading for calm.

Silurian flicked a look at the messenger, withering the old man where he stood. "Don't," he said, sickened by his inner demon that fought for release. If he had to go through Alhena, so be it.

Another emotion flitted about the periphery of his roiling thoughts. Compassion. For Alhena. And with that thought came a suffocating shame, but instead of quelling his rage, it stoked it further. He was done fighting the good fight. That path always led to needless death.

Soul Forge

Innocent people suffered because no one had the wherewithal to stand up and exorcise the foul deed that needed to be done.

Ignoring Alhena, he focused on Thetis. She was the source of his unease. Another pang of doubt questioned his motives where Thetis was concerned. A niggling feeling screamed at him that this didn't make sense, but it was overridden by his lust for vengeance.

His conscience beseeched him to disengage—something was amiss. An underlying deception hung in the air, but he couldn't tell where it originated from. He had known it for a while. Long before entering the Under Realm. The little creature's insinuation had simply rung true, unlocking a hidden door within his convoluted mind. He sensed truth in the creature's words but he didn't know where the truth lay.

The hiss of a projectile split the air.

A blow dart struck Thetis in the left shoulder. She emitted a high-pitched screech and jerked back a step. She pulled the dart free, staggered, and dropped to the ground.

Thetis cried out and Rook released his arrow. The missile flew unerringly at Silurian's heart.

Faster than thought, Silurian sidestepped. His sword took the arrow in flight, cleaving it in two; the shattered halves brushed harmlessly by him.

Nobody else moved.

Rook shot Silurian a dire look and dropped to his knees to attend to Thetis.

The spell of rage broken, Silurian lowered his sword, still glowering at Rook—his body visibly shaking.

Nashon rushed to Thetis' aid, his sudden movement snapped everyone else from their mesmerized state.

Nashon relieved Thetis' hand of the crude dart and sniffed its pointed end. He questioned the shorter creature. "What is the substance on the dart? Is it lethal?"

The small creature stared back at him saying nothing.

Silurian sheathed his sword. Without looking at anyone, he exited the circle and stood a few paces behind the captain.

Thorr ordered the company back to their fires to finish their meals and then spoke to the taller creature. "Go. Find the one you call Menthliot. Your friend will remain with us until you return."

Soul Forge

Darkness hadn't fallen yet when an emissary from the wall came forward with several other odd creatures.

Silurian watched them approach. Thorr, Pollard, Sadyra, Ithnan, Ithaman and Olmar met the contingent before they reached the camp.

The creatures stopped, their beady eyes flitting everywhere at once. The oldest looking creature stepped forward, sporting wisps of manic grey hair and nary a tooth.

"Are you in charge here?" The captain extended a hand.

The wizened creature ignored the proffered greeting, his yellow eyes crazed. When he spoke, he did so with animated hands, "I am Menthliot. We haven't much time. Blackness is near. The Sentinel will find you. Gather your people. Leave your stuff if you must and follow. We offer you a haven from the beast. Come. Come." The creature motioned for everyone to follow him to the cliffs.

Thorr searched out Thetis, sitting beside Rook and Nashon Oakes. "What of the lady over there?"

Menthliot's beady eyes grew big. He gazed at Thorr as if he were a lunatic. "Demons are not permitted. Now come."

Rook stormed over and stepped in front of Thorr. He towered over the strange, little creature. "The lady you call evil is a valued member of our quest. This *demon* you refer to has guided us to this hell you call home. What evil has she done?"

Menthliot scowled. He turned his head and spat. When he looked back, his wrinkled mien broke into a diabolical grin. "She has led you to your death."

292

Soul Forge

Sentenced to Death

"**Demon.** That's what she is. Evil." Menthliot gestured wildly. "We deny her entrance. There is foulness about her." He hopped about, arms flailing. "You seek a power equally foul in the company of a devil. You stumble about our world, fortunate not to have encountered the Sentinel. It *will* find you. When it does, your quest will come to an abrupt end, that is certain. You seek to harness the same foulness the Stygian Lord employs to mutate us into what you now behold. We offer sanctuary, and yet, you ask us to sanction evil within our home." He spat into the sand at his feet.

Without waiting for a response, Menthliot's voice dropped to a low growl. "You lack the enlightenment we have achieved enduring this living hell. You're blind to the evil amongst you. This I grant but heed our warning. Terminate the demon before she leads you to ruin."

He folded his scaly arms across his bony chest and looked away in disgust. His head snapped back just as quick. "The darkness is almost upon us. Decide quickly. If you remain out here when it falls, we will pray for you, for that will be the only hope you will have left."

Menthliot walked back toward the cliffs with his entourage in tow.

The Marrow Wash seeped past, inches from Silurian's feet. He studied its bizarre flow. It had a consistency more like lava than water. The repulsive stench stung his senses whenever the flow sputtered and gurgled as gas bubbles rose to its surface and popped.

293

Soul Forge

He struggled to quieten his hammering heart. It felt like he had drawn upon a dormant energy deep within himself and channeled it through his sword. A sensation similar to that of Saros' enchantment.

He held his ancient blade in one hand and ran his fingers along its runes. If he didn't know better, he'd swear a warmth emanated from the strange characters.

Avarick stood a few paces behind him, warding his back. He offered the Enervator a weak smile.

Watching the river ooze by, he shivered as the adrenaline seeped from his body, leaving him oddly cold. Dizziness threatened to topple him into the flesh dissolving water, so he lowered himself to sit on the bank and placed his sword across his lap.

A high-pitched voice sounded behind him, approaching quickly. "Master. Master."

Several cave dwellers struggled to push past Avarick. Avarick grabbed the hilt of his black sword but Silurian stayed him with a nod that it was okay.

Menthliot stood over him with several other of the strange creatures circling around. Eight furry faces in all stared at him with grave concern.

Beyond the creatures, Pollard bounded over to help Avarick deal with them should the need arise.

Menthliot knelt before Silurian, his big eyes searching Silurian's. The closeness of the vile looking creature made Silurian lean back, but the cliff dweller leaned over him.

Menthliot tilted his head, slowly one way and then another. He reached out his hands—one hand resembling that of an ape.

Unable to lean back any farther, Silurian cringed as Menthliot traced the scars on his temple left behind by the wolf attack over two months ago. Menthliot's fingers slithered down to caress his cheek in a soothing, circular motion.

Avarick and Pollard moved to intervene but Silurian held up a hand to stay them. Whatever the creature was doing, it served to ease his tension.

Menthliot broke contact and for a few moments afterward, Silurian didn't have a care in the world. The whirling emotions concerning his confrontation with Rook and Thetis seeped back into his thoughts, but Menthliot's voice soothed them away.

"You are the warrior we have waited for."

The cave dweller pushed aside a stray wisp of silver hair from his eyes. He glanced over his shoulder to his peers. "Allow me to present to you, my Voil brethren, the warrior our songs revel. Ward him well, for he is your salvation."

Voil brethren? Silurian tightened his grip on the hilt of the Sacred Sword Voil. Why were these creatures named after his sword?

The other seven creatures bent in to converse with their leader in a squeaky, foreign tongue. Finally, Menthliot nodded. "Aye, our future draws nigh. This I sense."

Silurian got to his feet and loomed over the group of elders. "What are you talking about? I'm here to avenge my family. No more, no less. I aim to kill Helleden Misenthorpe."

The cave dwellers shrunk down and shivered.

All except Menthliot. "Yes, you can end the Stygian Lord."

Silurian sheathed his sword. "Look, we need you to direct us to the Soul Forge."

The creatures shuddered.

Menthliot gave Silurian a sympathetic look. "Allow me to relate the crux of our legend."

Not waiting for permission, Menthliot broke into song.

"From ancestry unknown,
a new race has grown.
We are Voil by design,
tools of the malign.

Minions cast in hell,
waring the Sentinel.
Hiding beneath the stone,
inept, we grant thee home.

Cower though we may,
we await the coming day.

Soul Forge

A warrior shall travel down our path,
and deliver his unhindered wrath.

Thus, the prophets do proclaim,
we may yet outlive this shame.
O warrior, pray, slay the Sentinel,
and grant us leave of our living hell.

Menthliot finished, gazing intently into Silurian's eyes. "You alone have been granted the grace to end the Stygian Lord."

You alone. You! Alone! The words reverberated through Silurian's mind. He tried to focus on Menthliot but couldn't calm his thoughts. He looked beyond the odd creature, to the base tent erected for Thorr, searching for something to quell the confusion addling him. The tent quivered. Ithnan ducked out through the large door flap and held it open for Nashon, Ithaman, Sadyra, Rook and Thetis as they stepped into the daylight.

Other than Rook and Thetis, the group exiting the tent walked toward him, their concern evident.

Nashon, pipe in hand, pulled Menthliot aside and had a few words with the creature, before he asked Silurian, "How fare you?"

Silurian shrugged. How was he supposed to feel? He had just been moments from killing his best friend.

"You have us worried." Nashon puffed upon his pipe before adding, "Menthliot claims he can see deep into a person's psyche. He fears you suffer from overexertion. I agree. It's too early for you to undertake a journey of this sort after what you went through at the portal."

Menthliot claims? They had just met the creature. Overexertion? Everybody suffered from exhaustion.

"Menthliot says you summoned a dormant ability within you…a kind of magic."

Silurian scoffed at the idea. "Pfft."

Menthliot nodded and moved off to join the others of his clan. Reaching a group of cave dwellers milling about the outskirts of the camp, he turned and said, "Assemble your people. Darkness is nigh. Join us in our stone sanctuary. Only there will you be safe."

296

Soul Forge

Thorr nodded and Pollard's booming voice gave the order to break camp.

Silurian remained where he was, staring at the wind-swept sandstone beneath his feet, unable to grasp the significance of the Voil. By the time he lifted his head to take in the activity going on around him, the tents had been taken down and stowed, the fires put out, and the quest milled about awaiting direction.

Close by, Alhena appeared paler than usual. The concern in his voice made Silurian focus on his words.

"What of Thetis and Rook?"

Thorr walked toward Alhena. He raised his eyebrows. "They have fled upriver. Toward Soul Forge. They felt it better this way. Their fate is in their own hands, let it not be ours."

A cold chill gripped Silurian.

Alhena frowned. "And what about this Sentinel thing lurking about? If it is as bad as we fear, they are doomed. Do we forget the fate of Seafarer and the scouts this quickly? If Silurian *or* Rook perish, so will the quest. We will be seeking sanctuary in vain."

"Thetis assured us she'll not allow the Sentinel to harm Rook," Thorr said. "And, Menthliot promised his people will ward their progress from secret entrances along the cliff walls. If Rook's life is imperiled, Menthliot assures me they'll offer him safety. Of Thetis, who's to say? For some reason they fear her."

Alhena leaned on his staff, "They may not have time to intervene."

"Fear not, my friend. Pollard and Olmar are preparing to go after them."

Alhena shot Thorr an incredulous look.

Thorr shrugged. "They're too big to fit in the tunnels. Blindsight has also agreed to accompany them, ensuring they have eyes at night, and Longsight has offered to be their eyes during the day. They will go after Rook and Thetis to keep them safe."

The four men in question were just finishing adjusting their gear before setting off up the Marrow Wash.

Alhena turned away, shaking his head. He watched the brave men as they started out. "We have sentenced them to death."

Soul Forge

Mesmerized

Menthliot led the members of the quest toward the base of the cliff, around the huge boulder where Longsight had originally restrained the first two Voil.

Everyone was surprised when the Voil elder disappeared. One moment he chatted with another of his ilk, the next instant he disappeared. Closer examination revealed a hidden cleft, its mouth so narrow and low that even the Voil had to duck to enter.

The quest dropped to their hands and knees and crawled into the dark tunnel.

It didn't take long in the tight confines of the dark passage for second thoughts to bombard Alhena. He could hear the anxiety of the quest members on either side of him—fore and aft. Claustrophobia had his nerves on end, the feeling more intense than when he and Rook had stumbled through the tunnels of the Splendoor Falls catacombs.

He couldn't get Silurian's confrontation with Thetis from his mind. Although there was definitely something off with the woman, it seemed a big mistake to abandon her now—especially if that meant Rook as well. What reason did she have to lead them astray?

What made the standoff more incredible, was the fact that nobody knew anything about the Voil. And yet, here they were, spread out on their hands and knees, totally vulnerable. If the tunnel was a trap, they were all dead. An eerie thought permeated his better judgment. Perhaps the Voil *were* the Sentinel.

He tried to shake the thought from his mind. There was little to do about it now. Inexorably he pulled himself along, his mind muddled with delusional thoughts. Would he ever be able to stand erect again? Were they going to crawl all the way to the Soul Forge?

Soul Forge

The scariest part was, there was really no way back. The constrictive tunnel forced them to travel one behind the other. As individuals contemplated their fears, the procession spread out.

Just before mayhem ensued within the suffocating tunnel, Alhena detected a faint glow ahead. Rounding a tight bend, he stopped crawling and closed his eyes to shield them against the intensity of a bright light directly ahead.

Sadyra, following closely behind, nudged his feet, prompting him into motion. Her muted voice reached him, "Come on, old man. Get that bag of bones moving."

Alhena smiled. He hardly knew her but he sensed the petite archer was full of spirit.

The tunnel opened into a small cavern, allowing him to stand, despite the protests of his aching back. He attempted to stretch out the kinks but Sadyra and the rest of the company emerged behind him, pushing their way into the hollow.

He found an open spot and stood still, mesmerized by the unnatural lighting that seemed to soothe his anxiety. Glittering sapphires, rubies, diamonds, and other priceless gems embedded into the ceiling rock cast brilliant beams of multi-coloured light into the subterranean cavern. The sandy rock surface they had interminably crawled upon had turned into veined, white marble.

He couldn't shake the feeling they were in trouble. He searched out Thorr, but before he had a chance to relate his suspicions, a sweet aroma wafted into the cavern, and his worries drifted away.

All around him, 'oohs' and 'ahs' filled the tightly packed grotto, as the quest took in the dazzling spectacle.

Silurian forced his way through the crowd toward him, his dazed expression cleft by a rare smile.

Alhena smiled back. The entire company smiled. Absently, he noted, the Voil did not.

Menthliot smacked his ape-like hand against its human counterpart with delight, his hypnotic voice grabbing Alhena's attention. "Welcome to our domain. You are now guests of the Voil." He broke into a hideous laugh.

The quest laughed with him.

Soul Forge

Menthliot turned his back to the quest and threw his hands over his head, his voluminous sleeves hanging off his arms. He waggled his fingers. "Come. Together we revel in the realm of our founder, Carmichael Voil. Know the sensation you are experiencing is but a hint of the euphoria that awaits you. You are free of the witch."

Distant alarm bells reverberated through Alhena's mind, but he couldn't concentrate long enough to vocalize his concern.

The mystic Voil bounded through an opening at the far end of the cavern.

Alhena was certain the opening hadn't been there a moment ago.

A maniacal laugh followed Menthliot into the tunnel.

Alhena's body no longer retained its aches and pains. The soothing atmosphere of the lights and smell soothed him. Deep inside, a little voice cried out for attention, warning him that the euphoria he experienced was similar to that of the portal. Before he latched onto the significance, the voice slipped away.

Prodded by those behind him, he was jostled into the queueing lineup, joyously following in the wake of Menthliot's laughter.

Rook trudged along in a stupor. What had just happened? Silurian had wanted to kill Thetis with no other provocation than the words uttered by a creature he had never met before. The next thing Rook knew, he had fired an arrow at Silurian and now, here they were, stumbling along the banks of the Marrow Wash in absolute darkness, at the mercy of the Sentinel and whatever hell spawn roamed the night.

He clutched Thetis' elbow for dear life. She had no trouble navigating the darkness. As they walked, she averred that the Voil were the evil ones, and he should fear for the company's safety, not his own. He shook his head. Nothing made sense anymore.

Regardless of her assurances, Rook couldn't help thinking about the beast that had destroyed Seafarer. He shivered.

Thetis squeezed his hand, but it gave him little solace.

He placed his arm around her waist, pondering what kind of demonic creature could actually live within the Marrow Wash's acidic waters. Perhaps it watched them now. He stepped away from the unseen river, pulling Thetis with him.

She steered him around outcroppings of rock and through sudden depressions, with tugs and pulls upon his arm.

At one point, he withdrew his saber in a futile effort to alleviate his mounting fear. A fat lot of good a sword would do him. He couldn't see the nose on his face. He slid the sword back into its scabbard, admiring Thetis' bravery, trying hard to believe in her steadfast assurances that they would be okay. What choice did he have?

Their progress proved slow, due to his blindness. Even with Thetis leading the way, he stumbled a lot. If anyone, or indeed *anything*, followed them, they would be easy prey.

He almost laughed out loud when he caught himself glancing at the Marrow Wash for the hundredth time, half expecting the Sentinel to rise out of its milky depths. How could he expect to see anything in the absolute darkness?

The sound of exotic bugs, unique birds and small wildlife had fallen silent when the darkness descended. Other than his heavy breathing and the soft scuffs of their suede boots, the only sounds disturbing the night came from the Marrow Wash as it burbled and slopped its way by. The noise of the river set his nerves on end. Every slap of the flowing ooze made him jump.

Silurian stood within the cavern, enthralled by the lights and smell, but he didn't jump into the fray departing the cavern. Something about Menthliot's words had unsettled him. The Voil elder claimed Carmichael Voil was their founder. Carmichael was ironically the name of the lost shrine where his sword had rested. That couldn't be a coincidence.

He wandered after the company in a daze as the men and women of the quest skipped and sang ahead of him. He grinned despite the nagging feeling that this was wrong. He tried to concentrate, to push aside the fog, but the hypnotic lights and sweet aroma massaged the knot of doubt from his mind.

He wasn't aware of much else, but he sensed his adrenaline mounting. The thought of enduring another episode like he had just experienced with Rook and Thetis unnerved him. As his mind drifted, a kernel of rational thought implored him to listen—the Voil were responsible for what was happening to them. The sensations wafting over him were just like those he had experienced at the portal.

The revelation gave his mind something to grasp. If he were to succumb to the Voil charm, they were all lost.

A lone Voil skipped along beside him, nodding to itself. Silurian had no idea where this Voil had come from. He hadn't seen it before.

Entering the tunnel in a daze, he forced himself to focus on the relics hung along the walls. Helms, shields, swords—all too large to have been wielded by any of the misshapen race. Between the pieces of silver armour, great tapestries hung, depicting colourful scenes of the Voil, usually within the confines of a tunnel or cavernous chamber, performing deeds, that at a glance, appeared heroic. The crystallized ceiling continued into the tunnel, refracting a kaleidoscope of colours upon the dirty, marble floor.

Side passages branched off at regular intervals on the right. Within each of the corridors stood one or two armed Voil watching them pass.

Silurian lost sight of the quest. Their singing voices diminished as they distanced themselves from him.

The Voil walking with Silurian made no effort to catch up.

A sudden, bone chilling sensation crept up Silurian's spine. The Sentinel.

The mischievous creature bound along beside him with nary a care in the world.

Silurian's mind grasped at the fleeting kernel of sanity and tugged on it for all he was worth, pulling his mind out of the haze and breaking the spell.

The strange, greyish creature stopped. Its yellow eyes turned on him. Its lips parted, revealing jagged, brown teeth.

Bile rose in Silurian's throat. He sensed the tendrils of the hypnotic environment attempting to reclaim him. He pushed the advances aside,

Soul Forge

his mind alive to the quest's peril, both inside and outside of the sand cliffs.

His right hand grasped the hilt of his ironically named, Sacred Sword Voil.

The Voil backed away, a serrated knife appearing in its hand. It made a sudden lunge at him before spinning around to flee, but it wasn't quick enough to escape the path of Silurian's sword. Its head thudded upon the marble floor, rolling away from its body—moments before the bedazzling lights went out.

Soul Forge

The Evil Within

Silurian stood alone in the dark, afraid. Mildew and rot had replaced the sweet aroma.

He swung his blade around, probing the darkness to deter the unseen creatures he sensed sneaking up on him.

He detected movement ahead. Someone whispered nearby. He stabbed the darkness and jarred his sword off a stone wall. There had been many side passages but he couldn't see them now.

His fear mounted. Sightless, and lacking the ancient charm of the Sacred Sword Voil, he was struck by how vulnerable he really was.

A soft scuffling sounded close to him. He hacked wildly about the darkness, never once striking what his instinct told him lurked just beyond his reach.

Common sense urged him to retreat—screamed at him to run, but where could he go? His friends were up ahead, caught unaware in the enchantment and lost within the Under Realm.

Heightened by terror, his adrenaline surged, thickening his neck and pounding at his temples. He forced himself forward, deathly afraid of what the sensation gathering deep inside him meant. He'd felt it before. The day he had returned home to the gruesome discovery of his family. He had managed to fetter it then, but there had been no one around to unleash it upon.

His mind reeled. The quest was in jeopardy. Tricked and lied to by creatures bearing the same name as his sword.

His control slipped. A radiant heat emanated from the pommel of his sword. Perhaps the relic retained some of latent power. He clung to that hope.

The sword became too hot to hang on to, but he refused to let it go. Imperceptible at first, a pale blue glow limned the runes of the Sacred

Sword Voil, clearly visible in the absolute darkness. Just like it had when it possessed Saros' enchantment.

He spun about, listening for the telltale whistle of air that denoted a blade cutting toward him. He envisioned claws shooting out of the darkness, ripping at the exposed flesh of his neck.

His sword pulsed brighter, illuminating the blood-stained floor, the metal so hot that its heat radiated upon his face, but his hands remained unaffected.

Laughter sounded behind him, taunting him from beyond the edge of the sword's light.

He spun around and the voices receded, but new voices sounded just beyond the fringes of darkness. He twirled, fast as a cat. The new voices receded just as quickly, replaced by the original ones, behind him again.

Ignoring whatever crept up on him, he leapt forward. Small, blue flames writhed along his sword's edges, coalescing momentarily at its tip before leaping from the blade into the darkness beyond.

He was just as surprised as the unfortunate creature that had gotten caught in the conflagration. Tapestries burst into flames, illuminating the tunnel beyond. The fleeing backsides of screeching Voil ran away from the charred victim writhing on the ground.

He paused, examining the devastation his sword had inflicted upon the pitiful creature as it cried out in agony and fell still. Spurred by his shipmate's imminent peril, he ran after the retreating Voil.

He came to an intersection and contemplated giving chase to those who had fled that way up the left tunnel, but he detected a malign presence directly ahead. He hadn't sensed an evil this profoundly since the day he had faced Helleden Misenthorpe upon the bloody plains of Lugubrius.

He took a deep breath and his fear fell away. He had agreed to join Alhena for the sole purpose of putting an end to Helleden's tyranny. If the cliffs fell this day, so be it. He started up the passageway, blue flames dripping from his sword and fizzling upon the marble floor behind him.

As soon as he entered the next tunnel, he was accosted by wave after wave of foul smells—death and rot so pervasive he wondered whether he ran through the underside of a graveyard.

Soul Forge

A passage branched off to his right, then three more to his left. Passing these, he slowed his jog to a hurried walk. In this labyrinth of tunnels, he was beginning to doubt which way he should go.

Another passage shot off to his right. He stopped and pointed his sword into its dark interior. His fine neck hair stood on end. The creature he sought waited for him at the end of this shaft.

The tunnel was no different from the one he left behind. Masterfully rendered tapestries adorned the walls, hung between countless pieces of metal armour, dimly lit in the blue aura cast by his sword.

He walked, endeavouring to perceive where the malign presence emanated from. The floor sloped downward toward the cliff face.

Doubt crept into his mind. It was his fault for allowing the Voil to mislead them. They were in the Under Realm. How could he be so naïve?

Dispatched by Saros himself, Thetis had led them through the portal, as safely as one could expect given the nature of the transition, and guided them to the shores of the Under Realm. Who else could have achieved that? Had someone else suggested such a journey feasible, he'd have thought them crazy.

Her relationship with Rook had given him grief, but reflecting back over the last several weeks, perhaps he was the cause of his own despair. Who was he to deny other people their happiness?

One unfounded allegation by a creature he had never met before had triggered a calamity. By his own hand, a grave injustice had been bestowed upon Thetis and his old friend, Rook.

It dawned on him who lurked in the shadows. Menthliot.

His pace increased. The Voil elder had manipulated him, accomplishing what Seafarer had warned them not to let happen. He and Rook were separated.

The vileness emanating from the Voil elder grew stronger. The Sacred Sword Voil pulsed and blue flames leapt into the darkness, igniting the wall hangings and scorching the tarnished armour.

His actions beside the Marrow Wash weighed on him. What had possessed him to turn on Thetis? The answer to that question had become obvious. Menthliot had coerced him into leading the quest into a trap. By siding with the Voil elder, he had thrown away their chance of reaching the power source capable of destroying Helleden.

306

Soul Forge

A fist-sized ball of blue-white fire coalesced along the top edge of his sword and leaped toward his unseen adversary. He slowed his pace. The creature was close.

Menthliot? The Sentinel? Were they one and the same? Perhaps the Voil wizard had killed Seafarer and the sailors. It made sense. Leaving a powerful sorcerer like Menthliot behind in his stead, freed Helleden to venture into the world to pursue whatever hellish intent he desired.

A jagged bolt of energy sizzled through the darkness, impacting the wall on his left. It detonated with a thunderous crack.

The concussion threw Silurian against the opposite wall. His sword flew out of his hands and buried itself almost hilt-deep in the marble floor—the sword's luminescence extinguished upon impact. The light in the tunnel dimmed considerably, lit only by the flames consuming the wall hangings.

Stunned, Silurian struggled to gather himself. The hair-raising sound of a second bolt singeing the air got him moving—the energy bolt blowing a small hole in the floor where he had stood. The concussion tossed him into the wall across from his imbedded blade. Rock fragments exploded outward—a shard of marble tore into his left cheek.

He didn't have much time. Ignoring the searing pain in his cheek, he grabbed the imbedded sword with one hand and pulled.

Nothing happened.

He grasped the hilt with both hands, braced his feet and gave a mighty tug. The pommel slipped through his sweaty hands, sending him staggering across the tunnel to knock against a smoldering wall-hanging.

The air crackled again.

He pushed away from the wall as the bolt impacted the tapestry. Chunks of granite erupted into the passageway.

Staggering to remain on his feet, he grasped his sword's handle.

From down the hall, an evil laugh reached him as another crackling ball of energy flew toward him.

If he were to die, his companions were doomed. His temples pounded. Gathering his resolve, he sensed his adrenaline surging. The sword hilt warmed in his grasp as he pulled on it for all he was worth.

Soul Forge

The rock around the sword exploded in a shower of debris that blew back at him.

The crackling energy bolt missed him by a whisper, but as it struck the wall beyond, he was thrown to the ground.

Dazed, he rose to his feet and stumbled toward the Voil wizard. Before he got any closer, the darkness was pushed aside by a storm of crackling energy. Bolt after sizzling bolt seared toward him.

In the tunnel's close confines, he had nowhere to go.

He intercepted the first bolt above the hilt of the Sacred Sword Voil, the impact knocking him backward a few steps, but otherwise it didn't affect him. The energy exploded into a series of arcs, fizzling out as they hit the ground, ceiling, and walls around him.

With renewed confidence, he intercepted the second volley and then the third, each one causing him to stagger momentarily. Moving forward, small blue flames dripped from the tip of his blade.

The hypnotic ceiling lighting blazed to life, blinding him. He looked up for just a moment, but the distraction proved long enough. Three fierce blasts smote his wavering sword and threw him to the ground.

He sat as fast as his stunned body allowed, but he couldn't get to his feet. He intercepted four more energy bolts, the last one driving him onto his back.

Flash after crackling flash smote the tunnel all around him, pelting him with rock and marble debris. Fighting through the pain, he rolled onto his side and scrambled to his feet but was immediately blown backward as an energy bolt tore up a slab of marble and dropped it on his legs. Try as he might, he couldn't pull himself free.

Menthliot let out a hideous laugh and the barrage ceased.

Silurian focused on channeling whatever power his sword possessed into keeping the slab of rock from crushing his legs. He shielded his eyes against a bright flash, but the ensuing scream had him staring straight at the wizard.

Menthliot approached, dangling a large object from his right hand—a bloody dagger in his left.

Before Silurian recognized what Menthliot carried, the Voil wizard heaved it at him.

The spheroid object bounced with a sickening crack in front of the gouge left behind by the uprooted chunk of marble crushing his legs.

Soul Forge

The object was some poor creature's head. The atrocity skidded into the gouge and came to rest, staring vacantly at him. Wisps of grey hair covered part of the face. A long grey beard, stained red, lay twisted around the agonized face. Alhena's vacant gaze stared back at him.

Silurian gagged. Adrenaline screamed through him. He no longer felt the weight of the slab. He glared murder at the Voil wizard.

Menthliot smiled, exposing row upon row of jagged teeth. The makings of another lightning bolt crackled along his dagger's edge.

Seething, Silurian slammed the Sacred Sword Voil into the marble slab pinning his legs. The massive rock exploded in a shower of stone shards.

Menthliot stopped walking. The energy sizzling along his dagger winked out as several marble slivers penetrated his hide.

Before the Voil wizard had a chance to defend himself, Silurian jumped to his feet and hoisted his sword high. The feral roar escaping his throat drowned out the crackling of white-hot energy materializing along Menthliot's dagger.

Silurian's sword slashed toward the marble floor, cleaving the vile wizard from shoulder to hip. As the dead wizard fell away, the unnatural lighting winked out.

Silurian stood in the ghostly semi-darkness, the tunnel lit by the muted light of smoldering tapestries and the waning glow of his sword. He dropped to his knees before the head of his dear friend and wept.

The charred tunnel became still as the remaining light failed him. He knelt, shaking with grief, desolate and alone in the absolute darkness of the Under Realm.

A wave of vertigo spun the tunnel around him as his exhausted body relinquished its hold on consciousness.

Soul Forge

Pursued

The burbling Marrow Wash played havoc with Rook's nerves. He had no idea how Thetis put up with his crushing grip on her arm, but he wasn't about to let go. His bow dangled uselessly in his left hand. In his own realm, he was lethal with it. In the Under Realm darkness, the bow was dead weight.

Thetis' movements were self-assured as she led him over, around and through obstacles unseen to him. She hadn't offered much in the way of conversation since the darkness fell, other than the obligatory, 'step right' or 'step up.'

During brief periods of time when Rook was able to calm his mind, he thought about Silurian. He knew the man better than most. As such, he appreciated the fact that he was still alive after their recent incident. Ever since their time in the Wilds, Rook had come to know that as benevolent as the old Silurian used to be, the new Silurian had no qualms of killing anyone who stood in his way. Thank the gods for whoever had shot that poison dart.

He tightened his grip on Thetis.

The Voil. Nothing else made sense. The Voil must have coerced Silurian into believing Thetis was evil.

Seafarer's words echoed through his mind, *"Heed my warning, Rook. Our hope, Zephyr's hope, depends on you two staying together. If you become separated, we may all be lost."* Perhaps the Voil also knew this to be true, and now he walked alone but for Thetis.

The Marrow Wash slapped loudly beside them. He swallowed. If the Sentinel rose from the river and slew them, would the result really be any different than if Silurian had killed them yesterday?

He shook his head. He shouldn't have allowed yesterday's events to dictate his future. He had been manipulated by…

Soul Forge

He pulled up short, yanking on Thetis' arm.

"What is it?" Thetis asked, a hint of annoyance in her voice.

"I shouldn't have left the company."

"What are you talking about? They cast you out."

"No, *they* didn't. The Voil did."

"More like the Voil cast me out."

Rook let her arm drop. He located her shoulder and gripped hard. "Whatever. It was a ruse. The Voil are in league with the Sentinel. I don't understand how they convinced Silurian to think you're evil, but they did. What matters is we are separated, and that's not good."

"There's not much we can do about it now," Thetis said and spun around, breaking his grasp.

Rook couldn't see, but he knew by her reaction that something had caught her attention. "What is it?"

She didn't respond right away. When she did, he heard the concern in her voice, "I'm not sure. Something is happening within the canyon walls." She paused. "I detect a strong magical disturbance somewhere behind us. A struggle is happening."

"What?" He located her arm and stepped closer. "The Sentinel?"

"Aye, yes," she said at once, then corrected herself, "no, actually, not the Sentinel. It's hard to tell. Someone conjures a powerful sorcery. The quest is in peril."

"We've got to help them," Rook said, trying to peer through the inky darkness in a futile effort to discover a passageway into the cliff face. He released his hold upon Thetis, ready to run blindly toward the canyon wall.

A distant laugh echoed up the canyon.

Rook sensed the malign sorcery at play—the foulness almost palpable in the air. He winced. How had he let himself become separated from the quest? Seafarer and Alhena had warned him not to let this happen.

He located Thetis again and pulled her to him, his free arm about her waist. He felt her shudder, and then the presence of the magic was gone.

He whispered, "I sensed it too."

"Aye. Such power rarely goes unnoticed. Perhaps it *was* the Sentinel."

Soul Forge

Rook bowed his head. "It's my fault. I shouldn't have allowed us to part company. If anything happens to Silurian…" He didn't know how to finish that statement.

Thetis started upriver.

He let his hands slide from her waist.

She stepped back and embraced him.

He buried his face into her neck and wept.

"I'm sorry," she said softly. "Their loss is profound. Let's hope we are equal to the task ahead."

Rook shook his head rapidly. "We shouldn't have left them. You and I aren't strong enough to do what must be done."

"And what could we have done to prevent their death?"

Their death? Silurian, dead? Her words confirmed what he refused to believe. It hit him like a battering ram. Tears rolled off his cheeks. "Anything. Everything! We should have tried. You could've made a difference."

"No, my love. My presence may have prolonged their death, but in the end, we would be dead too. I am not strong enough to face the Sentinel. We made the right choice."

"The right choice?" Rook shouted. "How can you say that? They're dead. The *quest,* is dead. Silurian is…" His voice cracked, "My best friend is dead. Without him our mission is impossible. Helleden has won."

"No. Never impossible," Thetis declared. "If we had been in the realm of the cliff dwellers with the quest, then yes, it would've been impossible. But you and I are still alive, and as long as we are, we maintain the ability to try. That much we can do."

Rook didn't respond.

Thetis hugged him, running her fingers through his matted hair.

When his heaving breaths abated, he broke free of her embrace and held her at arm's length, his bow still clutched in his left hand. "The cave dwellers offered the quest sanctuary from the Sentinel. They claim to have lived long within the wall of stone without the Sentinel reaching them. If what they say is true, how has the Sentinel managed to invade their domain now?" He fell silent for a moment. Everything seemed so confusing. "Unless."

Soul Forge

Thetis completed his thought. "Perhaps the cave dwellers are the evil ones. I fear it is as I said, but Silurian's mind was poisoned against me. I sensed a vileness from the moment we descended into the canyon. I didn't know where it emanated from until it was too late. They poisoned Silurian and the rest of the quest against me before we even knew they were there."

Rook swallowed. He released her arms and prodded her into motion, never losing touch as they continued upriver. Anger started to overpower his grief. If this was how it was going to play out, he was up to the challenge. "Let's get on with it then."

Thetis took a few steps and stopped. She stared back the way they had come. Her whisper raised the hair on the back of his neck, "We're not alone."

Rook's blood ran cold.

"Several creatures trail us. None of them gifted, but two are much larger than the others."

He neither sensed, nor saw a thing. "Attack or run?"

"If we wish to prevent them from following us, we need to take them out. Other than the Sentinel, I'm sure I can handle whatever comes our way."

She grabbed Rook's arm and led him toward the canyon wall, taking him behind a mound of fallen rock. He crouched low, keeping his eyes downriver, although he couldn't even see the rocks they hid amongst.

A pinprick of orange light emerged around a bend in the canyon wall. In the dead silence of the gorge, the scrape of boots sounded harsh on the rocky terrain.

As their pursuers got closer, the bobbing light grew and separated into three burning torches. Rook discerned a silhouette jogging several feet in front of the burning brands.

He felt Thetis move away from him toward the lead runner, the one without a brand. It wasn't unusual for creatures to see in the dark. This type of darkness, well, who knew, but Thetis and the Sentinel obviously saw well enough. So did the sailor…

"Thetis, no." Rook scrambled forward, almost knocking her over.

At the sound of his voice, the torch bearers threw their brands to the ground and dove behind cover.

313

Soul Forge

Thetis gained her balance and scanned the banks of the Marrow Wash. "Great. Now I have to search them out."

Their pursuers spoke hastily amongst themselves, and then a familiar voice echoed toward them, "Bowman? Is that you?"

Rook almost collapsed with relief. The voice belonged to Pollard Banebridge. That meant the rest of the quest wasn't far behind. They had realized their error in time.

"Over here. By the canyon wall."

Blindsight traipsed up to them, followed closely by Pollard, Olmar and Longsight, the latter three had reacquired their torches.

Rook shook their hands. "Are we glad to see you. We were afraid the Voil had killed you. How far back are the others?"

The newcomers looked at each other.

"They ain't," Olmar said.

Rook gaped. "What do you mean, they aren't?"

Pollard had sheathed his sword, but he quickly drew it again. "What's wrong? Are they in danger?"

Rook couldn't speak.

Thetis grabbed his free hand and squeezed. "We fear they have been betrayed. Offered false sanctuary and led to their doom."

Pollard let the double tips of his sword "*chink*" into the soft stone at his feet. "That cannot be. They are safe within the wall. Safe from the night terrors. Safe from the hell beasts skulking about. You are mistaken. The Voil keep them safe."

Thetis' braid waggled as she shook her head. She pursed her lips to speak but didn't look the big man in the eye. "The Voil *are* the hell beasts."

314

Soul Forge

Forbidden

Knives continuously being thrust into his skull without killing him. That's what Silurian thought was happening to him as he fought his way back to consciousness. His stomach also pained him, but neither condition was worse than what greeted him when he opened his eyes.

He lay in a room with the same ceiling lighting that had illuminated the entrance tunnels. Several mutated faces hovered over him, talking in earnest amongst themselves. Seeing he was awake, their conversation ceased. As one, they leaned in to inspect his face.

Silurian tried to sink deeper into whatever he lay upon, but the bed held firm. He threw his hands up before his face, to ward off the press of Voil bodies.

A chair scraped on stone somewhere behind him. "Easy Silurian. They mean you no harm."

That voice?

The strange creatures parted to allow a wispy haired, old man with strange white eyes to step between them.

What kind of demonic trickery is this?

"Easy, my friend," Alhena soothed. "You have endured more than any man should."

Silurian peered around his upraised arms. "Alhena?"

Alhena smiled as only Alhena could. "Aye, my friend. It is me."

Silurian's eyes filled with tears.

"Let it out Sire. You have endured a lot."

Silurian's lip's trembled. He tried to say something but couldn't. Instead, he wrapped his shaking arms around Alhena, pulling his head to his chest. He held his face against the top of the old man's head and wept. Nothing made sense anymore, but all he cared about at the

315

Soul Forge

moment was that Alhena was alive. He opened his eyes wide—that meant the rest of the quest were probably alive as well.

They cried together for a while, Silurian unwilling to let him go.

When Alhena straightened up, Silurian clasped his wrists and pulled him closer.

"I-I can't believe it. I saw it myself. You were…" He couldn't bring himself to say it. Just the thought made him shudder. "I thought you lost."

Alhena smiled. "Nay, I still dodder about with my head attached."

"But…" Silurian trailed off.

"It wasn't real. My death at least."

"But I saw you."

"Please, Sire, I'm not easily offended, but I do hope I look a wee bit better than that," Alhena said.

"Where is the Voil wizard, Menthliot? He attacked me."

Alhena nodded. "Aye, that he did. The Sentinel had taken control of him. If not for the aid of the rest of these kind creatures, we would *all* be dead. Trust me when I tell you they lost many lives seeing us out of harm's way."

Silurian didn't know what to think. He closed his eyes. Was the company still under the spell cast by the hypnotic ceiling lights? The air was close and a bit musty, not sweet like before. He studied the ceiling, still basically the same, but the light seemed different somehow. Brighter perhaps.

Avarick burst into the chamber, out of breath. He started to say something, but seeing Silurian awake, he stopped. His eyes grew wide for only a moment before he declared, "Pollard and the others have returned. They bring Rook and Thetis with them."

Captain Thorr's voice sounded from a corner of the room, "Where are they? Take me to them."

"This way," Avarick said, pointing into the corridor. "They're being fed and briefed on last night's events."

Thorr brushed past Avarick and left the chamber.

Avarick lingered long enough to say, "That was some demonstration you put on. Remind me not to anger you." He raised his eyebrows. "We feared you lost. Apparently, you had other ideas. As did Pollard. He ended up killing five Voil as he forced his way into the tunnels

316

before we were able to calm him down. Thetis told him the Voil had killed us. Imagine that?" That said, the Enervator left the chamber to catch up with Thorr.

Silurian sat up, totally confused. He still wore his regular clothing, but the rock dust had been brushed away.

Alhena walked behind the bed and retrieved the baldric containing his sword and handed it to him.

Silurian unsheathed it long enough to inspect the blade. Whatever damage it had sustained during his battle with Menthliot, someone had taken great care to clean it up, leaving it in better condition than it had been before the confrontation.

"Avarick saw to its welfare, if you can believe that?" Alhena offered him a faint smile. "Come, if you are up to it. Let's see what turmoil we can stir up."

Silurian limped after him.

Exotic aromas of unknown dishes reached them long before they entered a cavernous room carved out of the solid rock. Ornate marble pillars soared in concentric circles, spiraling outward, many stories high. Large shards of illuminated gemstones encrusted the domed roof, each one worth enough to purchase a small kingdom.

Servants scurried about the cavern delivering trays laden with food. A steady hum filled the hall—the voice of hundreds of Voil and sailors settling down to eat. As Silurian and Alhena entered the vast chamber, all conversation ceased.

Silurian turned to walk right back out, but a familiar voice called to him.

Pollard lumbered forward, beaming a mighty smile. He slapped his hands around Silurian's in a crushing handshake. "Well met, Silurian. You are a welcome sight."

"Thanks Pollard. It's good to see you safe." Silurian said, distracted, searching the cavern for Rook. He found him sitting at a table with Thetis. Their eyes met briefly. He forced a grim smile. Rook nodded, his expression unreadable.

Soul Forge

"Ach. Take more than a dark night and a river beastie to stop Pollard, let me assure you."

Silurian sighed. He resigned himself to the knowledge that things would never be the same with Rook. He responded to Pollard as the big man's words registered, "From what I've been hearing, this particular beastie isn't your normal nasty."

"Ach." Pollard led them to a couple of empty chairs. Seated about the large stone table were Tara and several other shipmates he and Pollard had enjoyed sparring with on the voyage to the portal. The rest of the quest sat about the surrounding tables, trying hard not to stare at their strange host who occupied the remainder of the cavern.

After an oddly satisfying meal, Silurian talked quietly amongst those nearest him until an ancient Voil entered the chamber and hobbled up to him, bearing his weight with a knotted, twisted limb of some dark wooded tree. The short length of polished cane, etched in snarling faces of creatures Silurian had never seen before, sported rows of sharp teeth and forked tongues. The walking stick appeared to writhe in the creature's scaly claws.

"Fear me not, Silurian Mintaka. Long have I awaited this day." The haggard creature gazed at Silurian with watery, yellowed orbs that were barely distinguishable amongst the wizened folds of his cheeks. He offered a shaky paw. "I am Wendglow, leader of these beautiful peoples."

Long have I awaited this day? Speechless, Silurian watched the little creature extend his twisted digits in greeting. He reluctantly shook the proffered paw.

Out of nowhere, two younger Voil scampered over to their location carrying a well-used, wooden armchair covered in layers of multi-coloured material. The aged creature gave his assistants a curt nod and sank into the chair's folds.

The diminutive aides scurried away.

The ancient Voil took in all those around him. "For those of you who didn't hear, I am Wendglow." His voice, gravelly with age, carried well. "I am the accepted leader of the Voil. On behalf of my peoples I offer a heartfelt welcome to you, our guests from a far-off land."

Wendglow turned his attention to Silurian. "I apologize on behalf of my people for the deplorable greeting you received at the hands of one

Soul Forge

of our elders. Allow me to explain to you the events that led to things getting out of hand."

Silurian fidgeted under the scrutiny of the bizarre creature.

Wendglow nodded to Thetis, sitting at the next table. Judging by the space the Voil gave her, they weren't overly keen about her presence.

"I also must ask the forgiveness of fair Thetis. Perhaps we have judged you prematurely, hmm? We left you to fend for yourself in the wilds of the Marrow Wash. Not many survive the river's banks when the light is extinguished. Fortunate for you, the Sentinel's attention lay elsewhere."

"Thank you, Master Wendglow. Without your timely intervention our quest would surely have been lost." Thetis said, her sweet voice a mollifying charm.

Wendglow's thin lips offered her a faint smile—one that Silurian construed to be fake.

Wendglow raised his voice, his eyes taking in the entire company from the *Gerrymander*. "I don't know where to begin, so I shall start by saying that, yes, the ceiling lighting can, and did, place you under an enchantment. You likely experienced a sweet aroma as well. More theurgy."

A ripple of conversation broke out amongst the quest members. Pollard stood, crossing his arms. The muttering stopped.

"You are right to be upset. Let me assure you, these measures are taken for your safety, and indeed, our own. When darkness falls, the Sentinel roams. The demon is too large to enter our tunnels, but he is able to control one's mind from quite a distance."

More muttering sounded. Pollard's scowl curtailed it.

"The enchantments are in place to combat the Sentinel's psionic ability. A type of mind control, if you will. Until you are deep into our cliffside home, you are susceptible to the Sentinel's reach. Many Voil also possess a psionic ability, but nowhere near the strength of the Sentinel. Those Voil in question, though, are unaffected by the enchantments we put into place. Menthliot was one of those whose job it was to control the hypnotic effect." Wendglow paused, letting his words sink in.

"Unfortunately, Silurian somehow blocked the effects of our protective enchantment. More unfortunate, for Menthliot indeed,

319

while trying to entice Silurian into the effects of the charm, his concentration lapsed, and the Sentinel entered his mind as well as a few others. Menthliot was powerless to resist. He became a conduit for the Sentinel. We tried…" Wendglow's voice dropped off, his eyes glossy.

After a few moments the Voil leader regained his composure. "We lost many good people last night in our futile attempts at wresting them from the Sentinel's grasp." He stared at Silurian. "We feared we had lost you."

Silurian was taken aback. *Lost me?* He had never met these creatures before yesterday. "If what you say is true, then why were we not warned about the hypnotic charm before you allowed us entry?"

Wendglow nodded several times. "Many times before have we offered sanctuary to wayward travellers. On each occasion we held out a false hope that the voyagers were the ones mentioned in our legends. If they were able to survive the portal, it seemed plausible that they were also capable of harnessing the river's power. On each occasion, we were sadly mistaken."

The Voil elder pursed his lips, considering his next words. "We sheltered them and showed them the way, but they were either killed by the river's touch, or driven mad. The few who survived the river's touch fell victim to its power. Each time, they went on to lay waste to everything around them, including our people. Learning from our mistakes, we developed a trial to challenge those wishing to attempt the river. The trial is designed to bring little harm to the candidates. Thus far, none have passed."

"Until now," Thorr's voice sounded from Thetis' table. He nodded toward Silurian.

Wendglow laughed. "Hah! He didn't pass the test. He ruined it. Because of Silurian's unforeseen response, Menthliot was forced to change the way he conducted the test and it cost him his life."

Silurian scowled. "Harmless testing? I almost died."

"That was the Sentinel. Let me explain. Our testing centres around the control we exert while the subject's mind is under our enchantment. When you weren't affected, we scrambled to keep you in check. It mattered little that we couldn't conduct the test. We feared the Sentinel might assume control of your mind before we were able to get you into the deep safety of our home. Judging by your response, that would have been disastrous."

Alhena stood up beside Thorr. "So, Silurian beat your test."

Wendglow shook his head. "Silurian proved he is the *last* person we want attempting the river. If he were to succumb to its evil touch, he will end up killing us all. He is far too dangerous. We forbid it."

Soul Forge

The Sword of Saint Carmichael

Wendglow struggled to gain his feet. Every member of the quest stared, openmouthed.

Thorr jumped to his feet and grabbed the frail creature by the arm to help him stand clear of the special chair. "Forbid it? What do you mean, forbid? Silurian must harness the river's power, or everything we have endured has been for naught."

Wendglow glanced at the sea captain's hands clutching his arm. "We forbid Silurian, or anyone else from your expedition for that matter, to approach the river. You have no idea what you are up against. It is much too dangerous. Now, if you'll kindly release me."

Thorr let him go.

The Voil leader waited for his handlers to remove his chair and followed them from the cavern.

"Master Wendglow?" Thetis' voice stopped him. "May I walk with you?"

Wendglow half turned. He gave her a long once over before gazing into her indigo eyes. "If you must."

Thetis caught up to him in the passageway—half a dozen armed Voil forming up behind them, and then they were gone.

The quest members glanced at Rook.

The bowman shrugged.

The bustle in the cavern had long since died off. A handful of Voil still lingered about, attending the quest member's whims, but for the most part, the company from *Gerrymander* had the hall to themselves.

Soul Forge

Silurian's eyes were closed. He rested his head within the crook of his arms upon the table. He sensed the movement of many creatures close by, and sat up, blinking.

A group of armed Voil entered the cavern. He instinctively reached for the Sacred Sword Voil strapped over his back but let go of the hilt when Thetis and Wendglow entered on their heels. Thetis led the ancient creature by a frail arm.

Wendglow's chair was brought forth and placed beside Silurian. His mole covered face smiled at those around the table as he lowered himself slowly into the chair's embrace.

The Voil elder allowed Thetis the courtesy of finding a chair herself before he addressed the quest. "I have erred in my judgment, Sir Silurian Mintaka."

Silurian blinked.

"Thetis has enlightened us about many of our misconceptions, especially where she is concerned. I fear we almost cast away our only chance at leaving this realm through our misguided treatment of *Saros'* disciple."

Silurian stole a glance across the table at Thetis—her smile barely perceptible.

"The Elder Council agrees with poor Menthliot. He was certain you were the one, but the rest of the council disagreed, feeling it prudent to let matters lie. I cannot blame them. We have endured much despair at the hands of those who have come before. After speaking with fair Thetis, however, we, the Elder Council, decree that you, Silurian Mintaka, are indeed the warrior mentioned in our histories. Twice have you proven yourself capable. You overcame the Sentinel's advances into our home." Wendglow paused out of respect for Menthliot. "More importantly, I am told, you are personally responsible for banishing Helleden from your realm, many years ago."

Silurian's cheeks reddened. He had no idea what Thetis had filled the Elder Council's heads with. There were a lot more people responsible for defeating Helleden at the Battle of Lugubrius than just himself. He had merely been the one to thrust the sword. As it turned out, he hadn't eliminated the threat at all, but if the Voil didn't oppose their quest to the river, he cared less what they thought. "Thank you."

Soul Forge

"Do not thank me yet. You underestimate what you are up against. Many souls have attempted to harness the river's power. Only one has ever overcome its maddening effects. He now lies dead at the bottom of Deneabola."

Rook, sitting with the captain at the next table, got up and stood beside the wrinkled elder. "Deneabola? That is the ancient name given to Saros' Swamp. How do you know that name?"

Wendglow nodded to the bowman, holding up a scaly paw to brook further comment. "No one else has escaped the Under Realm without first being corrupted. Did you know that Helleden Misenthorpe was once an adventurer like yourself? Intent on harnessing the mystical properties of the river? Aye. So, too, were the Sentinel and the Morphisis. They found their way to the Under Realm a long time ago, separately mind you, but each with their own agenda. Helleden was the first and is still by far the worst—or the best, I guess, depending on whose side you're on. Helleden is one of only four creatures known to have reversed the portal's effect, allowing them access to the Upper Realm. For reasons of its own, the Soul itself is unable to accomplish this, and fortunate for all that it can't. Yet." Wendglow let his last word linger.

Soul? Morphisis? Silurian's frown matched many of those watching on.

"Saros is the second and sadly we now know his fate. Of the third, the Morphisis, we have no idea where this creature is. It might be in this very room right now and we would be none the wiser."

Silurian glanced around at the people from the Gerrymander and the few Voil scattered about. Looking back at Wendglow, he asked, "What of the fourth?"

Wendglow raised his unkempt, bushy eyebrows. "The Sentinel. But, we don't think it can do so without Helleden's assistance."

Silurian swallowed. He couldn't imagine the havoc a creature like the Sentinel could unleash in Zephyr.

Wendglow's next words surprised him. "Let me see your sword."

Avarick and Pollard sat up straighter.

Silurian eyes narrowed. *'The Morphisis might be in this very room.'*

Wendglow chuckled. "You fear a man half your size? One barely able to stand?"

Soul Forge

Against his better judgment, Silurian reached behind his left shoulder to unsheathe the gleaming weapon. He looked at the sword and then at the ancient creature.

Everyone in the room held their breath.

Turning the razor-sharp blade around, he handed it hilt first to Wendglow, who accepted the Sacred Sword Voil with reverence.

"Ah, it is as Thetis claimed. Saint Carmichael's Blade. Saros' Sword. I never thought I would see this cursed weapon again."

Silurian gaped. *Saint Carmichael's Blade? Saros' Sword? Cursed weapon?* How did this little creature know its history? It was centuries old. Crafted by Saint Carmichael himself. Saros, Lord of the Innerworld, had been its guardian for as long as the histories recalled. And yet, this Under Realm creature claimed to have laid eyes upon it.

Wendglow muttered sarcastically to himself, "Some saint Saros was. Hee-hee." His eyes misted over. "Aye, I'll grant him that, now that he's gone. A saint he was. Bless him."

The Voil elder traced the mystic runes with an outstretched claw, his touch causing the etched lines to radiate in a warm, blue glow.

Silurian didn't know whether to snatch the sword away or run. Instead, he leaned in closer.

"Integrity. Honour. Courage. Hope. Faith," Wendglow intoned, his face awash in the blue radiance.

Wendglow turned the blade over and repeated his ministrations. "Only. The. Worthy. Shall. Prevail. Hmm. The Law of the Five."

Ten runes in total, etched into the two faces of the blade, glowed softly, casting those closest in soft blue light.

Wendglow reverently handed the sword back. "Silurian Mintaka. I present to you Saint Carmichael's Blade. You are the one the sword speaks to."

Silurian reclaimed the sword from Wendglow's shaky grasp, having no idea what the crazed creature referred to. "You can read the runes?"

"Of course I can. I engraved them."

325

Soul Forge

Legend Found

Had he not been penned in by the close proximity of those around him, Silurian might have fallen from his chair. "But how? This blade belonged to a deity in our realm."

"A deity now, is he? Hah! Aye, but I can see it clearly." Wendglow chuckled. Shaking his head, he continued, "Before you became its rightful wielder, the sword belonged to Saros. Saros Carmichael to be precise. As to being a deity, who knows." The wrinkled creature's shoulders shuddered. "It certainly sounds like something he would dream up. He most assuredly thought himself a god."

"But..." Rook sputtered.

Wendglow held up shaky hands. "But nothing. Saros was many things. Apparently, a saint in your realm. I do grudgingly admit, he was a warrior of great repute, of that there is no doubt, if you believed even half his stories...hmm? A philosopher too, or so he would have you believe. You might even say a decent healer. But a god? No. He was far from that. He was my brother."

Goosebumps flooded Silurian's skin.

The cavern became deathly still.

Rook knelt between Wendglow and Silurian, gazing into the old creature's eyes. "Your brother? How can that be? There's no possible way you forged that sword? That would make you—"

"Four hundred and fifty-three," Wendglow grimaced. "Give or take a year or ten. I can't keep track anymore."

Rook gaped and looked Silurian in the eyes. Silurian shrugged, as baffled as everyone else from the *Gerrymander*.

"'Tis a convoluted story, for certain. Suffice it to say, the rigours Saros and myself have endured over the years have served to alter our body's chemistry. Some may see a long life as a blessing. I might tell you different."

Rook stared straight into the creature's watery eyes. "He never mentioned a brother."

"He didn't know he had one…at least not one that lived." Wendglow sighed. "Four centuries ago, yes four, Saros and I were part of a quest, similar to your own. Our leader came in search of the fabled power of the river with the intention of overthrowing our emperor. That would've been fine had Emperor Zarlothe deserved such a fate. Zarlothe…" Wendglow smiled at the memory. "If the emperor had a fault, it was his willingness to do the right thing." He paused to consider his thoughts. "It's a funny thing…I don't remember any names other than the emperor's and my brother's…I have a hard time remembering the name of the empire we hailed from, ever since I was captured and taken to the Soul Forge. Anyway, our misguided war leader was bent upon exploiting the emperor's weakness to his own ends, but he lacked the forces to overthrow Zarlothe. So, he embarked upon a wild course that led us to the portal. All on the whim of a crazed witch woman."

Silurian stole a glance at Thetis.

"Let me assure you, the lucky ones died during the transition. The rest of us found the river. Although Saros and myself weren't much better than the company we kept, we didn't support our leader's vision of assassinating the benevolent emperor. With the help of a few others, we staged a mutiny at the river. The ensuing battle with the witch woman and our former cutthroat companions was brutal. It's a good thing the Carmichael boys were decent fighters, hmm?" Wendglow drifted away for a few moments.

"Anyway, we had no intention of entertaining the trial with the river, but the witch woman convinced us otherwise. As she lay dying at our feet, she informed us that the only way back lay in the river."

The ancient Voil sighed again. He took measure of the quest members around the table. When he spoke, he averted his gaze to his withered hands, folded in his lap. "Three other members of our band survived the mutiny at the river's edge. None of us were up to attempting the river, but what choice did we have? So, we made a pact to attempt the river simultaneously."

Soul Forge

He shook his head. "Not a good idea. I don't know what the others experienced, but I know what happened to me. Thankfully, it is but a fleeting memory. I was drawn into the river's depths, into…nothingness. I remember intense pain. Something tugged at what I could only believe was my soul, and then…" He shrugged.

"As for my brother, he had no way of knowing whether I lived or not." Wendglow lifted his odd limbs as if examining himself. "In reality, I guess I died that day. At least the person I used to be, died. In the end, the rest of us were either dead or taken. Saros, however, attempted the river and won. He discovered a way to unlock its secret and defeat its maddening allure. He also figured out how to return, obviously, to wherever it is you hail from. So, that being said, we most likely hail from there too. Who knows? Of the other three, I have no idea. They may have been desecrated and tossed into the Marrow Wash as garbage, or they may have been transformed into legions of the Soul."

There was that name again. The *Soul*. Silurian wanted to ask about who or what the Soul was but he didn't want to lose the question he had poised on the tip of his tongue. "I'm confused. You said you made the blade."

"I said I engraved it. Saros forged it. He made many weapons in his time. He is a master weapon smith. Or was, I guess. He created it. It was his blade. I just made it unique."

Silurian grasped the ivory handled dagger in his belt, but let it go when Wendglow smiled.

"Aye, that is his as well. He called it Soulbiter, or something silly like that."

Nodding at the name of the dagger, Silurian asked, "If what you say is true, how did the sword get the name, Sacred Sword Voil?"

"That, my troubled friend, is a story best left for another time. Let's just say it was named in our honour. A pledge if you will, that Saros would one day come back to discover what had happened to the rest of us." The ancient's ashen demeanour parted in a sad smile. "Alas, now he is dead."

An uncomfortable silence descended upon the hall.

Rook broke the mood, reaching behind his back, but before he unslung his bow, Wendglow nodded.

Soul Forge

"I recognized your bow earlier. My brother is responsible for that also, and yes, I engraved it four centuries ago. Being wood, I'm surprised it has weathered so well. Have you been able to unlock the runes?"

"Unlock the runes. I don't know what you mean."

"I didn't think so. The bow was originally crafted for someone adept in runic magic. I don't believe there were many people left still practicing the secret art even in my day, so it is not surprising. I'm afraid the secret to unlocking the runic magic is long lost."

Silurian thought about the other weapons wielded by the deceased members of the Group of Five. "Did you also shape three other special weapons. A warhammer, a scorpion flail, and a crossbow?"

Wendglow stared through Silurian, contemplating his words. "Hmm? Possibly. Every weapon Saros made was special. He truly was a Master, but I'd never tell him that to his face. There isn't a weapon known that Saros couldn't fashion. I dare say, when he made a weapon, it was superior in every way."

"How did he imbue them all? Surely, he didn't wield all five," Rook asked.

"Ah, there you err. He was quite adept with every weapon he created. It's a strange coincidence that his favourite weapons were your bow and Silurian's sword. Of the others, your friend Seafarer played a major part."

"Seafarer?" Rook and Silurian said together.

"Aye. That is also a long story I'd rather not discuss right now. We digress from what is important. You said you hail from where?"

"Zephyr," Silurian said, confused. "We hail from a kingdom called Zephyr, and you're right, if we don't get back soon, everything your brother fought for will have been for naught."

"Zephyr, hmm? Can't say the name sounds familiar," Wendglow shook his head. "Let me fill you in on what we will face."

"We?" Silurian and Rook asked together.

Wendglow looked from one to other. "Aye, we. You don't think we are going to allow you to wander near the Forge without us? Your little company wouldn't get three steps from the exit tunnel." He paused to let that sink in.

Soul Forge

"Rest assured, the Sentinel knows why you're here. He knows where you're holed up, and he most certainly knows the terrain leading to the river. Nor is he alone. He commands a number of intermediate beasts." Wendglow paused, as if considering his next words. "By intermediate, I mean creatures more intimidating than Voil. Creatures mutated by the Soul and kept here for defense."

"Don't sell yourselves short," Silurian mused. "You guys scared the life out of me."

A slight chuckle escaped the elder's lips. "Be that as it may, the creatures your company will encounter will be scarier still. There's also the matter of the Morphisis. No one has ever laid eyes on that demon and lived long enough to identify it. It rears its ugly presence whenever a river attempt is made. Where it comes from, we have no idea. Once the threat passes, it disappears again, not to be seen for decades on end."

Rook frowned. The Morphisis sounded worse than the Sentinel. "How do you know it will appear this time?"

Wendglow looked at Rook as if he were an idiot. "Oh, it will appear. Pity to any who stand before it."

Rook swallowed.

"More importantly, however, is what Silurian will encounter, should we survive the trek across the Dead Plains to the river."

The ancient leader directed his next words at Silurian. "When you immerse Saint Carmichael's Blade into the river you will be drawn into the clutches of the Soul. When this happens, and it will happen fast, one of two things will occur. You will either go mad and lay waste to everyone around you, or something much worse will happen…"

Worse than killing everyone around me? What could be worse than killing everyone around me? Silurian's brows knit. Perhaps the ancient Voil was mad.

"Do not doubt the Soul's intent. It covets power. It feeds on it. We fear what it seeks to find in you."

Wendglow's words felt like an accusation. "In me? What can it find in me?"

"A partner."

Silurian sat back, flabbergasted. "A partner? For what? What is this Soul thing?"

Soul Forge

Wendglow nodded. "Forgive my presumption. Of course, you have never heard of the Soul before now. Let's just say, the Soul is your real concern. It controls Helleden."

Silurian swallowed, his mind reeling. There was a creature more sinister than Helleden?

Wendglow patted his forearm. "I will present to you the Soul as a trapped, ethereal being that seeks escape from the Under Realm. Our legend proclaims that when the Soul locates the person mentioned in our histories, it shall be set free."

Silurian fidgeted, expecting he already knew who the 'person mentioned in our histories' was. "That doesn't make sense. If Helleden can come and go, why not the Soul?"

"It cannot leave on its own for it lacks a corporeal entity. It requires a vessel strong enough to contain the power it exudes. That is quite a statement, considering Helleden, the Sentinel, and the Morphisis all answer to it, and yet, they are obviously not worthy of such a task. Otherwise, we wouldn't be having this conversation. Helleden's responsibility is to search out further sources of power to feed the Soul's insatiable hunger. It requires the power Helleden harnesses to keep its ethereal form alive.

"That being said, my earlier misgivings still hold true. I believe you are that vessel. Our legend speaks of the coming of our redeemer. Someone strong enough to confront the Soul and put an end to our nightmare. Our fear is not how this shall transpire, but what that actually means, 'put an end to our nightmare.' Killing us would be a sure way of ending our suffering. Through his contact with you upon the banks of the Marrow Wash, Menthliot believed that our prophecy points to you. Thanks to Thetis, I see that now." Wendglow's voice dropped so that only Rook and Silurian heard him, "We need to find a way to keep you from killing us all."

Stunned, Silurian went cold. Realizing Wendglow was attempting to stand, he leaned forward and assisted the elder to step free of his chair before handing him off to the aides scurrying up beside them.

As the ancient creature shuffled away, Silurian heard him mutter, "May the gods save us all."

Soul Forge

Yarstaff

$\mathfrak{Silurian}$ stepped into line beside Alhena, down a wide passageway, three days and forty-one leagues after the meeting in the great Voil Hall. A disciplined company of the creatures hurried past on their way to the exit tunnel. The thunderous steps of the rest of the quest trailed after them, followed by hundreds of other padded footfalls.

Though the tunnel was wide enough for four people to walk abreast, the bejewelled ceiling wasn't high enough for the taller members of the quest to walk upright. Avarick, Pollard, Olmar, and many others from *Gerrymander* were forced to duck or bend over double.

The tunnel they traversed paralleled the Marrow Wash canyon, deep enough into the stone to prevent interference from the Sentinel.

Perspiration shone upon Alhena's brow, denoting the brisk pace the leaders set.

"How fare you today, Sire?"

Silurian shot his friend a stern glance at his insistence on using the honourific. If it had been anyone else he would've berated them on the spot.

Unperturbed, Alhena indicated the continuous parade of tapestries and various pieces of armour and twisted weapons lining the walls. "All these weapons once belonged to the Voil...well, at least they belonged to who the Voil had been before they were mutated at Soul Forge."

Silurian said nothing, but after digesting Alhena's words, he cast him a quizzical look.

"Aye. That is what Wendglow told me. The Voil were once as we are now. Before they were captured. He claims that whenever an adventurer is captured they are taken to a place known as Iconoclast

Soul Forge

Spire. A great, mountainous tower straddling the mystic river we seek. Within the bowels of this black mountain burns the hearth known as Soul Forge. People are experimented upon, altered, and if they are *unlucky* enough to survive the mutilation, they become members of Helleden's legions."

When Alhena fell silent, Silurian raised his eyebrows. He knew all this. Wendglow had inferred as much, and yet, a small part of him sounded an alarm. Perhaps that was what was happening. The Voil were herding them toward Soul Forge. If the Voil had assisted other travellers, how come they hadn't seen any sign of them, other than the hanging armour?

Alhena's next words eerily drove that point home. "According to Wendglow, the armour and weapons hanging along the corridors are reclaimed pieces salvaged from the killing fields around the river. Aye, from the very place we are headed."

The large group of Voil and quest members passed many side tunnels branching to the left and a few to the right, but as the days rolled on, the side passages became less frequent.

The Voil kept to themselves during the long march, except when the company halted for meal breaks, at which point they assisted the quest members with whatever needs they might have—directing them to privies, explaining certain tapestries, and providing Nashon with various healing salves and advice. Through it all, it was obvious the misshapen creatures remained wary of Thetis.

Alhena was ready to collapse by the time the fourth day of their trek ended. A shout from ahead brought the company to a halt as it emptied into an immense cavern devoid of the unnatural ceiling lighting. Torches sparked to life around the perimeter walls.

Coming up from behind, Wendglow announced, "We go no farther today. Tomorrow we pass beneath the Marrow Wash. We are beneath the upper forge now."

Everyone from the *Gerrymander* looked up.

Soul Forge

Alhena and Silurian stepped aside to allow the sweating litter bearers room to muscle the ancient Voil leader along.

Wendglow nodded to them from his perch of shabby pillows. "In the morning we will place the company under our protective charms once again to prevent the Sentinel from detecting our advance."

Silurian tensed.

"A necessary evil if we are to continue down this road."

Alhena pitched in to help clean up after a tasty meal of an unknown meat, and a blue, earthy vegetable nobody from the *Gerrymander* had seen before. When he finished, he sat beside Silurian. Pollard, Avarick and Sadyra hovered nearby.

"I need to speak with you." Torchlight cast eerie shadows on Alhena's face. He glanced around, seeing who was within earshot. "It is about Thetis."

Silurian's eyebrows shot up.

"I do not know where to start, but since the first day we met her, I have had misgivings. I know, it sounds silly."

Silurian urged, "Go on."

Alhena leaned in close. "She claims to be Saros' disciple, but if you actually think about it, she has yet to do anything to contribute to our cause."

"She led us to the portal," Silurian offered. "Without her we might have sailed off the edge of the world. She directed us to this land and led us here. What more can she do?"

"Yeah, yeah, that is all fine, but what did she do when we were threatened by the portal? She was nowhere to be seen. We lost some good men. We almost lost you."

Silurian shrugged. "She told us what to expect *and* how to protect ourselves. She practiced what she said."

Alhena nodded, acknowledging the explanation. "What about the disappearance of the sailors at Debacle Lurch? She did nothing to prevent that."

Soul Forge

Silurian frowned. "I can't believe I'm defending the woman, but what could she have done? She said she's never been here before. I don't know how she could've foreseen the outcome."

"True, but...does it not strike you as strange? I would think a disciple of Saros, capable of, um...I do not know, but I think she should be capable of doing something."

Silurian mulled over Alhena's words. "You already know that I have felt the same mistrust toward her, pretty well from the outset of our meeting in Madrigail Bay. Even though we almost came to blows on the canyon floor, I have no proof of any wrongdoing on her part. She has led us to this point. Granted, not entirely safely, but she achieved what none other could have. Don't forget, she was the one who was instrumental in convincing Wendglow and the Voil council to allow us to continue our quest."

Alhena nodded impatiently as he listened. As soon as Silurian finished, he said, "Do you not think it strange, that once ashore, she knew which direction to follow?" Out of character, his next words dripped with sarcasm, "For someone who claims she has never been here before?"

"Aye, I guess."

Alhena pulled back and stewed. After a bit, he leaned in close again, speaking with even more determination. Pollard, Avarick and Sadyra hunched in to listen as well.

"What about Menthliot? Who knows the evil of this realm better than the Voil?" He raised his hands to point to the pockets of Voil huddled about. "Look around. They still do not trust her."

Silurian had nothing to say to that.

"Thetis and Rook were alone in the darkness, along the banks of the Marrow Wash, and what? Nothing? The Sentinel never sought them out. Why?"

Silurian rolled his eyes. "Wendglow already went over this. The Sentinel was preoccupied with his occupation of Menthliot. They were lucky, I guess."

"Pfft!" Alhena clenched and unclenched his fists.

"I don't think I've ever seen you this worked up. You are normally as laid back as my old friend, Alcyonne. That's saying something."

335

Soul Forge

Alhena knew that Alcyonne was one of the deceased members of the Group of Five but beyond that, the reference meant little to him. Thetis was the one he was concerned about.

Silurian shrugged. "I admit, there is something peculiar about her. Of that there can be no doubt. If she has ulterior motives, I have no idea what they may be." He patted Alhena on the forearm. "Fear not, my friend. If she is up to mischief, it will become apparent soon enough and I will deal with it. For now, we must trust she is true."

Silurian stood and offered him a hand up. "Come. Something tells me the days ahead are going to be difficult."

Silurian made his way back to a remote part of the cavern and laid out his bedroll. Sleep was an ever-elusive beast in the realm of the Voil, but he lay on his back, propped his head upon the bulk of his pack and closed his eyes. His discussion with Alhena had unsettled him more than he would have thought.

Pockets of soft murmuring slowly replaced the sound of eating. He awoke from a light slumber to the melodious voice of the tallest Voil he had yet encountered. One of Wendglow's litter bearers, Yarstaff.

Silurian yawned and rolled onto his side to watch the creature covered head to foot in short orange fur that stuck out in tufts from the edges of his drab clothing.

Sporadic torchlight flickered throughout the chamber. The smell of burning pitch accompanied the acrid clouds of black smoke wafting up to the stalactite infested ceiling.

Silurian had learned that every Voil possessed their own personal song, written and composed by themselves. Whenever the Voil gathered, they sang them to pass the evening hours away. The *Gerrymander* crew had come to look forward to this peaceful time, losing themselves in the lyrics and melody, forgetting their worries for a while.

Silurian leaned back and let Yarstaff's sweet voice wash over him.

The orange furred Voil sang softly at first, but his voice grew quickly to fill the entire chamber,

Soul Forge

"Sapling sprouting, eyeing sun,
guidance yearning, life begun.
Worship warmth, commanding respect,
images of a pleasant reflect.

Innocent chase of life's grandeur,
making choices, oft to wonder.
Searching the meaning,
my gaieties weaning.

Warmth shimmers, cries out in pain,
ominous clouds settle, my future in vain.
Pleasant images fade, losing their hold,
the void of absence filling with cold.

Harsh are they, those above,
fate outstripping eternal love.
Flounder do we, to live in vain,
to yearn again, of warmth's refrain.

Alone and bending,
wind never ending.
Warmth omniscient,
but nary present.

This path, which is before me face,
craving new warmth, oh please embrace."

Silurian's eyes closed, recalling his conversation with Wendglow the
previous morning, while the elder's litter carriers marched him along…

… "Yarstaff is unique amongst the Voil." Wendglow had spoken in
hushed tones, motioning with his chin to the peculiar, orange furred

337

Soul Forge

Voil bearing the right front, litter handle. "He is the only one of us that still has both of his human hands *and* feet. No other Voil has that."

Silurian scrutinized the tall creature loping along in front of him.

Wendglow said with reverence in his voice, "He is special to us. The epitome of why we remain free of the Soul and its minions. If you look closely, Yarstaff is not like us. He successfully made it through the transformation process at Soul Forge. Beneath that orange fur, his skin is red. He was groomed to be a field commander in Helleden's army. But..."

So enrapt in what the Voil elder related, Silurian nearly tripped. The tunnel they followed had dropped over a shallow ledge. He caught himself on the side of the litter.

Wendglow smiled and waited until he collected himself. "For some reason, Yarstaff's mind wasn't as affected as the usual victims of the forge. As time went by, the core of his real self, buried within the recesses of his simple mind, resurfaced. Unknown to his captors, he found his way back to independent thought, and realized that what happened at Soul Forge was wrong. So, he took steps to correct it.

"Through his courage, many of us, unsuccessful in our transformation into minions of Helleden's army, and slated to be cast into the Marrow Wash, were saved."

Silurian mulled over the elder's words. "That means..."

"Yes. Yarstaff is the eldest Voil. The first of us. He saved us and sheltered us. He used the power he gained at the forge to create the original wards of our cliff side home."

Silurian's eyes widened, listening to Wendglow's words.

"There have been other, much more powerful mutants who have been rescued from imminent destruction in the Marrow Wash, Menthliot for one, but Yarstaff was the first. He rescued himself."

Silurian studied Yarstaff with a new respect. The litter bearer's stooped back and slouched shoulders showed he wasn't immune to fatigue.

"No doubt you wonder why the founding father of the Voil is required to bear a litter." Wendglow's voice resonated with pride. "That is his choice. He wants no special treatment, nor the accolades he most certainly deserves. You see, I was his first rescue. He considers me more his child, than a rescued victim. For some reason

Soul Forge

known only to his simple mind, Yarstaff feels obliged to watch over me. He has done so now for over four hundred years. What better way to protect me than to be one of my litter bearers, hmm?"

Soul Forge

The Gods Must Surely Be Crazy

When the call came early the next morning, Alhena had trouble shaking the stiffness from his aging body. Easing his pack onto his shoulders, he sighed. He wasn't getting any younger. The last few months had taken their toll on everyone, but especially on the older members of the original quest, of which, Alhena had everyone beat by more years than they knew. If he survived this quest, he had only one more task ahead of him to ensure his life was complete. He adjusted his shoulder straps and formed up behind Avarick who busied himself behind Silurian.

Pollard assumed a position directly in front of Silurian and boldly stated, "If anyone wants to get at you, they'll need to go through me first."

Wendglow's litter stood beside Silurian. The Voil leader appeared more robust than they had seen him before. He dropped from his cushioned platform to stand next to the man he professed to fear the most.

Silurian grasped his proffered paw.

Wendglow cleared his throat for all to hear his frail voice. "Today we embark upon the last leg of our journey. If all goes well, we will reach the river before nightfall."

Murmurs rippled through the cavern.

"When we leave this cavern, you will once again be under our protective warding spell."

People shuffled their feet.

Wendglow directed his next words at Silurian. "You will also need to be under its influence until we exit onto the Dead Plains. I cannot express this enough. Do. Not. Panic."

Soul Forge

Thorr stood with Olmar in front of Pollard. "How do we know the Sentinel won't be waiting for us at the tunnel's end?"

"Rest assured, Thorr Sandborne, we have sentries posted along the Marrow Wash day and night. We also have a few spotters hidden in the foothills of Iconoclast Spire."

Thorr raised his eyebrows, unconvinced.

"We will egress from a point close to the forge. We have never used this exit before, other than to usher the odd rescued victim from the forge into our sanctuary."

"What about this Soul thing?" Avarick spoke up.

"The Soul is an ethereal creature, unlike us." Wendglow replied. "It resides far below the mountain, beside a bottomless lake. That is the location of the true Soul Forge. Subterranean lava vents fuel it. The Soul cannot survive elsewhere." He turned to Silurian. "Unless..."

Silurian fidgeted.

Wendglow winked at him. "The magic of the river is a byproduct of Soul Forge. The farther away from Iconoclast Spire, the less danger there is in entering its waters." He nodded. "We will try to get you as close to the source as possible."

An eerie chant rose within the cavern as members of Wendglow's people began the hypnotic process of warding. A faint glow radiated from the exit tunnel—the passageway beyond pulsed softly.

"Captain?" Wendglow turned his gaze to Thorr. "Are your people ready for the evil that awaits us?"

Thorr squared his shoulders and puffed out his chest. "Aye, Master Wendglow. They will take the day."

As if on cue, Pollard unsheathed his mighty, twin-bladed broadsword, and held it high. "Onto the power! Into hell and out the other side!"

The lead scouts disappeared down the steep slope of the exit tunnel, weapons drawn and Pollard's battle cry upon their lips.

The morning slipped by unnoticed—everyone's mind under the Voil's thrall. Most embraced the wondrous enchantment, opening

Soul Forge

themselves to the blissful peace it provided while Wendglow's people kept them moving along at a brisk, sustainable pace.

Silurian, however, found it difficult not to resist the charm. If the Voil meant them harm, now would be an opportune time. It took a considerable amount of convincing before Wendglow was able to place him under the warding spell.

Past midday, the quest passed beyond the Soul Forge and were startled by a peculiar sensation of travelling through a shimmering wall. One instant they hadn't a care in the world, and the next, the bright light of the outside world assaulted their vision through a narrow exit. It took a few moments for the reality of their situation to seep into their bedazzled minds.

Longsight and Blindsight were the first members from the original quest to leave the safety of the tunnel. A sheer rock face shot skyward on their left. Straining their necks to look up, the lofty peak of Iconoclast Spire was hidden behind a large promontory, hundreds of feet up the face of the cliff. They were bumped ahead by Olmar and Thorr who stopped for a few seconds before they too were jostled forward by Pollard, Silurian, Alhena and Avarick. The sequence repeated itself many times over until the entire company made its way outside the hidden tunnel.

They had travelled beneath the Marrow Wash and although its milky slag wasn't visible from where they stood, vestiges of its putrid stench still managed to reach them.

Silurian stepped away from the milling throng to survey the breathtaking vista that stretched out before them. Around the incredible bulk of Iconoclast Spire, a vast expanse of rolling hills fell away toward a ribbon of turquoise. The river. Between the company and their destination, fields of waist high, crimson reeds dominated the gently sloping river basin. Unlike the cliffs, there wasn't a sign of sand anywhere.

Silurian took in the scene with mixed emotions. He was finally here. The river lay within his reach. The trauma and hardship of his exhaustive journey from the Nordic Wood felt like a distant memory. He smiled, caring less if anyone saw him. Twenty-three long years mulling over what ifs and hungering for a vengeance he thought he would never realize. He now stood within striking distance of the first step toward turning his fantasy into a reality. Within walking distance of the power source that would help him rid the world of Helleden Misenthorpe.

He knew it wasn't going to be quite that easy. Life never was. The Soul stood in his way.

He resisted the urge to run to the river and get it over with. Wendglow had advised him not to rush into the confrontation with the Soul.

From where he stood, the task ahead appeared straight forward. Approach the river, immerse Saint Carmichael's Blade, and let the sword soak up its old enchantment. Simple. But, if Wendglow's warnings held any merit, the Soul had other things in mind for him.

There were also the matters of the Sentinel and the Morphisis. He sighed. At least he was here.

Boundless leagues of gently swaying reeds spread out below them upon the Dead Plains. What a strange name for a sight so wondrous.

Pollard's gentle nudge snapped him out of his musing. The lead Voil scouts had begun moving from behind a mass of tumbled boulders, and descended into the river valley, spreading out as they went.

Pollard towered over him, resplendent in his brass cuirass—his eyes scanning everywhere at once. Silurian took comfort in the fact that anyone wanting to get at him would have to go through the beast of a man first.

Already half a league away, the upper halves of Longsight and Blindsight bobbed about above the crimson reeds, scouting the quest's landward flank, while Ithnan and Ithaman were barely visible along the base of the ominous bulk of Iconoclast Spire.

Dark silhouettes of large, vulture-like birds turned great swooping circles overhead. Wendglow had called the birds, Terrors, and claimed they were a lot bigger than Olmar.

Silurian wondered how the Voil were going to navigate through the high reeds, but then again, he thought, they would be hard to spot by the enemy, so perhaps their height worked to their advantage. Unfortunately, the presence of men like Pollard and Olmar would certainly negate the company's stealth.

Thetis and Rook sidled between Silurian and Avarick, and as a large group, the men, women and Voil started forward.

Soul Forge

The lead ranks set a good pace. Armoured Voil disappeared amongst the foliage, their progress leaving trenches of freshly downed reeds. It wouldn't be hard to follow their trail. Silurian laughed to himself. So much for the Voil advantage.

Wendglow's litter trudged along behind Avarick and Sadyra, upon the shoulders of Yarstaff and three husky Voil while Alhena and Thorr kept pace with the litter on its far side.

Silurian pondered the usefulness of the ragtag collection of warriors charging forward with the aim of providing him a chance at attempting the river. From aged men to seafaring women, from misshapen creatures of all shapes and sizes to washed up warriors. Everyone moved across an alien landscape on a fool's errand to reclaim the lost enchantment upon his fabled blade. In his mind's eye, he pictured High Bishop Uzziah rolling his eyes. The gods must surely be crazy.

They were farther away from the river than it had first appeared from the promontory outside the tunnel. Their hurried pace ground to a slow trek. Pushing through the high reeds and traversing the soft loam beneath their feet proved an arduous task.

More Terrors appeared in the sky overhead. According to Wendglow, they were the shock troops that usually preceded the Soul's minion army. Thankfully, the massive birds had kept their distance thus far.

Iconoclast Spire dominated the landscape to the left of the river, forcing them to drift farther into the Dead Plains to circumvent the rough terrain surrounding the mass of granite. The spire's flat top was home to Helleden's keep, complete with jagged black walls and gnarly towers spread around its perimeter. The Terrors flight seemed to originate from the direction of that ghastly fort. Others followed Silurian's gaze as a collective shiver rippled through the masses.

Reports filtered back that the forward scouts neared the river's edge. The quest's pace increased—a pall of nervous expectation fell over the company as it trudged over the sodden ground.

It wasn't lost on Silurian that their progress seemed far too easy to this point. He almost jumped out of his boots when Alhena touched his shoulder.

344

Soul Forge

"Wendglow fears the Sentinel lurks within the river. I think our best course may be for someone else to approach the river to draw its attention."

Silurian swallowed. Who would willingly volunteer for that duty?

Wendglow's litter came up beside them. Silurian couldn't help himself staring at the gargoyle faces decorating the Voil elder's staff. If he didn't know better, he would think they were alive.

Wendglow must have overheard Alhena. "Nay. The Soul would use that person as a conduit to channel its power. For as long as that person survived, which wouldn't be long, the power they discharged would create havoc amongst our ranks. As it is, we'll be lucky to fend off the Sentinel long enough to give Silurian the time he needs. The last thing we want is to defend against a rogue wizard. Nor must we forget the Morphisis."

Before anyone digested his words, Wendglow added, "Perhaps there is another way, hmm?"

Soul Forge

Betrayal

$\mathfrak{Silurian}$ stood atop a grassy knoll, a long stone's throw from the river's edge. Wendglow had informed him that the slow moving, brackish water of the mystic river slipped by the Dead Plains on its way to Debacle Lurch. Across the river, broken trees littered the river bank, fronting a row of jagged hills beyond. They were as close to the where the river flowed from beneath Iconoclast Spire as the rugged terrain permitted. Half a league upstream, Iconoclast Spire shot skyward—a formidable bastion of evil. How anyone got up there, short of flying, he had no idea.

Beside him, Pollard stood defiant, his strong hands clutching his unique sword. Sadyra stood a few paces farther back, a dozen arrows sticking out of the ground around her, ready to be quickly utilized. Behind them, a small contingent of heavily armed sailors and Voil wizards awaited Silurian's direction. Movement, a quarter of a league downriver, caught their attention.

Crouched within the crimson reeds, the remainder of the quest, including Alhena, Rook and Thetis, watched as a hunched figure approached the river. Nashon Oakes, and others of his ilk, hunkered down a safe distance behind the second group, the healer's presence an omen of what was likely to come. The entire quest held its collective breath, but the ancient Voil never hesitated.

Wendglow hobbled to the water's edge supported by his twisted, dark wood cane. He made an exaggerated show of raising the cane above the water's surface before lowering its tip into the mystic river— the faces etched along the cane's length squirmed in response to the river's touch.

As soon as the cane's tip marred the water's surface, a bone chilling howl sounded from the direction of Iconoclast Spire. A writhing black mass of hollering demons swarmed over the Iconoclast Spire's foothills at an unbelievable pace while ear piercing screeches sounded overhead.

The black Terrors no longer turned lazy circles overhead. They coalesced into ragged formations and dove at Rook's group. Several Terrors broke away from the flock and winged toward Silurian's smaller band of warriors upriver, their disjointed flapping making them appear like giant rags fluttering on the wind.

"To the river!" Silurian ordered his troop into motion.

Before Silurian's group covered the short distance to the river, the first Terror dropped into their midst. Fourteen feet long, the bird's black-haired body, all muscle and sinew, sported great, leathery wings that proved to be more agile than its clumsy flight let on.

As the monstrosity swooped, its red eyes searched for someone to clutch within its rows of jagged teeth—foamy drool dripped from the corners of its elongated beak. Silurian ducked to avoid being raked by its meat rending talons.

A second Terror dove into the wake of the first, deftly avoiding Pollard's mighty swing. Silurian sidestepped its flight and brought his blade whistling around with both hands. As erratic as the Terror's flight was, it avoided the attack and twisted away toward the river.

Silurian followed its flight over the water. It banked hard and came again. All around him, bow strings twanged.

The Terror over the river dove at Silurian, its unpredictable flight bringing it in behind Pollard who concentrated on the flight of another. Silurian stepped behind the big man and swung a well-aimed cut, but before his sword connected, Sadyra's arrow took the Terror in the shoulder and it veered out of harm's way.

Stumbling with the momentum of his miss, Silurian's eyes never left the beast. He caught himself in time to see Pollard react—his mighty sword severing the creature's left wing, sending the Terror careening into the human and Voil warriors behind him.

The flailing bird knocked aside rows of fighters as it scrabbled to its feet. It charged at Pollard, dragging its damaged wing behind it.

Before it could reach Pollard, a sword lashed out of the crowd and took its left leg. The bird fell to the ground, but Pollard still found himself hard pressed to avoid its snapping beak. Jumping sideways to avoid being bitten, he hacked at the creature's neck. Blood spurted from the wound, temporarily blinding him.

Pollard forced his eyes open and brought his twin blades up. Behind him, the screech of another bird sounded right on top of him, accompanied by the swish of a sword slicing air. Spinning around, a headless bird slammed into his shoulder and pinned him against the ground.

Pollard rolled out from beneath the corpse and tried to stand, but fell back to his knees, half stunned.

Silurian slid an arm under his armpit and helped him up, bracing himself to face another swooping beast. Blood dripped off his infamous blade.

And then the sky went dark.

Wendglow whirled about to witness the brooding mass clambering over the foothills and swarming into the river basin. He watched for but a moment before he realized that the contact of his cane with the river had caused the wood to begin smouldering—the enchanted cane of protection another of Saros' great inventions. He withdrew it and discovered to his dismay that the intricate faces carved along its length had gone still.

He began chanting warding spells to protect himself from the Sentinel, but the creature never materialized.

"'Ware the skies!" Thorr's voice commanded from somewhere behind him.

Wendglow cast a warding spell over those nearest him and incanted an offensive spell to deal with the incoming Terrors. Seeing the group of Terrors break formation to head for Silurian's group, he aborted the spell and hobbled away from the riverbank, throwing his arms in the air. "To Silurian!"

Yarstaff and his husky crew crashed through the tall reeds bearing the elder's litter, but the Terrors descended into their midst. When darkness replaced the light, they stumbled to their knees, spilling their burden.

Soul Forge

Screams sounded all along the riverbank.

Wendglow rolled free of the upturned litter and strained the limits of his rapid spell casting to create a shroud of light, its boundaries hardly sufficient to make a difference to the members of the quest floundering around in the darkness at the mercy of the Terrors.

Other Voil wizards followed his initiative, but their combined spells did little to illuminate the skies overhead.

The Terrors fell upon the wizards commanding the illumination spells, forcing the wizards to drop their light enchantment and summon a warding spell. Several Terrors burst into flame and dropped to the ground, their burning carcasses igniting the tall grass.

The regular fighters were hard put to evade the plunging birds. If Wendglow's group were to have any chance of living to see the morning, they had to get to Silurian.

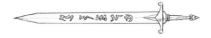

Wendglow's handlers ignored the dangers snapping at them and gathered up the fallen litter. Yarstaff plucked him from his feet and threw him back into the litter without losing a step, following in the wake of the illumination wizards and Blindsight.

Wendglow puzzled over the Sentinel. Why hadn't it been heard from yet? Since it hadn't taken the bait when he touched the river with his cane, it had to be lying in wait for Silurian.

The frightened faces of the quest were grim shadows in the faint light provided by the spell casters around him. It was difficult to make out individual faces, but whenever a Terror dropped from the sky, the gruesome result was plain to see.

Wendglow concentrated harder, expanding his cocoon of protection as far as possible, but he struggled to ignore the destruction wreaked by the large birds of prey. Coupled with the war cries of the approaching land demons who sounded like they were almost on top of them, his anxiety heightened. Where was Thetis?

Soul Forge

Rook clutched Thetis' arm tight, letting her guide him through the chaotic scene unfolding around them. Several times, he went down hard, tripping over the moaning remains of one of their company or slipping on slimy bits of gore from one of the downed Terrors.

They had been running ahead of Wendglow's litter, farther from the river, but when the light disappeared they lost contact with the main group. That struck him as strange. Thetis' vision wasn't hampered by darkness.

He sensed, rather than saw, the beasts diving at them, only to bank away at the last second when he threw his arms uselessly over his head. She must be diverting their flight.

All around them, sailors and Voil alike were being picked off and ripped apart. If not from the air, then from the ground by birds that had been downed but not killed.

Why wasn't Thetis protecting them?

Rook stopped and spun her around to face him. The press of men and women bumped them about in their frantic attempt to reach Silurian's group.

He stared hard into her eyes, her pretty face visible in the flickering light of burning grass.

"Why aren't you fighting back?"

Thetis gave him a contemptuous look.

Taken aback, he swallowed. "For the gods' sake, do something!"

Her upturned lips turned his blood cold. She laughed, but not in her normal voice. Her laughter resonated deeper. Raspier.

Releasing her, he backed away. A passing warrior striving to get by brought him up short.

A maniacal laugh escaped Thetis' lips, drowning out the death cries around them.

The woman Rook thought he had fallen in love with began to transform. Her face oozed. Melting lips exposed bloodied, jagged teeth. Beautiful golden hair mutated into blotchy, grey fur. Bulging muscles tore the clothes from her increasing frame.

Soul Forge

Mesmerized, Rook gaped. Others around them screamed at the sight, not sure of what they were seeing, and ran into the night.

A massive beast, covered in clumps of bloody fur that sloughed away the last vestiges of Thetis' skin, transformed before his eyes. The beast's head consisted mostly of bone. Scraps of skin dangled from the chin and cheeks of the beast as it transformed into something resembling a gigantic wolverine. Twice the size of Pollard, it rose up onto powerful leg muscles that ripped away Thetis' knee-high, leather boots—its clawed feet shredding the material into ribbons.

Three sailors charged in to confront the beast. A lightning swipe of the beast's forepaw raked the first man's face from his skull.

The second man ducked the beast's initial swing and jumped into the air, bringing his sword down in a mighty, overhand chop. His sword shattered upon the creature's head.

The beast ripped his throat out with a savage snap of its jaws.

The third sailor vaulted onto its back, wrapping her arms around its neck. The sailor Silurian had spent many hours sparring with and learning the sailing craft. Tara.

The beast reared up with a mighty roar, trying to throw the woman, but she held fast. It twisted its head, snapping, but its mouth couldn't reach her.

Tara smote the beast's spine, her hard leather boots impacting like warhammers cracking rock.

Unaffected, the beast reached behind its back with a massive paw and grabbed Tara by her jerkin, pulling her free.

She thrashed about in the beast's grasp, trying to stab a dagger into the arm that held her, but it shook her so hard, she dropped the blade.

Its claws tore through her leather armour like she wasn't wearing any.

Tara screamed and blood spewed from her mouth.

The beast extended its claws to wrap around her spine. With a sudden snap of its wrist, it tossed Tara's corpse into a knot of fleeing warriors—her disembodied spine still hanging from its grasp.

A Voil wizard ran into view and shrieked, "'Ware the Morphisis." The misshapen spell caster stumbled and fell over. Mumbling a few words, the wizard waggled his fingertips at the feral beast, but before he completed his spell, the Morphisis reached out to clutch the wizard's head and squeezed. The wizard's head popped, spraying the beast in gore.

The Morphisis flicked the pulp aside and stomped on the wizard's carcass, snapping his bones with a sickening crunch.

Rook stood alone. The last of the warriors had disappeared into the darkness, or worse. He stared at the horror that had been Thetis. His love. The Voil *were* right but it didn't make sense. She was Saros' disciple. Seafarer had vouched for her.

It dawned on him why he and Thetis hadn't been attacked. The demonic birds must have sensed the Morphisis and let them be. He suddenly understood why their flight up the Marrow Wash, in the dead of night, hadn't been cut short by the Sentinel.

"Rook!" A familiar voice called from the darkness.

He dared not look away from the creature looming over him, but he knew the voice.

The chinking of Avarick's armour came up behind him.

Without taking his eyes from the creature, Rook called out, "Stay back!"

"I'm coming!" The chinking of armour increased its cadence.

"Avarick! Stop!"

The chinking slowed.

"If you come any closer, I'll kill you myself!"

The chinking stopped. "Is that the Sentinel?"

The Morphisis laughed. It cocked its head, eyeing the Enervator amongst the broken reeds and death piled all about.

"The Sentinel has been summoned back to your pitiful kingdom by Helleden. It has fled this realm. Come at me, Thwart. Let's see how dangerous you really are."

"Don't, Avarick," Rook pleaded.

The Morphisis cackled, "It seems your friend is a coward."

Rook winced. "Don't rise to the bait."

Ignoring Avarick, the Morphisis changed its tact. "What's the matter, my sweet? Am I not to your liking anymore?" It tried to put a pout on its near fleshless lips. "Won't you come lie with me?"

Rook shouldered his bow and ran at the creature, drawing a dagger from his belt.

Soul Forge

The Morphisis jumped into the air, vaulting him. For a creature so large, it landed behind him with nary a sound.

Rook charged again.

The Morphisis hopped sideways.

Rook faced the beast. He wasn't going to catch it unless it let him. He dropped the dagger and pulled his bow from his shoulder. "What did you do to Thetis?"

The Morphisis cackled, "Why, my sweet, absolutely nothing. I am she, she is me."

"Saros sent Thetis to guide us. You're not..." he trailed off.

"Yes, my sweet. Saint Saros Carmichael," the Morphisis' voice sounded like Thetis again, but its words dripped with venom, "sent unto you his great, great granddaughter. Thetis Saros. Sad about that one. She met an unfortunate end." The Morphisis' voice turned raspy and deep, emitting a wicked laugh.

"You and I met at the docks, when you first arrived in the Bay. I offered to help unload the Seagull, or whatever you call that garbage scow."

Rook's mouth hung open, recalling the wart covered man on the docks.

"You also gave me money. In an alleyway, though *you* were reluctant to do so. Silurian had to guilt you into it."

"The old crone?"

"Yes, my sweet. If you had only taken the time to look closer, you would've met the real Thetis," the Morphisis cackled. "You see? I can take many forms. Thetis is but my latest. A useless body really. Too soft. I prefer this one, cast at Soul Forge."

Rook's breathing grew ragged. He recalled the image of the hag in the alley. In particular, he remembered seeing the body lying in the pile of garbage at her feet.

The Morphisis cackled like the hag, *"Grans will see to you."*

Quick as a thought, Rook withdrew an arrow, nocked it and let loose. The missile struck the Morphisis' chest and bounced harmlessly away.

The Morphisis cocked its head. "You *can* kill me, but you won't. You lack what it takes. Weapons can't hurt me."

Soul Forge

Rook trembled with fury. A metal sword had no effect. His arrow was useless. He doubted even Saros' enchantment would have proven effective.

In the distance, new cries sounded out. He couldn't see those responsible, but he knew the land demons had engaged Silurian's group.

Silurian! He had to get past this beast and get to him. Alhena's words echoed in his mind, *'If you wish to confront Helleden and survive, you must be united.'* He shuddered. How had he let himself be so deceived?

"Come, my sweet. Let me save you. They are nothing. They will be dead soon," the Morphisis purred. "Join me in the river."

Resist as he might, his feet carried him toward the mystic river. He twisted the upper half of his body away from the riverbank but couldn't stop his feet from moving forward.

Upriver, flames shot into the sky, illuminating the river basin.

A guttural howl sounded behind the Morphisis, breaking the creature's hold on him.

Rook winced. The rapid cadence of chinking metal armour marked Avarick's approach. In the eerie light cast by the burning grasses, Avarick charged at the beast.

The creature turned to intercept him.

"Avarick, no!"

The Morphisis swiped at the Enervator, but Avarick dodged the blow, rolling beneath a deadly swath of claws. In one fluid motion he gained his knees, unslung his crossbow, and hammered a bolt home.

Rook heard the snick of the crossbow releasing its deadly missile.

The creature had no time to react, but the bolt bounced harmlessly off its forehead.

The Morphisis kicked out.

Avarick was quicker. He got his feet beneath him, threw the crossbow over his back and vaulted the beast's outstretched leg. Barreling headlong into the creature's chest, he drove his serrated black sword point at its neck.

The blade rebounded uselessly aside, but the resulting collision toppled the two combatants in a flurry of swatting claws and lightning fast sword jabs.

Soul Forge

The Morphisis landed on its back, sending a shower of embers into the air, crushing a patch of burning reeds beneath it.

Avarick's attack, as brutal as it was, proved ineffective. The marks he left on the creature were superficial at best, but as they rolled about in the smoldering reeds, he pulled a dagger from his belt and drove it deep into the creature's left eye, opening a gory wound that showered him in green ichor.

The Morphisis lurched to its feet and staggered about, roaring in agony. It latched onto Avarick and hurled him screaming through the air.

Avarick's broken body landed in a heap of bashed armour and broken bones. The acidic ichor from the Morphisis' wound had dissolved holes through his thin plate and leather armour—smoking and sizzling into his body.

The Morphisis howled in rage. Heaving great breaths, it clutched at its damaged eye. The hilt of Avarick's dagger fell to the ground at its feet—the metal blade dissolved within its eye socket.

The ichor hissed as it ate into Avarick—the air rank with the smell of his burning flesh.

Delirious, the stricken man tried to regain his feet. He made it to one knee and placed his other foot beneath him. He paused, glaring through the veil of blood covering his face, and fell over sideways. He rolled onto his back, his legs sprawled beneath him at an unnatural angle.

Rook ran to him and dropped to his knees, taking in the grisly sight. Avarick's blackened eyelids were clenched shut. His body convulsed. Rook fretted at his inability to help the suffering man. The only release for the irascible Enervator would be death.

Avarick opened his eyes. The searing pain evident behind them made Rook shudder.

"Its other eye," Avarick said through clenched teeth. Choking, he coughed up blood, splattering Rook's face. He shut his eyes tightly and trembled violently one last time.

Rook stared hard at the lifeless Enervator. The Chamber's hired thug. He hadn't been the easiest to bond with, but he had accounted for himself well. His death had offered Rook a chance at life.

Soul Forge

Rook grabbed Avarick's crossbow and the small quiver of bolts attached to the weapon's sling. He threw the straps over his shoulder and stood, eyeing the foul beast. The creature who was supposed to safeguard the quest.

The clatter of weapons and horrific screams marked a furious battle not far away. He had to get to them.

The Morphisis growled, "He was a foolish man. His actions have served to quicken your demise, my sweet." Its steps impacted the ground with a discernable tremor.

Rook's hands trembled, but a strange calm washed over him.

The ground shook again.

Rook yearned for the death of the creature responsible for luring his people into the Under Realm to be butchered, while Helleden Misenthorpe wreaked untold havoc back in Zephyr. Decades of training and self-discipline forced his mind to focus on what needed to be done.

Another burst of fire upriver allowed him to see the Morphisis more clearly. The wretched beast stopped its advance—a bloody paw pressed against its damaged eye. It squinted its good eye and snarled, baring dagger sized teeth.

Rook stepped in front of Avarick's corpse, daring the beast to attack. Rage consumed him, but he honed his anger and funnelled it into resolve.

The Morphisis' eye opened wider as it launched itself into the air.

Rook withdrew an arrow, strung it, and loosed. The arrow flew true, piercing the Morphisis' good eye—the shaft burying itself to its fletches.

The Morphisis shrieked as it fell upon the man who had killed it.

Rook put his hands up in a futile attempt to block the ensuing collision.

A furry, orange missile flew from the burning reeds, painfully driving into his side and knocking him out of harm's way.

Struggling to regain his breath, he let Yarstaff help him to his feet. Without a word, the quiet Voil ran back to Wendglow's litter and led the last of their group upriver to join the slaughter.

Soul Forge

Soul Forge

The Soul

Pollard. Silurian couldn't ask for a better ally. Even in the near darkness, the tired, bloodied, and bruised giant held his own.

Together they made their way to the river's edge. If he was going to immerse his sword in the river, he knew he must do it now. All around them, Terrors swooped in for the kill.

Spellcasters, archers and swordsmen fought for their lives amid the burning reeds, raking claws, and snapping jaws, but the worst was yet to come. The hellish din raised by the oncoming land demons sounded like they were almost upon them.

He hesitated. Doubt crept into his mind. Was he strong enough to face the Soul? How could he fight something he knew nothing about? If he failed, Wendglow claimed he would end up killing them all. He had spent most of his life battling that never-ending fear. A fear that forced him to remain hidden deep within the Nordic Wood. The fear of destroying everything he strove to preserve.

Pollard stood over him, cleaving a Terror's head in two. The creature's bulk shook the ground behind him. A chunk of the creature's head splashed into the river and sprayed Silurian with water.

The Voil were right about the water's compelling touch. He immediately experienced an insatiable desire to wade into the river.

A woman's scream pierced the chaos of battle. A man cried out for help. The demon flyers were decimating the company at will.

Adrenaline throbbed in his veins. The same phenomenon that had gripped him when Menthliot had gone berserk. A finger of blue flame eddied along the tip of his blade—the runes softly glowing. He felt better equipped to handle the sensation this time.

Concentrating on honing the latent power, he trusted his protection to Pollard's capable hands. The colossus slashed at the air above their heads, slicing another Terror before it hit them. The wounded bird splashed heavily into the river.

Silurian winced, but no water hit him. Before he opened his eyes again, Pollard had stabbed at another Terror and missed. The bird's large wings lifted it into the darkness but Sadyra stepped forward and felled it with an arrow to the neck.

Flames coalesced along the length of Saint Carmichael's Blade, illuminating the immediate riverbank in a light blue glow. Another woman's scream provided the catalyst for the flames undulating along his sword, further pushing away the darkness.

Given the extra light, Sadyra and the rest of the archers made quick work of the nearest Terrors just in time to turn and face hundreds of red demons bearing tridents and polearms that charged into their midst.

Wendglow's group fought their way toward them, their progress marked by flickering wizard light. They were too late.

The flames along his sword dwindled. He could barely see Pollard. He had to immerse his sword now, but he hesitated. If he wasn't up to the challenge, more people would die because of his actions.

Faces bombarded his memories. So many lives lost over the years. Most he couldn't place a name to. Menthliot came to mind. Helvius, Alcyonne, and Javen, all fleeting thoughts. Saros. Seafarer. King Peter. Thonk. Hairy. The wild ones. Queen Quarrnaine. *Gerrymander's* crew. Bregens. Siaph and his children! Hundreds of people dead because of the choices he had made. Blurred faces, nameless to him, all shared the same thing: they had died because he hadn't done what he had vowed to do all those years ago—vanquish Helleden Misenthorpe.

A warning shout from downriver broke his reverie. It was the giant helmsman, Olmar. "'Ware the Morphisis! Thetis is the Morphisis. Rook is lost!"

Silurian's eyes snapped open. *Rook is lost?* Flames shot skyward from Saint Carmichael's blade, almost incinerating Pollard.

The sound of battle was deafening as the devilish beasts thrust into the line of defenders. Men, women, and Voil gave their lives to afford him the opportunity to do what must be done, and yet, he remained still.

Soul Forge

Pollard left his side to join in the fray as the company's defensive lines collapsed around him.

The thrum of bowstrings loosed, and the constant clicks of crossbows releasing, mixed with the clash of metal on metal. The missiles had no trouble finding targets in the thick ranks of demons. Even so, the archers had little effect on the unrelenting horde.

Standing defiant, several paces away, Pollard nearly fell to the ground by the press of their own fighters being pushed back toward the river. He found his balance and ferociously fought back.

Olmar joined the fray along the riverbank, leading a flanking attack into the demon horde, attempting to reach a dwindling pocket of surrounded sailors. He swung a massive warhammer, clearing a swath through the demon ranks

Just when all seemed lost, a furious battle cry stopped the minions in their tracks. Thorr, with the aid of wizard light, led a large group of sailors into the back of the demon line.

The red beasts' advance slowed. Pollard rallied the troops around him into a cohesive unit. Following the battle crazed goliath, the small group of fighters pushed the creatures back, but the reprieve Thorr's charge had given the quest was short lived.

Silurian couldn't take his eyes off Pollard. The Songsbirthian brute had just dispatched a nasty demon while another one charged at him, its massive trident aimed at his chest. Pollard intercepted the polearm between both blades and twisted his sword, snapping the trident in two. The disarmed demon never slowed its advance—it came at him with fangs bared. Pollard jockeyed for position in the limited space around him, avoiding the brunt of the creature's impact. The demon's outstretched claws scraped down his brass cuirass with a tooth rattling screech and tore Pollard's left side open below the armour's bottom edge, before Pollard's backswing bit the demon in the small of its back, nearly cutting it in half.

Silurian winced at Pollard's wound, but the man seemed unaffected by the nasty gash. He brought his double blades up to confront his next victim.

Silurian swallowed. They were running out of time. He turned to the river. The small flames licking at the edges of his sword illuminated the water at his feet. He didn't like the image reflected back at him. Taking

360

a deep breath, he immersed the tip of Saint Carmichael's Blade in the river—the resulting steam enveloped him.

The Soul's touch was instantaneous. A malevolent presence entered him through the blade and tore into his mind. Icy tendrils of someone else's thoughts wrapped about his brain and squeezed. He screamed a silent scream as his feet carried him into the river.

Knee-deep in water, he fought to yank his sword free, hoping it would stop the pain in his head. With an agonizing pull, he wrenched his sword out of the river and held it above his head.

An unbearable hurt squeezed the inside of his skull, demanding he lower his sword back into the river—the impulse so strong he feared he was losing his capacity to think on his own. The presence felt like a large parasite had burrowed into his brain, wriggling and biting, tightening its grip and probing deeper. It clawed its way into his subconsciousness, overcoming his feeble attempts to block it.

Vaguely aware that he couldn't prevent himself from wading deeper into the frigid waters, flames shot skyward from his sword.

You cannot resist me, he thought, but it wasn't *his* thought.

You are not strong enough to vanquish my hold upon you.

Losing control of his limbs, his sword plunged with a hiss into the river. He fleetingly thought of Wendglow's fear as the Soul seized control of him.

You are mine now. The words reverberated like a canyon echo.

A maniacal laugh escaped his lips.

A detached vision of the raging battle upon the shore distantly registered in his mind. All action on the battlefield had stopped momentarily to look at him. He stood shoulder deep in the river—his eerie facial features outlined by the glowing aura of his sword beneath the river's surface.

From somewhere deep within himself, he mounted a small measure of resistance. He raised his sword above his head and sent a geyser of blue flames crackling high over the river.

The icy tendrils constricted further, threatening to snap the life from him. The fury of his geyser ebbed.

You are strong. This pleases me.

Silurian struggled to make sense of his addled thoughts. From somewhere in his mind, a nuance of inner strength sparked to life. The

Soul Forge

pillar of flames shot higher into the air. He wanted to scream, to force the Soul's thoughts from his head, but the Soul tightened its hold and his thoughts skittered away.

Laughter sounded upon the river again, emanating from his mouth.

You don't know it yet, but you are already mine. The more you resist, the stronger Helleden becomes. Fight harder, my pet, let us devastate Zephyr together.

In spite of the Soul's power over him, Silurian shouted, "No!" He surprised himself. Perhaps the Soul's hold upon him wasn't as strong as it believed.

Come, my pet. My strength doesn't weaken. You haven't begun to appreciate my full power, but you shall feel it now!

Silurian's head tossed back and forth as wave after wave of excruciating pain bombarded him for what felt like an eternity.

Rook's voice called out to him, urging him to be strong. Letting him know he wasn't alone.

Although Silurian could no longer see past the grip of the Soul, he heard the thump of arrows guarding the sky above him, taking out one black Terror after another.

Sensing a warmth he hadn't known in a long time, a feeling he thought he had lost forever, he plunged his sword into the river. The water around him bubbled. When the ensuing steam faded, he was gone—pulled beneath the surface by whatever had invaded his mind.

He thought his fingers would break as he tried to maintain his grip on Saint Carmichael's Blade. He opened his mouth to scream at the stabbing pain in his head and his lungs filled with water. Swifter than a strong current he was being drawn upriver through the depths of the mysterious waters. He knew he should be drowning, but somewhere in the vortex of his whirling thoughts, he understood the Soul wouldn't permit that.

A prisoner locked within his own mind, he disentangled his last reserve to form a coherent thought of his own, *I will never serve you. I will die first.*

Laughter bubbled from his water-filled mouth. *That, I won't allow. You will come to understand that the longer you resist, the more complete the destruction of Zephyr shall become.*

No! I will never help you.

362

Soul Forge

Ah, my pet. Still do you fail to comprehend. Helleden lays waste to Zephyr as we speak. Your continued resistance is facilitating the destruction. Helleden draws from the energy we expend battling each other. Our struggle amplifies his sorcery.

Silurian fought to withdraw further—to back away from the intrusion and sink deep into his mind.

If you think you don't command power, you are sadly mistaken. If you didn't, you would already be mine. Know, however, that should you stop resisting, even for a moment, I will have you. And if you don't, Zephyr will be destroyed. The choice is yours. Remember the Innerworld? Or the queen?

That last statement jarred him. He almost slipped. Mulling over the Soul's words, Silurian searched his mind for a way to stop resisting. If what the Soul said was true, their struggle provided Helleden the strength he needed to destroy everything the quest had come to the Under Realm to protect. Zephyr.

He thought again of Wendglow's warning. If he stopped resisting, the Soul would gain mastery over him, thus justifying the Voil elder's ultimate fear.

He was trapped. If he resisted, Zephyr was doomed. If he gave in, the Soul would acquire his corporeal form and break free of its ethereal shackles. Silurian couldn't even begin to fathom the ramifications of that eventuality. His thoughts whirled in confusion and despair. His grasp on sanity was slipping fast.

Ah, my pet. You see the futility. Let it go. You can end the devastation. Together we will cleanse the world.

Destroy it, you mean?

Semantics. In the end you can be the means to Zephyr's destruction, or you can concede the deed to me. Either way, the result is the same.

Silurian's ire rose. The madder he became, the harder he fought back. The more he struggled, the more the Soul entrenched itself within his head.

Your resistance fuels Helleden's power. The harder you resist, the greater Helleden's destruction becomes. Only you can stop the suffering of your people. Let me in, and Helleden's power dies. Surely, you do not wish to be the one responsible for your people's annihilation. Succumb before there is nothing left of Zephyr to return to.

The Soul withdrew its presence enough to allow Silurian room to think clearly. If what the Soul claimed were true, the people of Zephyr were being slaughtered—right now. More were about to die if he continued down this path. A small part of him tried to convince himself that the Soul lied to trick him into lowering his barriers—to achieve its mastery over him. For some reason, he knew that wasn't the case. Reaching out, he sensed Helleden's presence flitting about the periphery of their conflict.

Even so, he couldn't willingly surrender himself. To become the Soul's doppelganger and free the beast wasn't an option.

Why me? Why not just occupy Helleden?

An icy finger tickled his thoughts. *The Stygian Lord is not strong enough to breach the barrier restraining me.*

Silurian sensed, rather than heard, a slight snicker. The transformation had already begun.

Aye, my pet. You were always mightier than the Stygian Lord, you just didn't know it.

Silurian shuddered. Realizing there was no way out, he did the only thing that made sense to him. He withdrew his power and gave up his struggle. He allowed his body's physical limitations to be overcome by the environment around him. He withdrew the essence of his power into the deepest recesses of his mind, exerting only enough resistance to thwart the Soul's icy tendrils from finding him. He effectively shut down the vital processes keeping him alive. His mind became dormant. He began to drown.

The Soul ripped through his tattered mind in a frantic attempt to locate him, panic clearly evident in its actions.

If Silurian could have smiled, he would have. He drifted in a dreamlike trance, the little he comprehended felt surreal, as if everything was but a nightmare he wouldn't wake from.

It dawned on him, at the edge of his thoughts, that his body had been enveloped in an unusual blanket of warm air. Even though his mind remained locked away, he sensed his body convulsing. His lungs vacated the water within them. A sulfurous odour upturned his nostrils. His body had stopped travelling. It had reached its destination within the bowels of Iconoclast Spire, and he was still alive. That wasn't good.

From somewhere beyond where he cowered within his mind, a dull reverberation vibrated through his body. If the Soul were able to locate his essence, he feared he would be powerless to slip away again—especially within the heart of the Soul Forge.

The Soul's pale apparition shimmered ghostlike on the floor of an immense cavern, deep beneath Iconoclast Spire. At its feet, Silurian's body twitched and gasped.

In the cavern's centre frothed a large, milky lake. Fed from overtop a great shelf of rock, viscous white liquid plummeted hundreds of feet to the lake below. The lake, in turn, spilled through a dark cleft at the cavern's far end, feeding the Marrow Wash.

Matted hair hung from the Soul's head, long enough to reach its knees. The specter stood so tall that it nearly brushed the milky white stalactites hanging from the voluminous chamber's roof. The only colour evident in its appearance came from its fiery orbs, sunk within an otherwise empty, fleshless skull.

Its eyes flared, illuminating the crypt. *How dare you deny me?* It boomed loud enough to vibrate Silurian's body.

Not receiving a response, it bellowed, resonating so loud within Silurian's mind it would have ruptured a normal man's brain, *Succumb to me!*

Silurian's body shivered despite the heat. The Soul's words reached him, finding their way into the mental fortress he had barricaded himself within. The thunderous drone shook his physical body. Fear seeped past his defenses.

Obey me, mortal!

The Soul was getting closer to prying him out.

Surrender now or forever know my wrath! I know where you are.

He wanted to reach out from behind his mental barrier and attempt to shut down his respiratory system or stop his heart, but he feared that if he ventured out for even a heartbeat, the Soul would claim him.

Soul Forge

Despite its boasts, the Soul hadn't found him yet. He couldn't be certain, but he clung to the belief that the Soul wasn't any closer to finding him than it had been before. The Soul's words weren't lost on him, however. Sooner or later, it *would* find him.

I have all the time in the world.

He ignored the taunt. His corporeal body required sustenance to keep it alive. All he needed to do was refrain from allowing the Soul's taunts to lure him out of his bastion until his body died of natural causes. Given his recent beating and lack of proper food, he predicted that wouldn't take more than a few days.

He needed to calm himself. Ignore the Soul and concentrate on other things. Visions flooded the simple thoughts left to him. He rode horseback, looking through detached eyes. His old black charger, Alcytwin, galloped at a phenomenal speed along Redfire Path. Ahead of him, a group of rough horsemen circled a frightened young man who stood defenseless in their midst, a scorpion flail wrapped tightly about his neck.

Bregens?

Silurian heeled Alcytwin, urging him into the circle.

Bregens' bruised and battered face beseeched his help.

Silurian offered the leader a wicked smile, and suddenly the man's warhammer appeared in his own hand. The circle of riders faded away.

A sad voice parted Bregens' lips, "Bregens is Silurian's friend?"

Silurian hefted the cudgel over his head. He wanted to recoil from the terror evident on Bregens' face, but he was helpless to prevent himself from swinging the warhammer and crushing Bregens' skull into a bloody pulp, splattering himself with the young man's blood.

No! Bregens, I didn't do it.

The Soul had found him. It had cracked his barrier. It wouldn't be long before it hammered a wedge into the crack and exposed him entirely.

In the blink of an eye, Silurian watched in horror as he fled along a smoky passageway. He didn't recognize the place at first, but familiar voices called after him as he ran from the flames licking at his heels. Cries of terror begged him to save them. Pathetic screams of those who fell behind, caught in the flames, cried out his name. A throng of

Soul Forge

chambermen raced after him, pleading forgiveness. He laughed and ran harder, his glowing sword igniting the tunnel as he went.

He slipped from the entrance shed and slammed home a bolt, locking everybody inside. They jammed their faces against the door's barred window, pleading for death as the flames consumed them.

Silurian's mind cried out, *that wasn't me!*

The Soul watched on in delight as the pitiful creature writhed in torment at its feet. It laughed. *You only have yourself to blame. You are responsible for their deaths. You have only begun to experience the terror your mind is capable of inflicting upon itself.*

Silurian strode into Nordic Town's centre. His sister Melody was being held by a filthy man with a rusty sword. Rook was there as well, fighting off the advances of another swordsman.

Silurian watched himself approach the filthy man. Without a word, the ruffian pushed Melody into his waiting embrace. Sobbing and babbling, she wrapped her arms about him.

Silurian threw her to the ground.

Rook looked over in disbelief. He dispatched his assailant in quick order and confronted Silurian.

Silurian brandished his sword. There could only be one outcome. He wanted to scream out, "Run," but he had no power over the visions.

Rook fought fiercely, but he was no match for Silurian's feints and offensive swings.

He forced Rook backward. A quick parry and a forward lunge had Rook scrambling unbalanced and falling over the lifeless body of Alcyonne.

Where did Alcyonne come from? None of this is making sense.

Unable to prevent the scene from unfolding, Silurian retreated further into his demented mind. This couldn't be happening. Alcyonne was long dead and nobody had heard from Melody since the feast of Lugubrius.

The Soul was manipulating his memories in an effort to exploit the crack he had exposed in his mental armour. The Soul wanted a confrontation. Even knowing this, Silurian couldn't escape the poignant effect the horrific scenes had on his psyche.

The creature wriggled another tentacle of thought through.

Silurian watched helplessly as Rook's sword arm sprawled out wide to catch his fall and lost his grip on his blade as he tumbled over Alcyonne's smiling corpse.

"I have waited many years for this day." He heard himself say as he hefted Saint Carmichael's blade above his head.

No! It's not me! he yelled, but Rook couldn't hear him.

Rook threw his arms over his face and cried out, "Why?"

His sword whistled downward with the killing stroke. "You shall betray me no more."

"No!" Silurian roared, withdrawing from the seclusion of his mind. In one fluid motion, he was on his feet and glaring at the ghastly apparition towering above him. As he located his errant sword and moved in to attack, he felt a strange presence within the cavern. It stirred the ashes of a fond, childhood memory. A pleasant calm washed over him. Not everyone in his world had died. The heartwarming awareness gave him the strength to do what must be done.

The Soul had thought it was impervious to any attack Silurian could muster, but it fell back a step, in surprise.

At its feet, the pitiful creature had broken free of its hold and was summoning all of his unknown power to throw back at it. More power than the Soul had thought a mortal capable of. Bolstered by the river's touch, no doubt.

The Soul hesitated. It hadn't expected this to happen, but so be it. Silurian's body was proving worthier than it had anticipated. Allowing

Soul Forge

Silurian to unleash whatever power he had at his command would augment Helleden's raging firestorm.

The pitiful swordsman located his errant sword. Flames burst to life along its length. His ice-blue eyes were crazed as he closed the gap between them and swung his fiery blade. "Enough!"

The Soul recovered from its initial shock. Appreciating its peril, it commanded all of its ancient theurgy to deflect the ensuing confrontation, comfortable in the knowledge that no matter what reserve Silurian drew upon, it was more than strong enough to absorb the assault without any lasting repercussions. Never in its wildest dreams had the Soul thought this kind of response possible. It smiled. What a perfect host. In moments, it would be free.

Appreciating that the aftermath of the resulting attack would kill Silurian if he were to bring Iconoclast Spire crumbling down on top of them, the Soul prepared itself to seize control of Silurian's body when that happened. Oh, how long it had waited.

As the ensuing blast erupted from Silurian's sword, the Soul knew fear.

Another presence made itself felt in the cavern. It drew exclusively from the Soul's immense power, preventing it from defending itself.

Helleden!

Enraged, the Soul fought to bring its defenses to bear but was unable to focus its energy.

High atop his mountain aerie, Helleden had waited for the Soul's concentration to fully focus upon the pathetic creature opposing it. Helleden's master hadn't anticipated his stealthy tendrils slipping in to seize control of *its* power.

Timing his move to perfection, Helleden siphoned the Soul's defensive magic, leaving the ethereal being vulnerable to the full might of Silurian's discharge. At the same time, Helleden channeled the immense power into the vast firestorm he was unleashing upon the kingdom of Zephyr.

Soul Forge

Silurian's blast ignited the Soul's bared power. The resulting catastrophic detonation blew the higher reaches of Iconoclast Spire hundreds of feet into the air, sending thousands of tons of shattered rock into the atmosphere.

Another presence made itself felt within Soul Forge—distant, yet powerful. As Iconoclast Spire collapsed upon itself, Helleden wondered where he had sensed this presence before.

Leagues downriver, the cataclysmic detonation of Iconoclast Spire levelled the battlefield. The Dead Plains lit up beneath a storm of burning debris.

The remnants of the minion horde scrambled away into the fiery darkness or flapped away.

The few quest members not rendered unconscious by the initial concussion witnessed the ensuing flurry of molten rock shooting skyward in a slow, agonizing arc. The killing detritus spread out like a mushroom cloud before beginning its lethal plunge while the bottom half of Iconoclast Spire collapsed upon itself.

Another concussion rocked the land, obliterating everything in a white flash.

Hidden from view, behind a sudden wall of mist, the river boiled.

370

Soul Forge

Until We Meet Again

Bobbing gently beneath an azure sky, an odd assortment of sailing craft made their way east upon what everyone hoped to be the Niad Ocean. *Gerrymander* cut through the waves at the head of the armada, a little worse for wear than when she had disappeared weeks before.

Rook stood behind Olmar on the wheel deck, leaning on the aft rail, gazing out to sea. His vacant stare followed the trail of the ship's wake to the horizon. Toward the portal—the gateway to the realm in which he had abandoned his best friend.

He kept reliving the final moments upon the Dead Plains when Iconoclast Spire erupted. He had believed the lives of the quest were at an end, and then the white flash. The next thing he knew, he was aboard *Gerrymander*. In fact, it appeared that every creature still alive—that had ever been captured by the portal—had been returned to the Niad Ocean in the vessels they had originally set sail in. Unfortunately for the Voil, most of their vessels had long since been destroyed or rendered useless, and they suddenly found themselves swimming for their lives in the frigid waters. Ironically, after finally being delivered from the Under Realm, many Voil were dragged to a watery grave by the heavy armour they had depended on to protect themselves.

Demons were also transported back through the portal but were quickly dispatched by *Gerrymander's* crew or left to flounder on their own.

Rook shook his head. The entire journey had proven too bizarre to contemplate. He ruefully listened to the songs of joy emanating from the curious collection of Voil craft—the strange little creatures skipping and dancing upon open decks, delighted to bask in sunshine.

The absence of the Sentinel during the battle left Rook unsettled. *Thetis,* he grimaced and corrected himself, *the Morphisis had said the*

Soul Forge

Sentinel had been summoned to Zephyr by Helleden. Wonderful. Now they had two devils to deal with if they ever made it home.

His eyes misted, blurring the vista before him. He couldn't accept that Silurian was gone. He was about to cry again when a giant hand slapped his shoulder.

"Come, my friend, they await your presence."

Rook nodded, not trusting himself to speak. Pollard patted him on the back and respectfully left him alone to gather himself. He wiped his eyes on the cuffs of his filthy green tunic, took a deep breath, and strolled across the aft deck.

Olmar offered him a grim smile as he passed the helm. He gave the helmsman the faintest of nods. With a heavy heart, he joined the throng of people assembled amidships.

The silent gathering parted to allow him into their midst. He stopped beside Alhena and wrapped an arm about the old man's waist.

Alhena put his arm about his back and squeezed.

Out on the ocean, the rag tag collection of Voil craft jockeyed to hold their position alongside *Gerrymander's* bulk.

At a signal from the captain, Alhena composed himself and stepped to the starboard rail, clutching his staff. A soft breeze played in his wispy hair—his fine beard fluttered over his shoulder. His peculiar white eyes were rimmed in red, but his voice held steady, "Our fateful journey has come to an end. An end full of mixed emotions." His words carried over the din of the lapping waves, flapping sheets, and creaking hawsers. "Many good men and women have fallen along the way. In their place, we have discovered new friends. The Voil. They, too, have suffered much grief while in support of our cause. Without their assistance, I dare say, none of us would be standing here today. Together we mourn."

Alhena bowed his head. Struggling to maintain an even voice, he sniffed, and looked up, his vacant gaze staring beyond those gathered around him.

"Life is ever fraught with danger. We were entrusted with a quest. A quest that was not only implausible, but outright impossible. We did not deviate. We sailed into hell and came out the other side. Together, we defeated an ancient evil. Together, we survived, and together we shall continue the fight."

Soul Forge

The breeze picked up, ruffling his flowing black cloak and underlying, filthy, white robes. "We gather today to honour those we left behind. Seafarer, Menthliot, Avarick, Tara…" He went on reciting scores of names from a scroll he fought to keep from blowing out of his wrinkled hands—most of the names, Voil.

He paused as he arrived at the last name. His eyes welled up. Biting a trembling lower lip, he took a deep breath, his voice on the verge of cracking, "Take not away the sacrifice of those aforementioned. They kept us safe."

He paused. Taking a shuddering breath, he continued, "At this time, I ask you to remember the man who led us into hell. He gave his life so that we might come through the other side. Take courage from his death. Grieve not for Silurian Mintaka. He gave his life to rid the world of an ancient evil and by doing so, he has provided us a way home."

Sad rumblings sounded amongst the crowd. Uneasy feet shuffled about.

"We know not whether he ultimately achieved his goal. I am certain we will find out soon enough."

Rook observed many heads shaking. If Helleden *were* still alive, Zephyr would be in a difficult spot as the one man capable of repelling the sorcerer was lost to them.

"Console yourselves with the knowledge that Silurian Mintaka, former king's champion and member of the Group of Five, has finally found the peace he desperately sought. He now lies with those he so loved. Find comfort in the knowledge that his peace could not have been achieved without you." Alhena's voice broke. He couldn't carry on.

Tears dripped freely from Rook's chin. He wrapped an arm around the old man and pulled him close. With his other hand, he nodded to Pollard, manning the davit.

Pollard cranked the gears controlling the ropes that supported a ceremonial coffin. The crudely constructed box symbolized all those who had died in the Under Realm. The grinding metal and creaking ropes did little to mask the sobs heard across the water.

Rook guided Alhena to the starboard rail.

The casket bobbed momentarily upon the low seas and slid beneath the waves.

Soul Forge

Staring at the spot where the coffin had disappeared, the old messenger whispered, "May you find the peace you have so dearly given us, Sire. Until we meet again."

The End...

...of the beginning

I hope you enjoyed 𝕾𝖔𝖚𝖑 𝕱𝖔𝖗𝖌𝖊.

Your opinion is important and means a lot to me.

Please consider leaving a review on Amazon and Goodreads.
Reviews are vital to an author's livelihood.

If you prefer, you can send me your thoughts at:
richardhstephens1@gmail.com

Chapter 1 of, *The Wizard of the North*, book 2 in the *Soul Forge* Saga

Wizard of the North

𝔄 storm was imminent. It promised to be a bad one. It would rain hard, and with the rain would come death.

Within a grotto, high atop an active volcano, a wizard hunkered over a vision within the flames of a modest campfire, holding back long wisps of golden hair.

Something strange was occurring hundreds of leagues south of the cave. Something catastrophic. Tears dripped from the tip of the wizard's nose. The omens foretold the return of a devastating power. A power that had annihilated the unspoiled tracts of the Innerworld a moon cycle earlier. The same power that had besieged Quarrnaine Svelte and her expedition four years before, but this time it was different. This time, the signs pointed to an absolute apocalypse—a total annihilation of Zephyr, and there was nothing the wizard could do to prevent it.

A cold wind swirled ash into the wizard's face, burning small holes in the silken robes fluttering about the magic user's slight frame.

Ignoring the acrid smoke, the wizard leaned closer to the flames, willing the vision to reveal a deeper understanding. Helleden Misenthorpe was at the root of this storm, of that there was little doubt, but there were other participants involved this time. One bigger than the malign sorcerer himself. If this magical storm of doom wasn't strange enough, there was also something familiar about it. Something that shook the wizard to the core.

The flames burned with more intensity than they had a right to, given the meagre fuel they fed upon. They flared up to singe the wizard's hair and abruptly went out.

The wizard quickly uttered an incantation to relight the fire, anxious to witness the unfolding storm, but the flames refused to come back. The wizard frowned and chanted again, paying attention to proper enunciation. Next to a divination invocation, a vision spell was the hardest one to enact correctly. The embers flickered with promise before fizzling out again, but the wizard had felt that familiar presence again. It was as if someone had mentally reached out, desperate for the wizard's attention.

"No," the wizard bemoaned the unresponsive ashes and made a frantic search of the dank interior. Passing over a pile of tattered tomes and brittle scrolls, the wizard found a grimy vial of green ichor—handling it with the utmost of respect. A little hesitant, but with no time to waste, the wizard thought, *why not?*

Pulling the cork stopper loose, the wizard shook the vial in an effort to hurry the gelatinous substance from the container. Excruciatingly slow, the ichor dripped once, and then a second time, sizzling as it oozed into the embers.

The wizard replaced the stopper and dropped the vial into a robe pocket. With both hands free, the wizard intoned the magical phrase of vision, pronouncing each word exactly as they had been learned.

At first, the smouldering fire hissed and sputtered, but as the wizard panicked anew, a small flame caught, quickly rearing to engulf the entire pit—threatening to climb out of its confines and onto the stone floor.

The extreme heat forced the wizard back against the cave wall. Concentrating like never before, the wizard drew from an unknown reserve, and the vision reformed within the leaping flames. The scene of a bloody battle waged in virtual darkness, except for the fires burning in the fields around a river and the sporadic bursts of what could only be magic, took shape, but this was not Zephyr.

It was difficult for the wizard to determine where the battle took place; certainly nowhere familiar. Immense birds of prey flitted in and out of the vision, swooping down upon hapless victims and then flying out of sight. Men, women, and small misshapen creatures battled for their lives along the banks of a wide river, against an insurmountable number of red demons wielding tridents and other malicious instruments of death.

The familiar sensation reached through the flames, taking the wizard's breath away.

"Silurian?"

Unseen in the background of the image until now, a cylindrical mountain blazed to life. So intense was the illumination that the wizard cowered behind an upraised arm.

The wizard's raging fire pulsed once in warning—the wizard oblivious to the omen.

The wizard locked onto the compelling pull from within the flames, desperately trying to make sense of what was happening.

The image of the blazing mountain exploded, erupting like a volcano. A visible concussion shot outward, the intensity of the blast obliterating the wizard's vision.

A violent wind emanated from the centre of the fire pit, stoking the wizard's flames, a harbinger of the fiery maelstrom that suddenly engulfed the cave.

Born in Simcoe, Ontario, in 1965, I began writing circa 1974; a bored child looking for something to while away the long, summertime days. My penchant for reading *The Hardy Boys* led to an inspiration one sweltering summer afternoon when my best friend and I thought, 'We could write one of those.' And so, I did.

As my reading horizons broadened, so did my writing. Star Wars inspired me to write a 600-page novel about outer space that caught the attention of a special teacher who encouraged me to keep writing.

A trip to a local bookstore saw the proprietor introduce me to Stephen R. Donaldson and Terry Brooks. My writing life was forever changed.

At 17, I left high school to join the working world to support my first son. For the next twenty-two years I worked as a shipper at a local bakery. At the age of 36, I went back to high school to complete my education. After graduating with honours at the age of thirty-nine, I became a member of our local Police Service, and worked for 12 years in the provincial court system.

In early 2017, I retired from the Police Service to pursue my love of writing full-time. With the help and support of my lovely wife Caroline and our five children, I have finally realized my boyhood dream.

Books by Richard H. Stephens

The Royal Tournament

The Royal Tournament has at long last come to the village of Millsford. For Javen Milford, a local farm boy, the news couldn't be better. Finally, Javen can perform his chores on the homestead and partake in the biggest military games in the Kingdom, hoping beyond hope that just maybe, he might catch the eye of the king. Javen enters the kingdom's flagship tournament only to discover that in order to win, one must be prepared to die.

Of Trolls and Evil Things
The (standalone) prequel to the Soul Forge Saga series!

Travel down an ever-darkening path where two orphans battle to survive upon a perilous mountainside, evading the predators and prowlers preying upon its slopes, and within its catacombs. When the dangers they face force them from their mountain home, they end up in the cutthroat streets of Cliff Face plying their hands as beggars to survive.

Soul Forge - The Epic Fantasy Trilogy

Soul Forge

Book 1

Loyalty, betrayal, fantastic creatures, breathtaking vistas and one man's need to rescue his darkened soul come together in this amazing epic fantasy.

Accompanied by a band of eclectic characters, Silurian Mintaka embarks upon a journey seeking revenge on the those responsible for the murder of his family. Those closest to him fear his decisions will end up killing them all, and the fate of the kingdom hangs in the balance.

Wizard of the North

Book 2

The Royal House of Zephyr is in shambles. A beast is unleashed, and the only hope the kingdom has to survive the imminent firestorm, lies in the hands of an eclectic band of giants, a rogue vigilante, an old man, an orange furred creature and a pair of female pranksters.

A catastrophic spell reunites two lost souls, setting them on an epic journey of discovery to discover the source of an ancient magic.

Into the Madness

Book 3

The epic conclusion of the Soul Forge Saga. A carefully hidden truth is revealed. The key to the kingdom's salvation if the Wizard of the North and her unstable companion can unlock its secret and survive an encounter with a wyrm bent on destroying the world.

Far to the south, a motley group of assassins set out to end the land's suffering. Waylaid by an eccentric necromancer, and suffering a tragic loss that threatens to ruin their poorly laid plan, they stagger toward a fate no one ever envisioned. An obsidian nightmare is summoned and Zephyr will never be the same.

Legends of the Lurker Trilogy

Reecah's Flight
Book 1

A young girl dreams of flying. Encouraged by her grandfather to follow her heart, Reecah forms a taboo relationship with a baby dragon.

Secretly opposing the mandate of her people, Reecah tests the boundaries of unquestionable love as she and her enchanting accomplice battle the discriminative edicts governing the land and the people bent on eradicating the magical creatures.

Reecah's Gift
Book 2 – Available Autumn, 2019

Fleeing from the only life she has ever known, Reecah Windwalker sets out to avert a terrible tragedy. One that will force the dragons to the edge of extinction. But first, Reecah must find herself.

Braving the perils of a cutthroat city, Reecah discovers that as bad as life may have seemed, nothing had prepared her for what her future has in store. Surviving hardships no one should ever have to endure, she finds herself face-to-face with those seeking her demise.

Without the intervention of an eclectic warrior, and the assistance of her dragon friends, Reecah might never realize the gift so many have died to protect.

Reecah's Legacy
Book 3—Available Winter, 2019
The culmination of the Legends of the Lurker series.

If you wish to keep up to date on new releases, promotions and giveaways, please subscribe to my newsletter by checking out the contact tab on my website.

www.richardhstephens.com

Facebook:	@richardhughstephens
Twitter:	@RHStephens1
Instagram:	@richard_h_stephens
YouTube:	https://bit.ly/2NKpOhn

www.amazon.com/author/richardhstephens